ASHES
OF XY

# PRAISE FOR ELIZABETH VAUGHAN

"Vaughan...recreates the delicious feeling of adventure and the thrill of exploring mysterious cultures created by Robert E. Howard in his Conan books and makes for a satisfying escapist read..."

—BOOKLIST

"Like the previous books, this was another emotional one that kept me hooked to the story. I couldn't put it down and finished it within a few hours."

—RED-HAIRED ASH READS ON *WARLORD*

The writing is vivid, and the characters are all individuals, complex and real."

—HER HANDS, MY HANDS ON *WARPRIZE*

"Over the course of the series, Vaughan has built a fantasy world that is believable, relatable and filled with well-loved characters."

—NOT A BOOK SNOB

"This is a wonderful series with engaging characters that grow and develop with each book."

—SHARYNN BLOOD, REVIEWER

"*Warsong* is a thrilling, romantic, and epic read filled with beloved characters and daring deeds."

—VICKI STIEFEL, REVIEWER

"Ms. Vaughan has written a wonderful fantasy...The story is well-written and fast paced."

—A ROMANCE REVIEW ON *WARPRIZE*

"A classic read for me right up there with Linda Howard's MacKenzie's series or Nora Roberts' The Donovan's Legacy series or Anne McCaffrey's Tower and Hive series. If those three are favorites...enjoy this one too!"

—KINDLE CUSTOMER ON *WARPRIZE*

"Full of daring, nobility, and great surprises!"

—LEIGH ANNE JENSEN, ON *WARPRIZE*

ALSO BY ELIZABETH VAUGHAN

### CHRONICLES OF THE WARLANDS

*Warprize*

*Warsworn*

*Warlord*

*Dagger Star*

*White Star*

*Destiny's Star*

*Warcry*

*Wardance*

*Warsong*

*Fate's Star*

# ASHES OF XY

ELIZABETH VAUGHAN

ASHES OF XY
by ELIZABETH VAUGHAN
© 2025 by Elizabeth Vaughan. All rights reserved.



Cover Illustration: Russell Marks
Cover Design and Interior Layout: STK Kreations

First Edition
Paperback ISBN: 978-0-9984501-6-2

Published by Birch Cove Press

*For Gloria Pelletier*
*Dearest Friend and Fierce Warrior*

# ACKNOWLEDGMENTS

*Ashes of Xy* comes out on the 20th anniversary of my first book, *Warprize*.

My writing journey started in 1998. The support I have received, the friends I have made and lost, the laughter and pain I have experienced and shared, the sorrow, the joy, and everything in between, how to sum that up in the space of a single page? I do not have the words.

Agents and editors, fellow writers, and my readers, all have enriched my life beyond measure.

So very many people have supported me in this process. Everyone who touched this manuscript improved it immensely. I am deeply grateful.


Maybe I do have the words.

Thank you.

Beth

*Xy was a mighty kingdom, with trade routes on both land and sea. The people were well ruled by the Sons and Daughters of the Blood. Peace and prosperity drew other kingdoms to pledge themselves to the Xyian Crown and to merge with Xy, creating an empire the likes of which had never been seen.*

*All hailed the Golden Age of Xy, and the circular stone beneath the throne, the heart of the Empire, rang with the cheers of the people.*

*But in time, the lessons of the past were forgotten. The Blood lost their way, and the Wasting erupted, leaving destruction in its wake, followed by war and death, plague and chaos.*

*All that had once flourished was lost.*

*The wise tell us that everything ends, but that all endings are beginnings. That in turn, beginnings always mark an end.*

*Now begins a new struggle. To restore what was lost.*

*For the restoration of the Blood of Xy.*

## CHAPTER ONE

—◦—

*Autumn Equinox, mid-afternoon of the last day of the
Reign of Xywellan and Queen Kara*

Vren crawled under the low pines to the edge of the ridge, keeping to his belly, his head down. The branches above him swayed in the wind, the movement helping to hide him. Dried needles shifted beneath him as he slowly lifted his head. The cool breeze hit his face, whisked away the sharp scent of pine, and replaced it with the stench of blood, smoke, and death.

The battlefield stretched out below him, filled with the heave of a pulsing mass of men and horses. The airion and wyvern banners were the only way to track the sides in the chaos and haze. Beyond that stood the House Airion camp, command tent at its center, flags flying. Beyond that lay the walls of Edenrich, where worried sentries no doubt stared toward the battle.

Vren's stomach clenched, in fear but also dread at what he had to do. He was of the marcusi. *Be the wind, be the shadow, be the blade, be the silence of the night.* How in the name of all the elements could he rescue a pregnant Queen from this nightmare?

A warm weight pressed against his leg, a soft whine rising to his ears as Dust crawled up to rest next to him. The vore was so large she stretched the length of his body.

The vore were fearsome fighters, true enough, with jaws that could crush a skull with a snap, but she too had no place on a battlefield. Her ears were flat to her head, taking in the sight with an intelligence equal to his own.

Although she would claim she was far smarter than any human.

He buried his fingers in Dust's coarse guard hairs, sinking them into her soft under-coat and giving a nervous tug.

Dust nudged him with her wet nose.

"King Xywellan's forces are losing," Vren whispered. "The Wyverns will take the day." Out of habit, he glanced for the sun but saw only the low, brooding clouds. "Probably before nightfall."

The vore growled low, voicing her concerns. He could feel the vibration through his fingers.

"I know," he agreed. "But I am summoned, and I am sworn to heed that call. I have to try." He hesitated. "You'd best stay here. I know not what awaits me–"

Sharp teeth gleamed in the shadows as the vore jerked her head and snapped at his chin. He flinched out of instinct, but she never meant for those dagger-like teeth to strike him. Just wanted to let him know what she thought of his suggestion.

Vren shook his head. "Dust, I am serious. We each have our

own missions. I am called to aid a pregnant Queen Kara in the midst of a battle. You are not, and the Wyverns would kill you on sight. It's too dangerous—"

The vore shoved her muzzle under his chin. Vren sighed and buried his face in her fur for a moment, breathing in her warmth and scent.

"Together then." He cast his eyes toward the low gleam in the sky that marked the setting sun behind the clouds, and started to crawl backwards.

They skirted the battlefield, making a wide curve so as not to be drawn into the great sea of combat, avoiding men and horses at all costs.

Vren noted the blue and white airion banners falling and the red and gold wyvern flags still waving in the wind.

Battle had already reached the camp in the form of looters intent on spoils. If any saw Vren, which was doubtful given his skill, they paid him no mind. But the command tent still held, with warhorses outside, saddled and waiting. Vren kept a wary eye on the beasts, but felt some relief at the sight; no doubt they were preparing to take the Queen to safety. He and Dust could act as the rear guard, covering their tracks and killing any pursuers.

Vren gave the horses a wide berth and used the shadows, only stepping into the light when he and Dust reached the entrance.

A fierce woman with hard eyes challenged his approach; her gaze flicked from him to the vore beside him. Not that Vren blamed her; vore were a rare sight, and enough to take any aback. At first glance a large dog, and then not, with the square jaw of a demon-spawn, bright fangs, and the focus of a killer. Dust drew the eye more than his own lanky frame.

"I am of the marcusi." Vren spoke, which caught the woman's

attention. She frowned at him. "I am summoned," he added and held out his token.

"Captain," the guard called over her shoulder, and another emerged from the tent, her eyes even harder. She gave Vren a nod, produced a similar token, and held out her hand for his.

The two pieces fit together with a click, creating a small figurine. A black panther with crystal blue eyes.

"Come," she said, turning back into the tent.

He followed, the vore at his side.

The tent was stifling. In the outer chamber warriors, all women, were arming themselves. Each one raked him with a glance, assessing and dismissing him. He was content that it be so. They had second glances for the vore, and those held respect and caution.

He was content with that as well.

The Captain held open another flap and Vren ducked through. A sleeping chamber, crowded with people. Here the air was thicker, reeking of blood and piss.

On the bed a woman was propped up by pillows, her black curly hair in disarray and pressed to her head with sweat.

A tiny babe nursed at her breast.

Vren sucked in a breath. Dust whined softly as she sat at his feet.

The white bedding was splotched with bright red blood. Between the new mother's spread legs, other women were frantically doing … something. Vren stomach churned and he dropped his gaze, not wanting to know more.

"Majesty," the guard said, and Vren found himself the focus of the room.

Even those ministering to the woman stilled for a moment as Vren knelt and said, "Hail to you, Kara, Queen of Xy."

The Captain stepped to the bed and handed the Queen the token. Kara took it, rubbing the smooth black side with her thumb. She lifted her gaze and gave Vren a weary smile. "You are the marcusi I sent for?" She fingered the token. "Your name?"

"Majesty, I–" he shook his head. "I am one of the marcusi, sworn protector of the Blood of Xy. Until the snows summon and the stars call."

Kara narrowed her eyes. "But which Blood?" she asked, then shook her head. "Never mind. It matters not. Very well, marcus. I will trust in your truths and in the ancient promise." She grimaced as the healer moved between her legs. "You will take my daughter and flee."

Vren's head jerked up. "Majesty?" She couldn't be serious.

Queen Kara ignored him, focusing on the other women in the room. "Well?"

"Majesty," one of them said, "lean back and let me try–"

"No," Kara was firm. "We both know the bleeding will not stop. I won't die bleeding out on the birthing bed. Better to ride into battle with my warriors, sword in hand. Pack me up with bandages and bring me my armor."

Vren's heart sank further at her words. This was not a woman seeking rescue.

The chief guard stepped forward. "Majesty, no–"

The babe at Kara's breast dropped the nipple and yawned. The newborn had a shock of black hair, just like her mother. For a brief moment the woman smiled down at her babe, then lifted a stark face to the others. "King Xywellan has fallen. I must rally our warriors or all is lost."

"Majesty, you will die." The chief guard placed her hand on Kara's shoulder. More than a guard, then.

"Death comes for us all in time," the Queen said. "I will not flee the field while one hope remains." She grimaced. "Finished? Help me up."

The Captain took the sleeping babe and the token. Many hands extended to aid Kara to sit on the edge of the bed. Her face was pale, breath coming in short gasps. "T'will serve. My armor."

"Wait," another healer offered her a cup. Kara downed it in one gulp, then grimaced.

"Give it a moment," the healer said. Kara nodded, breathing heavily. Then she jerked her head to the Captain.

"Give her to him. And the token."

Vren took the swaddled child, but not without protest. "Your majesty?"

Kara took a shuddering breath, then straightened her shoulders. "My armor," she commanded.

The women started to help Kara into her padded jerkin. "Marcus," she said, again with the tone of command, "Hide her. Keep her safe."

"Majesty?" he asked. He shifted his gaze to the Captain, as if to confirm the Queen's madness.

The woman met his stare with her own and gave him a nod.

Queen Kara continued as her attendants dressed her, "My warriors and I will rally the army. Give strength to the weakening hearts. I will not leave these warriors whom Xywellan led to their deaths."

"Majesty," Vren argued, "she'd be safer with you, with a host of warriors–"

"This has already been decided, Marcus," Kara interrupted. "Even before the birth pains started, this was the path. If I live through the day, you will bring her back to me. If not, there is no one else I can trust with her safety. Or with the raising of the true heir to the throne." She held out a hand. "Dagger."

One was handed to her.

Half clad, Kara sat on the edge of the bed and nicked her left palm. Blood welled on her pale flesh.

The healer made a soft sound of protest; Kara gave her a cynical look. "As if it matters now."

Someone handed her a small glass phial. She held it beneath her injured hand, letting the blood fill the glass. "Know what I know," she recited. "Feel what I feel. See what I have seen and known. See what comes within this day." Kara stared at Vren but he doubted that she saw him; her eyes were wide and slightly unfocused. "I give these memories freely unto you and to those you so choose." She took a deep, steadying breath. "Quickly now."

The phial was stoppered with cork and wax and placed in his hand as a healer bandaged her wound. Holding the babe tight, Vren managed to tuck the phial away securely as all the women, even the healers, started to armor and arm themselves, preparing for battle.

Queen Kara's voice was muffled as her chain shirt was eased over her head. "Wellan extended his hand in peace to those poisonous Wyverns," she said. "Brought them to court, treated them with honor."

Someone brought out the chain leggings, but she shook her head. "No, the weight will be too much. Just the leathers."

They pulled her to her feet. She paled for a moment, none too steady. But after a breath she nodded and was aided into the trous. To his horror, he caught a glimpse of blood on the bandages between her legs before they were covered up.

She stepped into her boots as another knelt to lace her in.

Kara looked him in the eye. He knew that expression. One who sees death approaching and has thrown caution to the winds. "And for his efforts to please, to placate, they turned on him, bringing this war, this civil war, this bloody, vicious, wasteful war." Her women tugged at her, fastening buckles, armoring their Queen. "There's no hatred worse than that between bloodkin," she finished.

A warrior approached, knelt, and held up her sword. Kara took the weapon and buckled it on. "Are we ready?"

"Aye," came the chorus. The others nodded, donning their helmets. They started filing past him, bowing their heads to the babe as they passed.

Kara was last, and she moved close, looking at her daughter. She gently drew one finger down the infant's soft check. The babe stirred in Vren's arms but did not waken.

"Forgive me, child." For the first time, Vren saw Kara's pain. "For I have brought you into a world of fire and blood and treachery and now must leave you. Such was never my intent." She cupped her babe's cheek in her hand. "Blessings upon you, Xylara, Daughter of the Blood, Daughter of Xywellan and Kara, Warrior Queen."

The tent flap closed behind her before he could say a word.

Horns pealed with rallying cries.

Vren looked down into the tiny face of the babe as the enormity of what was happening hit him. A babe. None of his training had prepared him for this. Be the wind, be the shadow, be the blade, certainly, but an infant? Where could he take her? How would he feed her? Doubts and fears flooded him. He looked down at Dust, hoping she had some idea—

The vore was staring at a corner, ear perked forward.

A young woman sat there on a stool, pressed into the tent wall, out of the way. She had golden brown skin and a sprinkle of dark freckles around her brown eyes. The tangled coils in her black hair trembled, her face filled with resignation and terror. She too had a babe in the crook of one arm, its skin a paler version of hers. The other hand held a trembling blade, poised as if she meant to defend herself.

Vren was speechless for a moment, then it hit him. "Wet nurse," he whispered.

"Aye," came the barest whisper in return. "I am Amari of–" Her voice cracked and she stopped. "It matters not." She tightened her grip on both the babe and the blade. "Kill us, please."

Vren stared at her.

"I am no warrior and the Queen had enough to worry on." She gulped, her dark brown eyes wide. "You must save her," nodding to the baby in his arms. "Save the hope of Xy." She took a ragged breath.

"But if you would–" she choked on her words. "I cannot kill him," she whispered, looked down at her own babe. "And I would not wait for what must come." She flipped the blade over and held it out to him, hilt first. "Please, have mercy. Don't leave us alive for them to ravage."

More horns sounded, pealing strong and clear.

Vren hesitated. Alone, he'd slip away with none the wiser. But the needs of the child in his arms outweighed his own.

"Can you keep up?" He moved closer to her, ignoring the blade. Dust whined, facing the tent flap, keeping watch.

Amari blinked at him as if not understanding his words.

"I will try to save you both," Vren said. "But if you falter, I will leave you behind." She was in skirts, true, but they were simple enough not to impede her much, and looked warm.

Hope dawned in desperate, swollen eyes. "You are truly a

marcusi?" she asked with disbelief. "And that is a vore? I have heard such stories."

"Only half are true," he said softly as he pressed her elbow, urging her to her feet. "If you can keep up."

"Yes, but promise me," she said, rising. "You will kill us, if–"

"If I can, without risk to my charge."

Dust huffed. She would deal with it, if necessary.

"Quickly," he continued. "Grab what you can and let us be off. How long will they sleep?"

The woman was already reaching for a sling and tying her babe to her chest. "The birth was less than an hour ago. The Queen nursed her; my own just fed. A few hours, perhaps more." She fumbled for an extra sling and handed it to him, then frantically gathered supplies, stuffing them into a sack.

"Good." He took the sling and bound Xylara to his chest, then covered her with his cloak. "We will try to avoid being seen, but we must move fast. They will search for her, once they know–" he cut that thought off, not willing to ill-wish the Queen.

But Amari nodded, painful reality in her eyes. "Where?" she asked as she swept up a dark cloak and settled it over her shoulders before drawing up the hood. "There is no safety hereabouts. All those that were loyal to Kara are in the field with her."

He paused, considering. The options were limited but … .

Dust whined, rising to her feet, her hackles up. From outside came the tramp of boots and the clash of swords.

Vren drew his dagger and slit the tent wall along one of the seams. "Where they would not think to look." He pushed through the canvas and reached back for her.

"Come."

# CHAPTER TWO

—◦—

Amari lost track of the hours as they fled through the rain, the dark, and the cold. With her babe strapped to her chest, she was free to focus on staying close to the marcus. She didn't question when he led her out of the camp, squelching through mud, the drizzle falling on her oiled cloak. She didn't question when they hid in trees as he scouted the way; her thoughts were constantly on the babes, hoping they would stay warm and dry and quiet. Thanks be to the Hearth that they slept.

Time blurred as she followed and obeyed. Stopping and hiding at the man's merest gesture, moving on when the vore nudged at her with its snout.

Ancestors, that creature was huge. It moved silently in and

out of the darkness, but she did not fear it.

She was too numb for fear.

She didn't question when the vore left them, or how the marcus somehow managed to get them into the city, didn't question when he led her through dark and winding alleyways. She simply kept putting one foot in front of the other and didn't let herself think on what she had seen, what had happened in a scant few days.

She didn't question when he led her up three flights of a wooden staircase, pausing for a moment while he picked the lock of a simple wooden door.

It wasn't until Amari found herself standing in the warmth of a strange kitchen, lit by a small night lantern, that questions even occurred to her, that fear began to creep into her very breath. She almost couldn't move when the marcus urged her to a seat by the stone hearth. Every muscle in her body sang with the urge to flee; they weren't ready to accept the idea of safety.

"Take him," the marcus whispered as he handed her Dalan. Amari let him tuck Dalan under her cloak, eased her boy into the crook of her arm. Lara was swaddled close to her already—she and the marcus had switched off, letting her take Lara's smaller weight—and the marcus pulled Amari's cloak closed over all three of them.

"I'll return in a moment," the marcus whispered, and then he was gone, leaving her in the dark, her heart still racing.

Dullness and weariness washed over her. Her damp shoes felt cold against her feet and every bone ached. Amari welcomed the exhaustion. The fog muted her fear and made it hard to think, hard to understand all that had happened in a few short hours.

Dimly they tugged at her heart, the grief and sorrow, waiting for her to see, to feel. But she couldn't let herself think on that. Not yet. For now, she would sit in the quiet shadows, huddle within the shelter of her cloak and hood, and wait.

What pierced her fog was the gurgle of a fussing babe. Dalan was rooting, turning his cheek toward her, eyes closed and mouth moving.

Alive. Her son was alive and warm, and they were safe, and relief started to creep under her skin, but she dare not trust it. She stared down at his sweet face and took in his heat, his scent. Alive, blessedly alive. Tears welled, but she couldn't let herself feel joy.

Not yet.

Her gaze was drawn to the smaller bundle, where she could see Xylara's tiny, sleeping face, so innocent, so small, so very precious.

Amari leaned back in the chair, looking around. She couldn't see much. There was a high, small window, rain pelting against the leaded glass. The place smelled musty, of dust and old paper. There was warmth, but no proper hearth, just an oven with metal doors set in the stones. A wooden table, chairs, and were those dishes stacked about?

Now that her breathing had slowed, she could hear the faint sounds of music and laughter below her, and a rhythmic pounding that didn't seem to be drums.

Dalan shifted against her side. He'd wake soon, both of them would, and they'd need tending. She blinked against her tiredness, determined not to sleep, and tightened her hold on the babes. The marcus hadn't said they were safe, and if the need came, she'd rise and flee again.

So long as he was willing to lead to safety, she would follow.

———•———

"Two babes? A wet nurse? Why in the name of all the gods did you bring them here, Vren?" Orval pushed back his blankets, shifted to sit on the edge of his bed and stared at the marcus in horror. The light of the small bedside lantern pooled around them, leaving the rest of his bedchamber in shadows. "This city is the first place the Wyverns will come, to secure the throne."

"They need shelter and warmth," Vren said as he shook his head. "The Wyverns will not think to look here for a babe." His voice was an urgent plea. "You are a known bachelor, distant cousin to both sides of the conflict, not often at court and—" he hesitated.

"A cripple," Orval finished for him bitterly. He ran his hand through his curls and over his face. "Vren, I have known you for years, and you have honored me with your name, but I have to say this is not the smartest thing you have ever done."

"Needs must, when the snows come." Vren sighed, his weariness showing on his face. Orval reached for his bed-coat at the foot of the bed and struggled into it. "You're sure that King Xywellan and Queen Kara are dead?" Orval asked gruffly, really not wanting to know.

"It's possible that they triumphed," the marcus said. "But even so—" He paused. "Queen Kara gave me her blood memories."

Orval closed his eyes in grief as it washed over him. He and Wellan and Kara hadn't been close; but they had been family. "They might take the child, raise it as their own."

Vren gave him a pitying look. "Orval, you fostered with Xyrath. Do you really think he would tolerate a rival for the crown?"

"Our fosterage overlapped, 'tis true, but thankfully, not for long." Orval grimaced. "And no, he would not. They will kill the child." He ran his hand through his curls. "Where are they?"

"The kitchen," Vren said. He paused. "Your servants. They are loyal?"

"Now you think of that?" Orval said harshly, then regretted it when fear flashed over the marcus's face. "Forgive me, old friend." he grumbled. "I am not at my best, roused in the middle of the night. I had to release my servants months ago. I hated to; they'd served my sister before–" His throat closed with fresh pain. Orval took a breath and pushed past the sorrow. "My Crown stipend was cut."

"Forgive me," Vren said. "I'm–"

"Forgiven." Orval took a breath, then eased to his feet, wincing at the cramps which spidered through his withered leg. "Of course I will shelter them until better is found. Is Dust with you?"

"No." Vren picked up the small copper lantern to lead the way. "She is laying a false trail toward Swift's Port. Besides," he flashed a grin, "she does not do well in cities."

Orval grunted his understanding as he reached for the bed post to steady himself. "I suppose you picked my lock," he asked, knowing full well the answer.

Vren flashed another grin.

Orval shook his head. "At least tell me you didn't break it."

Vren lifted the lantern. "Of course not," he said, taking mock offense.

Orval took his first painful step, knowing the cramping would ease as he moved. He gestured for Vren to take the lead, then followed as quickly as his leg would allow. It dragged worse when he was tired. The floor was cool beneath his bare feet and he could hear rain striking the windows. It was no night to be out.

Vren lifted the lantern as he walked, taking care to avoid the piles of books and papers. "Bad enough your rooms are a warren," Vren said. "One day you will be buried in these piles of history, biography, philosophy, etcetera, etcetera."

Orval snorted. "I know where everything is," he muttered as

they made for the kitchen. An old, familiar, and oddly comforting argument. "How much time do we–"

The city bells started pealing, reverberating through the stone walls.

"Never mind." Orval said, clutching his bed-coat tighter. The marcus brushed against a pile of scrolls on one of the side tables and knocked a few over. "But have a care," Orval snapped.

"Sorry," Vren murmured.

Even before they reached the kitchen, the deeper church bells had joined in.

"Figures the Holy Matriarch would be quick to support the victor," Orval snorted.

"Aye," Vren agreed quietly as he opened the door to the kitchen. "All the more reason to protect them."

The light of the bed lantern joined that of the one kept burning in the kitchen. Shadows fell from the bulky cloaked figure by the hearth.

"It's safe," Vren said.

Orval stepped in as the figure pulled back its hood. He sucked in more air than he knew he could hold.

She was glorious.

Golden-brown skin, dotted with dark freckles just under her eyes. Tousled, black, tightly curled hair, pulled back with a simple cloth band, framed her face. Deep, dark brown eyes focused on him warily from beneath black velvet lashes.

Orval stepped forward and walked into his own table, sending dishes rattling.

A small cry came from beneath the cloak.

Those lovely eyes dropped to her burden. Orval took a breath at the lines of exhaustion there, the circles under her tight, weary eyes. The mud caked to her shoes and skirts. The wet cloak.

"This is Orval." Vren sat the lantern down on the mantel. "He is a cousin to Xywellan and an honored scholar. He is trusted. You can shelter here."

Those eyes rose again, and Orval was lost. "I," he stumbled, "I," the words caught in his throat. "You are welcome, lady."

"Amari," came her husky whisper, with the faintest trace of an accent. "I am Amari, lord."

"No, no," Orval straightened. "I'm no lord. A distant cousin, no more. A fourth cousin, once removed, in point of fact. No title, that is certain." Flushed, embarrassed, he cleared his throat again. "I, er–"

Vren, all the elements bless him, moved. "Let me help you," he said. "Perhaps something warm to drink," he suggested as he drew a bundle out of Amari's arms.

"Of course, of course," Orval moved then, to open his oven doors. Heat and steam billowed into his face as he used the sleeve of his robe to pull out the kettle. "There are clean mugs some-place... ." Orval glanced around at the shelves and reached for a mug that didn't seem quite as dusty as the others.

Vren held a babe in one arm and he cleared old dishes off the table. Amari was untying her blouse with one hand.

Orval averted his eyes. "We'll get you warm, not a kav drinker myself, too expensive for my purse these days, but I've tea and some honey here somewhere." He could hear himself babbling and forced himself to take a breath and set the tea brewing.

A thin cry drew his attention and he looked back at Amari to see her cradling a tiny babe with a shock of black, silky hair.

"Is that her?" Orval asked.

Amari looked up and nodded. "This is Xylara. Could you

take her for a moment?"

"Oh, I–" Orval put the tea down and wiped his hands on his robe. "If you are sure," he said, nervous. "I'm not much for babies–"

Amari rose, graceful and lovely, and put the babe into his arms. "You won't break her," she said.

"Oh," Orval said softly as the infant yawned and blinked up at him. She had Wellan's hair and fey blue eyes, a true Daughter of the Blood. So small, so new, born into a rough and dangerous world. A world where even a tiny babe could be deemed a threat.

Tears welled up. Orval blinked them away as he remembered the ancient pledge, the words spilling from him in a joyous flood. "My hand to yours. Bless you, Xylara, Daughter of the Airion House of Xy, Daughter of Xywellan and Kara, Warrior Queen."

He looked up to find Amari looking at him, something in those deep pools of brown that had not been there before.

Hope.

## CHAPTER THREE

—⟨•⟩—

*Autumn Equinox, the same day, the first few hours of the
Reign of Xyrath and Queen Satia*

arriors of Xy, behold your King!"

The cheers rose around him as Xyrath greeted his bloody and exhausted warriors as they returned from the battlefield.

Finally, victory was his.

He stood tall and proud before his command tent, bathed in the light of the setting sun, certain that he could be seen by all in his gleaming armor despite the gathering clouds. The torches that surrounded him glowed in the light mist that was starting to fall. Overhead, his banner, red with the rampant gold wyvern, snapped in the breeze.

What a glorious day. What an image to burn into the hearts of his warriors.

Xyrath held his pose, hands on his hips, chest lifted proudly, and watched as Lord Marshal Tarwain walked toward him, covered in gore and dirt, his beard thick with filth. The man's white teeth practically glowed as he grinned in triumph. In his hands was the crown of Xy, gleaming despite the mud and weeds that clung to it. Tarwain wiped at the metal with his bare hands as he drew closer, throwing clumps of muck to the ground.

Xyrath doffed his helmet and shook out his blond hair as the men around him cheered. Tarwain went to one knee before him and offered up the crown. "All hail King Xyrath, Son of the Blood, King of Xy!" Tarwain boomed.

Cheers rose as Xyrath took the crown, careful not to grimace at the feel of the chilly mess still clinging to the gold. He lifted the circlet high before placing it on his own glorious blond head. The cheers rang out again and continued as he pulled Tarwain to his feet. Xyrath put one hand on Tarwain's neck and pulled his head close, as if in fond embrace. "Wellan?" he asked under his breath.

"Dead," Tarwain said. "I pulled the crown from his head myself."

"And the Ring?" Xyrath asked.

Tarwain shook his head. He drew from his belt the traditional red leather gloves also smeared with gore and mud, and dropped them at Xyrath's feet. "Lost. I pulled these off his hands myself. The Ring wasn't on him," he murmured. Tarwain straightened up as he took a step back and took off his own helmet, running a hand through his dark, sweat-soaked hair. "Hail to King Xyrath," he shouted.

Cheers washed over Xyrath, even as a wave of rage passed through him at the loss of the Ring. But he kept his face stern and solemn. There would be time for that later. He raised a hand for silence.

The bloodied and exhausted men around him all went to one knee, bowing their heads. Tarwain waited a breath, then he too knelt.

"My friends, my faithful brothers," Xyrath half-shouted, "we have won this day. I give thanks to the Lord of the Sun for his aid and strength in ending this civil war. Once more, the Crown has been claimed by the Blood. Let us march upon the gates of Edenrich and restore the Throne of Xy!"

Cheers followed his words, but they seemed to be a bit less enthusiastic than moments before. Lord Marshal Tarwain rose to his feet stiffly, his armor rattling. "My King, perhaps you mean to march upon the morrow? I've a report on our losses and we must see to the wounded."

Xyrath frowned at the man. "We must present ourselves to our people, Lord Marshal."

"Aye," Tarwain said, hesitating. "But Your Majesty needs to–"

"Wait," finished a feminine voice.

The flap of the command tent opened as Xyrath turned to see Satia emerge, looking calm and cool in blood-red robes, her beautiful heart-shaped face bearing a slight smile. Her golden brown skin glowed in the torch light, her long black hair gathered in a single thick braid.

Two of her bondmaidens followed. Surprisingly, they were not dressed in their usual, matching finery. Satia had armed and armored them, so they stood in black leather and chainmail, swords and daggers at their sides. The pair framed Satia, in her lovely red dress, her dark eyes warm and filled with admiration for him.

Every inch his lovely queen.

She was going to stop him, he could tell, just as she had restricted him from the battlefield. A necessary precaution, but it had still stung.

Her alluring dark eyes focused on Xyrath as if she knew his thoughts. "His majesty needs to wait before his triumphal entry to Edenrich. The time is not yet right. There are tasks that need doing."

Xyrath returned her smile, hiding a twinge of annoyance. She was right, and she had good reasons, but he disliked being denied. Still, there were tasks that only he could do. He held out his hand.

Satia stepped lightly to his side and took it.

"Warriors of Xy," Tarwain bellowed. "Behold her Majesty, Satia, Queen of Xy."

Cheers rose again. Xyrath was pleased they were not as loud as *his* had been.

———•———

Satia smiled as she emerged from the tent, focused on her glorious golden god of a man, now king. King.

*Finally.*

But even as she stepped forward and took his hand, turning her gaze on the cheering warriors gathered before them, she knew this wasn't the end, it was just the beginning. They had seized the crown, now they had to secure it.

"My King," she said placing extra emphasis on the title. "We must needs see to our injured and our honored dead." She tilted her head to the northern sky and lowering clouds. "The winds will bring rain this night. A sorry sight to stagger into the city, bedraggled and muddy." He flinched at muddy, as she knew he would. She pressed her point. "We will make a glorious procession of victory in the bright light of the morning, with all the fanfare you can imagine, if the people are given time to prepare."

Xyrath hesitated ever-so-slightly, then smiled and nodded. "You are right, my fair Queen," he said. "In the morning light, I'll ride at the head of my warriors with the trumpets sounding, banners flying, and all the people cheering."

"Besides," Satia leaned into him to whisper, making sure that he caught the scent of her perfume as her breath tickled his ear. "All know that a warrior is most potent after a battle." She half-closed her eyes, letting her dark lashes mask them. "We must celebrate, you and I. After you have seen to the … business. Upon your return."

That caught his interest, as she knew it would. She could see the pulse in his neck beat faster at that invitation.

"What better way to celebrate than with your rich, sweet body," he whispered back. "And perhaps, finally, an heir in the making." He kept his eyes on hers as he lifted her hand to his mouth and kissed it. "Let it be so," he whispered.

Satia dropped her eyes demurely. "Walk among your warriors, then run your errand," she murmured. "I will make the prepara-tions." She pulled back and raised her voice. "Escort the King to walk among our ranks. All Hail the King of Xy!"

"Hail, Hail, Hail," came the chant.

King Xyrath lifted his hand and basked in their admiration, heading into their midst.

Satia watched Xyrath go with silent amusement. For every-thing that Xyrath lacked, he did make an impressive sight.

Lord Marshal Tarwain stepped to her side, gesturing to his own escort. "Go with him. Keep him out of trouble."

The guards hurried off, leaving him alone with the Queen.

"What word?" she asked quietly.

"I've no numbers yet, but their dead outnumber ours. Once Kara fell, it was a rout."

"Kara is dead?" Satia asked sharply. "You are certain?"

"Aye," Tarwain nodded. "I saw her body with my own eyes."

"Had she given birth?" Satia pressed, keeping her voice low. Her Bondmaidens had moved to shelter them, making sure there were no prying ears and eyes.

Tarwain seemed taken aback. "My Queen, I don't know. She was wearing armor–"

"You didn't strip it off?" Satia asked.

"No, of course not," Tarwain stared at her.

Satia managed not to roll her eyes. Men. Useless. Instead she gave him nod of understanding. "Of course not," she echoed. "But we need to know."

Tarwain nodded and glanced behind her. "Perhaps your hand-maidens–"

"Bondmaidens," Satia corrected him. The nervousness in his eyes pleased her.

"Perhaps they could, er," Tarwain said.

"We will see to it," Satia said. She smiled at him again, offering reassurance. "Are you securing the enemy camp? How many noble prisoners do we have?"

"Not many," Tarwain said, his shoulders relaxing slightly. "Most died on the field. I will order the rest executed."

"No, no," Satia shook her head, making sure to keep her voice gentle. "We will show mercy and imprison them instead. We can hold them for ransom, seize their estates. There's time. And some things are worse than death."

"As you command," Tarwain gave her a bow. "I've given orders that there is to be no looting," He assured her. "I don't have a full count of our dead yet, but we lost quite a few. Lord Asyith is dead, as is Lord Eijer."

"Leaving a trail of broken hearts and promises, no doubt." Satia looked again at the clouds building in the sky, thinking of next steps. "We need to secure the city and the treasury. If there is one left."

Tarwain nodded. "I will send Lord Roredge and his men. If the gates open to them, they will secure the castle."

"The gates will open," Satia assured him. "We have enough agents within to see that done." Satia folded her hands over her stomach. "Does Roredge have the list of those of the Blood?"

"He does, and Captain Ussin was assigned the task." Tarwain glanced up as the winds rose. The wyvern banners snapped on their poles. "Is that really necessary?"

"Those of the Blood must be found and secured," Satia said firmly. "We need to ensure their … safety. Make certain of them. Be sure to find Orval especially."

"The cripple?" Tarwain snorted his disbelief. "When I knew him, he was always lost in his books."

"Xyrath has given me to understand he is clever. Dangerous in his own way," Satia said firmly.

"I'd worry more about Tithanna, the Dowager Queen." Tarwain glanced toward the city.

"We will see to her. You will arrange an escort?" At his nod, Satia smiled at him. "We have won the Crown, Tarwain. Now we must secure it. We must be seen to be gracious and merciful in public. Retribution will come later."

Tarwain glanced around, then moved closer and bent his head

toward hers. "Perhaps we could discuss the details of our plans in your tent this night?"

Satia gave him a warm smile, then did her trick: half-closed eyes above a slow, sensual smile. She shook her head ever so slightly. "I must celebrate with the King this night, Lord Marshal." She extended her hand for him to kiss. "Later, perhaps?" She put a promise into her voice.

Tarwain bowed over her hand, letting his lips linger on her skin. "Majesty." He strode off as the first drops of rain began to fall.

She watched him leave as her Bondmaidens, Mira and Avice, stepped to her side. "The Lord Marshal doesn't know," Mira stated. It wasn't a question.

Avice retrieved the red leather gloves from the ground.

Satia still watched her departing lover. "I see no reason why he should," she said softly. "In a few weeks, I will proclaim I am with child. Xyrath will puff with pride, and the people will rejoice that I have finally produced an heir. Who will question then?"

Mira smiled, her dark eyes warm as her reddish-brown skin and dark hair caught the last rays of the sun. Such a contrast to Avice, tall, ivory-skinned, and golden-haired, but with a face as cold as it was lovely.

Satia turned and went back into the tent, followed by her Bondmaidens. Where there should have been tables with maps and battle plans, there were only thick carpets and a large, luxurious bed. Xyrath's command tent was for his personal comfort.

The maps and plans were in her chamber.

The new Queen stepped into one of the smaller sections, where her three other Bondmaidens waited.

Caris and Iris made an odd picture, wearing their black leathers and chain while seated and working at their tatting and knitting. They too were opposites. Caris, with her auburn hair and brown eyes, tawny and tanned. Iris, dark as obsidian, black eyes, black hair, as deadly as she was dark.

No needlework for Nora, she of the sharp cheek bones, her skin like a lustrous pearl, her hair black as night. She merely sat and waiting, poised for action. Now she looked up, eager to be unleashed.

Satia stood for a moment, thinking. Who best for the tasks at hand?

"Avice," Satia decided. Regal and commanding, one look from those blue-eyes would cut through any who challenged her. "Take some of Tarwain's men and go secure Wellan's and Kara's bodies."

"She is dead?" Nora asked.

"Yes," Satia said.

"The babe?" Caris asked.

"Unknown," Satia sniffed. "And the men did not think to check her body. Avice will make sure," Satia turned to her and the young woman gave a firm nod. "Make clear our regrets that the babe died within her. Claim her body and Wellan's on my behalf. Say it is so they are not dishonored, so we might tend to their burial with all due respect." She made a face, looking at the disgusting wet leather in her hands. "I don't suppose these gloves will burn."

Avice shrugged. "Eventually."

"Bury them with him," Satia said, then paused. "No. With Kara. She should have worn them."

Avice bowed her obedience and Satia dropped the gloves into the Bondmaiden's hands.

"Caris, Iris, Nora, ride to the enemy camp and secure the command tents. I want any documents preserved, as well as any valuables." Satia narrowed her eyes in thought. "But first seek out Kara's tent and report what you find. If she gave birth, and the child is there, kill it and any witnesses."

Caris flinched ever so slightly. "Majesty–"

Satia narrowed her eyes and swiftly sent a pulse of pain through the bond to all of them. Caris stiffened and clenched her right hand about her left wrist.

"You are bound, you are all bound, to me, to my House, to my command." Satia concentrated harder to drive the point home and now they all flexed their left hands. Nora pulled back her sleeve to expose the bond mark on the pulse point of her inner wrist.

Its red hot glow contented Satia and she eased up on her focus. "That babe, that Airion bloodline, is a threat," Satia said firmly. "Babes die, from fever, from colic, in their cradles asleep. Smother the get, conceal the body, and bring it here. I would see it with my own eyes."

"I meant no disrespect," Caris bowed her head.

"If you find that the child was born yet find no trace of the babe, hunt it down." Satia turned to Iris. "Pursue any information, any hint. Do not stop until it is dead in your hands."

"We could gather some warriors," Iris said. "The more eyes–"

"No," Satia said. "I want no whispers, no gossip. You will hunt, and you alone."

"We will see it done." They gathered up their needles and thread and bowed while Nora rose smoothly to her feet, then bowed as well.

"Go then." Satia smiled as her poison darts left swiftly. She sighed and stretched as the tent flap closed behind them.

"Mira, we must prepare for the King's return. He will be some time, but we should be ready." Satia lifted a hand and started to take down her braids. "Stoke the braziers and warm some towels." Satia looked up at a new sound: a hard rain had begun to strike the tent. "Bring my oils and perfumes. We should prepare hot food and drink as well. His Majesty will be wet and chilled."

"I'll mull some wine," Mira said. "And lace it perhaps? A touch of herbs to aid his Majesty?"

"Yes," Satia nodded absently. "He will return to bury himself in my arms even as his men work in the rain to clear the field and bury the dead. He will think only on his victory, not on the cost."

"Or what must be done to keep you safe on the throne." Mira said.

"Our throne," Satia said, dropping one hand to her belly. "Our throne."

# CHAPTER FOUR

Yfin sat on the hearth stool in the corner, leaned against the warm stone of the fireplace, and tried not to let his eyes close.

It was good, being hearth boy in the Palace, not as good as kitchen boy, but better than cleaning the midden or catching rats. Best an orphan like him could expect. He was fed and warm, better than when he'd been running the streets.

His duty was the hearths and naught else. Normally, this late, he'd be bedded down already, on his own pallet, with a blanket all to himself.

But this night he'd been sent to serve Queen Mother Tithanna. Usually, she took to her bed fair early. The Queen Mother was old, as old a person as Yfin had ever known, wrinkled and tall, with bright white hair she kept in a thick braid. She liked her chambers warm, for her old bones, she'd said.

Footsteps roused him and he glanced up as she paced by, circling the chairs before the hearth, back and forth. She'd been doing that since he'd come on duty, her heavy robes swishing against the floor as she walked.

Yfin yawned and rubbed at his face. He'd already got a good stack of wood, so easy enough to keep the fire bright.

The Queen Mother made a turn and stopped. Yfin heard footsteps, coming towards the door. He rose to answer it.

"No," she said quietly, picking up a candle. "I'll see to the door."

Yfin stayed put, laying in a bit of kindling and blowing on coals. The flames licked at the wood as he heard a sharp sound behind him.

He turned and saw the Queen Mother just standing there, looking all hollowed out. Her face was as pale as the moon, her eyes glittering like dark stars.

Two men had entered. One of them, bloody and filthy, knelt before her. "I broke off when I saw Queen Kara go down, Daughter of Xy." He coughed and clutched at his ribs, his face gaunt with pain. "Thought it best to bring you word before-"

Yfin inched closer and smelled the iron tang of blood, the sharpness of smoke, and the sourness of sweat. But the Queen Mother's face was still, as if the smells and the blood did not exist.

"You've done well," she said, her voice oddly strong. She reached out and put her hand on his sweat-soaked head. "May the Lord of the Sun bless you for your service to our House," she continued. "But you need to go, get away from here. They will come."

The bloody man nodded and rose with the help of the other man. "I will, Your Majesty." He bowed his head. "Lady, Xywellan died fighting. Swinging his sword, cursing them to the last—"

"My thanks," the old lady said gently, looking past him to the other man. "Can you get him out and away?"

"It will be like he was never here," came the gruff response as the man stepped into the light. Yfin recognized Captain Roth of the Palace Guard. A strong man with a short gray beard and hard eyes, tonight his face was tired and lined. Yfin wanted nothing so much in this world as to be a Guard and carry a sword and be just like Cap'n Roth. But he'd no chance of that.

The wounded man wasn't done. He reached out his hands, palms up. "My hand to yours. Bless you, Tithanna, Daughter of the Wyvern House of Xy, Daughter of Xyvoth, Wife of Xykahn, Warrior King."

A thrill passed through Yfin at the words of the old oath.

The Queen Mother reached out and pressed his hands together between hers. "My hand to yours. Blessings upon you, Warrior of the Airion House of Xy."

The fire spat and Yfin started and turned back to his duty, using the poker to spread out the coals and adding another log. He heard the Queen Mother say something to the Captain, heard the door close. There was a whisper of cloth and then she stood over him, looking into the flames.

Yfin looked up as the firelight danced on her face. He was young, true enough, but he knew something had happened, something bad, because he knew that there was war. He was afraid to speak, to ask, because, well, she was old and kind, but scary at the same time.

She took deep breath, then gave a sharp nod, like she'd made up her mind about something. "Build up the fire, lad," she commanded. "I'll see to more candles."

Yfin scrambled to obey, out the door and running for another armful of wood.

When he returned to her chambers, Captain Roth was in the room with the Steward. The Queen Mother stood by the fireplace, arms crossed over her chest.

Yfin darted in, dropped the wood by the hearth with a clatter, and bent to work with a will while they argued. The boy watched them out of the corner of his eye.

He knew Steward Paulin, 'cause the man had a tendency to kick boys out of his way. Normally, Yfin was frightened of him. But right then, the Steward stood there, sweating, shifting his weight from one foot to another like he had an itch. He pulled out a large white handkerchief and mopped his balding head. Now, he was the one that looked afraid.

The Captain, now, he was like a rock, his voice soft but firm. "We could fight."

"What good would that serve?" The Queen Mother faced them, her voice clear and sharp. "More blood spilled and to what end? Open the gates," she commanded. "Welcome the victors."

The Steward bowed and scurried off, closing the door behind him. Captain Roth waited.

"Instruct your men as well, Captain." The old lady's voice was firm. "They are to offer no impediment."

"I'll pull them off the gates." The Captain's voice was low and rough. "The Steward can have the honors."

The Queen Mother snorted. "He'll bow his head and not have the courage to look them in the eye."

Captain Roth's smile was grim.

"Just as well." The Queen Mother lifted her hand to smooth down her hair. "Just as well that I sent my women to safety weeks ago."

"Majesty," the captain's voice grated, low and thick, "you should go."

"Go?" she said, her voice sounded so regal Yfin had to look up from his work. She seemed to grow taller as he watched. "Go where, good Captain?"

"There are those that would shelter–"

"And what of the harm I would bring down on them? No." She shook her head so hard the braid swayed down her back. "I stay. But what of you, Captain?"

Captain Roth gave a slight shrug. "The Palace Guard has walked a fine line of neutrality, ma'am. I will be well, or not, as it may be." His face went hard. "I will not leave my post."

The Queen Mother nodded, then shivered, rubbed her arms, and sank down into her chair. "I would ask for more wood. The boy will build up the fire and we will wait."

The Captain bowed and next thing Yfin knew, guardsmen were tramping in with arms full of wood, stacking it up by the side of the hearth as tall as he was. They'd come in, stack the wood, and bow to the old lady, seated in her chair, her eyes hooded, staring into the fire.

At last, they were finished and the room grew silent. It was just the Queen Mother and the hearth boy and the crackle of the fire. Yfin could hear the castle stirring beyond the door and people moving about with voices raised.

Queen Mother Tithanna rose from her chair, went to the door, and bolted it. "Come," she bid Yfin, and he followed her into her bedchamber.

"Under the bed," she gestured. "The long, narrow chest."

Yfin went to his belly and pulled the chest out in a cloud of dust.

"Lazy maids," she muttered, then gave a dry laugh. "As if that matters now. Come, lad."

She led the way back to the fire and slowly lowered herself to the floor, close to the hearth. "Open it," she commanded.

The box was a narrow thing, of old, thin pine. It took Yfin a minute to wrestle the stiff latch. Once he had it opened, the old lady reached in and pulled out a dagger, with a bright blade and a sheath decorated with an airion. She drew the blade.

"Still sharp," she said, testing it. She held it for a long moment. "This was mine, when I was young. Wellan would not wear it for fear of offending the Wyverns. He was too trusting, too eager to please."

After a long pause, she set it aside and pulled out a tabard of blue and white velvet and embroidered with an airion, rearing up, its sharp claws extended.

"He wore this at his investiture, when he was named Prince and Heir. I embroidered it myself." The Queen Mother held it up. The cloth glittered in the firelight, on the silver and gold threads. "He was so proud that day, so glorious. Handsome, the sun shining on his sweet face as his father placed the coronet on his head."

Yfin knelt beside her, admiring the crest. The airion looked so fierce, with the head and wings of a bird, and the body of a horse, and the legs of a lion.

The old lady gripped it firmly in both hands and brought it up to her nose, her eyes closed tight. Like maybe she could still smell something on the cloth.

Then she tossed it into the flames.

Yfin jumped, reaching for his poker, sure she'd made a mistake, but she gripped his arm and stopped him. "Let it go," she commanded. The cloth burned and the gold threads curled up and melted.

She hesitated over a sheaf of letters tied with ribbon. "Ah, Kahn, my love," she whispered, letting her fingers linger over the ribbon. "You wed me to bring the Airion and Wyvern families together and it only drove them all further apart. It might have worked, but for your death. Our Wellan just was not strong enough."

Yfin shifted his weight from one foot to the other. She didn't look at him, just tossed the bundle on the fire. The paper sizzled and turned black.

"Build up the fire," she commanded. Yfin placed two logs and added more kindling to create the brightest, hottest flame.

The Queen Mother reached into the box again and pulled out old cloth gloves, stained brown.

"His first kill at the hunt," she said, placing the gloves in her lap. "My golden boy, laughing in the courtyard as his father the King smeared the blood on his cheeks and forehead. So young, so happy, and his father and courtiers all gathered around, praising him. He basked in everyone's approval. I was so proud, but I hurt as well. I lost my little boy to manhood."

With a flick of her wrist the gloves went into the fire, landing on a log as if they'd been put there to dry.

Yfin watched them blacken, then returned his attention to the old woman to see her drawing a leather cuirass from the box, clearly made for a little one even smaller than him. The leather was dry and cracked, worn thin from use. Something clattered to the floor as she pulled it out; a small wooden sword and shield had been tangled with the leather.

Yfin couldn't resist; he reached for them, eager to swing, then froze, realizing what he'd done in his excitement.

The Queen Mother eyes crinkled at the corners. "Go ahead," she said.

Yfin grasped the sword and took up the shield in his other hand, taking a stance like he'd seen the guards do at practice. He slashed at his enemy bravely, holding his shield high. The weapons felt so good in his hand, for all that they were toys.

Would that they were real. He closed his eyes and took up the stance again, standing strong, seeing the monster before him, and his blade … .

He stopped, taking a breath. Yfin's shoulders slumped as he came back to himself.

The Queen Mother's blue eyes were fey and wise as she stared at him. "What is your name, lad?"

"Yfin, lady," he said awkwardly, then remembered his lessons. "Your Majesty."

"How old are you?" she asked.

Yfin shrugged. "Last I remember, my mam told me I was ten. She died before the war," he mumbled the last, not really wanting to think on it.

The Queen Mother's smile dimmed. "So you, too, know of loss," was all she said as she gave a nod toward the fire.

Yfin bowed his head in obedience and tossed sword and shield into the flames, trying to ignore the stab of pain it gave him.

The old lady tossed the leather cuirass in as well. Yfin thought for sure the smell would drive them out, but the smoke just grew black as the leather curled and darkened. The wood of the shield was dry enough that it was soon burning, the sword as well. They watched for a bit as the flames consumed everything.

"More wood," she commanded. Yfin quickly obeyed until the flames roared up the chimney and it seemed to him that the stones of the mantle were turning red. Sweat poured off him like rain.

The old lady's face also glistened in the light. He thought it was sweat.

But maybe it was tears.

She tossed smaller things, then, a bouquet of dried flowers, tied with a blue ribbon. Those crisped before they even touched the coals. Next was a child's wooden tablet, with faint chalk marks. She brushed her fingers over them, tracing the letters. That went fast, the fire crackling around it.

The last thing, as Yfin stood and watched, the very last things she brought out, were a white baby gown, with ruffles and ribbons, and a tiny white cap.

The Queen Mother laid it in her lap, gently smoothed out the fragile cloth with her old, wrinkled hands. For a moment, just a moment, she smiled. But pain returned and her face grew tight with anguish. She balled up the cloth and cap and flung it into the flames. It fell like a blanket of white over the wood and fire, but black scorch marks appeared as quick as thought, and then it was gone.

She struggled to her feet, grasping the dagger she'd taken first from the box. Yfin offered his hand and helped her up as best he could.

"Strong young man," she puffed, then steadied herself on the back of the chair. She drew herself up to her full height. towering over Yfin. Once again she pulled the blade from its sheath, then tossed the sheath into the flames.

She held up the dagger, the steel gleaming in the light. The image froze in Yfin's eyes. The tall, old woman, made gold by the fire. Every detail seemed clear; Yfin could see a small sigil on the hilt's cross-piece, glittering in the firelight. The blade glowed in the light, drawing his eye, bright and hard and sharp.

Yfin's heart leapt to his throat.

Tithanna, Queen Mother, shone in the firelight as she lifted her braid, cut it from her head, and flung it into the flames.

The smell of burning hair filled his lungs, and Yfin knew that he'd never forget the heat, the stench. The sight of her face lit by the fire, the short strands of her hair starting to curl without the weight of the braid. She looked no less a Queen.

She stood there tall and unbending, and watched it all burn, the dagger still in her hand. The sheath melted, the gemstones turned brown and cracked. It was something to see.

"Now the chest," she said. "Push it against the wall and fill it full of wood."

Yfin scrambled to do as she bid as a knock came at the door. She placed the dagger on the mantle and went to open it.

There was a blast of cooler air as she pulled it wide. Captain Roth stood there, his eyes going wide as the heat hit his face.

"Your Majesty," he bowed. "A small group of riders approach. They fly no banners, but they come from the field."

"They didn't bother to tend the wounded or see to the dead. Typical." She turned away. "It matters not. I will await them here."

"As you wish, Majesty."

Captain Roth bowed himself out, but she held up a hand. "Captain, this lad is Yfin. He has served me well this night." She gestured Yfin to her side. "He would be wasted as a hearth boy. I think he'd make a fine warrior. Take him into the Guard."

Yfin's heart leapt into his chest at those words. He was sure he looked the fool, mouth wide open and eyes bulging out of his head. "Really? Really?" He trembled as his voice cracked.

Captain Roth didn't hesitate. "As you command, Majesty. Come, lad. Come with me."

Yfin ignored him and fell to his knees before the Queen Mother, his heart so full he could barely croak out the words. "My hand to yours," was all he could manage as he held out his hands, stuttering as he tried to say her name.

The Queen Mother smiled. She reached out and pressed his hands together, between hers. Her palms felt cold and thin against his skin, but her eyes were bright and her words warm. "My hand to yours. Blessings upon you, Warrior of the House of Xy." She released him and reached out to brushed his hair from where it was plastered to his forehead.

The sound of bells came at that moment, city bells, then temple bells, all pealing the news of the victory.

Captain Roth pulled Yfin to his feet and toward the door. The Queen Mother turned back to the fireplace. Yfin blurted out "Lady, what will you do?"

Tithanna looked at him and her smile was bitter. "I will endure," she said. "I have endured the death of my husband. I have endured the death of my sons. I have endured the marriages and departures of my daughters, only to hear of their deaths in letters from distant lands. I will endure the sundering of this House and the triumph of Xyrath, my third grand-nephew, once removed, or whatever he claims to be. I will endure," she repeated.

Captain Roth went to one knee. "My hand to yours. Bless you, Tithanna, Daughter of the House of Xy, Daughter of Xyvoth, Wife of Xykahn, Warrior King." He bowed his head.

The Queen Mother stood silent and still for a moment. "My

hand to yours. Blessings upon you, Warrior of the House of Xy." For the first time, Yfin heard a tremor in her voice. "Ah, Roth," her voice the barest whisper. "Xywellan was such a golden child. And such a terrible king."

She stood there, a dark figure before the raging fire. Captain Roth put his hand on Yfin's shoulder and they both stepped back, bowed, and closed the door behind them.

## CHAPTER FIVE

————⋅(•)⋅————

Amari's weary heart leapt as Orval pledged himself to Xylara.

She'd loved Queen Kara and been grateful for the offer to be a wet nurse, but she was no warrior. For months now, she'd been surrounded by fierce soldiers, men and women with hard muscles and harder eyes, ready to defend their rights with sword and shield. Even the marcus had carried with him a sense of edgy danger.

But this man was different. Short and stout, wearing a bed-coat of all things, he walked oddly. He ... bumped into things. He had plump cheeks and a high hairline under short black curly hair, with skin so pale he must never go out in the sun.

He took Lara into his arms like she was a precious thing he feared to break.

And his face … his face glowed like the sun when he looked up after he spoke the oath. Her heart, weary and tired, drew strength from that calm. He felt … safe, not like a warrior, all sharp of eye and blade. His light blue eyes were warm; they crinkled in the corners when he smiled. One of his front teeth had a slight crook to it, which made him all the more fetching. In the warmth of the kitchen, in the quiet darkness, something eased in her chest.

Then Lara gave a soft cry and all of Amari's worries came crashing back.

"Is she well?" Orval looked at the babe in his arms with terror.

Amari started to struggle out of her cloak. "She needs to nurse," she said shortly. Her fear rose again, that the poor, motherless child would not take her nipple, would not suck, would not– "Unwrap her, please. She might needs a change."

"Oh, uh," the poor man seemed perplexed by the bundle in his arms.

"Here," the marcus took pity. "I'll do it. Take the boy."

Orval took Dalan in his arms as the marcus unwrapped Lara on the table. The room had warmed considerably once the oven door had been opened. She'd be warm enough.

The marcus moved quickly, unwrapping the swaddling. With the babe exposed, he froze for a moment, staring down.

"Is it bad?" Orval asked, balancing Dalan as he averted his gaze and wrinkled his nose.

Amari stifled her smile at his apprehension.

"No, no," the marcus said. "She's good," He quickly changed the cloths, stuffing the old one away in a pocket.

Lara lay quiet, her lips moving, which was a good sign. To

Amari's relief, the birth cord looked healthy, with no signs of irritation or infection. She bared her breasts.

"Ah," Orval looked away, his cheeks turning slightly pink. He dug out kitchen rags, handing them to both of them.

Amari took some warm water from the kettle and a cloth and wiped her nipple. The marcus handed her the newborn and Amari offered a soft prayer as she positioned the child at her breast. "Please," she whispered softly as she tickled Lara's lower lip with her nipple.

She needn't have worried. Lara opened her mouth, latched on like a leech, and started to suck greedily. Amari sagged in relief at the strong, healthy tug at her nipple.

Orval still had his eyes averted, but the marcus was staring at Lara. He lifted his eyes and Amari gave him a nod. He returned it.

"Tea," Orval cleared his throat. "You will want something warm, both of you. There's pease porridge in there as well, warm and filing, if a bit bland."

"A bit?" the marcus said with a sly smile, then shook his head. "I can't stay, Orval. I need to–".

"I've a pot in the hearth," Orval gave him a glare. "You will eat and–"

"Dalan will need seeing to, then I can feed him as well." Amari interrupted gently.

"Two at once?" Orval glanced at her and then quickly glanced away. "Oh, well, yes, of course, I–"

"Here," the marcus reached for Dalan.

"No, no," Orval said firmly. "Get her tea and put something in your stomach. I can do this; it doesn't seem so hard." He placed Dalan on the table and started to unwrap the swaddling.

The marcus shrugged, poured tea, and handed the mug to

Amari. She kept it well away from Lara and sipped eagerly. It was dark and bitter on her tongue, but the welcome warmth pooled inside and made her stomach growl.

"Who do we have here?" Orval asked as he pulled back the swaddling cloth.

"Dalan," Amari said.

Her son was nearly naked on the table. Her eyes filled to see him smile at Orval, healthy and happy as he waved his arms. Orval was peeling back the old nappy hesitantly, as if something was going to jump out and bite him.

"Oh," Amari said, "you might want to cover–"

A small fountain rose in an arc. The proud baby chortled as he decorated Orval's robe.

Orval blinked in surprise. Then he laughed, a lovely, warm belly laugh, his eyes sparkling. "Well, aren't you a little whizzer," he exclaimed.

Dalan chortled and let loose with another stream.

"Oh no, not again, you little scamp." Orval threw a clean cloth over Dalan, cutting off the flow. "We'll get you under wraps right now."

"Don't bother swaddling him," Amari said. "I'll tuck him under my other arm and give him the breast."

"Oh," Orval looked uncomfortable but willing. Amari used her finger to break the suction with Lara, who protested with a small cry as Amari repositioned her under her arm. Thankfully, Lara went right back to sucking fiercely.

Amari took Dalan next, having no fear that her son would have trouble. He too went right for the teat, and she settled with both under her arms as she cradled their heads.

"You need to eat," Orval said.

"After they do," she insisted. "I can eat after they finish." The tugging at her nipples was pleasurable to both her body and her heart as her milk flowed.

"Then you eat," Orval said to the marcus as he pulled a covered crock from the oven with the sleeve of his robe. He used a rag to remove the top, revealing a thick, yellow paste.

The marcus grimaced but pulled a stool to the table. He took a bowl and spoon from Orval and took a bite. "As good as I remember," Vren teased, but started shoveling the porridge in quickly.

"Cheap, plentiful and easy," Orval retorted and poured more tea.

They sat in silence for a moment; the only sound was Dalan snuffling as he nursed. Outside, the bells still rang, muffled and distant. Rain pattered against the window, a steady rhythm. Below them, Amari could hear low talk and that thumping, but the laughter was gone. The tea had given her enough energy to focus. "Where are we?" she asked.

"In Edenrich, in my apartments, over a whorehouse." Orval answered, pouring his own tea.

Amari's eyes went wide as the marcus sighed. "Perhaps a little less honesty," he said to Orval.

"I'm a terrible liar," Orval said with a smile. "This was a warehouse, long ago, and these were the accounting halls. It's now a pleasure house, the House of the Weary Traveler, run by Madam Winter. She caters to an older clientele. Not bad neighbors, and these rooms are perfect for an impoverished scholar like myself. All these shelves, you see. Copper lanterns, so no open flames. The ancient pipes still run water, and the privies are water-flushed. Uses the heat from boilers. Really quite ingenious, when you–"

"He'd go on about the history if you let him." the marcus interrupted. "It's safe. An older, fairly impoverished neighborhood, and his locks are decent."

"You're the only one that picks them," Orval snorted. "No one else bothers now that they know my treasure is a collection–"

"Hoard," the marcus interjected.

"Collection," Orval emphasized. "Of books, papers, scrolls." He puffed up. "Almost as large as the Royal Library."

"Almost," Vren said.

Their expressions told Amari that this was an old game between them. Orval, looking offended, and the glint in the marcus's eyes. But then the marcus's face grew serious as he stared at Orval. "I can't stay," his eyes dropped to the almost empty bowl. "We were seen, before we left the battlefield."

"We were?" Amari clutched the babes to her, then willed herself to ease up. They both kept sucking, unconcerned, innocent of the danger.

The marcus nodded. "We lost them in the rain, well before the walls. But they will hunt, and I must lead them off." He looked at Orval and then nodded to Amari. "And the babes can't risk going further."

Orval nodded, and the humor was gone from his eyes. "What do you need?"

"Dalan's dirty nappy, to go with Lara's," the marcus said. "If I can lose them, I will double-back. Then we will need to find a safer place to hide them. No offense."

"None taken," Orval said. "How long?"

"A few days," the marcus scraped his bowl clean with his spoon. His eyes were hooded. "Maybe more. My guess is that it won't be safe for my charges to move until the Wyverns are occupied with the coronation."

Orval looked at Amari with worry in his eyes. "This place is not set up for babies," he said. "I don't know what they need, or … ." his voice trailed off.

"They need warmth," she reassured him, "dry nappies, and my breasts. That's all, really."

"Well, then," Orval nodded. "We'll cope, yes? I've never entertained such before, but we will find–"

A wooden door creaked open, and a voice called. "Orval! Orval, have you heard?"

The marcus rose, pushed the bowl and spoon in front of Orval, and with a backward step, vanished into the shadows.

"Orval! I know you don't like me to use the inner door, but–" The door to the kitchen opened and a woman stepped in, dressed in gauzy fabrics of green and gold, with her hair decorated with spangles. Tiny bells rang as she closed the door, focused on Orval. "Have you heard? Queen Kara and Xywellan are killed on the battlefield, and the Wyverns are–"

She stopped dead, staring at Amari. "Who's this, then?"

## CHAPTER SIX

O rval's heart surged to his throat as he struggled to rise, his leg cramping. "Madam Winter," he said, then stopped and cleared his throat, trying to stall, to think of what to say.

The older woman had brought a cloud of perfume in with her, as well as her bright silks and the rattle of bracelets and bells. The silence of her abrupt halt was jarring. As was the stunned look on her face.

Echoed by Amari's expression, equally startled, although her gaze seemed focused on Winter's wrists.

Orval cleared his throat, resorting to old customs. "May I introduce–"

"Stop." Madam Winter raised her hand. "I don't want to know. I have enough drama with my ladies downstairs. I came through the inner door to tell you the gossip and you were at your books. I have seen nothing else."

"And what is the gossip?" Orval asked carefully.

"The news is flying through the streets. The Airions have fallen in battle. The Wyverns are securing the city with an advance force and proclaiming their victory." She sniffed. "There's to be a triumphant procession in the morning, with Xyrath and his Queen Satia entering the city in all their glory. They've declared a holiday for all. What comes after is anyone's guess." Winter's eyes narrowed as she stared at Amari.

Orval glanced over. Lara yawned, releasing Amari's nipple. He took the babe, leaving Amari a free hand to deal with her son. He turned back, the naked infant in his hands.

Winter stared.

Nervously he placed the little one back on the table, intending to wrap her, fumbling to find a cloth big enough.

The silence grew.

"My thanks for the news," Orval said, desperate to fill the void. "I don't–"

"No, you don't, do you?" Winter demanded. She stepped over, pushed him aside, and with a deft hand swaddled the babe. "Cover your shoulder," she said. "This one needs burping."

"Oh, er," Orval lifted the little bundle to his shoulder and gingerly started to tap her back. "Of course she does."

"Of course," Winter snorted, and stared at Amari. Dalan had finished nursing and was now in her arms.

Amari lifted her chin. "We can see to the care of my twins," she said, her voice trembling.

Winter lifted an eyebrow and then swept past him, to the inner door. "Orval, I don't know what trouble you are bringing into your home, but leave me and mine out of it. I will go the way I came. Be sure to bolt that door after me and keep it locked. Trust that I will bolt my side." She paused at the door jamb. "Two things."

"Yes?" Orval asked.

"Your sister's clothes would fit her," Winter nodded toward Amari.

Orval's stomach knotted. "And?" he snapped spitefully.

"If you are trying to pass those children off as twins, don't let anyone see that birth cord." Winter snorted. "At least, no woman. And for the love of all that is holy, don't feed them that crappy pease porridge you live on."

She closed the door behind her with a quiet thud.

"That was three things," Orval grumbled as he glared at the door.

Vren emerged from the shadows. "What do you think she knows?" He asked, a blade in his hand and his quiet voice suddenly filled with menace.

"Madam Winter has thrived in this city a long time. She has a strong sense of survival coupled with an edge of paranoia. She is a friend," Orval said firmly, his heart still racing. "A passage runs from her inner chambers to my storage room. Go and bolt that door."

Vren paused in the doorway to look at him. Orval shut his eyes against the pain that welled up and nodded in answer to the unasked question. "My sister's trunks are in there. Shift them to my bedroom, if you would."

Vren nodded and left.

Amari had sat in silence all this time. She looked sad and

defeated. "I should have thought," she whispered. "About the cord. I didn't think—"

"It's no matter," Orval assured her, taking a breath, trying to calm himself. "Winter said she saw nothing, and she means it."

Amari nodded, patting her boy's back with hard firm pats. Orval frowned and tried to copy her method with Lara. The babe was a warm burden on his shoulder, her tiny face close to his.

"Your sister?" Amari asked, her eyes averted.

It was hard to try to talk past the lump in his throat. "My sister and her husband died two years ago, of the Sweat. She was expecting—" he couldn't find the words.

"I'm so sorry," Amari whispered. "I don't really need—"

"No," Orval managed. "Those things have been sitting in storage for long enough. Use what you need. She would have liked that."

Lara sneezed in his ear.

Orval started. "Was that a burp?" he asked.

Amari smiled and nodded.

Orval managed a smile back. "Then let me hold these two while you eat a bowl of porridge. I know it's not much and rather bland, but it's warm and filling." He heard himself babble on, about porridge and tea. He must certainly sound like a complete fool, but that glazed look in Amari's eyes told him that the words didn't matter.

She sank to the stool and reached for the pot to serve herself. He saw that her hands trembled; he suspected she was exhausted. He wanted her to feel safe and distracted long enough to get her into his bed—

No, no, that wasn't what he meant. Into a warm bed, that was all, and he blushed hot at the very idea and sputtered to a stop, praying he hadn't said it out loud.

He must not have, praise the elements. The poor woman seemed to sink into herself as she ate, clearly worn and tired.

Vren slipped silently back into the kitchen. "It's done," he said. A flicker of a grin flashed over his face. "I didn't even knock over any books."

Orval rolled his eyes, grateful for the distraction.

"Could you spare a few pounds of dried pease?" Vren asked. "And a sack or two to carry them?"

"Of course," Orval said. "I've a few dried apples as well, and some bread. Some dried beef for Dust." He gestured to the shelves.

With a few swift steps, the marcus gathered up the swaddling clothes and Dalan's dirty nappy as well as supplies for himself and Dust. Then he went to Amari's side and knelt. "I must go," he said.

Amari nodded wearily. "My thanks to you, marcus. You saved–"

"Lady, you saved us both. I've little knowledge of babes and your courage allowed me to save us all. The Airion House of Xy owes you a great debt." The marcus reached within his cloak and produced a small carving of a panther. "Take this," he said, pressing on the figure so it came apart in two halves and handing one half to her.

"This is a token of the marcusi, we who are sworn to the protection of the Blood. If one comes in my name, he or she will bear the other half. And if you have a dire need, hold your half tight, think on aid, and aid will come, as quickly as it can." The marcus rose to his feet and swung on his pack and cloak.

"I do not even know your name, to ask the Hearth to bless you." Amari said.

Vren flashed that grin of his and glanced at Orval. "And you can see why I trust this man, who has not once used my name in front of you. But I am Vren of the Marcusi, and all your blessings are welcome."

"You have them," Amari's voice trembled with tears.

"I'll keep them hidden," Orval assured them both, wishing he felt a bit more confident.

"I'll be as quick as I can." Vren hesitated. "I have her blood memories," he held out the vial, holding bright red liquid. "Should it stay with–" he nodded toward Lara.

"No," Orval said, handing him the supplies. "It's useless without a mage, and Kara gave the permissions to you. Besides, if aught happens, others will need to know. Take it with you."

"I'll go," Vren said. "I'll let myself out a window and go over the roofs. Best you don't see me leave."

"The skies be with you," Orval said. "And the stars light the way."

———•———

Amari was so tired she didn't even realize the marcus had left until the door closed softly behind him. It was an effort to drag the spoon through the porridge, and bring it to her mouth, but she forced herself to focus, to chew and swallow. It was bland and rather chewy, but it was warm and filled the empty spaces in her stomach. She needed to eat and drink, needed her strength to feed both her babes.

Blinking, she suddenly found the bowl empty, her spoon scraping the sides.

Numbness crept over her and everything seemed distant. Her tiredness went to the bone.

"Up," Orval urged, and she obeyed. He held both babes, one in each arm, and nodded to the door. She opened it, grateful that it moved smoothly, and trailed after him, putting one foot in front of the other, reaching out to the walls for support.

Another door, this one to a bedchamber. There sat a large four poster bed surrounded by thin curtains of various colors, faded and worn. A small mountain of brocade pillows at the head, the blankets tossed back. The walls were covered in faded tapestries of landscapes and airions dancing in the clouds. Every surface was covered with books and papers and pens and bottles of ink. The smell of old paper and dust filled the air.

Here and there hung tiny copper lanterns, flames dancing within. It felt safe and warm and … she almost sobbed with relief.

"Here now," Orval set the babes in the middle of the bed. "They can sleep here this night, close to you. I'll make a wall of pillows, so they don't fall."

"They won't roll," Amari said.

"Still," Orval looked up. "I will feel safer." He gestured to the open side. "For you. You'll probably find something to wear in those trunks and the privy is through that door." Eyes averted, he was busy arranging pillows that weren't needed.

Amari opened a trunk to find women's clothing, bundled haphazardly. She didn't have to dig deep to find a bedgown, smelling faintly of lavender. She pulled it out and retreated to the privy.

She returned to find Orval waiting, all the lanterns out but one. He gestured her to the bed.

"What of you?" she asked as she climbed in and pulled up the covers.

"Oh, I'll be fine," he said. "I fall asleep at my desk regularly."

"But your leg," she said, blinking.

"I've lived with it a long time, lady," Orval said softly. "Now sleep."

"I don't think I can." Amari leaned back against the softness, looking at the babes beside her, surrounded by a fortress of pillows. So many cushions, oddly placed. Was that for his comfort, with his leg? He'd been so kind. Such warm blue eyes … another wave of tiredness crashed over her and she fought a yawn.

Dalan yawned as well, smacking his lips in his sleep. Her son, her boy, safe and warm and beside her. She was still in disbelief. But the pillows behind her were soft and supportive and the blankets were thick. She lay back, eyes wide. "So much has happened, I don't—" she yawned. She was exhausted, but her mind was racing. She had to sleep; the babes would need feeding again in another few hours.

"I have the perfect remedy," Orval said. He cleared a chair of a stack of books, then went to one of the shelves. In the light of the lantern, his pale skin glowed; he seemed very pleased with himself. "It's the *Epic of Xyson*. This is Botswell's interpretation. Not that I agree with all of his ideas, mind, but it's a fair enough representation."

Amari blinked at him. "I don't know that book," she said, and curled on one side, facing him. The bedding started to warm around her body.

"Oh, it's a classic piece of Xyian literature, although its historical accuracy is challenged regularly. Let me read to you." Orval settled in the chair, opened the slim volume, and started to read. "Consider the tactics necessary against horse archers."

The words meant little to her, but his voice was warm and steady, droning on, drowning out her racing thoughts. She took a breath, and then another, and then … .

———•———

Never failed. Orval watched Amari, waiting a moment to make sure she was really asleep, before he rose and left the room. The

*Epic of Xyson* was old and ancient and fascinating to him, but well, even he had to acknowledge it had its dry parts. It had never failed to lull his sister to sleep when she'd … .

He'd caught the whiff of lavender from the chests. Lara's favorite. Grief rose up in his heart. His sister Lara had been lovely and loving, and … .

And she'd have scolded him about the dishes in the kitchen, embarrassed to see it in such a state.

Orval smiled at the memory, rose, and quietly left the room. They'd be safe enough with that copper lantern. He didn't want to leave them in a strange place, in the dark. With the door open, he'd hear if they roused. He wouldn't be able to sleep himself; his blood still raced with the start Madam Winter had given him.

And there were dishes to be done.

He'd set another pot of pease porridge going, then close the oven for the night. The morning would bring more worries, and the elements knew he had questions. Amari had a faint accent, and she didn't know the *Epic*, so she was certainly from a distant land. How had she come to be wet nurse to Kara?

Thunder rolled overhead as he set to work. Vren would be out in the wet and cold, but Orval knew that he'd the skills to move quick and unseen. Safe.

The marcusi, secretive and secret, were sworn to the Blood. He'd take word to his superiors and they'd find a place of safety for Amari and the babes. Someplace better than a crippled scholar's quarters. Which reminded him … he took down the butter crock, where he stored his extra coin. No books this month; that was certain. He'd need the funds to buy better food. He'd been saving for that original volume of *Ancient Tribes of the Plains*, but he set that aside with only a twinge of regret. Amari deserved better than pease porridge, that was certain.

Of course, that was assuming that he'd still receive a Crown stipend under the new King. But worrying wouldn't bring answers and his own exhaustion was creeping in.

Orval put the crock back and returned to his tasks, working until the dirty dishes were cleared, more water and porridge placed in the oven, and clean mugs set out for tea in the morning. It had taken longer than he'd thought; light was starting to spill through the small windows. Orval yawned, taking up the copper lantern. He'd nod off at his desk and—

Pounding at the kitchen door, startled him wide awake, his heart once again racing in his chest.

"Open! Open, in the name of the King!"

## CHAPTER SEVEN

—◦—

"Open! By order of King Xyrath!" The person outside was shouting now.

Orval's heart leapt madly against his ribs. He stood frozen, in his stained and rumpled robe. Staring around the room like a fool, not sure—

The pounding came again, four hard blows. The door seemed to bulge in the frame.

"Coming, coming," he yelled as he limped to the door. Whoever it was seemed intent on breaking in. He offered to the elements, and unlocked the door only to stumble back, nearly falling, pushed aside by a pair of tough-looking warriors, all in chain and leather, bearing the crest of the Wyverns. They smelled of rain and rust and death.

Orval caught himself on the table as they stormed in, setting the crockery rattling. "See here," he began, but was interrupted.

"Awake, were you?" That was a voice he knew only too well. Captain Ussin walked in, one hand on his sword. He'd been a big, burly bully when they'd fostered together; now he stood a bigger, burlier soldier. More gray hair, the same piggish eyes.

"Who wouldn't be, with all this clamor." Orval said, hoping the weakness in his voice was taken for anger. "Ussin," he nodded. Damned if he was using the man's title. "I understand that Xyrath has triumphed on the field."

"By the will of the Lord of the Sun, he has," Ussin boomed, still using his battlefield voice. He looked around, peering into the corners while his two men took up positions by the hearth. "My King sends me to you to greet you and ensure your safety."

Orval blinked, steadying himself against the table. "Well, my thanks, but that is hardly necessary. I am a distant cousin, a minor member of the royal family, after all."

"Still," Ussin boomed as he prowled about the room, "my king has commanded that two guards shall be posted outside your door, to keep you safe and escort you on your daily errands."

*What was the man looking for?* Orval pulled his robe a bit tighter around himself. "I really don't see the need–"

"Orders," Ussin said firmly. "For all the family of the House of Xy."

"Very well, then, if that's His Majesty's command, we must obey." Orval straightened. "You might stop in and mention that to my landlord, Madam Winter of the House of the Weary Traveler. She has a great deal of respect for the king's men, you know."

The two soldiers perked up at that.

"My thanks to His Majesty for his care of us," Orval started, just as a shrill cry cut through the room.

The wail of a babe.

Ussin's head jerked up, as did those of his soldiers. Ussin glared at Orval, then stomped though the open door and into the corridor.

"Here now," Orval protested, limping after him. "Ussin–"

The babe wailed again, then went quiet. Ussin stopped in the doorway of the bedroom. Orval limped up behind him.

Amari was propped up on the pillows, clutching Dalan at her breast. Her eyes were wide with terror.

"Captain Ussin, I must insist–" Orval started breathlessly.

"I am also commanded to keep an eye out for a newborn babe," Ussin growled. "Who is this?"

The moment froze between one heartbeat and the next. Dazed, Orval felt his lips open, not sure where his words were coming from but speaking with an authority he didn't know he had. The lie flowed easily from his lips. "Ussin, I'd like you to meet my wife, Amari, and our twins."

Amari's expression changed ever so slightly, like a shutter closing over a window. Orval's heart sank as he struggled for words. She'd deny it, of course. A cripple. Elements forgive him, he'd–

"Wife?" With Ussin's question reality kicked back in.

To Orval's relief, Amari spoke, her voice soft, but steady. "We were blessed with twins a month ago. A boy and a girl." She gave a nod to the bundle beside her on the bed.

"Dalan, our first born," Orval babbled. "And Lara."

Fear flashed through Amari's eyes, but Ussin just gave an abrupt nod. "Blessings on you, lady, and yours. Forgive the intrusion."

Ussin backed out of the room, closing the door behind him.

It felt like he filled the hall and towered over Orval. "I did not know you were married," he rumbled.

"You have been long from the city," Orval said, the strength of fear starting to drain from him. "Life goes on, Ussin, even in war."

"And now, I've woken them and disturbed your rest." Ussin grimaced as he strode back to the kitchen.

"They were due a feeding. Not much rest for us, these first few months, or so I'm told." Orval felt himself starting to babble and clamped his mouth firmly shut. Less said, the better.

"Explains the odd smell in the kitchen," Ussin grimaced. "Baby cack. You will be up to your neck in nappies for some time."

"Aye, aye," Orval said. "I haven't gotten much sleep this night." He paused as they returned to the kitchen. "What with the storm and the bells ringing."

"My bookish friend here has been blessed with twins," Ussin boomed to the warriors as he slapped Orval on the back. "Sly dog, making hay while we were at war. Didn't know you had it in ya."

"Er," Orval decided to take it as a compliment.

"I'll have the men guard at the bottom of the stairs, with orders to disturb you as little as possible," Ussin said. "Although I've no doubt you'll be summoned to Court."

"Well," Orval hedged, trying to think of an excuse. "It will be some time before—"

"Of course," Ussin boomed. "But the House of Wyvern is triumphant, and you will want to congratulate their Majesties."

Orval managed to keep his thought to himself as they left, striding out into the rain and down the stairs. He threw the bolt, glad of the silence, then sniffed the air. He didn't smell anything out of the ordinary, the babies hadn't pooped … .

Unless it was the pease porridge.

Orval frowned, and then took a breath, dreading what must come next. What had he done? Married? Where had that come from?

He'd committed that poor woman to a lie, at least until the marcusi could get her and the babes to safety. He poured some tea, admittedly fairly strong by now, but maybe a peace offering. He limped down the hall to the bedroom, careful to open the door quietly.

There was peace in the sight. Dalan was still suckling, his tiny hand up by Amari's cheek. She nuzzled his fingers, cooing at him softly. It was only when she lifted her head that Orval saw her worry and fear. "Are they gone?" she whispered, glancing at the door. "What happened?"

"I fear I married you, milady." Orval limped forward, set the tea by the bed and settled slowly in the chair, stretching his leg out in front of him. "I'm truly sorry, but it was the only thing I could think of–"

"You told them she was Lara," Amari's voice stayed soft, but the accusation was there. "He will know that–"

"Oh, that. No, no," Orval shook his head. "Lady, you are not from Edenrich, are you?"

"No," she averted her eyes, "I am not."

"Trust me in this, every family with any link to the Xy-ian bloodline has a 'Lara'. It's a common enough name." Orval rubbed his face, feeling his tiredness catch up with him. "It was my sister's name."

Amari drew a breath and let it out slowly. "I did not know."

"I fear that I have besmirched you, claiming you and the babes, but I could think of nothing else," Orval continued, rub-bing his aching thigh. "Taking me on as a husband in name is a poor bargain, but it buys us time. Still, I fear I have besmirched your honor."

"No, Orval" Amari's mouth quirked ruefully. "That is not a concern. You offer protection, shelter. We will disrupt your household as it is—"

Orval chuckled. "Such as it is, lady." He yawned, slumping in the chair. "We'll make do, until the marcusi return for you." He yawned again, feeling the pull of sleep.

Amari smiled at him, warm and bright in the light of the lantern. It seemed he was forgiven. He liked the way she said his name, with her accent. Dalan was making little snorting noises against her breast, her skin was brown and warm, glowing in the light. Such a picture, even better than his brief dreams of a loving woman in his life, content and happy—

His eyes closed and he drifted off to sleep.

———◆———

Poor man. Amari watched as his chin hit his chest. She admired his quick thinking. She'd never have thought, never have dared, really, to assert herself so. But he'd done it as if it were truth.

Dalan's tiny hand hit her chin, and she looked down as he released her nipple, fast asleep. She took up the swaddling cloth, and rewrapped him carefully, setting him back in the fortress of pillows. Lara still slept, so she'd let the child tell her when she was hungry. Amari drank the tea that Orval had brought, then settled back, reciting a small prayer to the Harmony of the Hearth with a grateful heart.

How long she slept, she didn't know, but Lara's fussing woke her. Amari set her to the breast, pleased when once again the baby girl latched on without issue.

Orval was still asleep, slumped in the chair, head back. She saw no reason to wake him.

Time enough for that.

Once Lara was finished, and burped, Amari re-swaddled her, and then eased out from the blankets to search out the privy. Bare foot on wooden floor, she yawned as she made her way there and back, then paused. There was a new noise, a scratching sound. Did Orval have mice? Certainly there was enough paper here to draw them, but his housekeeping hadn't seemed quite that bad. And on the third floor, surely not.

But the scratching continued. There was enough light through the windows for Amari to make her way farther down the hall, away from the kitchen, to what had to be the storeroom Orval had mentioned, hours earlier. There was a door there, bolted on this side; the scratching came from the other side.

"Is someone there?" Amari asked.

"Finally," came a soft, female voice. "Open the door."

Amari hesitated, but Orval had seemed to trust the woman she'd met the previous night. She pulled the bolt back.

"Here," Winter was quiet, her bells and those lovely bracelets gone. She thrust some bundles and blankets, and at least two baskets of food, into Orval's rooms. Amari took them carefully. "Wait," the woman said, and disappeared into the gloom beyond the doorway, returning moments later with an armful of cloth and hammer and nails. She slipped through and shut the door.

Amari opened her mouth, but Winter shook her head. "Wait," she whispered. With a sudden clash, drums and music vibrated through the wall.

"Help me," Winter said, speaking in a normal tone, and together the women nailed the old tapestry to cover the door. It was faded and tattered, with at least one hole. Winter stepped back and gave it a nod. "Perfect. Looks like its always been there."

"Orval is sleeping," Amari said.

"We need to wake him," Winter gathered up two bundles and one basket. "I don't have much time."

Orval was already waking as they came into the room. "Winter?" he asked, his voice rough. He winced as he moved, stiff from sleeping in the chair.

"What possessed you to claim her as your wife?" Winter asked softly, after glancing at the babes on the bed.

"I–" Orval sat straight up.

"Smarter than I gave you credit for, that's certain." Winter put her burdens at his feet. "Here's some worn nappies, and swaddling cloths."

"How did you know that I … ." Orval glanced at Amari.

"Because that swaggering fool Ussin swaggered in and demanded housing for his men and wanted to know if I knew your business." Winter put her hands on her hips. "And I told him that you are a crazy old bookworm who never ventures out and rarely deigns to talks to whores, and that for all I knew, you preferred men for bed partners."

"I always talk to you!" Orval sputtered. Amari covered her smile.

Winter rolled her eyes. "I lied, Orval. I also told him the cost to house his so-called guards and that it needed to be paid up front, in good, solid coin and that until then they could stand in the rain for all I cared, wyvern, airion, grass snake, or whoever.

"And when he announced to my lounge, which was full of guests, that you'd twins, I said that I thought you were out to increase your royal stipend so you could continue to live off the backs of people who pay their taxes."

"What?" Orval covered his face. "Winter–"

Winter knelt by his chair. "Orval, I fear he means you harm. I fear *they* mean you harm. What better way to solidify their hold on the throne than to rid themselves of those of the Blood?"

"But why?" Orval uncovered his face, looking so very miserable that Amari's heart ached for him. "Winter, I am no threat. I have no political power, no wealth, no contacts. How can I threaten him?"

Winter glanced at Amari. "Whatever else you've gotten pulled into, you *are* of the Blood. The Wyverns just fought a bloody, vicious civil war. King Xyrath can't yet be confident in his rule." Winter struggled back to her feet. "I've covered the passage on both sides. Get your sister's things out, make the place look more lived in. Clear away some of your clutter. I brought enough food for a few days. It's better than that crap you eat. The empty baskets can serve as cradles. Make sure it appears that you share that bed."

Orval flushed red. "The procession is this morning?" he asked, clearly changing the subject.

"The procession was this morning," Winter snorted. "Pathetic and sad, but Xyrath looked glorious. He enjoyed the cheers, right enough."

"He always did," Orval agreed. "It came through here?"

"This part of town? No. They wound straight from the main gates to the castle. They're up there now, probably sorting through the spoils." Winter looked grim. "There's one more thing," She glanced at Amari, then put her hand on Orval's shoulder. "There's word from the Palace." She paused and swallowed hard. "Queen Mother Tithanna was found dead in her chambers, a dagger buried deep in her heart, they say by her own hand."

## CHAPTER EIGHT

S atia was still cold from the procession when the palace staff knelt at her feet, their blue and white dresses puffed out around them on the floor.

She refrained from showing her irritation at their insubordination. One glance at their reddened cheeks and eyes swollen from crying, and she resigned herself to a show of patience. But the least they could have done was to have mulled wine ready for her.

"We have all suffered a loss," she said softly. "I share your grief at the loss of the Queen Mother Tithanna. But we must take care not to disappoint the King on his first night in residence." Satia paused. "I would not wish to see him angered with you."

"No, Your Majesty," the Royal Housekeeper said without

lifting her gaze from the floor.

"Best to bury ourselves in our tasks and leave our mourning for later, outside the presence of the King." Satia looked around. The Queen's Suite was as she expected it to be, cavernous rooms, every inch covered by the blue and white of the Airions. Stuffy and cold, with the stale scent of dried lavender and no fire in the hearth.

Her Bondmaidens surveyed the room, checking behind curtains and in cupboards. Mira sniffed. "Filthy," she said disparagingly.

"Apologies, your majesty." The Royal Housekeeper still had her eyes down and was sniffing back tears. "We are somewhat disarrayed. The King and Queen have not been in residence for some time, you see."

"The King and Queen are now in residence," Avice said sharply.

The woman's face went pale. "The Queen Mother's chambers would be warmer, although they have not yet been cleaned. We were not allowed to–"

"Understandable," Satia said, although it was not. But allowances needed to be made. Satia reached down and urged the Housekeeper to her feet. "We must see to the comfort of the King." Satia gave her an encouraging smile. "Rosemary, wasn't it?"

"Rosalind, Your Majesty." An older woman, with a worn face and graying hair. Her wrinkles were deep with exhaustion and grief.

"I know this is a trying time," Satia murmured as she gestured for the rest of the staff to rise to their feet. "But let us be about it. First things first, we need to remove all the airion tapestries."

Rosalind paused. "Majesty, it will be terrible drafty without–"

"Take them down," Satia firmed her voice. "We would not wish to anger the King."

"The oldest ones are fragile and require careful–"

"They must all be removed before the feast tonight," Satia insisted, more sharply this time, allowing her irritation to show, just a bit.

"Yes, of course, Your Majesty."

"To work, then." Satia dismissed them all. "Quickly now. I know you have suffered a great loss and are pained and hurt. But come, mop your faces and turn grief to action. There is much to be done to see to His Majesty's comfort. The King is currently inspecting the guards and talking to his Council, but he will want to refresh himself soon enough."

The staff fled, hopefully to get to work without too much delay.

"Rosalind," Satia stopped the woman at the door. "Please tell the Royal Steward to attend me here as soon as possible."

"And a hearth boy, to see to the fire," Avice added.

"I will see it done, your majesty." Rosalind bowed and left, shutting the door behind her.

Satia allowed herself to collapse into the padded chair by the cold hearth as a sudden wave of exhaustion swept over her. Her gorge rose and she pressed her hand to her stomach. It was far too soon to declare the pregnancy. She'd need to wait a few weeks before making her symptoms known. "That bitch Tithanna must have mellowed in her old age, if they are all heartbroken over her death." Satia shook her head. Xyrath shouldn't have acted so impulsively. But what was done was done.

"Majesty, are you well?" Mira knelt at her side. "The procession took forever and I fear you are chilled."

"It was needful for the people to see us, and for Xyrath to hear their cheers." Satia rubbed her arms. "We can sort out the staff later. We can weed out the disloyal slowly. No need to seem the butchers." She shifted in her chair, trying to ease her discomfort.

A cheer went up outside. Avice crossed over to the windows. "The King is in the courtyard, speaking to the guards."

Satia rose and peered out. Xyrath was indeed out on the cobbles, strutting like a cock, gesturing as he spoke. She'd have to remember to have any large mirrors moved to his chambers. He did so like to look at himself.

Tarwain stood near to the King, with a slight frown on his face. She cracked open the window.

"… peace and mercy to all who pledge their loyalty," Xyrath announced. "If not, you are free to return to your homes with your weapons and armor."

"Oh, that was not well thought out," Avice muttered.

Satia stifled a grimace. She was about to pull back when Tarwain spotted her and gestured toward the window.

"All hail Her Majesty, Queen Satia," he called.

The Queen smiled, leaned out and waved to the cheering men, then threw a kiss to the King. Withdrawing, she closed the window and considered. Her lover might become a nuisance. "Doesn't Lord Tarwain have a daughter?"

"Aye," Avice made sure the window was bolted. "A dowdy thing."

"I should make her one of my attendants," Satia mused. "Perhaps his lady should come to Court as well and bring their younger children." Satia settled back in the chair. They could be given apartments here in the Palace. Useful, to keep him and his family under her eye.

A knock at the door, which Avice answered. A hearth boy stumbled in, arms piled high with wood, kindling clutched in his fists. Rosalind followed him, her hand on his shoulder. "Make your bow, Jarris," she reminded him. "Then see to the fire. Be quick, now."

The boy bobbed a hasty bow, nearly dropping the wood, then rushed to the hearth and dropped the logs with a clatter.

Rosalind bowed. "Your Majesty, the Royal Steward awaits your pleasure."

"Show him in," Satia commanded, then rose to stand facing the door. Better to be on her feet for this interview.

"Queen Satia, gracious majesty, I am Paulin, Royal Steward." An older man, bald of pate and with tired eyes, went to one knee before her. Not without an uneasy glance at her Bondmaidens.

"Rise, Paulin," Satia commanded. "There is much to be done and little time. It is the pleasure of the King that there be a small dinner this night in the Great Hall. There will be no more than a hundred people or so, only the most loyal of our supporters."

The man nodded. "Yes, your Majesty."

She continued, "Please see that the Great Hall is prepared. Remove the airion banners and replace them with ours." She paused for dramatic effect. "Do not clean our banners. They will be stained from the battlefield, but those are honors hard won."

"Of course, gracious lady," Paulin's head bobbed.

Saita paused as if thinking. "Are all the solid gold place settings still here?"

"Aye, Majesty, locked up tight." Paulin looked nervous. "Would you have them used this night?"

"No, no, the everyday ware is fine for men fresh from the field." Satia's stomach chose that moment to flip. She drew a breath and gave Paulin a smile, hoping she looked more tired than sick. "Royal Steward," she said more seriously, letting her smile fade, "before I let you go, we must speak of other matters. I would ask the status of our coffers."

The Royal Steward bowed his head. "I fear I anticipated your question, Majesty. Your coffers are almost bare."

Satia was practiced enough that she didn't even flinch, though this was not what she wanted to hear.

"We are in arrears with all the tradesmen and the Guild of Mages," Paulin continued. "I fear that soon–"

"The Guild of Mages?" Satia's voice was sharper than she intended. "Why so?"

"For the Chained Mage," Paulin lifted an eyebrow. "Ruinously expensive, but Queen Kara insisted."

"A Chained Mage? Here?" Satia demanded, feeling the stirring of her Bondmaidens. "I didn't … ." All the possibilities of what she could accomplish with a Chained Mage under her control flooded into her mind.

"He is outside, awaiting your Majesty's pleasure." Paulin's expression was an odd combination of anticipation and dread. "Majesty, if I might offer a word," Paulin paused. "He is rather … difficult at times."

"Bring him in." Satia ignored the probably well-meant advice.

The door opened and darkness walked in. A man, tall, long black hair streaked with gray cascading down his back. His robes were black as night; the only brightness to his appearance was the glint of the silver chains that ran from neck to wrists to ankles, loose enough to allow movement, but obvious marks of what he was.

Satia controlled her excitement. A chained mage.

The chains made a soft rattle, glittering in the firelight. They did not bind his movement as he flowed into the room. His dark gaze flicked over her and then to her maidens, no doubt seeing more than she wished. Satia kept her face still as his lips tightened.

She'd a moment to wonder if there was elven blood in his lineage as he came to stand before her and gave her the barest of nods.

Paulin cleared his throat. "Your Majesty, this is Ritathan, Chained Mage of the Guild of Mages of Edenrich."

Satia smiled warmly. "I welcome you to our service."

"I do not serve you," Ritathan said coolly. "You do not hold my key."

So they were not to be friends. Satia dropped her smile and gave him a narrow look. "A small matter." She turned to Paulin and held out her hand.

Paulin shook his head. "Majesty, I was never entrusted with the key. To my knowledge, it was carried to the battlefield and may be lost."

"And the spare?" Satia clamped on her anger as the smirk on Ritathan's face grew.

"Your Majesty, I beg pardon, but I was never told of a spare."

Satia glared at Ritathan. "Where is the spare key?"

"You are not the master of my chains," Ritathan intoned. "You do not hold my key."

Paulin studied the ceiling. "That's rather a common refrain."

The two men exchanged looks that told Satia much that did her little good now, but could be stored away for the future. "You cannot cast," she said flatly.

Ritathan gave her an insolent nod. "I cannot cast unless commanded by the master of my chains, the holder of the key. I am bound by key and contract." Satia didn't miss his glance at her women. "Such are the strictures of the Guild of Mages and the Royal Contract from the time of—"

"No matter," Satia interrupted, to regain control of the interview. "We will find the key."

She turned her attention away, deliberately, and focused her attention on Paulin. "Royal Steward, we need prepare to celebrate our victory–"

"Your victory?" Ritathan's voice cut through hers, smooth and strong. "You have won a civil war over the carcass of what was Xy. 'Tis now but an outlying city of what was a vast empire. This city and its surrounds can barely sustain itself and your army just trampled over many of the crops that would have aided its people."

"Mage Ritathan," Paulin protested, but the man continued.

"The surrounding baronies no longer acknowledge you as suzerain, owe you no fealty, if they even communicate with you at all. Swift's Port and Athelbryght do not even trade with Edenrich. The foreign ambassadors have fled to their homes long ago, the Palace is falling to ruin about your ears, and the coffers are empty. So, yes. All hail the King and Queen of Xy. The King and Queen of Xy, all hail." Finished, Ritathan bowed his head with the slightest of impudent tilts.

"I should have you executed," Satia spat.

Ritathan nodded. "Guildmaster Forterran would not be pleased, but he would not be surprised. I have a reputation for telling truth to power. It makes him grind his teeth."

Satia turned away and focused on Paulin. "Take him away and confine him to his quarters. Contact the Guildmaster. I do not want a mage I do not control loose in the castle. Are the fees current with the Guild?"

"No," Paulin said. "Nor with the tradesmen and laborers."

"We will see to the accounts when the war chest arrives and the King's household is set up. A matter of days, no more." Satia closed her eyes, then opened them and smiled at Paulin. "Perhaps you could find a few musicians to play at the evening meal? The King likes revelry and we should see him amused."

"I will see it done, Your Majesty." He bowed and gestured for Ritathan to precede him as they left. Satia's stomach heaved again as the door closed behind them. Wretched man, telling her things she'd rather ignore.

A soft knock. Avice opened the door, took a tray of tea things from someone, and shut the door again. She placed the tray on a small table near Satia's chair, saying "The war chest is empty."

"Yes," Satia settled back in the chair, "I know."

"Let this steep for a bit, then drink." Mira set to work with her satchel and herbs. "Should settle your stomach."

"We can sell the airion tapestries, and take note of who buys them," Satia took a breath as her stomach knotted again. "That solid gold dinner service can be melted down and coins issued. Xyrath can announce a new coinage to replace the old, debased coins."

"Were the old ones debased?" Nora asked.

"They were if we say they were," Satia said firmly. "I also have a list of the richest merchants and bankers that offered us no support. We can accuse them and see their property confiscated."

A cry from out in the hall. "Our Lord, the King!"

The door flung open and Xyrath strode in, golden and beaming. "Satia," he boomed, smiling.

"Your Majesty," Satia got to her feet, then sank to the floor before him, lowering her eyes. Avice and Mira followed suit.

"Now, now, my Queen," Xyrath put his fingers under her chin and lifted her head. "So lovely, my dear wife and Queen. What do you think of the Palace?"

"Sorely neglected, my King," Satia took his offered hand and rose. "But we will restore it to its former glory."

"Well said," Xyrath said with his usual winsome smile. "Captain Ussin reported to me that all of the Blood on your list are safe and well-guarded."

"Good," Satia said.

"They're no real threat, you know," Xyrath watched the hearth boy as he struggled with his bucket of ash, then turned back to Satia, his eyes sparkling. "You'll never guess what I heard from Ussin. Remember my cousin, the cripple, Orval? Crafty dog got himself married and they had twins a few months ago!"

Satia held herself still.

"Can you believe?" he snorted. "I always thought he leaned toward men, just goes to show one never knows. We will have to increase his stipend, what with him supporting three now and being a cripple and all."

"He is of the Blood," Satia said slowly. "Didn't he need to seek permission to marry?"

"No, no, distant cousin really." Xyrath wandered over to the window, clearly trying to catch a glimpse of himself in the glass. "No claim to the throne at all."

"Who did he marry?"

"Captain Ussin didn't say," Xyrath ran his fingers through his hair. "Only said he was overwhelmed by nappies and dishes. No threat to us, surely."

"We have just won a war and must secure the throne," Satia gently reminded him. "Who knows where their loyalties lie? Therefore we must protect them. With all honor, of course."

"Of course, of course," Xyrath turned back to her. "Is there to be a banquet tonight? For our brave warriors? I should change. Bathe, perhaps."

Typical, leaving the details to her. Still, it suited her. Satia nodded. "The baggage train should arrive soon. Let me order a bath prepared for you."

"Would you join me, dearest?" Xyrath gave her a look under his lashes. "Before the bath? Help me out of this armor, perhaps?"

"My King, you honor me," Satia leaned in close. "Just let me finish this tea, and I am yours."

Xyrath swept her into his arms and twirled her around, laughing at her squeal. "Don't be long," he said, striding out and calling out for the staff.

Avice shut the door.

"The tea is ready," Mira poured out a steaming cup. "It will help."

"Good," Satia steadied herself on the back of the chair, waiting for the dizziness and nausea to pass. She took the cup from Mira, feeling the heat on her fingers.

A knock sounded on the door. Nora and Caris slipped in when Avice opened the door, their armor caked in mud and grime. Avice closed the door firmly behind them, first glancing into the hall to make sure no one was near enough to overhear.

"A child was born," Nora said, her voice low. "It was taken, and they were seen fleeing, a person and a large animal. From the tracks, a vore."

Satia hissed. "Iris?"

"As you commanded," Caris said. "Iris hunts."

## CHAPTER NINE

Vren squirmed out through a small window in one of Orval's back chambers, making sure to close it firmly but quietly. A moment to orient, crouched in the rain, before he moved off over the slate roofs. *Be the wind, be the shadow, be the blade, be the silence of the night*, he recited to himself, grinning.

Far easier without a wet nurse and babes in tow.

Visibility was almost nil, so he let his eyes adjust before he increased his speed.

He crossed the city, the rooftops changing underfoot from slate to clay to wood to thatch. He wanted to be swift but knew that a mis-step, a clatter, or a patch of rotten straw would cause a ruckus.

The rain grew heavier, coming down in dark sheets, the wind cutting like knives. Few would be out-and-about. Perfect weather for prey.

And prey was what he intended to be.

Once over the city wall, he skirted the sides of the road, staying where the trees were thickest, heading back to the battlefield. Dust would be there, keeping a watchful eye. He suspected the Wyverns would be searching and he needed to be seen by them, if Dust hadn't already been spotted.

The road was quiet, the only sound the rain. Still, he was wary. At this point there would be warriors clearing the dead, or at the very least, tending the wounded. With a bit of luck, and the favor of the skies …

Horses coming down the road. Riders with lanterns on poles, making no secret of their presence.

Vren darted to the side, hunching down. If that light swung his way, he'd be seen. He clutched his knives and waited.

A rustle under a dead tree behind him caught his ear. Yellow eyes gleamed for a moment, then disappeared.

Dust had found him.

He slid toward her through the grasses, quiet as he could. He saw her scramble back, on her belly, leaving an opening, and crawled after her, dead leaves and branches scrapping against his oiled leather cloak. The smell of mold and wet filled his nose as he crouched beside her, turning to face the road. Her breath was warm on his cheek as they watched through the branches.

Illuminated in their pool of light, the warriors wore their hoods up. The jingle as they pounded past spoke of armor and weapons beneath their cloaks. No banners were displayed, so no way of knowing their allegiance. Vren lowered his gaze, for fear his eyes would catch the light. Dust pressed her muzzle against his cloak, ears twitching.

The light passed over them; the hoofbeats faded off into the night.

Still, Vren waited silently, pressed against Dust, until she shifted and gave a huff.

He waited still, until she nodded. Then, at last, he shifted to sit cross-legged at her side. Water showered down on them as the dead leaves rustled in protest.

Vren buried his cold hands in her warm ruff, and put his head to hers. "Well, they weren't beating the bushes, so they weren't hunting you. You lost them?"

Dust's ears twitched with a "yes," then perked with a tilt of her head.

"All's well," he whispered. "They are with Orval." He hesitated. "I checked. Neither bore the birthmark you seek."

The vore drew a huge sigh and then pressed her head into his chest, a rare sign of affection.

"I need a minute," Vren said, reaching for his pack. "Orval sent some dried meat for you." He dug it out. Dust, with a flash of fangs, snapped it up. "He fed me a bowl of pease."

Mid-bite, Dust huffed, giving him a side look.

"Well, you know," Vren kept a straight face. "Warm, cheap and filling."

Dust paused in her chewing, bared her teeth and clicked her tongue. The vore version of a laugh. Vren smiled as well. "I asked for a bag of dried pease."

The vore sneezed, effectively rolling her eyes.

"No fear," Vren chuckled. "I won't be eating it." He pulled out the bag of pease and dug further for some leather cords.

Dust tilted her head.

"I am making a baby," Vren explained. One of the dried apples, after some rough carving, would serve as the head. "Something to sling to my chest, make it look like I am fleeing with the child." He worked fast, tying off the head and then forming rude legs. "We need to pull them from the city." He dug deeper in his pack, drew out a cloth. "This was Xylara's nappy."

Dust gave the cloth a sniff.

"It's dry, she hadn't dirtied it yet. But look," He opened the bundle. In a corner of the cloth, two things were sewn in place with wild, loose stitches. A key and a ring.

The vore's ears went up.

"My heart about stopped," Vren said. "The Ring of Xy. I don't know what the key is for, but it must be important."

The vore's ears went flat.

"I can't let these fall into Xyrath's hands, much less the blood memories. How many warriors are hunting us?"

Her response startled him. "One?" Vren asked "Just one?"

Dust stopped chewing, focusing her yellow eyes on his. Her message was affirmative, but there was more. Vren's heart started beating faster.

"Bondmaiden?" he whispered, hoping he was wrong.

After traveling with Dust for so long, he'd learned much of her language of body movements and sounds. He didn't always pick up the subtler meanings, but this was absolutely clear. Hate, cold and terrifying, aimed at their pursuer.

There was nothing a vore hated more than blood magic. Dust wanted the Bondmaiden dead.

Blood magic. *Unwilling sacrifice, unwillingly made.*

Vren shuddered. His hands stilled as the implications started to sink in and fear rose in his throat. Not for himself. "Orval," he whispered. "Orval doesn't know … I never told him that–" he swallowed hard. "Skies as my witness, I never thought–" he clamped his jaw tight.

He'd first met Orval when he'd approached him years ago, offering protection to a child of the Blood of Xy. But Orval could have cared less for the Crown and the Court. He had snorted, pulled Vren into his rooms, offered kavage and pease porridge and pulled out charts of family trees, reviewing blood lines and explaining 'fourth cousins twice removed' to show that he stood in no danger of that fate. 'Not to mention,' Orval had said, "they'd never let a cripple sit on the throne.'

Vren should have faded away then, but he kept coming back. It was a breath of fresh air to sit and talk with the man. Well, in truth, Orval did most of the talking, often asking questions that Vren couldn't or wouldn't answer. When that happened, Orval just shrugged and offered more pease or kavage. He kept treats on hand for Dust, when she deigned to enter the city.

Orval hadn't been shy about quizzing the vore either, with Vren to interpret as best he could. Dust seemed to find it amusing that Orval pestered her with questions about her home in Athelbryght and its history.

Not that she was willing to share many details.

Now his friend was in danger, more danger than he knew, and Vren had placed him there. Vren hadn't told him about the Bondmaidens, how blood magic had been used to create them. How that taint was one of the reasons why the marcusi had withdrawn their protection from the Wyvern Blood of Xy.

"I am a damn fool," he whispered, lifting his head, his first instinct to go back into Edenrich.

Dust nudged him with her nose, reading his thoughts.

"I can't risk it," he agreed. "I know I can't. And killing her is not an option. Best thing we can do is draw her attention to us and lead her away."

Still, his gut churned for his friend. He had work yet to do, even as his mind raced, so his fingers moved while he thought.

"Why just one?" he asked.

Dust had resumed chewing her meat, but he knew she was listening.

Vren dug out more rags and twisted them into a semblance of limbs. "Ah, they don't want anyone to know, do they?" he answered his own question. "So we need to keep her on our trail. Does she use magic?"

Dust denied that. And she'd sense if it was being used.

So the woman was just tainted with blood magic. That was one worry off his mind. He focused on tying the legs and arms to the doll.

The sling was next; he had to wiggle around to get it in place under his cloak. The branches rustled, and showered them with droplets. At least the rain had settled into a soft patter on the leaves.

Dust gulped down the last of her meat and rose on her haunch. She rubbed her muzzle with a forepaw, cleaning her face. Moments like this made it clear she wasn't just a large wolf of some kind. There was something feline in her as well.

"Believable?" he asked as he shoved the doll into place.

Dust snorted.

"Well, not everyone has your senses," he said. "It has to serve."

Dust made another suggestion.

"I am not finding a piglet to strap to my chest," Vren started to squirm out of their hollow, staying low. "It might sound and move like a baby, but you just want a meal."

Dust emerged behind him, her tongue lolling out of her open jaws.

"What would a desperate man with a newborn baby fleeing through the dark cold night do?" Vren mused. He took a breath of the cold, damp air and answered his own question. "Put as much distance between him and his pursuer as possible. Find food for the babe."

He looked at Dust. "So, we will let her find us." Vren said, pulling up his hood and adjusting the sling. "If you scent a farm or sheep holding, we will head there. Make her think we're getting milk for the baby."

The vore shook herself in agreement.

Vren rose to his feet. "Let's give her something to hunt."

## CHAPTER TEN

W inter?" Orval ducked under the tapestry, pulled the bolt back, and desperately scratched at the passage door, clutching a whimpering babe in the other arm. "Winter, please be there. Please help me," he begged softly, fear catching in his throat. He scratched again, sweat dripping off his face and under his tunic.

"Orval?" Winter's muffled voice was followed by the sound of the bolt being thrown back on her side. "Orval, what's wrong?" Winter's worried face appeared; her eyes widened as she took him in. He knew he was a mess, tears streaking down his face, his tunic stained.

"Winter, please, Dalan won't stop crying," Orval choked on

the words, knowing, just knowing he'd done something wrong, something awful. "He cries and cries, and he's going to wake Amari and she's exhausted, and but I don't know what I did or—"

Winter took the child he desperately thrust into her arms. "Hush," she said. "He seems fine, just miserable." She stepped into the storeroom and pulled the door closed behind her. "Let's take him into the kitchen and see what we see."

Orval nodded, feeling weak and shaky. It would be all right, Winter knew what she was doing. As they walked past the bedroom, Orval glanced in to see poor Amari had fallen back asleep, with Lara in her basket by the bed. Thank the skies they had not woken.

Winter opened the door to the kitchen, and stopped dead, looking around.

Orval sidled around her, shame-faced. "I've tried to keep up," he said, quickly limping forward to clear a place on the table. "But it's hard. Babies are … ." he swallowed the lump in his throat. "Terrifying," he whispered. He'd failed miserably, not just at taking care of Amari and the babes, but by letting everything fall apart.

Winter put Dalan down on the table and unwrapped the swaddling. Not that it took much effort, since he apparently couldn't swaddle a baby to save his soul. It was always too loose, too—

"He's fine," Winter said, checking the little boy's nappy. "He's clean and dry and there's no rash. Did he nurse?"

"Just a bit ago," Orval said. "Lara went to sleep but even after I burped him, he fussed, and now he won't stop crying."

"Orval, sometimes babies just cry." Winter stroked Dalan's tummy. The babe squirmed, his face puckering up. "You burped him?"

"I did," Orval insisted, heart sinking as Dalan sucked in a breath and wailed like he was dying.

"Well, then," Winter said. "We'll see about the other end, then, shall we?" She took one of Dalan's small, perfect feet in each hand and started to pump his little legs back and forth, crooning to the little one. "Poor, poor lamb."

Dalan sniffed, his eyes wide as he stared at Winter.

"What are you doing?" Orval looked at her in horror. "He's sick, he needs–

"No, no," Winter chuckled, keeping a gentle rhythm, gently churning the chubby legs. "Sometimes, just like with adults, things get sort of plugged–"

Dalan's eyes got wider, his face screwed up, and—

*pop, pop, pop, pop, pop, pppppppop.*

"Gas?" Orval gasped, sagging against the table with relief.

"Gas," Winter confirmed. "And, oh dear," she said, looking down, "slightly more than gas."

"There should be a book," Orval sighed, swaying as exhaustion replaced relief that replaced horror at yet another change. "Something that explains all this. I'll get a cloth."

"With babies, experience is the true teacher. Hand me the cloth, I'll do it." Winter said. "Go wash yourself and change while you have a chance. Get into a clean night robe."

"Not sure there's any clean," Orval staggered as his leg started to give way. He caught himself on the edge of the table as the room spun. "I thought he was dying, Winter."

"I know," she looked at him with sympathy. "You are learning what every parent learns, Orval. Babies are wonderful miracles of love, joy, and chaos embodied. Noisy, messy, stinky blobs of demanding bedlam," she cooed at Dalan, who yawned in reply.

Orval frowned. "That's not a very nice thing to say." He lurched away from the table, heading for the door. "Dalan might hear you."

"It's the truth," Winter said. "Besides, it will be a while before he understands."

"Lara smiled at me the other day," Orval smiled himself at the memory of those tiny lips curling up. He fumbled for the doorknob. It seemed to be moving away from his hand.

"Babies don't–" Winter sighed. "Never mind. See to yourself, Orval."

Orval staggered down the hall, using the wall to brace himself. It wouldn't be long before the babies woke again, hungry. He'd need to get Amari something to eat, poor thing, and then–

He blinked, trying to remember why he was in the privy.

After he figured that out, he washed and shaved and changed into slightly cleaner trous. He staggered back out, blinking at the sight of Winter standing in the doorway to the bedroom. "Thank you," he whispered in a daze, looking down at Dalan sleeping, his tiny face at peace. So peaceful, so wonderfully, wonderfully … quiet.

"You need sleep, Orval." Winter led the way into the bedroom. Amari never stirred. The older woman placed Dalan in his basket and pulled back the bedding on the empty side of the bed.

Orval stared. "I can't. Amari's sleeping."

"You can." Winter pulled him over and gently pushed him down. "Sleep, Orval."

"I don't want to wake her," Orval protested even as his treacherous body sank onto the bed. Winter pulled the blankets over him. "She's so good with them and so lovely and–" the yawn caught him by surprise and his jaw cracked. He blinked up at Winter. "Maybe just for a few minutes," he mumbled. "It's so scary. They're so tiny, what if I break them?"

"Orval, you're doing fine." Winter straightened. "But you do need help."

"Can't afford–" Orval gave up the fight, letting his eyes close.

"Leave that to me," Winter said. "I'll see to it."

Sleep swept over him, pulling him down before he could muster a word of protest.

———•———

Amari woke to a heart beating steadily under her ear.

She drowsed, listening, feeling warm and secure, until consciousness flooded in and she lifted her head.

She'd been sleeping on Orval.

The poor man was sprawled next to her, on his back, his one arm wrapped around her as she cuddled close. Amari looked at his face, relaxed in sleep. Orval looked exhausted, and rightly so. He'd aided her at every turn, even when she was almost too tired to nurse the babes.

Light was flooding in through the small windows. Amari shifted to check the baskets, but both babes were sleeping as quiet as could be. She relaxed, letting her tiredness wash over her, hoping to slip back into sleep herself, until her stomach rumbled.

She needed food, and she'd best be about it while everyone was sleeping. Orval might not like it, but she didn't have the heart to wake him. He needed the rest, poor man.

She slid out from under the blankets and wrapped a robe around herself before quietly easing out of the room. A quick visit to the privy and then she headed to the kitchen, dreading the sight. She and Orval had tried to keep up with everything, but the room was a wreck, She'd see what she could find to eat, even if it was pease porridge. Amari wrinkled her nose, but she had to eat.

But she opened the door on a warm, well-lit and clean kitchen, filled with the wonderful smell of kav. Winter was at the sink, finishing washing the dishes. Amari couldn't have been more surprised. "Winter?"

"Good, you're awake." Winter started to dry her hands. "I was going to pretend to be you, but now you can answer the door when they come."

"What?" Amari took a step in and closed the door behind her, not wanting to wake anyone. Every dish was clean and there were bundles of bedding piled by the door.

"Here," Winter handed her a mug. "Here's some weak kav with lots of cream and sugar. I've an egg pie with tubers in the oven, no spices, mind, and there's bread and butter. Best get food in you while you can."

Amari took the mug and held it close, enjoying the warmth on her fingers and the wonderful smell. "Kav …" she breathed out a prayer of thanks and took a sip. The warmth traveled down her throat and pooled in her belly. "You are an avatar of the Ancestors," she said reverently.

Winter snorted. "Orval woke me because Dalan was having a bout of gas." She would have said more but a knock at the outside door cut her short. She moved out of sight of the door, gesturing for Amari to answer it.

"Mistress Amari, how be you this day? And the twins?" A small, wrinkled woman was standing there, a younger girl behind her, their arms laden with baskets of clean linens.

Amari blinked and opened the door wider. "Well, thank you," she said as the two women bustled in, exchanging the clean for the dirty bundles on the floor.

"We'll get this back, quick like," the older one muttered, half under her breath. "There's bedding and nappies here that will tide you over."

"This bundle be the dirty nappies?" The young one grinned as Winter nodded. "Hope those pisspots search it."

A flood of thanks overwhelmed Amari; it had been miserable trying to keep up with the wash. "I don't know how to thank you," she whispered.

"If'n he looked up from his books now and again, the Master would see that he's well-liked, especially by the booksellers." The older woman rolled her eyes. "He's been scribing for us and figuring for us whenever we comes around."

"He's got our respect and affection," the younger one said. "And there's many a hand willing to pitch in."

"After all Master Orval's done for us, tucking a few extra things in the wash is no chore." The older woman smiled, then sniffed. "What them guards don't know is none of our business."

A chill ran down Amari's spine. She'd forgotten the guards.

"Best we come more like every other day instead of weekly, Mistress." The older woman raised her voice loud enough for the guards to hear as they both headed down with their bundles.

"Many thanks," Amari called behind them. She could see the guards at the base of the stairs, nodding to the laundresses. She shut the door and turned to Winter. "Can Orval afford this?"

"He gets a small stipend from the Crown." Winter opened the oven and was using a cloth to pull steaming dishes from within. "This part of the city is working men and women, most with a deep and abiding distrust of the Crown and the Guard. No good comes of association." She paused and looked closely at Amari.

"But Orval has lived here a long time, and while he is of the Blood, he is one of us. He makes time to aid those that knock at his door and takes nothing in return. Even if on occasion he walks into people in the market when he tries to read as he walks." Winter rolled her eyes.

"There won't be talk of coin. And there won't be talk of the oddness of a sudden marriage. People here ask no questions and offer no information."

Amari sank onto a stool by the table and watched Winter dish up a plate of food. "We tried to keep up–" she started to explained, but Winter made a hushing noise.

"Or course you did," Winter said. "But it's been ten days and I should have checked on you before this. Eat now. Those babes will need feeding soon. Once Orval wakes, we'll change the bedding and get that room set to rights."

Ten days? Amari had eaten her first mouthful before that sank in. She'd lost track of all time, awash in the cycle of feeding and cleaning and sleeping. How could ten days have passed?

She frowned at the plate and took another bite, only to look up when Winter cleared her throat.

The older woman's eyes had gone suddenly hard.

"I don't know, and don't want to know, what you are doing here. Your business is your own. But don't hurt him, you hear me?"

Amari nodded, the threat clear. But the woman deserved honestly, if nothing else. "I hear. I will try not to."

Winter grimaced. "He's getting attached to the babes. It may already be too late. I fear–"

The inner door opened. "Too late for what?" Orval asked, yawning as he limped into the room. He was wearing nothing but trous and looked sleepy and rumpled. To Amari's eyes, he looked oddly boyish without the thick robes he usually wore.

"Too late in the day for your stipend to be delivered." Winter said firmly. "Your rent's overdue."

Orval nodded absently, looking at the table. "Is that egg pie?" he asked, his eyes lighting up. Amari smiled as he hastened closer.

"And kav," Winter offered him a mug. "Strong and black. You need it."

"The skies bless and keep you." Orval sat and took the mug with a grateful sigh.

"Eat while you can and I'll give you the news, such as it is," Winter said as she dug into the clean linens. "Here," she tossed Orval a tunic.

Orval pulled it over his head as Winter prepared him a plate. To Amari's amusement, dressing rumpled his hair even more. Orval caught her eye and gave her a sheepish grin as he dug into the food. "Good news?" Orval asked Winter before sipping his drink.

Winter waited for him to swallow then spoke, her tone flat. "Queen Mother Tithanna was interred in such haste, they didn't even pull the dagger from her heart."

Amari closed her eyes and offered a soft prayer.

Orval froze, staring at his food. "She wouldn't have done that. She'd never have done that, killed herself. She was too old, too tough, too–" Orval snorted softly. "Too strong, truthfully."

"Be that as it may," Winter said, some of the clean dishes clattering as she stored them away. "She's dead and buried, and it was done in haste and with little honor." She looked over her shoulder at them. "Eat."

"I don't think I can." Orval said. Amari nodded. Her own stomach was lead.

"There's worse to come," Winter said. "Force it in if you have to, but you need to know what's happened in the last ten days and I've not much time."

"Ten days? Orval's eyes widened as they met Amari's. Amari shared his disbelief. She dropped her eyes to her plate and then forced herself to take another bite. Orval followed her example.

Winter settled at the table, her own mug of kavage wrapped in her hands. She wasn't as calm as she seemed; Amari noticed her knuckles were white.

"Lord Jazan was executed for treason this morning. His lands and assets seized."

Amari's heart grew heavier in her chest.

Orval set his mug down, his lips pressed thin. "Lady Jazan? Their sons?"

"Their sons were both killed on the field." Winter's voice was dry and matter-of-fact, grating to Amari's ears. "Lady Jazan has fled. Other supporters of the Airion House have fled as well, or been imprisoned, and their lands and coin forfeit."

"I have no lands," Orval said.

"No," Winter agreed drily. "You have the newest generation of the Blood. Healthy twins, of which your Captain Ussin has made their Majesties very aware."

Fear gripped Amari, fear that was reflected on Orval's face.

"But there is soon to be another," Winter said. "Queen Satia is pregnant." She huffed as she took a sip of kavage. "Odds are it's not Xyrath's. For all his cavorting in his youth, never once heard that he got a woman pregnant. Loyal to Satia, I grant him that, but he's a poor breeder."

Orval sputtered, coughing. "Winter!"

Winter ignored him. "The King holds revels in celebration as the cold creeps in, and now there is talk of raising taxes to pay the good warriors who fought for the throne." Winter's lip curled. "Which no one believes, but all will have to pay." She looked up at the darkening windows. "I best get back. We'll open soon enough for the evening hours." She stood, leaving the mug of kavage on the table. "Orval, more people will come to aid you, for all that you have done for them. Accept their help, don't be foolish. I'll slip out quietly. You can bolt the door after the babes wake. Finish your food."

Amari watched Winter go, leaving the door ajar behind her. She reached for her kavage and found Orval staring at her. "Ten days?" he asked. "How did we lose ten days?"

"Exhaustion," she said glumly. "Babies. Honestly, Orval, I had no idea. It's all been a blur since I fled–"

"The marcus," Orval sat up straighter. "Ten days and the marcus has not returned.

I thought he'd be back by now, to spirit you and the babes somewhere else, somewhere safe and suitable for babies." He stared ruefully down at his plate. "I also thought it would be easy caring for babies. It's not like they would wander about and disrupt my stacks of books. A few days at best. How bad could it be?" He looked up at her. "Feel free to roll your eyes at my stupidity."

Amari stared back as a bubble of laughter rose up in her throat, and the next thing she knew they were both laughing giddily, though with a hint of desperation. She wiped her eyes and reached over the table for Orval's hand. He covered hers with his long, warm fingers, still laughing. When the fit passed, they both held their breaths, waiting to see if the babies had roused.

"You are so good at this," Orval whispered. "I'd thought I'd killed poor Dalan."

"I helped raise my younger siblings and cousins," Amari explained.

"A large family, then?" Orval asked.

"Yes," Amari pulled her hand back, not wanting to explain. "We'd best finish eating."

Orval's forehead puckered, but he drew his hand back as well. "It was only my sister and me, and we were fostered at an early age."

"Fostering? That is not done where–" Amari paused as a wail cut through the air.

"I'll go," Orval stood. "Eat."

Amari managed to clear her plate as she listened to Orval talking to the babes. One long, last drink of kavage, then she started to unlace her top to bare her breasts.

"Dalan is still sleeping," Orval said and brought both infants into the kitchen. "But Lara's ready."

Lara cried again.

"More than ready," Amari smiled as she took the swaddled baby into her arms and put her to the breast.

Orval sat down, cradling Dalan in one arm as he reached for the food. "Do they ever sleep through the night?" he asked, mumbling through a mouthful.

"Eventually." Amari smiled, enjoying the feel as Lara suckled her nipple.

"Eventually," Orval echoed with a sigh as he rolled his eyes. Then he grew quiet. "I claimed you as wife and now these two are considered of the Blood. Maybe we should use that token to send for the marcus. We could have you all catch fevers and die. I could become a grieving widower." He glanced down at the babe sleeping in his arms. "Or maybe," he said with an odd, tentative note in his voice, "maybe I could come with you."

"Leave your books?" Amari asked in surprise.

"Well–" Orval started, but was interrupted by a ruckus of some kind on the stairs. A shrill, old voice called out.

"Orval, tell these scallywags to let me in!"

Orval rolled his eyes. "My Aunt Xydell, a terrible gossip. Nothing for it, I guess." He rose, balancing Dalan as he opened the outer door. "Welcome, Aunt–"

Her voice entered first; she must still have been climbing the stairs. "Foolishness, guards following an old lady around, and more foolishness guarding a bookish fool who doesn't bother to let family know he's wed." Her cane clicked the floor as she appeared, well wrapped against the cold, silver-haired and tall, with sharp blue eyes that peered over a scarf. "Shut the door, nephew. You're letting out the heat."

Orval stepped back to let the woman in. "How nice to see–"

"Doubtful," she said as she unwrapped her scarf. "But since you are holding a babe, the rumors must be true." Xydell fixed her gaze on Amari and her eyes narrowed. "What is this brazen hussy doing here? If you've hired her as a wet nurse, I'll be having harsh words with your wife. Why would she hire a whore?"

## CHAPTER ELEVEN

Queen Satia swept into her solar, irritated, nauseated, and concentrating on keeping a pleasant expression on her face.

The ladies of the Court cut off their chatter, rose from their seats, and curtseyed low as she passed. Her Bondmaidens entered behind her. Caris, Nora, and Mira took up strategic positions around the room while Avice moved to a small desk next to Satia's seat of state.

Satia took some satisfaction that the ladies' blue and white dresses had been replaced with garments in other colors. Given the range of styles, some of them fairly antique and faded, many had been pulled from storage.

None of the women wore mourning black, since Satia had made her displeasure clear on that point.

Except the Royal Housekeeper, Rosalind, with her black armband.

Yet another irritant.

Satia stepped to the dais and stood before her throne for a moment before taking her seat.

Once she did, the ladies rose from the floor and seated themselves, all taking up their sewing. Satia had encouraged them to start sewing baby things for the future heir, pleased to see the wives and daughters of the noble houses, ranging in age from graying to nubile, working on behalf of her unborn child.

At least Xydell was not among them, the old bat. Always ranting about her perfect dead husband, Jerrold. Her shrill voice gave Satia a headache.

They'd all best keep their voices low and their gossip to harmless matters, if they knew what was good for them.

Her stomach flipped, turning sour. "Tea," she snapped, and Mira hurried to obey. Satia huffed out a breath and settled back, closing her eyes.

She could feel her nearby Bondmaidens, attentive, obedient, and watchful. But Iris … .

Satia relaxed and focused.

Long ago, before his death, her Lord Father had explained that the bond felt like having a fish on a line, hook deep in its mouth. You couldn't see it, but you could feel it, its movements, its strength or weakness. Once in a while, perhaps glimpse a silvery figure darting through dark waters.

She wouldn't know. She'd never been fishing.

But she could feel Iris, feel her moving away from Edenrich, feel her strength. The hunt for the babe continued. She had to be satisfied with that.

As expected of a solar, the room was well lit and warmed by the sun coming in through the high windows. The tapestries around the walls had all been changed, airions replaced with landscapes and scenes of hunting. They were older and worn in places, but that would be dealt with in time. For now, Satia was content with drafty halls and old tapestries, and the airions banished from the walls. As she had commanded.

Ten days, she reminded herself. Ten successful days since they'd triumphed. So far, all was going well, but securing a throne wasn't done so easily or so quickly. She'd accomplished much in that ten days, but there was much yet to do.

Regardless of her stomach.

When she'd told Xyrath of her condition, he'd been beside himself with joy. He'd proclaimed it to the Court and sent heralds through the city. She would have preferred a bit less of a stir, at least until the third month. Nonetheless it was a relief to be able to be sick publicly, now that the announcement had been made.

It was also quite useful for cutting off unwanted conversations.

However, it was also making her cranky. Emotional. She didn't care for that at all.

"Your tea," Mira murmured as she placed a tray on the small table at Satia's side. "Some dry crackers, as well."

Joy. Satia was tiring of ginger tea and dry crackers. She took a sip and reminded herself to control her temper.

"Steward Paulin requests an audience," Avice murmured.

"Granted," Satia said.

Nora bowed and headed for the door.

Satia drank a bit more, nibbled on a cracker, and let her gaze drift over the women in the room. All daughters and wives of supposedly true supporters. Some would leave Court for the winter soon, others would stay. She'd need to sort out their loyalties by then.

Tarwain's daughter Halithe was seated close. A plump, plain, partridge, that girl, with hair black as night, thick ankles, and a snub nose. She was not very good with a needle. Mira had set her to hemming nappies. The child did not adorn Satia's chambers, but it was useful to have her close. Tarwain had not become the problem she'd feared, never seeming to question the pregnancy.

But one never knew. Today's ally is tomorrow's enemy. A lesson she'd learned long ago.

"Steward Paulin," Nora announced.

Satia set down her cup and smiled warmly. "Steward Paulin,"

He advanced into the room and bowed as low as she could wish. "Queen Satia. Lovely to see you surrounded by the delightful flowers of the Court."

"Rise, Paulin. We have much to discuss." Satia gave the man a warm smile. "Do you have the accountings I've asked for?"

"Majesty, yes." Paulin was sweating as he held out the account books. Interesting. Satia wondered if he was skimming from the accounts.

Avice stepped forward and took the books from his hands.

"I am pleased to tell you that the treasury has plumped up nicely, thanks to the recent deposits," Paulin added.

"The palace accounts have been brought current?" Satia asked. "The vendors are satisfied?"

"Well, you have directed that your accounts be paid," Paulin stuttered a bit. "We haven't brought the accounts current from when–"

"We will not pay the debts of the false pretenders." Satia said firmly. "Let them understand that clearly. Clearly." She repeated.

"As you command," Paulin bowed again. "There is one, however, that is insisting the full balance be paid, unless you wish to break the contract." He looked uncomfortable, looking everywhere but at Satia. "The Mage Guild?"

Satia reached for her cup. She didn't hold Ritathan's key, as it had not yet been found, but she didn't want to lose control of such an asset. "How much would it take?" she asked.

The sum Paulin named was staggering. Satia took a sip to hide her dismay.

Paulin shrugged apologetically. "Chained mages are ruinously expensive, Majesty."

Satia gave him a nod as her thoughts raced. The funds flowing in would be one-time surges from the seizures. Any steady income would have to come from taxes, which would not be popular.

And there was the matter of the cost of Xyrath's "projects."

She didn't want to drain her funds, but she wanted to know the secrets the mage held, and the only way to get them was to maintain the contract. She gritted her teeth. "Pay it in full," she said, as graciously as she could manage.

Paulin bowed.

"There is another matter, Steward." Satia set down her cup. "Rosalind. I know she has served as the Royal Housekeeper long and well, and change is hard for all of us. But please speak to her about her attitude. It is upsetting that she continues to express her grief so publicly."

"Majesty, I hadn't noticed." The Steward frowned. "She is quite skilled, Majesty."

"She wears a small black armband," Satia said. "Subtle yet defiant."

"Majesty, I will speak with her." Paulin shrugged. "But Rosalind has always been fairly strong-willed."

"Perhaps just a gentle suggestion," Satia smiled. "Maybe she will listen to you." She ignored the doubt in his face and gave him a dismissing nod. "My thanks, Steward."

Paulin bowed deeply and backed away, through the door that Nora held open. Turning to watch him go, Nora looked down the hall and sank to the floor, her head bowed.

"Xyrath, King of Xy," a male voice boomed, and all the ladies rose and curtseyed low, their heads down.

Xyrath bounded in with a smile, followed by Lord Tarwain. Her love was armored in dark leathers, sword and dagger at his side, with brand new, red leather gloves tucked into his belt. He looked so handsome and dashing … and ready for battle they could not afford.

Satia clenched her jaw and made as if to rise to greet her husband,

"No, no, my love," Xyrath protested. "I pray you, be seated. How fare you this day?"

Satia sank back down on her chair. "Well, my love," she said. "Although I have had to instruct the Royal Cook to prepare only the plainest of foods for our future meals." She pressed a hand to her stomach. "I fear I can't tolerate strong smells or rich foods."

"Oh," Xyrath looked taken aback, then nodded. "Of course, of course, anything for the babe. Your every wish will be my command."

Tarwain was glancing around the room. When he spotted his daughter, to Satia's surprise, he frowned. Odd, that. She'd need to learn more about that tension.

"Ladies, I must speak with my Queen about things not fit for your gentle ears," The King turned his charming smile on them all. "Leave us, if you would."

The ladies returned his smile, although a few were not warm, Halithe included. Also interesting, and something Satia noted for the future. The King opened his arms wide and pretended to herd the chicks as the ladies picked up their various projects and scattered to the door, giggling.

Her Bondmaidens stayed. Both men took little notice, since that custom had been well-established years earlier.

The King returned to Satia's side, scowling. "Tarwain has word of the old baronies. They defy me!" He started to pace, agitated.

Satia looked at Tarwain who stood rock still, a scroll in his hands. "Majesty," he bowed his head. "I was attempting to review the situation with the King."

Xyrath prowled back and forth, scowling.

"Most of the baronies are neutral," Tarwain continued. "Athelbryght is under the control of one who bears the birthmark of the Chosen, of course. But the Black Hills are in open rebellion and–"

"*War!*" Xyrath boomed. "I will don the traditional red gloves of war. We must teach these upstarts to respect our sovereignty. If they do not respect our commands, they will respect our blades."

Tarwain's face was shuttered; this had obviously been a point of contention. Satia knew better than to argue reality with Xyrath. "Your Majesty is right, of course."

"You agree?" Xyrath threw Tarwain a triumphant look. "We can march–"

Tarwain opened his mouth but Satia jumped in before he could say a word. "Beloved, were you to march, you would not be here for the birth," she put her hand on her stomach. "I so desire your presence at the birth of your heir."

"Oh, yes," Xyrath knelt next to her, his agitation fading. He took her hand in his. "It will be such a celebration," he said. "I'd even a mind to plan it. But the baronies–"

"War might force you to neglect your projects," Satia put a worried tone into her voice.

"Oh," Xyrath said. "True."

"There is also the cost of a winter campaign," Tarwain offered. "Instead, we could use these months to train and prepare the men. We could indulge in diplomacy as well, sending our demands even if we know they will be rejected. That would put us in the right in the eyes of the people. Show them that we did everything we could to avoid bloodshed."

"Well, as long as we don't avoid it completely." Xyrath rose to his full height.

Tarwain coughed. "There is also the issue of security within the Palace. I have concerns about Roth, Captain of the Guard."

Satia's attention was caught. "You question his loyalty?"

"Not to the Crown," Tarwain said. "But to the current holder of the Crown. Nothing overt, mind you."

"Give him time," Xyrath said. "Change is hard, and he must know in his heart that I am the rightful King. As does the rest of the family, I am sure, now that we have seen to their safety."

"But others have not supported your cause," Satia said. "I have a list of the merchants and guild leaders who spurned us. Avice?" The Bondmaiden rose and handed Satia the list—one the Queen had dictated from memory the night before.

Xyrath took the paper, frowning. "I remember how they scorned us. Even now–"

"Let Tarwain see to them," Satia said. "You have a war to

train for."

"You are right," Xyrath passed the sheet to Tarwain. "Make recommendations as to who should be accused of treason."

"And compile an accounting of their lands and properties," Satia murmured.

"I will see it done, Your Majesties." Tarwain bowed.

"I am glad that the Blood is all safe," Xyrath said. "In the ancient days, they'd have all been granted lands, held in the Blood and through oaths of fealty to the Crown. Pity the family has fallen so low, however distant."

The stirring of an idea occurred to Satia. "My love, you are now the head of the House of Xy, so noble, yet so diminished," Satia said slowly. "I am sure the Blood will rally to you and lend you every support, to aid you in securing your lands."

Xyrath gave her a bright smile. "We must find a way to honor them all," he said. "Let us discuss this further tonight, at the entertainment I have planned. Paulin found a new group of jugglers to perform."

"Tonight, my King," Satia raised her hand for his kiss, looking at him through her eyelashes.

"Tonight, My Queen," Xyrath held her gaze as he swept her hand up and pressed his lips to it, letting his tongue touch her skin. "Until then. Tarwain, let us consider the preparations for battle in the spring!"

Xyrath swept out. Tarwain gave Satia a bow, then followed.

Nora shut the door firmly behind them. The Bondmaidens gathered close as Satia wiped her hand on her skirt.

"I fear the Steward supports the Royal Housekeeper," Avice observed. "He didn't seem pleased to be told to talk to her."

"The Steward will support me if he knows what is best for

him," Satia snapped. She covered her mouth to burp, her throat burning with ginger, crackers, and bile. She made a face at the taste. "Mira, the ginger tea isn't working. Find me something else."

Mira nodded. "Let me mix in some lemon. Sometimes sour cancels sour."

"Caris, Tarwain seems to be out-of-sorts with his daughter. See if you can find out why. Nora, I want to know more about both the Captain of the Guard and our Royal Housekeeper. Something I can use to pry them from their positions."

"They are well-established," Avice said. "It may be difficult."

"Perhaps 'pry' is too harsh a word," Satia took yet another cup of tea from Mira. "I will find a way to honor them." She took a sip and the bile cleared from her throat. "Yes. She smiled as her stomach settled. "Whatever the cost."

———•———

Ritathan felt her approach through his wards. He frowned before the door even opened.

"Halithe." He kept his voice flat.

Halithe stepped within and closed the door of his outer chamber softly. Ignoring his frown, she took a seat in the student chair before his desk. She sat straight, folded her hands in her lap, and met his glare squarely. Every black hair in place and her dark eyes steady.

He admired that. Few students could be so composed.

"This is unwise," he said firmly. "Dangerous, even, given the new regime."

"She has us doing sewing." Halithe's voice was almost as deep as a man's. "I loathe sewing."

"Appropriate, for ladies of gentle birth," Ritathan pointed out. "Safe, and so useful in your future wedded life."

Halithe didn't blush and didn't look away. "I am here for my lesson," she said firmly.

"I will give you no more lessons." Ritathan said, just as firmly.

"Queen Kara required you to give me lessons," Halithe said.

"Kara is dead," Ritathan pointed out.

"She is," Halithe gave a slight nod. "Yet her command has not been rescinded."

Ritathan narrowed his eyes. The chit before him didn't even blink. "Queen Satia will rescind it."

"She is not the master of your chains," Halithe intoned, "her dark eyes sparkling with glee. "She does not hold your key."

"Delightful," Ritathan dripped out the word. "How clever of you. Yet the contract for my services may terminate at any time. Or Queen Satia may get irritated enough to have me killed."

"I will take that chance."

Ritathan snorted. "Halithe, you do not understand what you ask. Queen Kara humored you in this, but now—'" He shook his head. "This path you would walk is fraught and even more dangerous for a woman. Turn away."

"No," Halithe said, her face unchanging, her determination clear.

"Halithe, you do not appreciate what you ask," Ritathan said. "We are not slaves, but we are bound. We chain our powers to the one who holds our key. In order to wield, we must surrender. In order to be free in our craft, we bind ourselves with chains and oaths and geases and contracts. Turn away."

"No," Halithe said.

Ritathan sucked in a breath through his mouth and let it out through his nose. "Halithe," he said again, for the third time. The last time. "You do not fully realize the sacrifice that will be asked of you. You will gain, but you will lose, in ways you can't foretell, and those losses are forever." Ritathan leaned forward, emphasizing every word. "Turn away."

"No," Halithe said. "The ritual is complete, Master. Three times you have asked, and three times I have answered." Now she leaned forward, and he saw the hunger burning in her eyes. "I want to learn," she continued, the same hunger in her voice. "I want to know."

"So be it." Ritathan sighed. "But this will all end in disaster, I just know it."

"So be it," Halithe echoed, but her lips quirked up in triumph.

# CHAPTER TWELVE

——⟨●⟩——

A whore as a wet nurse? If your Uncle Jerrold was still alive, he'd have something to say, certain sure. What is the world coming to?" Aunt Xydell shrieked again.

Orval shut the door behind her as quickly as he could so the guards wouldn't hear, not that that would make a bit of difference. Aunt Xydell's shrill voice could pierce rock.

"You're mistaken," Orval said, feeling his nervousness in his throat. "This is my wife, Amari, and–"

"Don't give me that, nephew," Aunt Xydell rapped her cane on the floor, waking Dalan. "She's Amari of Uyole, one of Eijer's castoffs." Aunt Xydell looked down her nose at Orval, her lip curling. "Which you knew," she spat, regally. "What have you done, you stupid boy?" she glared at Dalan. "Those twins are no more your get then I am."

Orval froze, the pressure in his chest making it hard to breathe. Dalan started fussing.

"Peace with the wyverns was doomed from the start," his aunt glanced around, wrinkling her nose. "I warned them, but no one listens to me."

Dalen snuffled.

Xydell ignored the babe's whines and raised her voice. "And you, slut. Seeking any who'd shelter you, eh? With Eijer dead in the field, you'd no hope of–"

"Dead?" Amari jerked. Lara lost the nipple and complained.

"On the field, with the other damn fools who supported Xywellan," Xydell raised her voice again as Dalan started full-throated wailing. "I didn't believe the gossip flying through the Court. This explains a lot, Orval. I wondered what woman would have you, what with your deformity and all your other failings."

Orval stood stunned as the wails of Lara and Dalan grew in intensity. His inadequacies, his flaws all pressed in on him, again, paralyzing him, bringing back memories of the past, constant reminders of what he lacked.

Yet, what made his heart twist was Amari, crumpled before him, her eyes filled with tears, crushed.

Xydell continued, hitting the floor with her cane for emphasis. "This is shameful. Always knew you didn't have it in you, but to do this? Dishonor the Blood? When word gets out–"

Something snapped within Orval. He found his breath "Enough," he thundered, even as he shook inside.

Xydell shut her mouth so hard her teeth clicked and fixed him with a glare. The babes still cried, but at least the woman had gone silent.

"Xydell," Orval refused to acknowledge their familial relationship. Rude deserved rude. "You are a nasty, vile woman. You have insulted my wife and children. Leave."

Xydell drew herself up. "You married this hussy so that you–"

Dalan was still crying. Orval set him on the table, well away from the edge, took Xydell's elbow and turned her firmly. "Out. You are not welcome in our home."

"Humph," Xydell threw her scarf around her neck even as she arched an eyebrow. "First time I've seen any spirit in you, Orval. Not that I would want to stay in this–"

Orval opened the door and managed to resist pushing the old harridan down the stairs as she continued her tirade. He waited until she was at least two steps down before he slammed the door and bolted it.

The babes were still complaining loudly. Amari wouldn't meet his eyes; she was sniffling and trying to get Lara back on her nipple. Orval swallowed the bile in his throat, picked Dalan up and started rocking him. "There's one in every family, you know," he said, trying to calm his own racing heart. "Rude, manipulative, never a kind word."

He started to walk back and forth a bit. His leg twinged but it was bearable. More important to soothe the little one.

Dalan blinked up at him, settling. Lara was nursing again, and in the quiet, Orval could hear Amari's sobs.

"She's never liked me, always made snide comments about my leg." Orval babbled as he steadied his own breathing. "My mother could always handle her, but my father and I–"

"You deserve to know the truth," Amari said softly.

Shame burned in her chest as Amari tried to stop crying. She was a fool, an utter fool, to think that the truth wouldn't come out at some point. Amari wiped at her cheeks, careful not to disturb Lara further.

Orval moved next to her. She forced herself to look up and meet his eyes.

Still rocking Dalan, Orval handed Amari a clean nappy for her face. "Only if you want to," he said. His eyes were warm and he gave her a quick smile, that one crooked tooth flashing at her. "You and I have suffered through enough baby cack and loss of sleep together to trust one another, yes?"

Amari took the nappy and smiled weakly before the tears started again. "But what she said–"

"That old gossip frames everything and everyone in the worst light," Orval eased back into his chair. "Never a nice thing to say about anyone or anything." He took a deep breath. "Trust me, I know."

"I don't think I can stop crying," Amari admitted as she clutched the nappy.

"We can talk later," Orval offered, but Amari shook her head.

"No," she said. "Best get it done and over with." She looked up at the ceiling, anywhere but at those understanding blue eyes. "I am Amari Misalyn Anouk of the Hearth of Misalyn in the Kingdom of Uyole, which acknowledged Xy as suzerain." Absently, she reached for her bracelets, her fingers finding only bare skin.

Orval nodded. "The farthest southern part of Ancient Xy."

For a moment, Amari forgot her shame and looked at him in surprise. "You know of it?"

"I've read about it, actually," Orval shrugged, with an embarrassed look. "A matriarchy, if I remember correctly." He paused, clearly thinking. "The men handle the military matters but the women rule."

Amari wiped her face, nodding. He had the wrong impression, most outsiders did. "It may seem so to outsiders, but it's more of a partnership. My mother is the Hearth Mother of a wealthy ... what you would call a barony." She struggled for the words as memories flooded in. "I am the fourth of eight children. After consulting with the Elder Aunties and Grandmothers, it was decided that I would be sent to serve Queen Kara, with an eye to establishing my own Hearth here." Amari bit her lip. "I so wanted to see the world, experience new places and people. It seemed a great adventure.

"Queen Kara was welcoming, and I was presented at Court as one of her ladies. It was there I met Eijer." She choked on his name.

"I knew him," Orval's tone was dry. "I suspect he saw you as a challenge."

"I learned that," Amari said bitterly. "Later." She drew a shuddering breath. "Among my people, one enters into a courting contract first. Marriage does not occur until after the joining has proven fertile and a child has lived six months after birth. Then and only then does a couple enter into a contract of marriage." She wanted him to know, to understand. She wasn't what that woman had said she was.

Orval gave her an encouraging nod, so she plunged on. "Eijer swept me off my feet," Amari choked out. "He was–"

"Everything," Orval nodded. "Handsome, witty, a wonderful fighter. Buckets full of charm and grace and lacking any honor or integrity."

Amari's eyes welled with fresh tears. "You knew him," she whispered.

"I fostered with him," Orval said. "He'd pretend to be a friend and then follow behind me, mocking my limp." Dalan gurgled and Orval shifted the babe to his other arm. "Most ladies at Court have mothers to warn them. I'm surprised Kara didn't warn you."

"The conflicts were rising: she wasn't much involved in the social aspect of the Court." Amari said. "It was all so bright, so glittering. Dances every night, with the Great Hall lit with a thousand candles. I was too stupid to realize it was also frantic, fearful. The nobles knew what was coming, but—"

"Party hard, for tomorrow we war." Orval said softly.

"Yes," Amari said. "And passion and fire overcame any sensibilities I had. I did ask Eijer about a contract, but he swept away my concerns with warm embraces and sweet kisses. We used my funds for a grand, glorious party that never seemed to end." She had to pause, her throat closing.

Orval's eyes were warm and sympathetic. He sat, her son in his arms, and waited. Patient, with no judgement in his expression.

"I discovered that I was pregnant, and I went to tell him the joyous news publicly. He rejected me—" Amari choked. "Publicly. With harsh words and fierce looks. Cruel in ways I had not thought possible."

Orval said nothing, just waited, giving her time.

Lara released the nipple with a yawn. Amari looked down into her tiny, sweet face. "I had no contract, no written word to protect me. My funds depleted, I sold what little I had, including my bracelets. I had no way to contact my family, due to the conflict." In truth, even if she had been able to get a message through, she feared what her family would say. Thrusting that thought aside, Amari stumbled on. "When Kara learned of what had happened, she sent for me. I expected harsh words and re-prisals, for I had shamed my Hearth."

Amari lifted her head. "Instead, I was offered sympathy and understanding. I think, in some way, she blamed herself for my plight. Although, in fairness," Amari's tears welled up again as her heart turned over, "with my heart filled with Eijer's soft whispers, I doubt that I would have listened. Kara told me that she too was bearing and offered me the position of Royal Wet Nurse. I accepted, gladly. She saw to my needs and brought me to a midwife to see me through the birth."

"Let me take her, if she's done," Orval said, nodding at Lara.

They quietly swapped babies, and Amari put Dalan to her other breast as Orval put Lara on his shoulder and started to pat her back gently. The kitchen was quiet, the only sound the drag of Orval's shoe on the floor.

Amari mopped her face with her free hand, trying to get her emotions in check. Eijer dead. That bright, handsome face, that sparkle. Despite everything, she'd hoped he'd have a change of heart once he'd seen his son, and return to her side, apologizing, becoming once again the loving, charming man she'd fallen for.

Now Dalan would never know his father and she'd never know— and yet, even deeper down, she did know. Had he ever really loved her? Had she really loved him? She'd thought she had, and yet … .

It was complicated and right now, it was all just a tangled bundle of pain.

Lara burped, the soft sound seeming to echo in the quiet room. Amari watched Orval switch the child to his other shoulder and resume patting as he paced, his eyes down, his face thoughtful. She felt lighter for having told him the truth, but dread crept over her. She waited for him to say something, anything, to condemn her for her—

Orval came to a stop, facing her.

"We need a courting contract," he said.

## CHAPTER THIRTEEN

Orval was pleased as he watched surprise replace the pain in Amari's lovely dark eyes, reddened from crying. His heart went out to her. What she must have gone through, this past year.

"What did you say?" Amari asked, as if she couldn't quite take it in.

"We need a courting contract," Orval repeated. Lara was snuffling in his ear, so he adjusted her on his shoulder. "We'll say that we are following the ways of your people in this."

"You do not condemn me," Amari looked like she was about to start crying again.

"No, of course not." Orval rocked a bit where he stood, keeping up a rhythm on Lara's back. "I know only too well how vicious life at Court can be. Even under Wellan and Kara, there was always cruelty and backstabbing. One of the many reasons I avoided the place. Except for the Royal Library, of course."

Lara burped and started to fuss. Orval hugged her to his shoulder as he turned away to gather up a fresh nappy and swaddling cloth, hoping this would give Amari a moment to gather herself.

How could he blame her? Eijer was everything a woman could wish for. Wealthy, handsome, charming, skilled at combat and dance, a sparkling addition to the Royal Court.

Everything that Orval had never been. A pit formed in Orval's stomach, filled with his own inadequacies.

Damn Eijer, for luring such a lovely lady on, then leaving her in such straits. "The nobility have sharp tongues," he continued. "They cheerfully vivisect one another for their dress styles, much less their private lives."

"Or for their physical differences?" Amari ventured.

"Just so. One of the many reasons I decided long ago on the solitary, scholarly life." Orval put Lara down on the table and unwrapped the swaddling. "While the royal library tempted me, the people didn't. Thus you find me, impoverished. And yet?" He glanced around at the kitchen shelves, stuffed with dishes and mugs, but also his books and papers. "Yet rich in what I value most."

Lara wiggled under his hand. Orval looked down and gave her a smile. "Hey sweetling, let's see to you, shall we?"

Lara blew a bubble of spit as he removed her nappy. He frowned as the birth cord came into view. "Is it supposed to be that black and nasty looking?" he asked.

"Yes," Amari's voice firmed up. "It will fall away soon. There is a small ritual," she offered hesitantly. "The birth cord is burned as an offering to the Ancestors, with prayers for the child's safety and welcome to the family."

Lara was kicking as Orval struggled to wipe her, making sure to dry her folds. "We could do that," he said absently. He glanced over to see Amari scanning the kitchen. She caught his look and dropped her eyes.

"You do not have a hearth-shrine in your kitchen," she said softly. "I wasn't sure that–"

"Father was of the Lord of the Sun and Mother revered the elements," Orval explained. "I am a mixture of both. We can set up a shrine, if you wish." He tucked Lara into a fresh nappy and started swaddling her. She stared at him with her eyelids drooping. "Hey, sweetling, now that you're changed and dry, then maybe you'll let us sleep a bit?"

"They will both sleep through the night," Amari said, "eventually."

"We need a contract," he said again. "We can draft it together and I can age it enough to pass muster. We'll count out the days and back-date it. No real problem."

"But," Amari looked down at Dalan, nursing hungrily. "Your Aunt," she started.

"My Aunt will be spreading the word far and wide, I am sure." Orval nodded. "But don't you see? That will–"

Steps on the stairs drew their attention. "That should be the stipend." Orval had been counting the days, hoping Xyrath and Satia would continue the funds and that they would arrive at the usual time. He gave Amari a swift smile as he opened the door, Lara in one arm, then stepped back in surprise. "Captain Ussin," he said.

"Afternoon, Orval. Milady," Ussin nodded at them both as he entered. "The King wanted me to personally deliver this, Orval. Said to make sure to hand it direct to you." Ussin handed him a leather pouch. "And this," Ussin added, holding out a sealed letter. "From the King and Queen."

"Er," Orval fumbled with the pouch, surprised by its weight. "Ussin, are you sure? This is far heavier than–"

"Certain sure," Ussin said. He chucked Lara under her chin. He stepped forward and dropped the letter on the table. "Best be leaving you to it, then. I might stop in and see how Madam Winter fares." Ussin straightened. "Fine woman, there. Smart."

Orval blinked at the man. "Yes, she is."

"I'm off, then," Ussin nodded again and was gone before Orval could say another word. Orval elbowed the door closed firmly and scowled.

"What is amiss?" Amari asked.

"This is more than I usually receive," Orval mused. He put Lara back on the table and untied the knotted cords of the pouch. The coins that spilled into his hand were gold. "Much, much more," Orval said.

"The note might explain," Amari said.

Orval broke the seal. "It's from Xyrath," he said slowly. "In his own hand. 'Cousin, word has come of your good fortune. Didn't know you had it in you,'" Orval rolled his eyes at Amari and was rewarded with a small smile. "'Be assured of our well wishes and our intent to honor you and yours.'" Orval stopped. Not sure he wanted to share the rest.

"Is there more?" Amari asked.

"A post-script," he said slowly. "In Queen Satia's hand. That we will be invited to Court after our Walk to the Well. She looks forward to honoring us in person." He paused, puzzled. "What is a Walk to the Well?"

Amari sucked in a breath and clutched at Dalan. "She knows." Her voice trembled. "I cannot go to Court, Orval. All those people, staring. They will know my shame, know the truth, and we can't–" her voice hitched and she started to breathe in short pants. "I can't, I can't, oh Ancestors, I–"

Orval reached over the table and put the tips of his fingers over her heart. Her heart was racing, her skin was clammy. Dalan had lost the nipple but mouthed it, trying to latch on.

"All's well," Orval whispered. "I'm here. Breathe."

She focused on him, then, and drew a long, shuddering breath. It took a moment, but she calmed, her pulse slowing.

He pulled his hand back, but she clutched at it, her fingers cold against his. "Orval," she started, but he shook his head.

"Think it through, Amari," he squeezed her hand gently. "Think it through. We will let all the gossips do our work for us. Some will think a cripple has taken advantage of the situation to secure children. Some will think that a loose woman has taken advantage of a poor cripple to secure an income for her children. Others will think that the rumors about you and Eijer were false and that the children are mine. We will not fight it, nor make a secret of it, nor acknowledge it. We will let them think what they think. In the meantime, as they talk and titter and tattle to one another, Lara is safer thereby."

Amari's gaze calmed as she took that in. She bit her lip, then nodded. "They will be so distracted by our outrageous behavior that they will not see the truth."

Orval nodded. "We may have to endure scorn, but Lara will be safe."

Dalan fussed. Amari squeezed Orval's hand, then shifted to help Dalan with the nipple.

"So, what is a Walk to the Well?" Orval lifted Lara back into his arms; the tiny girl was already sleeping.

"A tradition of my people," Amari shifted Dalan. "Hearths rarely have the water flow into homes as yours do," she nodded toward his sink. "We have wells for our water sources. If the child survives ninety days, the parents take the child and walk to the well. Family, friends, and neighbors gather to rejoice. The child is blessed with the water and named before the entire community. It is a great event among my people."

"Ninety days," Orval mused. "And you said that Dalan was born a month before Lara?"

Amari nodded.

"So you have bought us time as well," Orval gave her a grin. "We have the perfect reason not to show ourselves before your traditions dictate. Time enough to draft a contract, to let Lara here lose her birth cord, and wait to hear from the marcusi. Although," Orval dropped his gaze. "Taking me on as a potential husband is a poor bargain for your courage, Amari."

Amari sniffed, wiping at her eyes. "Orval, you offer protection and honor for myself and my son. I would accept your offer of a courting contract with gratitude and joy."

Warmth flooded his chest as they exchanged a long look. Amari's eyes warm and bright and so very lovely, that he– realized he was staring and dropped his gaze.

"Good, good," Orval cleared his throat. "We can work on the wording between feedings."

"Dalan's finished," Amari said. "I'll change him and see him settled."

Dalan fussed as she put him on the table and started to close up her tunic.

"No let me take him," Orval said. "You can clean up in here, then come to bed." Orval rose carefully, waiting for the pain in his leg to pass before gathering both babes in his arms. "I'll read to you, shall I?" he asked Dalan. "Where's that copy of the *Epic of Xyson* that I gave you? Still tucked in your basket? Let's go look."

"My thanks," Amari said as he headed for the inner door.

"I don't see what for," Orval cast her a glance over his shoulder and grinned. "I am leaving you with the dishes, after all."

Amari's laughter followed him out the door, filling his heart with quiet joy.

## CHAPTER FOURTEEN

T here's blood on your sleeve."

Caris dropped the bound feet of the would-be assassin to look at her elbow. The prisoner grunted through his gag as his feet hit the dungeon cell floor.

"Oh, dear," she cursed. "That will never come out."

"It will," Nora said as she dragged the prisoner further into the cell. "Just put it to soak in cold water when we're done."

The prisoner thrashed on the cold stone floor, trying to kick them. The noise fell flat against the damp stone walls.

"This is nice," Avice held the lantern high as she lifted the wooden lid off the privy hole. "It's not a cesspit. There's flowing water down here, under the grating. Nice large openings. No stink. Remember that midden in–"

"I wonder where it flows out," Caris said quickly, not wanting to remember that particular incident. "Is it a potential escape route?"

Avice reached down and tugged on the metal grille. "Seems strong." She wrinkled her nose and wiped her hand on the stone wall.

Mira, who had followed them in, closed the cell door. "Won't the body parts raise suspicion? She asked, frowning at the prisoner.

"Not if they're small enough," Nora was already loosening her laces. "I brought my knives and cleavers. Help me with this, Avice."

Caris watched the wide-eyed prisoner, who was trying to talk through the gag. An older man who served at table, with a graying, pointed beard and a mostly bald head. She'd seen him about, of course, although she couldn't remember his name. She did remember his annoying habit of humming under his breath as he went about his duties. He was struggling, but not effectively. "Poisoned cake," she said, kicking his bound ankles. "What were you thinking?"

Mira settled on a stool in the farthest corner. From the look on her face, she was stewing on something. Caris left it to her. Sooner or later the worry would come spilling out of her.

Nora and Avice stripped naked, piling their garments in Mira's lap and taking off their slippers.

The prisoner's eyes bulged.

Nora laid out her kit on the floor. She and Avice knelt on each side of the man, untied his hands, and used painful joint holds to stretch his arms wide and pin him down.

Caris couldn't help rolling her eyes; despite everything, his gaze was locked on their breasts. Men.

"Your life is already forfeit." Caris stood at his feet, glaring down at him. "What happens next depends on you. We need to know who hired you, who gave you the poison. Tell us, and your death is a quick one. Refuse, and–"

The man shrieked against his gag, his body arcing as he writhed in pain.

Nora tossed his little finger into the privy, her knife in her bloody hand.

"Nora," Caris scolded.

Nora looked up, her face filled with lust. Blood had splattered her neck and chest. Her eyes were glazed over; her lips parted as she licked them.

"He's not going to tell us," she crooned as she leaned down, letting her hardened nipple brush against his remaining fingers. "He's going to let me cut and cut and–"

"Nora," Caris deepened her voice into a command.

"Fine." Nora leaned back but kept her grip. "Talk him to death."

Caris huffed, shaking her head and turned back to the man. His eyes were filled with tears, and he was still thrashing. She lifted her voice, drawing his attention back to her. "Information," she said firmly, "and this will end." She nodded to Avice, who pulled out the gag.

Their prisoner spat with rage. "Death to House Wvyern, death to the bitch queen and her spawn." He drew in a sobbing breath, then screamed again as Nora took another finger.

"No one can hear you," Caris raised her voice. "And if they did, no one would stop us."

He cursed again, spitting his words.

"Fine." Caris said and nodded to Avice, who shoved the rag back in his mouth. "Break his elbows," she said. "Then start on his feet."

She went to stand by Mira, watching as the others worked.

"Don't you already know who gave him the poison?" Mira asked softly, holding the mass of skirts and underclothes that came almost to her chin.

"We have suspicions," Caris nodded. "But having it confirmed would be good. Besides," she leaned her head down and lowered her voice so she wouldn't be heard over the muffled screams. "Nora needs to work off her malaise. She's been vexed lately."

"We all have." Mira looked glum. She picked at a bit of lace on one of the sleeves. "Iris has been gone for so long; we have never been separated like this before. I keep looking for her, thinking I need to tell her something, but I turn and she is not there." Mira drew in a breath that was almost a sigh.

Caris gave her a questioning look.

Mira spoke slowly and carefully. "The Bonded is suffering. So far, her orders are rational, but I fear … ." Mira gave her a side glance.

Understanding her caution, Caris gave her an encouraging nod.

"Our Queen is smart and clever and manipulative and vicious," Mira let the words out in a rush. "But she always has a purpose. Lately she is just lashing out like a wounded bull. It can't continue, Caris." Mira seemed about to say more, but that foggy look entered her eyes and the words never came.

Thankfully, a clear scream drew both their attentions. Nora was pulling at the man's privates, clamping down hard. Avice was waving her knife before his face, whispering something.

"Lord Calfar, Lord Calfar, his steward paid me, paid me—" the hoarse, terrified rasp was cut off when Avice stuffed the rag back in his mouth.

"Ah," Caris said. "Good enough. Kill him. We can't be about this all day."

Nora and Avice just looked at her. "It's more fun when they struggle," Avice said. "If they're dead, it's just work."

"Twenty minutes more," Nora promised.

"Fine," Caris agreed. She glanced at the stone behind her, decided that her dress was already dirty, and leaned against it. "We're all concerned, Mira. She's bearing and—"

"No, you don't understand." Mira shook her head. "I'm doing what I can, what I know. But Caris, my training was solid, but my experience … ." After a breath, the words tumbled out of her. "I have basic healing skills, yes and I've birthed some babes on my own, and nothing's gone wrong during those times, but—

"She won't hear of another midwife. I fear that–" she gulped in air and tears filled her eyes. "I can't even ease her nausea. What if she starts to lose the child, or the babe comes out wrong, or–"

"Mira," Caris pulled a handkerchief from her sleeve and handed it to her. She glanced over to see that Nora was starting to drop parts into the privy. The muffled screams had dropped to moans.

Mira sniffled. "She gets so worked up about the mages and Tarwain's daughter and that sculpture that the King wants and the money worries." Mira blew her nose. "She's becoming more and more irritated and irrational, and she won't listen to me, and I am so afraid for her." She dropped her voice to the barest whisper. "And for us."

Caris tightened her grip, then released it. "A very real fear," she said.

"What is?" Nora asked absently, staring down at the wreckage that was left. She prodded the body with her toe, inducing a whimper.

"Fear of the Bonded's wrath," Caris said.

"Fear of failing her," Mira spoke loudly, as if afraid to hear her own words. "Fear of what happens if the child dies." She shivered. "Fear of what happens if she dies."

Instinctively, they all looked at their brands. Caris rubbed hers, frowning.

"I only speak to protect the Bonded," Mira said.

"Nothing is going to happen," Avice said firmly. She thrust her dagger into the man's belly and sawed down. The stink of guts and bowels rose as his back arched and his legs thrashed weakly.

"If Iris were here, she'd listen to her," Mira pouted. "She always listens to Iris."

"She doesn't *always* listen to her," Avice was put out; she always wanted to be the one in charge.

"Iris is not here and we don't know when she will return," Nora said.

"Still, we can't ignore Mira's concerns," Caris said. "We will have to try to talk the Bonded into thinking it's her own idea."

"That might work," Mira said, though she looked doubtful. She plucked at a piece of invisible lint on one of the dresses. "It's just that …" she sighed. "Nothing is right without Iris. We've never been apart this long before."

There was a final gurgle. Nora knelt down and poked. "Dead."

"Perhaps we didn't quite think this through," Avice said, cutting the soiled clothing they'd taken off him into strips. "We are not going to get the large bones through that grate."

"Leave them," Nora said. "They'll make quite the impression."

"The Queen will want the head on a spike," Mira reminded them.

"We'll take it to her, after we get you cleaned up." Caris said as Avice kicked the remains over to a corner. Caris looked over at Nora. Her once-wild eyes were calm and clear. "Feel better?"

"Much." Nora stood and stretched with a languid smile. Then her eyes sharpened. "Mira is right, you know. Iris–"

"Iris does the Bonded's will," Avice said sharply. "Nothing more need be said."

Caris felt it then, the familiar tightening, the pulse through her flesh that started at her wrist. She nodded in obedience.

They all did.

———•———

Iris crouched under the shelter of a pine and watched as the icy rain coated the needles. Her armor was sodden, her boots squished, she was cold and wet and none of that mattered.

She was close, so close.

She had to admire the vore and the marcus. She'd caught a glimpse or two, outlines on a ridge at sunset.

How was the babe being fed? She'd no experience with babies, perhaps the marcus was female and had brought milk to its breasts? For all she knew newborns didn't need to eat that often. But this hunt had taken days so far.

If there was a babe. She had to face the thought that she might be chasing a wild rabbit. But if that was the case, why not just try to kill her and be done? She'd been careful to watch her back trail for fear that the vore would circle round and take her from behind. But there'd been no sign of that.

The marcus, the vore, they'd tried everything in the book to lose her, but she'd found the trail each time. Not much, admittedly. A buried nappy at a cold camp, a babe's wail on the wind. The rare print in snow and ice.

Oh, they were good, she'd grant them that. She was better, and if the weather hadn't stopped her, she might have caught them this night.

She rubbed her wrist where the bond pulsed, driving her forward with an urgency that beat with her heart. But she and the others had learned long ago of the danger that the bond would push them past exhaustion and hunger until they staggered with fatigue or just collapsed.

The urge was softened now, muted. No doubt the Bonded slept.

She'd left Satia's side carrying the barest of food, thinking this chase would be an easy one, and had stretched those few provisions as far as she dared. Obedience stopped short of wasting herself. She needed food and rest. If the weather was forcing her down, it was a safe bet that it would force her targets down as well, especially with a babe. The trail was there, and clear, and the risk that she would lose it small.

She'd skirted farm fields a while back. She'd backtrack and see what she could find. Still, Iris hesitated. Her belly ached with hunger, but another pain bothered her more.

Her hands were cold. She stripped off her gloves, undid a few buckles, and thrust her left hand under her right breast to warm it. Her fingers rubbed against the puckered scar there, the skin rippled and rough under her fingertips. An old habit, an old comfort, to rub the old burn, long healed. She had no memory of the fire that had burned her as a child. The scar had always been there.

Even the Bonded could not break her of the habit, and had

given up trying long ago.

She focused on the feel, the touch, and knew the source of her unease. She'd never been this far from the others before this, and it felt … odd. Wrong. Like she was incomplete. She missed Avice's assurance, Mira's gentle worry, Caris's warm smile, and Nora's quick fierceness. Her longing for their presence was an ache.

Rain dripped off the edges of her hood.

There was another source of discomfort. She'd never been this far from the Bonded before, or for this long. Never operated without instructions or supervision for so long.

Even as that thought rose, the strands of the Bond tightened and she focused on her task. Farm fields meant a farmhouse. She'd steal what she needed. If an alarm was raised, she'd kill any unfortunate who crossed her and sleep in their bed.

The morning would bring a pulse of the drive to hunt again and she'd be off on the trail.

Iris shivered as some cold rain got under her hood. She distracted herself from her misery with the idea of the end of her task.

She'd finish this. Stalk them, kill the marcus, gut the vore, and wrap the dead baby in its hide.

Her grip on her knife tightened at the picture that formed in her head.

The Bond within Iris coiled in pleasure.

## CHAPTER FIFTEEN

Halithe glared at the nappy in her hand as if her will alone would straighten the hem. The lace of her dress scratched her skin; the sleeves were too short and it smelled of mothbane. She shifted in her chair, trying hard not to make it squeak.

The solar was over-warm, the women around her quiet and subdued. All heads were bent over baby clothes, swaddling cloths, blankets, tiny booties the babe wouldn't wear more than twice. Normally, there'd be the titter of talk, but lately the only sound was the quiet clack of knitting needles.

Well, that and the noise of Queen Satia heaving in the other room. Halithe was glad the inner door was closed. It sounded like the woman was trying to rid herself of her lungs.

With a sigh, Halithe turned her attention back to the offending fabric and twisted it, thinking that might even out the hem. She plunged the needle in and the thread promptly twisted and snarled.

"It's not an enemy, you know." Long, cool, pale fingers came into view and covered her own.

Halithe stilled, suddenly surrounded by the faint scent of fruit and spice. It was Caris, the Queen's lovely Bondmaiden, of the rich, red-brown hair and brown eyes flecked with amber. She was everything Halithe wanted to be and wasn't.

"It might as well be," Halithe grumbled to cover her flustered confusion. A quick glance showed that the other Bondmaidens were not in the room and the women around them were focused on their sewing.

Caris knelt beside her and took the wretched nappy from her hands. "You are glaring at it like a hawk after prey," she chided softly.

Halithe snorted under her breath. "A bat, maybe," she muttered. "Never a hawk."

To her joy, Caris chuckled. "Here, let me help."

Halithe risked a breath then, taking in that wonderful scent, and rested her hands in her lap. She watched as those long, lovely fingers worked magic. Threads untangled and the hem straightened before her eyes. Halithe looked at the result with both admiration and dismay. "You have a gift," she said grudgingly, knowing it was one she'd never learn.

"This is no gift," Caris said. "This is just practice. It will come to you, as it came to me." There was the slightest hesitation. "I have other gifts."

Halithe raised her eyes to find Caris's brown ones focused on her intently. She felt hot and cold at the same time. She opened her mouth to dare a question, but before she could draw breath, a crash of breaking pottery and a shout erupted from the other chamber.

"No more of that damnable ginger tea!"

The ladies froze, waited, and then relaxed when no more shouts were heard.

The moment was gone and Halithe's courage, fled. She dropped her gaze back to the nappy. "The Queen is in a foul mood," Halithe said.

"The Queen is finding bearing difficult," Caris agreed.

Halithe snorted, twisting her lips.

Those perfect, cool fingers clamped on her wrist. Halithe's heart beat faster. She stared at them, their paleness such a contrast to her olive skin, the blond wisps so unlike the darker hairs on her arm. She could see the brand on the inside of Caris's wrist. The pattern floated in front of her eyes, burning itself into her brain.

"Have a care," Caris's voice was the barest whisper. "Have a care, little hawk, that you do not offend, do not stand too far out among the chicks. Her temper is foul and it does not bode well to have her attention."

The door to the inner chamber creaked as it started to open. It was enough warning for Caris to be up and gone to her position by the main door before the Queen swept into the room, followed by the three other Bondmaidens.

Halithe rose with the others and curtseyed low as the Queen made her way to her seat. The chair had been replaced with a cushioned couch so that the pregnant woman could sprawl in comfort.

The Queen's face was screwed into a scowl. "You said it would stop," she snapped.

Mira was close behind her, carrying a chamber pot. "Majesty, I said that for most women it stopped. But sometimes these things linger and must be borne."

Satia sank down on the couch, one hand pressed to her stomach. "Rise," she commanded, but there was a weakness in her voice.

Halithe rose and reseated herself, making sure to focus on her stitching. The room that had been over-warm and silent moments before was now chill and tense. A brief glimpse of the Queen's face was enough. She might sound weak and deserving of sympathy, but her expression was … petulant. The hairs on the back of Halithe's neck rose. It felt like the Queen was seeking a target, if only to distract herself from her misery.

A knock, then. "The King, majesty," Caris announced. "With Lord Tarwain and Steward Paulin."

The door opened wide as the men strode in. The King was his golden, sunny self, smiling as he strode among the chairs. Lord Tarwain, Halithe's father, followed close behind. The olive skin and dark hair she'd inherited looked handsome on him.

Halithe rose once again, with a sense of relief and dread. Sure enough, the Queen focused on the King and the tension eased from the room. Sure enough, her father's eyes found her and glared his disapproval.

Halithe flushed with resentment and shame.

"My Queen," Xyrath walked forward, smiling, but in an instant, his face filled with concern. "How fare you?" he asked, sinking down on the couch next to the Queen, making sure his sword was out of the way. He gestured for everyone to sit.

"Not well, my husband," Satia leaned against him, putting her head on his shoulder, making such a pretty picture. "Not well."

"Ah, my sweet," Xyrath wrapped his arm around her shoulders.

"We should consult other healers. Perhaps our Chained Mage might have some ideas, eh?"

"Him." Satia scowled. "All I ever hear from him is 'no.' It's always 'I do not serve you; you do not hold my key.'"

Xyrath chuckled warmly. "Well, you do keep trying to have him cast for you, dear heart."

"I sent for the Mage Guildmaster, too," Satia sulked. "He would not come."

Xyrath's eyebrows climbed. The Steward cleared his throat. "Mage Guildmaster Forterran suffers from gout, Your Majesty. He has episodes. He did send word that as soon as the pain abides, he will attend the Queen."

"I want that key," Satia pouted. Her eyes filled with tears. "I want this nausea to stop," she added in a faint, childish voice.

Xyrath nodded. "Well, then, I'll just ask our Chained Mage for suggestions, eh? I am sure he will wish to ease your suffering, as we all do." He kissed her temple. "What you suffer is for the sake of this Kingdom."

Satia put both hands over her stomach. "For the Kingdom," she intoned.

Halithe bit her cheek and kept her face expressionless. The rest of the women were uttering soft murmurs of sympathy and support.

Xyrath smiled at everyone, then took Satia's hands. "We had thought to discuss the outer baronies with you but perhaps–"

"It's my belly that's ill, not my brain," Satia snapped. "What has happened?"

"It's the Black Hills, majesty," Lord Tarwain started. "They are in rebellion; the messengers we sent have been found dead at the border. I don't know if you are aware of the history between the Black Hills and the Crown, but–"

"I am not interested in history," Queen Satia said sharply. "I am interested in obedience. We must–" she cut herself off, looking around the room. "Ladies, leave us," she commanded. "Matters of state. Go flirt with the young men of the court, you are all released from your duties for a time. Leave your work and go."

Halithe rose hastily, dropping her hemming on the chair, and willingly fled the room with the rest. There was only one man she wished to speak to, and it had nothing to do with flirting.

————•————

Halithe settled in the chair in front of Ritathan's desk and looked at him expectantly. She loved his chambers, with its dark curtains, its massive maze of shelves, filled with scrolls, tomes, and papers. It always smelled faintly of incense and burnt wax.

"Today's lesson is based in history," Ritathan started.

Halithe slumped in her chair, staring at the candle sitting on the desk before her. "But I thought–"

"How are you to know what is to come, without knowing what has been?" Ritathan chided her. "What do you know of the history of magic?"

Halithe heaved a sigh.

Ritathan lifted an eyebrow and gave no sign of relenting.

"Fine," Halithe said, lifting her chin. "There was a time when magic flowed like water. Everyone could use it and everyone did. Great cities were constructed and many wonderful and marvelous things were created with it. Thus the Empire of Xy grew, and in its golden age all the surrounding Kingdoms were absorbed or acknowledged Xy as suzerain and all paid homage to the Heart.

"But then came the Mage Wars, where mage turned on mage. The force that once created was used to lay waste to all that was good and fair. Magic turned on itself and on its users and all that was perfect and lovely was utterly destroyed."

"I see that you have memorized your lessons," Ritathan said. "But have you learned from them?"

Halithe let all her frustrations boil over. "I have learned to wait in this drafty old castle for what might happen to me. Wait for the war to resolve, wait for my father to arrange my marriage. I am always waiting for things to happen." She drew a deep breath. "I want control, I want freedom, and I see it in your chains."

"Few are those that can muster the will, the drive." Ritathan said. "Yes, we have power, but it is restrained and constrained." Ritathan shook his head. "I am not sure you have sufficient mastery of your temper, Halithe. You have one, and a fiery one at that."

"I want this," she gestured at the candle. "And if that means reciting history at you for hours on end, so be it."

To her surprise, Ritathan laughed, his face open for the first time, relaxed and to her surprise, younger. "Well do I remember my frustration with the history, until I became fascinated by it. Very well, then," he mimicked her gesture at the candle, and the wick sparked and flamed. "Let us begin."

Halithe leaned forward in her chair.

"We project meaning upon the world," Ritathan said softly. "It is up to each of us to manipulate the forces, impose our will upon the world. When we do, we create order from the chaos. Concentrate on the candle flame. See it for what it is. Impose your will. Extinguish it."

Halithe frowned. "How?"

Ritathan raised an eyebrow. "How do you breathe?" he said. "What is the nature of the flame?"

Well, that was not helpful. Halithe stared at the flame, concentrating. Maybe it was like a riddle? Impose her will on it? She could just reach out with her fingers and douse the flame. But that wasn't magical. Or was it?

The flame danced on the wick, the colors within varied in hue, but the light was bright and constant. Ritathan didn't move, or even seem to breathe, as if he was content to wait until the crack of doom for her to—

The flame flickered.

Halithe jerked up. "Did I–"

"My wards," Ritathan pulled the candle nearer. "Someone comes. Hide. There." He nodded to the shadows that filled a corner, where the darkness in the shelves seemed deepest.

Halithe fled, whisking her skirts close even as the door to the chamber opened.

"Your Majesty," Ritathan said, chains clinking as he rose from his chair. "You honor me."

"No, no, just a bit of a friendly visit." King Xyrath's voice boomed. "Sit, sit," he said, and Halithe heard him take her chair, his scabbard rattling against the wood. "Nice chambers, you have. Lots of books, I see."

"I study many things, Majesty," Ritathan's chair creaked.

Halithe tried to peer through the stacks of books and papers but couldn't see a thing and didn't dare try shift anything.

"Good, good," King Xyrath lowered his voice. "I have some things to ask of you."

"Majesty, I do not serve you, you do not hold–"

"I know, I know," Xyrath chuckled as if that wasn't his concern. "No this is more in the way of advice, really."

"If I can, Your Majesty, I will aid you."

"Excellent." Halithe heard his chair move closer. "Now, I was wondering if the mage guild had access to any spells that might help," his voice dropped even lower, "with hair loss. Along the hair-line."

"Ah," Ritathan said. To Halithe's surprise, his voice held a note of sympathy. "Majesty, I have colleagues who have worked on this problem, but they have yet to solve it."

"They can't make hair grow?" Xyrath asked.

"They can," Ritathan said. "But they can't seem to make it stop. Nor can they localize it. When the spell is cast in its current form, the hair grows everywhere, uncontrollably." Ritathan lowered his voice too. "Everywhere, Your Majesty."

Halithe covered her mouth to stifle her snicker.

"Well, that is disappointing," Xyrath said. "They are still working on it, yes?"

"Oh yes," Ritathan replied. "Have no fear of that, Your Majesty. Many have an interest in such a spell."

"Well, that's fine, fine." Xyrath's chair creaked again. Halithe peered around piles, trying to see, but not daring to even breathe hard. "There's another matter, more of history than anything else." His voice was grown serious, with no trace of his prior humor. "Atira blades."

"Majesty?" Ritathan seemed startled. "I know that some in the Guild have attempted to make magical weapons, but no one has succeeded that I know of."

"Not yet," Xyrath said firmly. "Although I appreciate that they try. No, I want an atira blade, forged in the ancient days."

"Majesty, they do not exist." Ritathan was just as firm.

There was a long silence then. The back of Halithe's neck prickled. This King was not one to be denied.

Xyrath chuckled at last, and when he spoke, the tension in

his voice had eased. "Well, if you come across a reference, you'll let me know?"

"Of course, your Majesty."

"I'd also ask if you know any who have cures for the morning sickness. My dear Satia is suffering from it terribly and her healers don't seem to be able to aid her."

"I do not," Ritathan said. "I fear that magical healing, both divine and arcane, has been lost to us, Your Majesty. Ever since the Mage Wars."

"'As if magic itself lashed out at us and tore those gifts away,'" Xyrath quoted.

"I see you know your Worious," Ritathan said.

"From his Chronicles," Xyrath said. "Hated them but had them beat into me in my younger days." His chair creaked again. "She's sent for your Guildmaster, you know."

"Guildmaster Forterran?" Ritathan asked. "I haven't spoken with him recently.

"He's got the gout," Xyrath said.

"Ah," Ritathan observed. Halithe could have killed to see his face.

"My queen is with child, my heir." Xyrath rose and his scabbard hit the chair again. "She is a bit ill-tempered, what with bearing and all. You understand."

"Perfectly," Ritathan's chair slid back as he rose.

"Your presence irritates her," Xyrath said idly.

"Your Majesty, I fear my breathing irritates her."

"Yes," Xyrath said agreeably. "Still, she must be indulged during this time. Even in whims and sick fancies." Xyrath paused. "You understand." It wasn't a question. Halithe seethed at the implied threat.

"Yes, Your Majesty," Ritathan said.

"Good, good," Xyrath's boots headed to the door. "You'll let me know about the other thing, yes? If they advance?"

"Certainly," Ritathan said. How could he be so calm?

The door opened and closed, but Halithe waited, her anger simmering.

"Come," Ritathan said.

Halithe stepped out. The candle flame caught her eye. In her fury she looked within and saw its nature. With a clench of her fist, she imposed her will.

The flame rose high, shooting up to the ceiling. The candle melted down, and the flame died as it scorched the table.

"Ah," Ritathan raised an eyebrow. "Your next lesson will be about control."

## CHAPTER SIXTEEN

————◦————

The courtier greeted Forterran in the palace courtyard as the Mage Guildmaster struggled to heave his bulk out of his litter. He was not yet in his dotage, but he was no longer young, and he was prepared to use his age to his every advantage.

He'd managed to delay this meeting for weeks but it was clear that the King and Queen were losing patience.

"Guildmaster Forterran, be welcome." The courtier bowed low. "I am instructed to bring you into the presence of their Majesties for a private audience."

Private audience? That did not bode well. Forterran took a moment to take a breath and adjust his robes and chains. He knew full well that the royal summons had to be about Ritathan's contract. And whatever else the rascal had done to irritate their recent majesties.

His gouty big toe throbbed with his heartbeat, purple and engorged. There was even a hint of black around the nail. He'd worn simple sandals, for ease, yet even the hem of his robes brushing his foot was enough to cause pain. The courtier glanced down and grimaced, hopefully in sympathy.

"My thanks," Forterran nodded to the lad, gripping his cane tight. "Let us proceed, with as much haste as I can manage."

The courtier bowed again. "Make way," he called out, heading through the doors of the castle. "Make way for Guildmaster Forterran, Guildmaster of the Mages Guild."

Forterran fixed his face into a pleasant, neutral expression. Having a caller was not an honor normally afforded him. Someone wanted the entire court to know of his presence. As if that was necessary. The gossips would have it about far faster than the crier. Still, he wouldn't need to worry about anyone treading on his foot, since the lad was clearing a path through the crowd.

There was quite the crowd, which shouldn't have surprised him. Regardless of the power, there were always those who sought favor. Yet as he walked, he sensed that the flavor of the corridors had changed. The bright white and blue of the airions was gone, replaced by red, gold, and black. Tapestries had been torn down and carvings obliterated.

There was no music, no dancing. No idle card games or quiet flirtations. Forterran didn't need magic to sense the fear and uncertainty in the very air. He kept his expression neutral and nodded to those he knew as he followed his guide.

There was always a need to be wary; it had been so even in

Kara and Xywellan's time. Forterran had warned Ritathan about taking a royal contract. But Ritathan was never one to listen or turn from a challenge. The Guildmaster stifled a groan that had nothing to do with his big toe.

Under Forterran's mastery, his Guild had remained neutral, and he hoped to keep it that way. But the path he walked was a wary one, like a steep track that dropped off on both sides. One misstep, one wrong word, and an ally became an enemy.

"Guildmaster," the courtier broke through his thoughts. "Up here."

"Stairs," Forterran grumbled before he caught himself. He gave the lad a weak smile. "Lead on."

As Guildmaster, his chains bound him to the Guild as a whole, which both restrained him and freed him in some senses. It was a simple matter to cast behind the courtier's back and boost himself up the stairs, light as a feather. Simple too, to breathe and groan at the effort, enough to make the courtier glance back in alarm.

At the top, Forterran paused. "Let me catch my breath, lad."

The corridor here was narrower, with no supplicants hanging about. Guards, of course, uniformed in gold and black. Loyal too, from the suspicious looks Forterran was getting. He made a show of adjusting his chains before nodding the courtier on. Chains offered reassurance and promised safety. Little did they know … and better they didn't.

They stopped outside a door deep within the private chambers. The courtier knocked. A woman answered and the courtier called, "Guildmaster Forterran, for their Majesties."

The door was opened. The courtier bowed and gestured Forterren forward. The Guildmaster stepped within the chamber; as he crossed the threshold, he felt the first pulse of magic. His mage sense opened immediately, sensing the change.

A magical cord of glittering gold with sparks of red surrounded the woman who held the door open. The cord spiraled around her, like a tangle of wool from a child's knitting. Below that level of binding, a web of golden netting sank into her skin, deep and confining. The end of the bond cord trailed behind her, leading directly to the woman on the throne.

Forterran's gorge rose but he managed to keep his face still and his reactions to himself. The room seemed to dim around him until all he could see were the cords, tainted and sealed with the blood of an innocent life.

The other three women who stood behind Satia's throne were similarly wrapped in the same golden and blood red net.

He almost couldn't think, overwhelmed by the hate and loathing he felt. But he could not afford outrage here.

A corner of his mind noted that Satia was supposed to have five attendants. Where was the fifth?

"Ah, Guildmaster," the King's voice cut through his thoughts.

Forterran could not let himself be distracted during this audience, even by this horror. Clearly, the bonds had been set long ago, maybe even at birth. None in the Guild would use such blood magic, and not on new-born babes. Which meant that Satia's family had had those resources some twenty-odd years ago.

Something he refused to acknowledge as fear stirred within him.

One of the women shifted position slightly, revealing the fifth cord, stretched out behind the Queen. So there was another.

Forterran dimmed his mage sight and walked forward as slowly as he could. The room was close, with the smell of ginger in the air … and sickness. Queen Satia lay side-ways on a lounge, looking pasty and bloated and very pregnant. King Xyrath was pacing, as he was wont to do. Another man stood at Satia's feet. Forterran took a moment to place him. Lord Marshal Tarwain, if memory served. Looking decidedly put out.

Xyrath was the picture of royalty, his golden head of hair gleaming under his crown. He probably wore it to bed, Forterran thought sourly, but in truth, he knew he was envious of that head of hair. Unlike his own wisps.

Pity they couldn't get that spell to work.

Forterran reached the appropriate distance from the throne and bowed as low as he could manage, leaning on his cane. His chains sagged forward, swinging freely. That he also managed to display his gouty foot was rather well done, to his way of thinking.

"Your majesties," he said, keeping his head down.

"Rise, Guildmaster," Xyrath commanded.

"You finally come, in answer to our summons," Queen Satia snapped, her voice as peevish as her face.

"Forgive my infirmities, Your Majesty," Forterran rose slowly and sighed regretfully over his physical failings.

King Xyrath winced at the sight of his foot. One of the Bondmaidens whispered in the Queen's ear as she offered a cup of tea. Forterran thought he heard the word 'chair'. But from the Queen's lovely scowl, that was not to be.

Instead, she waved the girl away and fixed her beady eye on Forterran's person. "So, where in this Guild contract does it state that a Chained Mage can claim an apprentice against her father's will?"

Ah. Forterran plastered a puzzled look on his face, strengthened the spell on his person, and resigned himself to an unpleasant afternoon.

———•———

The only warning Halithe had was when Ritathan suddenly lifted his head, with an odd, sardonic smile.

She turned in her chair, the bowl of water sloshing in her hands, as the door opened. A large, thick-waisted, older man walked in, candlelight bouncing off his bald head with its wisps of white hair. "Had to have a tower room, didn't you?" he wheezed as he closed the door.

"Apprentice Halithe, may I introduce my old friend, Guild-master Forterran?" Ritathan said.

Halithe caught her breath at that, and swiftly rose to her feet, keeping the bowl steady.

"Don't 'old friend' me," Forterran growled as he settled his girth in the other chair. He eased a disgusting-looking foot out sideways, avoiding the desk. Halithe wrinkled her nose; it looked painful.

"Apprentice?" Forterran continued. "By what right? By written agreement? By consent of her family? By consent of the Guild?"

Ritathan gestured toward the scorch marks on his desk.

Forterran hummed, then looked at Halithe. "Your work, chit?"

Her anger rose and the water in the bowl sloshed a bit. But she controlled herself and set her face. "Yes, Guildmaster."

An eyebrow raised, and she could have sworn she saw a glimmer of approval. "Well, I can see why you have her working with water."

"And why I have accepted her as my apprentice," Ritathan said. "Subject to your approval, Guildmaster. Of course."

"Of course," Forterran repeated, his voice laced with sarcasm "Since I just spent a very long session discussing that very fact with an angry father, a peevish Queen, and a bored King."

Halithe's heart started to pound.

"And?" Ritathan asked. His voice sounded silkily dangerous.

"And I did what I always do when I've no forewarning. I stalled. I explained the long process of accepting an apprentice into a guild and the difference between one who shows promise and one who can achieve mastery. How rare it is to find one with the gift these days." Forterran leaned back. Halithe opened her mouth to argue but the glare he shot her had her closing it with a snap.

"And we left it there. The Queen has reasons of her own to be in the Guild's good graces. So, the girl-child, one Halithe, should be left to continue with her lessons. But as Guildmaster I will make the final determination as to whether to advance her."

Halithe caught her breath, her heart rising at his words, beating as if to escape from her chest.

"Have you bound her?" Forterran demanded.

Ritathan nodded. "Immediately after that," he gestured to the charred mark.

Halithe didn't wait for her master to instruct her. She thrust forward her left hand, where Ritathan had placed the apprentice bond bracelet. "I am forbidden from using magic except in the presence of my master," she blurted out.

Forterran huffed at her. "In the meantime, you will also continue with your duties as a lady-in-waiting upon the Queen." He raised an eyebrow. "Speaking of which … ."

Halithe placed the bowl on the desk and rose. "My thanks, Guildmaster," she curtseyed deeply to him. "My thanks, Master." She repeated the curtsey to Ritathan, then grinned at him before she darted to the door, fleeing before her joy could spill out. Then she was flying down the stairs, laughing.

Free, free, free! She'd found an escape from the prison of marriage and a life she'd dreaded and feared for so long–

She raced down, her feet almost dancing as she grabbed at her skirts. At the bottom, she turned, and twirled, and ran smack into Caris.

"Caris," Halithe breathed, grabbing her hands. "Caris, something wonderful–"

 Caris's face was stark white, pale as a wisp of cloud. "Halithe," she whispered and Halithe's heart leapt. The sound of her name, from Caris's lips; it sounded so different. Powerful. Beautiful. For a moment Halithe was overwhelmed.

Which let Caris push her into a curtained alcove, glancing around to see if anyone was about. Halithe found herself in shadows, the light faint through dirt-encrusted windows.

"Caris, I'm free," Halithe stumbled over her words as they rushed out in time with her racing heartbeat. "I'm going to be trained, going to be–"

Shaking her head, Caris set put two fingers over Halithe's mouth. "No, no, I've come to warn you." Caris put her head close, her lips to Halithe's ear. "You must have a care. Your father, the Queen," Caris shuddered. "Her rages are terrible, cold and focused, when her plans are thwarted. I fear–"

Halithe evaded Caris's fingers, darted forward, and kissed her. Soft. Her lips were so soft.

Halithe felt Caris inhale sharply, and then oh glorious wonder, her lips moved as well, opening, welcoming, and only the need for breath broke them apart. Halithe had both of Caris's hands and grasped them between hers. "I swear," she murmured. "I swear, I will become powerful and dreadful and I will break these chains." She pressed her lips to Caris's marked wrist. "I will free you and claim you and …" Halithe stopped.

Caris was silently weeping.

"Don't cry," Halithe whispered.

"Don't think it," Caris whispered back. "Don't breathe it, don't dare to hope. This bond is deep and dark and I am powerless."

"Think it," Halithe pulled Caris's hands to her breast. "Breathe it, dare to hope. It will be so."

"I must go," Caris said, in an oddly wooden tone. "They will be wanting me, and I must be where I am supposed to be. Do what they say I must. I only came to warn you."

"Go," Halithe claimed another kiss, then released her. "I will take heed." She reached out to stroke away the tears. "You have a care, yourself."

Caris didn't meet her eyes, just nodded and slipped away through the curtains.

Halithe closed her eyes, enjoying the feeling of endless possibilities. Then she drew a deep breath, reminding herself that there was work to be done before she would be truly free.

When she opened her eyes, she spotted a long hair clinging to her sleeve. A long, auburn hair. She pulled the strand off and coiled it carefully. She tucked the hair into a handkerchief and tucked that into her breastband.

Another breath before she slipped out through the curtains, a new determination firming her spine.

Even if she had to sew a thousand nappies.

———•———

"My thanks," Ritathan watched as Halithe left, amused at her happiness. "She does have potential, Forterran."

Forterran stared at the scorch mark, an odd look on his face. "Rage?" He asked.

Ritathan nodded. "Her response to a veiled threat from Xyrath."

"I remember when my mother came into her full powers, triggered by rage." Forterran chuckled, then remembered himself and gave Ritathan a glare.

Ritathan raised an eyebrow. "I did warn you," he said mildly.

"Hmmph." Forterran made a gesture and the pressure on Ritathan's ears changed. Indistinct, vague voices began to mutter near the door; they would be unintelligible to anyone outside.

"If there were listeners, I would know," Ritathan said.

"Never hurts to be cautious. You might have mentioned the extent of the corruption." Blood magic is pure evil and that bond seethes with it."

Ritathan opened his mouth but Forterran cut him off. "Yes, yes, don't think to give me a history lesson. In certain faiths, in certain cultures, self-sacrifice is a special form of blood magic. Don't try to tell me those women consented."

"I don't think even Satia consented," Ritathan mused. "I doubt she was old enough to know what was happening."

"Please don't expect me to be sympathetic. That young woman could seek to break the bonds."

"Could it be done?" Ritathan mused. "The bindings have been there so long they are woven into the women's very breath."

"I don't have the answer to that," Forterran rumbled, "and no time to speculate. Your apprentice wasn't the only thing they wanted to discuss."

"How much beer did you have to drink to get your gout to flare up?" Ritathan rose and took Halithe's chair.

"Not as much as I would have liked," Forterran groaned. "It will take a week of weak herbal teas and water to flush it out. I hope you appreciate my sacrifice."

"I would," Ritathan said with a straight face. "But I know how much you love beer." That drew a rueful chuckle from his friend. Ritathan leaned forward. "What did they want?"

"Your head on a pike was my impression." Forterran rolled his eyes, amusement gone. "But we danced around the issue, discussing the terms of the mage contract. They spoke of the cost and asked not so subtle questions about what happens if you die. I pointed out the relevant provisions." Forterran heaved a sigh. "Where is your key?"

"I do not know," Ritathan sat back in his chair and heaved his own sigh. "Kara had it when she left for the field, that is all I know."

"Queen Satia is a very unhappy woman." Forterran mused. "She does not wish to pay the fees, yet she does not wish to release you, for you would then be free to take a new contract."

"A pity, that she suffers so," Ritathan curled his lip.

Forterran shook his head. "Why not hit that hornet's nest a few more times?"

Ritathan gave his friend a helpless shrug.

"Oh, please." Forterran grimaced. "Our new Queen has strange ideas," he said slowly. "She pressed me to make sure that all suspected blood mages are presented to the King and Queen before they are executed. Some nonsense about a fair hearing before their majesties to assure them justice." Forterran snorted. "Can you imagine, hauling a struggling blood mage into the court for a hearing?"

"That does not bode well. That one schemes well into the future." Ritathan said. "Did you promise to do so?"

"Of course." Forterran gave him a look. "But any blood-mage I find will die in the struggle. I will apologize later."

Ritathan smiled. "If their Majesties even hear of it."

"There is that," Forterran said as he eased his foot out in front of him. "I know your loyalty to Kara, but you risk much, staying here. We could do an early termination of the agreement with a clause that indicates you will serve only the Guild."

Ritathan opened his mouth but Forterran raised his hand. "Take shelter in the Guild Hall. Claim the girl as apprentice formally and spend the next few years teaching her." Forterran looked pensive. "You could even train to replace me as Guildmaster."

"Please," Ritathan smiled, echoing his friend. "Can you imagine? We'd end up with mage wars within the halls, smoke and fire from every window."

"Very well." Forterran sighed in resignation and then frowned. "Their majesties also wanted to know the cost of a portal, since you cannot cast for them."

"A portal?" Ritathan puzzled over that. "Where to?"

"The Black Hills," Forterran said.

"Why?" Ritathan rubbed his chin. "There's naught out there but bandits calling themselves rebels."

"Probably to seek marble for Xyrath's newest obsession. He wants a life-sized statue of himself as the conquering warrior. Naked of course." Forterran's grin was malicious. "Can you imagine? The entire court ogling his bits?" He chuckled. "At least, that's got his mind off atira blades. Man bounces from one obsession to another."

"You are the worst gossip I know," Ritathan said.

"I don't gossip." Forterran raised his eyebrows in all innocence. "I listen. And I made no comment as to their reasons, just made sure their majesties knew the cost of a portal was high. I thought of a price and then trebled it. It would not serve for them to think it cheap or easy, or that the Guild is at their beck and call."

"Dangerous," Ritathan said. "Should they learn of your secret taunts."

"Dangerous?" Forterran shook his head. "So is your path, staying here, pissing them off. Know that as Guildmaster, I do not approve."

"So noted," Ritathan nodded. "If something happens to me–"

"When." Forterran said pointedly.

"When," Ritathan accepted the correction. "See to her, would you?"

"Better if you survive," Forterran said.

"I'll see what I can do." Ritathan smiled. "Shall I send for beer before you go? They stock fine ones here."

Forterran groaned.

## CHAPTER SEVENTEEN

———◦———

Go," Orval told Amari. He kept his smile firmly in place, determined not to let his nervousness show. "We'll be fine." He held Dalan to his shoulder, patting his back.

"You're sure?" Amari's forehead puckered. She stood in the kitchen, resisting Winter's efforts to wrap her in Orval's warmest cloak. "We could get one of the laundresses, or one of Winter's—"

"Orval will be fine," Winter said firmly. "The twins are both fed and Lara's already asleep. Orval will watch over them. We'll not be gone that long."

"I'll change Dalan and put him down," Orval said, ignoring the flutter in his stomach and assuming all the competence he could muster. "You'll be back before they wake, if you leave now."

Amari clutched her cloak and looked at him with anxious eyes. "But–"

"You need something nice for the Walk to the Well," Orval said. "And we've coin enough. Winter knows where to go and drives a hard bargain."

"And you've not been out of this hovel since you arrived." Winter said.

"Hovel?" Orval sputtered at his landlady, which made Amari smile, as he intended. "I'd point out it's a hovel we rent from you, madam."

Winter waved him off with a dismissive "pfft" and urged Amari to the door. "We'll have the guard that goes with us carry packages." She gave them both a wicked smile. "If Ussin's hovering, we'll make him come. Serve him right to have to go clothes shopping."

Amari laughed, casting a worried glance back at Orval as the door closed. He smiled and waved and nodded reassuringly.

The latch clicked and he was left to his doom.

Alone. With babies.

Dalan burped. Orval shifted him to his other shoulder. "At least now, I am wise to your tricks, young man," Orval said as he patted Dalan's back and waited for the child to burp again.

He started pacing back and forth; the rhythm of his limp always seemed to help rock the babes. As he walked, he looked around his kitchen.

Had it only been weeks? The changes Amari had made had been rather amazing. Gone from the kitchen were his piles of books and scrolls. Room had been found for them elsewhere. Clean linens and crockery—all of which had been there before, in a jumble—were now placed where they could be seen and used.

The pantry shelves held more than just his pease porridge.

On the hearth mantel, above the oven, Amari had created a small shrine to the Harmony of the Hearth. It wasn't much, really. Amari had taken a blank piece of parchment and with a quick and steady hand, had drawn two hands with their fingers intertwined.

"You can draw?" he'd asked, and she'd blushed and denied it. But he suspected she had more skill than the simple sketch showed.

She'd propped the parchment up with one of his smaller copper lanterns. Every morning, she'd light the lantern, recite a prayer, and then extinguish the flame. Orval smiled. Sometimes she was fairly rushed doing it, as one child or another cried. But even in a harried state, she was always lovely.

Dalan burped, loud and long.

"Finally," Orval started back toward the privy. "Not much time. A clean-up and then a nice nap, if the skies allow."

He peeked in on Lara, sleeping peacefully in her basket, then gathered fresh nappies and swaddling blanket and started to work.

"Now, remember, you have to do your share of the work," Orval said as he stripped off the dirty nappy, covering Dalan to prevent getting pissed on.

Dalan chortled, then yawned, waving his arms.

"You need to go to sleep, just like we told your momma you would," Orval said. "There's a bit of research I want to do, back in my shelves. But first," he took each tiny foot in his hands and started to pump those baby legs. "Let's see if you–"

Dalan chortled and messily farted.

"Whew," Orval leaned back, waving his hand in front of his face. "There we go," he said, and started over with fresh cloths.

Dalan focused on him, his tiny arms moving as he yawned. They had started weaning him from the swaddling. *Wean him.*

"Who knew of such a thing?" Orval asked as he scooped Dalan up. "But your momma does, so now we're to leave your arms free. Isn't that something?"

Dalan yawned, a good sign.

The babies grew so fast, every day something new. Skies above, both Dalan and Lara were growing like weeds. They'd soon outgrow those baskets, that was sure. It gave Orval the oddest sense of pride and yet … .

He carried Dalan into the bedroom. His sister Lara had talked of her pending child and Orval had looked forward to having a niece or nephew to spoil. But the Sweat had taken that away.

There were times when the babies made him want to retreat into the comfort of his shelves, his books and scrolls. He wanted to hide from the crying, the screaming, the various bodily fluids that came from every orifice.

But he'd miss them when they were gone.

Dalan's face wrinkled as Orval set him in his basket. He started to fuss.

"Well, I know what will settle you." Orval cast an anxious glance at Lara. He reached under Dalan, pulling out the old, tattered copy of the *Epic of Xyson* from below the cushion.

"I will have you know that *The Epic of Xyson* is the most boring epic poem ever written, in the entire history of Xy." Orval settled in the chair beside the baskets. "Scholars have argued for years over its translation from the archaic Xyian." He opened the book with a fond smile. "My father gave me this when I was very young. See, it still has my notes, tracing back our family blood line." Orval shook his head at his childish writing. "He was furious that I wrote in it, but he forgave me when he saw the depth of my research."

Dalan stared at him.

"And look, here is the most boring section. 'On the Preparations for Marching.'" Orval started to read in the softest, most boring tone he could manage.

Dalan's eyes kept opening, and closing, and opening, and closing. At last, with a soft yawn, he drifted off.

"And … three … . ton … .of … .blackstone … for … the … smiths." Orval droned to a stop and waited.

Dalan's eyes popped open and his face wrinkled up.

"Oh, no," Orval said softly, quickly tucking the book back into Dalan's basket, careful to cover it well. "Don't you dare wake your sister." He swept the boy back up into his arms. "We're running out of time. You'll just have to help me."

Dalan gurgled and grabbed Orval's ear, tugging on it.

Orval winced, trying to pull away. "Those little nails are sharp, Dalan."

Dalan chortled.

"Have it your way," Orval said. "Our goal is back here," he headed into the stacks, where Amari's touch had not yet quite reached. The familiar scent of old paper and dust filled his lungs.

Dalan sneezed.

"You know something?" Orval said softly. "I have my old picture books from when I was a babe. Maybe I should find them for you. You'd like the stories and colors, I am sure."

Dalen reached for Orval's mouth.

"Ah," Orval pulled his head back. "Maybe we should wait until you are a little older. So you don't rip the pages, eh?"

Dalan chuckled and shoved his fists in his mouth.

Orval knew he had at least one history of Uyole and certainly something on customs.

Ordinarily he could have spent hours on research, but they'd be back soon. He wanted to surprise Amari, impress her with his knowledge. "Yes, here," he struggled to bend down while holding the child securely. Dalan grabbed his hair, tugging hard.

He had two, no, three books, but they were mostly history and records of treaties with Xy, fairly old. He rifled through them quickly, looking for anything on babes or wells.

Nothing.

Orval paused, thinking. Dalan patted his cheek.

"I'm sure," he said to the boy. "Sure I have a reference ..." Where had he read about Uyole ...? He crammed the books in his hand back into the shelves. It had been a more general reference, and it was ... he switched Dalan to the other shoulder. "Let's try over here," he murmured.

Dalan yawned and babbled.

A book on birth traditions around the Old Empire. Orval moved to a different shelf and had it in hand in a minute. Standing between the shelves, turning so Dalan couldn't reach the other books, he flipped though the old, yellowed pages carefully.

Interesting. Bracelets carried meaning. Signifying the passage into adulthood, marriage contracts, wealth, status, and births. There. That was what he was looking for.

*'The Hearth Mother is honored with bracelets upon the birth of her children, grandchildren, and great-grandchildren. The first birth is celebrated with a bracelet of braided leather. If the Hearth Mother has birthed twins, beads of red jasper are intertwined. Upon the second birth—'*

Dalan shrieked and yanked on his hair. "Hey," Orval pulled his head back. "That hurts, young man."

Dalan looked at him, and then crammed his fist into his mouth, eyes fluttering closed.

*Bracelets are presented during the Walk to the Well, by the Hearth Father. If no Hearth Father has been chosen, the father of the child presents the bracelet.*

Wait. Hearth Father? Orval frowned. What reference was that?

*The Walk to the Well also signals the renewal of physical relations with the male of the Hearth Mother's choosing.*

Elements above. Orval felt heat rise in his face at the very idea. But Hearth Father … he paged forward, looking for–

*Each Hearth Mother chooses the sires of her children, as she wills. But the requirements for a Hearth Father are stricter, according to custom. Preference is given to the warrior who triumphs in battle, who exceeds in swordsmanship and riding, who embodies the–*

Orval's gut rolled, with oh-so-well-remembered pain. He snapped the book shut.

Dalan protested softly, his face now firmly pressed against Orval's neck.

Orval put the book back on the shelf. He had the information he needed and he didn't want to read more, didn't want to know more. Wasn't that always the way of things?

He shifted Dalan gently and sighed. "Let's get you to your basket, shall we?"

Dalan's blood father, Lord Eijer, had been a paragon of all the manly virtues, except that he lacked any morals or integrity what-soever. But he'd had all the qualities of a Hearth Father, all right.

As Orval himself did not.

Story of his life, really.

Dalan let out a soft snore and went boneless in his arms.

Orval limped back to the bedroom and slowly lowered Dalan into his basket. The boy was fast asleep.

The scholar stood still for a moment, watching Lara and Dalan. The pain over what he lacked, his inadequacies, faded a bit. It was an old familiar pain, that voice in the back of his head. But babies didn't worry over such things. They needed food and shelter and care. When Amari had first walked into his kitchen, Orval had been shaken, taken aback, but determined to aid them. And now, he couldn't imagine life without them.

It had all turned out better than he could have hoped.

Still, he reminded himself that this was temporary. Once the fuss died down, the marcus would appear to whisk Amari, Dalan, and Lara off to someplace safer. These rooms would once again smell only of old books and dust. It was foolish to hope for anything else.

Amari would be back soon and hot kavage would be welcome on such a cold day.

Orval took a deep breath and headed for the kitchen

————◆————

They were back before the kavage finished brewing. Orval looked up and smiled as Amari bustled through the door, her brown skin flushed, her eyes bright. She was followed by Winter and Ussin, his arms filled with bundles.

"It's cold, but sunny," Amari started to unwrap her scarves. "The well's not far—" she took a breath and laughed. "Winter bargains like a hawk after a mouse, wait until you see what we found! Even a matching tunic for you that you must try on. Are they sleeping? Is everything–?"

"They're sleeping," Orval assured her. "Go see for yourself."

Amari rushed through the door, taking off her cloak as she went.

Ussin piled the packages and bundles on the table.

"My thanks, Ussin." Winter added her bundles to the mix.

"Any time, Madam Winter." Ussin said cheerfully.

"Wait for me downstairs and I'll warm you … with a hot drink." Winter said, a note of playfulness in her voice.

"Much appreciated," Ussin said. "Lord Orval." He nodded and left, closing the door behind him.

Orval raised an eyebrow, but Winter just shrugged at him, then checked to make sure Amari was out of earshot. "Did you find what you were looking for?" she whispered.

"Yes," Orval whispered back. "Braided leather and red jasper beads."

"Good choice, not too expensive. I know a leather worker who does a lovely corded braid. The beads shouldn't be a problem."

"Good," Orval quickly reviewed the other things needed. "You'll take care of it? In time for the Walk?"

"I will," Winter turned to the door. Orval rose to follow. "You worry about them." She nodded back toward the bedroom.

"To the best of my ability," Orval said. As the door closed behind her, he leaned his head against the rough wood. "And ever after."

## CHAPTER EIGHTEEN

I ce," Vren smiled under his hood as the pellets came down. "Perfect."

Dust's ears flicked in agreement.

"She's going to have to go to ground," Vren said. "We should take advantage."

Dust rumbled a half-growl.

"We won't lose her," Vren replied. "If necessary, we'll back track and I will cry like a babe again. For now, we need to see to us."

The vore sneezed and pulled away, pointing her nose towards the woods off to the west.

"Lead on," he said, and followed.

His shoulders were tight with exhaustion, but he fought it

back. They needed shelter, secure from prying eyes. The icy rain was just a drizzle now, the leaves under his feet sodden and wet, ice forming on the branches. Vren walked soft, leaving little trace, as he had been trained.

Dust led him to a deer path, then trotted along it, her head moving from side to side. Vren knew she was scenting for threats, human or otherwise. He trusted her judgment; her senses were far more dependable than his.

As he'd been taught, he kept his mind clear, not thinking of what had happened or would happen, focusing on the "now," eyes open and aware. Each step came after another and another.

Dust stopped and Vren raised his hood to see a small mud and waddle hut, deep in the woods. He stood, listening. "Abandoned?"

As Vren ducked his head and entered, Dust shook water out of her fur, then followed.

It was clear that the hut had not been used in some time. There was a dirt floor with a fire pit in the center and a smoke hole above. It was small—Vren couldn't straighten up. But it seemed sturdy, with no sign of leaking. Everything else that might have indicated human inhabitants was gone, stripped bare.

Vren frowned. As safe as it seemed, the hut was not a good idea. "Risky," he said. "I was thinking a cave, or maybe a nice hollow tree, if–"

Dust grumbled and leaned against his hip.

Vren considered. He wasn't the only one tired and hungry. One night seemed safe enough, if he set wards and took precautions. He nodded, then put down his pack to take off his cloak. "We'll risk it." He shifted to hang his cloak over the door.

Dust slipped back outside before he secured the fabric.

He knelt by the empty fire pit, facing the circle, took a breath, and centered himself.

"The death of earth is the birth of water, the death of water, the birth of air, the death of air is the birth of fire, the death of fire, the birth of earth. Elements, aid me in the circle of birth and death and birth again until the skies darken and the stars no longer shine."

It was harder here than in the Wastes; the elements here were not used to being roused. The earth responded slowly, in ever wider circles around him, expanding out around the hut and through the forest. Vren closed his eyes, feeling the air and water around the hut grow heavy with mist and fog.

"Ward us," Vren asked, chanting the ancient words. "Warn us. Whisper of those that tread within."

The earth rumbled reassurance and sent him echoes of Dust's movements. She was hunting. There was a small stream close by; its waters sought to comfort him. The elements offered strength to one who walked with them, and he drew it in, grateful that they shared their power. After another breath, Vren opened his eyes.

In the center of the fire pit danced a small flame, without tinder, kindling, or smoke.

"We thank the elements," Vren whispered. He stretched, feeling his tension ease. Taking off his baby sling and wrapping the doll in it, he set it to one side. Still on his knees, he unfolded his bedroll. The air around hm warmed and the thatched roof rustled as the heat rose.

A soft whine from outside told him that Dust had returned and he eased out to find her with two fresh rabbit carcasses in her mouth. She dropped them at his feet, her tongue lolling.

"Yes, you can have my gizzards," Vren said. "But I am cooking my meat."

Dust led him to the stream, where he got to work gutting the rabbits, flicking the innards at Dust, who caught them neatly. The trees held back most of the rain and ice, but it was cold. Vren made short work of it, then washed his hands and knife and filled his water skin.

Back at the hut, he held the cloak aside just enough for them both to slip past, trying to keep any escaping light to a minimum. A wave of heat swept over his face.

Dust settled by the fire and blinked at him sleepily. Vren set her share of the rabbit in front of her and sat on his bedroll. He cut his meat from the bone and spitted the strips.

Yawning, he dug a small bowl from his pack and piled the bones, and what meat still clung to them, into it. He added water and set the bowl by the fire to stew. He'd have something warm for the morning.

Dust had finished her meal and was starting her grooming routine.

Vren's shoulders eased further, as warmth surrounded him. He snatched at the sizzling meat strips as soon as they'd cooked, sucking the juices from his fingers. A few sips of water and he'd be ready for sleep.

Dust yawned. Her coarse black fur was drying and she rolled onto her side, belly toward the fire. With the wards in place, neither of them needed to keep watch, but Vren wasn't sure he could relax enough to sleep. He stretched out on the blankets, stared into the dancing flame, and tried to organize his thoughts. Sleep claimed him between one breath and the next.

Hours later, an odd crackling pulled his eyes open and Vren sat up, blinking at the flame, which now pulsed with a faint blue light at its core. Dust lifted her head as well, then rose, shook herself, and came to sit beside him.

Vren arranged himself sat cross-legged, facing the flame, rubbing the sleep from his face and running his fingers through his hair. He cast his senses out and the elements sent back a pulse of peace and safety.

Dust was already staring at the flame. Vren narrowed his eyes, and his focus, and cast his thoughts within.

The blue flame rose around him and embraced him before fading.

Vren opened his eyes to find himself sitting in a senel circle, within one of the winter lodges of the Wastes.

A brazier burned before him, but he felt no heat. The marcusi around him, passing gurt and mugs of kavage, nodded their welcomes with warm smiles. Elements, he could almost smell the kavage.

All his training had taught him to control his reactions, but his spine still stiffened to see The Liam seated across the flames. The eldest of their order and master of the elements, the man sat tall and straight, his mostly bald head shining in the light of the fire, which limned the wisps of white hair off to the sides of his face.

"Vren? Dust? Welcome, both of you," the Liam said. "We decided to risk contact, though the link is tenuous and could fail. How fare you both?"

Vren braced himself, then turned his head. Flickering beside him was a woman, outlined in blue light. As she always chose, Dust was naked, one leg drawn up with her arms clasped around the bended knee. As she always chose, she was ageless, her eyes wise and weary.

Behind her, in the shadows, other images moved and blurred. Other animal shapes. A wolf was one, a fox another, with others not easily identified. They never came to the fore, always in the background when she was in spirit form.

Here, only here, could he see the vore in her human guise, hear her speak, try to know her mind and thoughts. Dust was timeless, eternal and a mystery. All the vore were.

"We are well," Dust said, her low and husky tones sending a shiver down Vren's spine. "For now, we are warm and safe. But we have tidings that will bring you grief."

That was also Dust. Never one to cushion pain.

"Speak," the Liam commanded. "We dare not risk keeping you here long."

Dust gave Vren the nod to speak.

Vren let his head dip, acknowledging the charge. "Master, Xywellan and Queen Kara are dead on the field of battle. The Wyvern House of Xy has won the day, and they move to secure the throne and the city of Edenrich."

Eyes glittered around the fire.

The Liam broke the silence. "May the skies hear our voices. May the people remember."

The response rose, "We will remember."

Vren joined in the chant as they all spoke in one voice. "Death of earth, birth of water, death of water, birth of air, death of air, birth of fire, death of fire, birth of earth."

As the last echo of the chant died away, the Liam spoke. "Is it perhaps too much to expect that the Blood of Xy that we were sworn to protect will now stop slaughtering each other?" His voice carried pain and frustration.

Vren opened his mouth to speak, but the Liam raised a hand. "Wait." He held his hand out to toward the fire.

The others followed his gesture. The flames rose. Vren felt the surge of power, strengthening him and the wards around them.

Dust shifted next to him, uneasy.

The Liam noticed. "Forgive us. But there is a need."

"Yes," she said shortly. All knew the vore hated magic after what had been done to them long ago. They tolerated the power of the elements so long as it was not used in unnatural ways, but took little comfort in it.

"Tell us your news, Vren," the Liam commanded.

Vren started at the beginning, telling of the summons through the token, of finding Xykara with the babe in her arms. Of his escape and flight with the wet nurse and the babes.

"What do we know of this wet nurse? Amari, you said," one of the other Elders asked.

"Nothing," Vren admitted. "But Kara chose her."

The Liam frowned. "Kara also chose to enter battle pregnant and close to her time. I can be pardoned for doubting her."

Dust huffed. "There was no other choice, in order to flee with a newborn."

"Amari gave me no reason not to trust her," Vren added. "Orval is known to us, and he swore the oath."

"You should have fled with the babe, brought her to us," another Elder insisted.

"Risky enough to flee with a newborn. Riskier still, to travel with one any great distance." Yet another Elder spoke. "Winter comes on."

"Then there is this," Vren reached out his hand and formed the mental image of the vial. The blood within shone bright red. "Xykara gave me her blood memories."

"You have the permissions?" The Liam leaned forward.

"Yes," Vren said. "And one other thing." He held up the key

and the ring he had found when he'd changed the babe.

"The Ring of Xy," the Liam breathed.

"Skies above, is that a mage key?" The elder closest to Vren squinted at the thing in Vren's hand.

"It was sewn into Xylara's nappy," Vren explained. "A few stitches secured it, as if done in haste."

"Xywellan had a Chained Mage, did he not? What do we know of him?"

"Little," responded another.

"What was Kara thinking?" The Liam lifted his eyes as if asking the skies themselves. "The Ring I understand, it rightly belongs to the child. But what reason would she have to pass the key to a babe?" The Liam shook his head. "The answers are in that vial."

Vren nodded.

The Liam heaved a great sigh. "We could debate for hours and still see no clear path. So I say this. In truth the child may be safer where she is for a time."

Vren glanced at Dust, who shook her head. "Master, Orval is trusted, but he is a bachelor who lives for his books and scrolls."

The Liam chuckled. "Well, he's in for a bit of a shock, but for now we will leave the babe with him and the wet nurse. Come to us, Vren. Bring Kara's memories to us. Others will be sent to ward the babe."

Vren bowed his head in obedience.

"Dust, you have our thanks for all you have done," The Liam said. "You are not a member of Our Order. Where does your path now lead?"

Dust inclined her head and spoke firmly. "The vore search for those Chosen, born with the birthmark of the Dagger-Star. Neither babe bore the mark." She paused. Vren's heart sank, then rose again at her next words. "I will travel with Vren as long as our paths intertwine. My goal is Athelbryght, where I can inform the Packmoot."

"My path takes me through there," Vren said quickly. Too quickly, perhaps. The Liam's look was sharp and knowing, but all he did was nod.

"Excellent," the Liam said. "The marcusi also watch. If the birthmark is seen, we will report to you and yours. Our thanks, Vore Dust."

The Liam raised a hand to end the senel, but Vren interrupted. "Where will you be, Master?" he asked. "Where will I find you?"

The Liam's mouth quirked. "Where our ancient Order was founded. Where we have always been, and always will be. In the Wastes, within sight of the Heart that was shattered."

## CHAPTER NINETEEN

The day had finally come.

Amari lit the small copper lantern on the mantel and watched the flame flicker to life. The glow illuminated the symbol of the Lord and Lady of the Hearth.

She drew a breath, released it, folded her hands, and recited the prayer she'd been taught by her mother and grandmother, the one recited by all the Hearth Mothers before her.

*"Gracious Ancestors, hold us in your hands,*
*May our windows open to light and knowledge.*
*May our hearth warm and feed all who sit beside it,*
*May our home shield us from the storms without.*

*May our love shelter us from storms within.*"

Sorrow welled up and caught her unaware.

Today was her walk to the well with her first-born, and her mother, grandmothers, aunties, and sisters were not at her side. Had she been home, they would have gathered around, talking and laughing, teasing and praying in the same breath. They would have admired her bracelets and helped her with her hair and dress.

Amari touched her empty wrists and sighed.

The men of the Hearth would have been there as well, holding red banners in readiness, bags of sweets in their hands. Some would have been seeing to the feast that followed. The air would have been joyful, even if the weather was bad. It would be the ceremony she had dreamt of since she'd first bled.

And yet … .

She paused and looked about her. The kitchen was warm and bright, with a pot of stew in the oven and kavage ready to be brewed fresh when they returned.

Orval was in the bedroom, talking to the babes as he did one last nappy change. No baby talk, for him. She was fairly sure he was reviewing the names of all the kings from the *Epic*.

He was so different from every man she'd ever met. There was no pretense, no blustering. Quiet, calm, even when taken aback by the arrival of a woman and two babes out of a storm. And smart? He took her breath away. For someone who never left his rooms, he knew so very much.

Regularly, someone would make their way up the stairs with a question or problem. Small things, really, a letter or contract needing to be written or a dispute between neighbors. They came because they had no trust of the local watch or judges.

Orval would welcome them, offer kavage, and listen intently. There'd be talk, then, discussions, and suddenly the matter was resolved, chairs being pushed back and nodding heads all around.

Had it been only a few months? Amari shook her head in wonderment. Three months since she feared for their lives, fleeing in the dark and cold. Three months since they'd sheltered here, from the weather and from those that would threaten them. She pressed a hand to her breast, where the marcusi token was hidden in her breast band. Those hours had been dark and fearful.

The flame in the lantern flickered, drawing her eyes.

She would be honest with herself. What she had dreamed of was never to be. Even if she'd managed to return home, she'd not receive a warm welcome, what with her shame of being deceived by Lord Eijer.

That life? That was over, as a dream dissipated in the morning sun.

Amari blew out the lantern.

This life? This unexpected shelter? Not what she'd planned, but so much better than she'd dared to hope. Although … .

She busied her hands, clattering dishes as she put clean ones away. Never once in these months had Orval imposed himself on her by either look or gesture. He'd not indicated any interest in her. They slept in the same bed, true enough, but babes had a way of quelling any idea of much more than sleep.

Maybe … maybe he had no interest in women? Surely, she'd have seen evidence of his interest in others.

It was much more likely that he had no interest in her, given her past foolishness. Xyians put great value on virginity, which made little sense to her, but it was their way.

Orval limped in, carrying Lara, who was well bundled against the cold. "One done," he said, handing her off to Amari.

Amari cradled her close as Lara blinked up at her from her wrappings. "Don't let Dalan piss on your new tunic," she said to Orval's back, and smiled at his laughter.

Amari nuzzled Lara, breathing in her sweet scent. Safe and warm and walking to the well. She'd snatch this joy and hold it in her heart.

A knock at the door and Winter bustled in. Amari had asked her to stand as her elder and Winter had been honored to agree.

"Whew," Winter said. "Sunny, but cold if you're not in the sun, we'll need to have the babes well wrapped. Are they sleeping through the night yet?"

Amari allowed herself to be distracted by the talk of the babes as Orval came in with Dalan. The adults bundled up for the Walk and headed down the stairs.

The guards were there of course, and Captain Ussin. They all headed toward the market, Ussin in front, clearing a path, with Winter close behind. Amari and Orval followed, side by side, each carrying a babe, with the two guards bring up the rear.

Stalls filled with wares lined the street and there was noise and bustle all around them. The scents of spices and baking filled the air, along with the squawking of geese and chickens, their legs tied to keep them from running amuck.

 Heads turned and greetings rose from the crowd as the small party headed to the well at the crossroads. Some followed as word spread.

Amari saw familiar faces, those who had aided them over these months. Laundresses, vegetable sellers, butchers, bakers.

People were laughing and smiling and calling out to Orval, wishing him well and congratulating him. He smiled and waved back, calling greetings to those he knew by name. He occasionally had to stop as older women would reach to hold his hand and pat his cheek and coo at Dalan.

"You know all these people?" Amari asked softly when he returned to her side.

"Well, not all of them, I mean, most of them, I guess." He seemed flustered at the attention, yet also pleased and excited. They both smiled at each other, sharing the warmth of the moment, then continued on.

The area around the well cleared as they stepped forward, the people forming a wide ring around the little group. A silence grew and spread.

Winter went to the well and took up the rope and bucket. It would not do to use the crank, not for this. She threw the bucket down, then pulled it out, brimming with fresh, clean water. A good omen.

Amari stepped forward. "Our Hearth has been blessed with twins," she announced.

Cheers rose.

"There will be burdens and blessings no matter what roads our children take," Amari continued. She'd worried that the recitation would feel forced, but it felt true. "We will teach them and guide them so that no matter what, they can always find their way back to the waters of their well. Their home."

Applause then, and the stamping of feet in approval. Amari unwrapped enough of the blankets to show Lara's face. The child blinked, her eyes bright, her black hair standing straight up from her head.

Amari lifted her high, with both hands. "Welcome our daughter, Lara Amari Orval," she announced to the crowd.

The people cheered.

Amari lowered Lara back to cradle her in her left arm. She dipped her right hand into the bucket and flicked the water into Lara's face. "May the waters bless and sustain you, until the Ancestors call you home."

Lara sneezed.

The crowd laughed and called out their own blessings as Orval handed Dalan to his mother and took Lara in his arms.

Dalan blinked at the light and waved his hands. Amari lifted him high. "Welcome our son, Dalan Orval Amari," she called out.

The crowd clapped, delighted.

Amari lowered Dalan to cradle him in her left arm and flicked the water of the well into his face. Tiny drops hit his eyes and gleamed like diamonds in the sun. "May the waters bless and sustain you, until the Ancestors call you home."

Dalan scrunched up his face and let out a hearty wail.

The crowd laughed and called out more blessings as Amari dried his face, cooing to reassure him.

A movement caught her eye and she looked up to find Orval standing close, Lara in one hand as he fumbled in a pocket with the other.

"I would honor my Hearth Mother," he announced loudly. He held something out to her.

Amari caught her breath. It was a bracelet, the traditional bracelet of the first-born, made of braided leather. Interwoven in the design were red jaspers, symbolizing the birth of twins.

She blinked back tears as she extended her hand to him and he placed the bracelet on her wrist. Now would be the time for the traditional kiss, for–

Orval hesitated.

Standing there, in the midst of the celebration, Amari's heart flared with joy. She looked deep into his eyes, wanting to save the moment in her memory, of this walk, this feeling—

"Kiss her, ya fool!" came a voice, and then laughter from the crowd.

"Don't be shy, sweetie," an old woman's voice offered encouragement.

Orval's eyes went wide and he drew himself up. "Give a man a chance," he called as he adjusted Dalan in his arms.

Amari laughed, and then he was there, and in some wonderful way, with two babes between them, he drew close and kissed her.

His lips were warm, dry, and wonderful, a firm pressure against hers, tasting of kavage and porridge and sweetness. Then the sensation was gone and Amari opened her eyes.

Orval stepped back, his cheeks red, and bowed to her.

Another cheer rose, and suddenly everyone started waving red cloths. Amari looked around, stunned. How did they know?

Orval cleared his throat. "I might have done a bit of research." He looked quite proud of himself.

Amari laughed. Dalan started wailing again, clearly unhappy.

Orval fumbled again, drawing out a bag. "Only coppers, my friends," he called as he scattered a few handfuls of coins in a circle. "Though there might be feathers among them, who can say? May they bring you luck this day!"

Amari didn't see any feathers in his hands, just bright copper coins that were scooped up by the crowd.

Winter tipped the water back into the well. "Time for home and hearth," she said, and the crowd laughed and started to dissipate.

They started back, and the return walk was quicker, because

the winds were picking up, the cold piercing cloaks and scarves. Still, more greetings were exchanged before the well-wishers who peeled off to return to their work day.

"Such a crowd," Orval said, his pride clear.

"What did you mean, feathers?" Amari asked softly.

"Ah," Orval gave her a grin. "A nickname for an old copper coin that can still be found, although rarely. It has an airion on the one side and a royal portrait on the other, although no one knows who, they are so worn. They're considered a token of good fortune. 'Good to have a feather in your pocket,' or so they say." Orval smiled. "I keep one in my pocket, one my father gave me."

When they got back to Winter's establishment the guards stopped at the base of the stairs, but Winter scolded them. "Freezing out here will do no good. Come with me and get warmed at the very least. These two will not wander off, not with babies to warm and feed."

Orval and Amari mounted the stairs, laughing at Winter's teasing as she hustled Ussin and the guards off. Amari felt the rush of home as the door opened and the warmth surrounded them. Lara was nuzzling, warm in her blanket but clearly in need of a feeding. She'd need to—

Orval stopped moving, suddenly silent.

There on the wooden table was a scroll, pristine and white, except for the red and black seal.

The Royal Seal of the Wyvern House of Xy.

## CHAPTER TWENTY

Caris's bond mark burned raging hot as she ran to the Queen's chambers, Mira close behind.

King Xyrath was exiting the room as they arrived, his expression forbidding. He raised a hand as they paused to curtsey. "Don't. Just get in there." He held the door open.

"Clumsy fool," Satia snarled, sitting on her lounge, weeping. Broken crockery and spilled tea were everywhere and the Queen was gesturing at the mess and screeching at the staff. Her eyes were red and swollen, her puffy, tear-streaked face set in a mulish pout. The air held the foul odor of vomit and ginger tea.

Caris exchanged a swift glance with Mira. They'd left her with a pot of tea and a full mound of honey cakes. What had—

"In the future, you'd best obey me the first time I speak," Satia spat at Rosalind, who stood silent before her, head bowed.

"Where have you been?" Satia focused on Caris and Mira, her voice tight and shrill. "You left me alone with these—" she choked back a sob, then spat, "these churls," gesturing at the pair of chambermaids, one of whom held a chamber pot, who were doing their best to become invisible.

Caris caught the glint of anger in Rosalind's eyes.

"My tea is cold," Satia sobbed. "And this stupid girl spilled it on me and dropped the tray and spilled the honey and just look at me," Satia grew angrier and redder as she waved her arms helplessly. "And my stomach ..." she groaned.

Mira took the chamber pot, looking in as she swirled the contents. Caris knelt at Satia's side, ignoring the mess. A quick glance showed no honey cakes left on the broken plates. She made soothing noises and offered the Queen a handkerchief. "Perhaps it would be best if you were to leave," she said to Rosalind.

"Yes, go! Get out, all of you!" Satia waved them away with an imperious gesture.

Mira shoved the pot at Rosalind, whose curtsey was swift and abrupt. The Royal Housekeeper drew the chambermaids out with her, departing with a sharp click of the door.

"It's in my hair," Satia wailed, holding out sticky strands. She heaved a sob. "It's all a mess," she said. "Nothing is as I want it to be."

Mira knelt at the Bonded's feet as Caris raced off for a basin and towels and Satia's favorite robe—a red one with tiny wyverns embroidered in gold thread on the sleeves. She snatched up a pair of comfortable slippers as well and returned, arms full, to hear Mira's soothing tones.

"We were seeing to your commands," Mira crooned. "Let's get you out of this gown and cleaned up. The others will be here soon."

Caris set the robe and slippers to warm by the hearth. She added a log, building up the fire.

Satia sniffed, letting Mira start to unlace her dress. "That stupid woman defied me and wouldn't give up the gold plate to be melted down."

Caris knelt and used the towels to mop up the spilled tea, gathering the broken dishes as she went. She didn't need to look up to know that Satia's face was puckered into a pout.

"I had to have the King order her to obey. Even then, she wouldn't shut up about preservation and history and tapestries. Doesn't she know that we have to pay that dratted Guildmaster an outrageous sum for that portal spell? Not to mention Xyrath and his stupid statue and his damned atira blades and plans for a coronation we can't afford. Spare no expense, he says." She paused for a ragged breath.

Mira whispered something comforting Caris didn't quite catch, easing Satia's dress off her breasts and down around her hips. The tea had soaked through to her breastband.

"We made promises to his uncles and cousins for titles and lands and there are debts that need to be paid, including to the Matriarch of the Lord of the Light." Satia wiped at her cheeks with the palm of her hand. "And I have to pay the Mage Guild-master because that damned chained mage will not do what I say." Her anger grew.

"Ritathan wanders around in those chains, smirking, with Tarwain's stupid, fat daughter following behind him like a puppy. Tarwain is nagging me about that, but I can't risk angering the

Mage Guild until after that stupid expensive portal is created. And they still haven't found me a blood mage." Satia cradled her belly. "Time is running out."

Caris bowed herself away to dispose of the broken bits of crockery. Taking up the kettle always left warming by the fire, she poured water into the basin, then soaked a cloth and tested it against her own skin before returning to Satia's side.

"There isn't any money in the treasury and I've learned that the Crown jewels are all tin and glass," Satia whined, clearly mortally offended. "That monster Kara melted down her jewelry and sold everything to feed the army. Who does that?"

Avice and Nora rushed in, breathless, making low curtseys, and clustered close, trying to help.

Satia glared at them and batted away their hands. "And I can't find the blessing gown handed down in the Xyian line for generations. I just bet that old crone hid it just to spite me." Her eyes narrowed. "I bet Rosalind knows where it is, the bitch."

Mira urged Satia up, with Avice and Nora helping her to stand. Her dress fell to the floor in a puddle of silk as Nora eased the Bonded's panties down to her ankles. Caris pulled all the cloth away as Satia lifted her feet.

Stripped bare, Satia stood in the center of their attention as they carefully washed her, regal and imperious and never once stopping her complaining. "Iris hunts, I can feel it, but she hasn't returned, and I still don't know if there is a stupid babe out there to threaten our throne."

Caris bundled the clothing carefully away in another room. The heat of the bondmark was easing and the pressure of the Bonded's displeasure left her chest. She risked a moment to gather up the silver mirror, brushes and combs, and returned.

"The invitation has been sent, the arrangements made," Avice said softly as she cleaned Satia's fingers delicately, one at a time. "Everything will go according to your desires."

Satia snuffled. "I might add a few people to my list."

Mira took up the brush and started to work on Satia's long, black hair with gentle strokes. Caris gathered the warmed slippers and robe.

Nora handed Satia a kerchief. "That always makes you feel better," she crooned. "And we dealt with the man that tried to poison you. He was an old retainer of Lady Jazan."

Satia huffed as Caris knelt and offered the slippers. Mira took the robe and held it while Satia slipped her arms in. Satia sighed, seeming to relax into the warmth and softness. The red of the robe made her bronze skin shine in the firelight. "I want her found and executed."

"As you command," Avice said. "All shall be as you want, Bonded."

"I want … ." Satia's face crumpled and they all froze as she heaved in a mighty breath.

"*I want this to be over,*" Satia wailed.

"This baby is making me fat, just look at my ankles. And my pretty rings don't fit over my knuckles. Look at these stretch marks," she sobbed, holding her belly. "I'm fat and ugly and nothing fits, and I hate this. And I have to endure months of this waddling. Months!"

She wept into her hands; her shoulders slumped, heaving with her sobs.

They clustered close, trying to offer comfort.

"The sacrifice you are making for the Kingdom," Avice whispered, and they all nodded and agreed.

"This is why we need a midwife," Mira said softly. "One with experience—"

Satia jerked her head up, her face distorted with rage.

Caris's bondmark flared blood-red and agony erupted at her wrist, catching her between breaths. She fell to her knees, gasping, as did the others.

"How dare you," Satia raged, lips twisted. "There will be no one else to witness my pain. Bad enough to suffer these indignities in your presence. I have said no, and yet you defy me. You defy *me*."

Caris tried to focus, to form words, but the pain squeezed the very breath from her body. She sprawled at the Bonded's feet, dimly conscious that the others had also collapsed. Satia had hurt them all before but never this bad, never all at once. Never like this.

She flung out one hand, instinctively reaching toward the Bonded, arm stretched in desperate supplication.

"*No*," Satia spat, drawing her robe closer. The burn in Caris's arm intensified, crawling up her forearm as frustration and fury poured out of the Bonded and into the bondmarks.

Distantly Caris heard Nora whimper. Avice writhed next to her, lips peeled back in a horrific grimace. Flat, unable to move, unable to breathe, Caris felt the heat of the poison weave up her arm toward her shoulder. She wasn't sure what would happen if it reached her heart. Probably burn it out of her body, as the Bonded willed.

Caris struggled to draw one last breath, make one last plea. She implored the cold face above her. "Bonded," she gasped, tears streaming down her face, "your plan."

It was too much. Caris collapsed in agony, face down on the stone floor, Satia's red slipper inches away.

"You're right," Satia said. "I am not myself."

The sudden absence of pain was a shock. The room was cold and quiet except for the breath that rasped in all their lungs. The memory of pain lingered in her muscles and her lungs. The burning receded down her arm, her bondmark returning to its normal black.

Caris dared to raise her eyes to the Bonded.

Satia stood, tall and straight, her red-hot, fiery rage gone, clarity returning to her eyes. "Lashing out like this, letting my emotions control my reactions, accomplishes nothing." She smoothed her hair with a graceful gesture, frowning as she looked off into the distance. "No one prepared me for this aspect of the matter."

"Perhaps no one can," Avice's broken whisper came. "Perhaps it needs to be experienced to know."

"Perhaps," Satia said. "At the least, I need someone who knows what they are doing."

She lifted her chin and cradled her stomach. "This is the key to my future. My survival. Suffer what I must." She deigned to look down at them.

"Very well, Guildmaster Forterran mentioned someone. Mira, find that midwife. Bring her to me." Satia gathered up her robe and stepped over the mess and her Bondmaidens' prone bodies, speaking over her shoulder as she strode toward her bedchamber. "I am exhausted. Avice, come and sing me to sleep."

# CHAPTER TWENTY-ONE

I t took Iris a full day to recover.

She'd had a little warning of the Bonded's rage, barely enough to hide in some brush and curl into a ball before the full agony hit.

Whatever had set off the Bonded, the pain had been the worst she'd ever felt, harsh and virulent. She'd no doubt she would have fallen if she'd been mid-stride. As it was, she just curled up tighter and tried to keep breathing. When the agony released her, its sudden absence left her gasping.

She managed to get to her pack, get her blankets and huddle under them, keeping every inch covered, trying to stop shivering. Never before had the Bonded lashed out like that, leaving her gasping and feeling bruised in every bone. The others had to have suffered as well; Iris had no way of knowing what shape they were in. Alive, hopefully.

It didn't help her recovery that her shelter was no more than a thick bush and she couldn't risk a fire. The rain had cleared at least, and thought the sky was heavy with clouds, there was no wind.

Long before she was ready, the bond pulsed. The sense of urgency returned, the push at the back of her throat like a terrible thirst.

Iris forced her tired, aching muscles to move. The Bonded wanted this, so it had to be done. Iris had only one purpose now, far from her Bonded: to hunt.

So be it.

Except that she had lost the trail.

She found the hut quick enough, but there was just a trace of their presence in the dirt around the fire pit. No ash in the fire, but two rabbit pelts buried in the woods a distance away, starting to rot

She bit her lip; she could not return to the Bonded with failure.

She walked a spiral pattern with the hut at its center, moving slowly, looking for any sign, taking her time. Rushing would only cause her to miss something.

It was sunset of the next day when she found a bit of fur snagged on a branch. The last dregs of light showed her a footprint and a faint paw print.

She looked up to orient herself. She'd knew from the Bonded's maps that they were roughly half-way to Swift's Port. But the signs were pointing north.

What was to the north?

Frustration welled up, but with the last of the day gone there was nothing she could do.

Iris made a rough, cold camp then and crawled under her blankets, impatient for daylight. With her armor loosened she could tuck her hand within and rub the ridges of her scar, trying to relax enough to sleep.

She closed her eyes and pictured the Bonded's maps. Swift's Port, with its deep harbor, the great river delta beside it, the swamp between Old Soccia and the area known as … Athelbryght.

Athelbryght. One of the oldest ancient Baronies, right up there with the Black Hills. Known for its farming, its wine, and its old trade routes, not much more than goat paths into the mountains. Trade routes that once had led to the fabled Kingdom of Xy but now ran only to the borders of the Wastes.

The Wastes, where none but the marcusi dared tread.

Iris pressed her lips together and glared into the darkness. It made sense for her quarry to flee to Athelbryght. From there, they could take the mountain pass to the Wastes, the perfect place for the marcusi to hide a child of the Blood.

Athelbryght was also the home of the vore pack, ruled by the Chosen, who bore the birthmark of the Dagger-Star.

Iris shifted in her blankets and bared her teeth to the night sky. The Bonded was wary, more than wary, of the vore. Iris wasn't sure if the Chosen would aid the marcusi, but the vore would.

The trail was growing cold and she dreaded failure. She pressed her fingers to the ridges of her scar, feeling her heart beat below. The ache returned, a longing for the others, a painful desire tugging her back.

But the Bond pulsed with the urge, the need, the mission, until her focus narrowed to her goal.

She could do this. It would be hard. Athelbryght was a settled area, of roads and towns and farms untouched by the battles that had raged. Come the morning, she could pick the trail back up. They'd make mistakes, and she could push herself to move faster. Once the marcus reached Athelbryght, she could find a way to send a message back.

She could do this.

She would do this.

A yawn caught her by surprise, making her jaw crack. She puffed out a breath and shifted in her bedding, getting as comfortable as she could. Dawn would come, and she would track, and find them, and kill them.

But first sleep.

———— • ————

"Do we have to do this now?" Avice demanded as she walked beside Mira on the crowded streets of the Stews. "We should not be leaving her side." Even with the Palace guards before and behind them, it was rough going, dodging people and refuse in the streets.

"We need to do it now, while she is agreeable," Mira said. "Who knows how long this mood will last or when another tantrum will come upon her?"

Avice had no answer for that.

They moved on. One of the leading guards kept peering at the buildings to the left and right. The street grew narrower and the road rougher until he finally stopped. "Here, lady. City Watch said she was here."

Mira stepped up smartly and rapped on the door.

It was opened by a man who looked a bit worse for wear, his hair all ruffled. He stared at Mira. From behind him, Avice heard the wail of a woman in pain.

"The midwife, Plumestra. Where is she?"

The man blinked and opened the door wider to show a family gathered by a hearth, every chair and bench filled. "She's in with me wife," he said, gesturing to a door, and before anyone could say anymore, Mira sailed past them all and into that room.

Avice ordered their guards to remain outside before she followed.

There were women only here, one at each side of the bed, one in the bed, laboring in pain, and another at the end of the bed, her hands deep in the woman's body.

"Plumestra?" Mira asked.

"Aye," the midwife grunted, clearly intent on her work. Her brown hair, streaked with gray, was plastered to her forehead. She gave the newcomers a look, then rolled her eyes. "I can already tell you are from some arrogant noblewoman, thinks she's the only pregnant woman for miles."

The woman in the bed wailed and flopped down, the women beside her wiping her forehead and offering encouragement.

"Nobles," Plumestra snorted as she leaned in, her hands getting deeper. "They won't follow advice, expect miracles, and forget to pay. Demanding or stupid or both. No, don't push," Plumestra warned the woman. "Catch your breath and give me a chance to shift the babe."

Avice winced. The room was over-warm and smelled of blood, sweat, and feces. The poor woman's legs splayed wide, her belly heaving. No effort at modesty here, that was certain.

All for a squalling mite that latched to a tit. Avice looked away.

Mira, however, was fascinated. "Breech?" she asked, getting closer.

"Aye." The midwife eyed her. "How much experience have you?"

"I have attended three births," Mira said.

"Three, eh?" Plumestra shook her head. "Then roll up those fancy sleeves and aid me. This one's decided feet first works just fine."

Mira shed her cloak without another word and started on her sleeves.

Avice lost patience with all of them. "The Queen requires your services," she announced over the woman's panting. "Immediately."

"I refused Queen Kara, who wanted me at her beck and call in the field of battle, what makes you think I will serve Queen Satia?" Plumestra removed one bloody, muck-covered hand and reached to guide Mira's. The wailing grew louder. "Feel its head?"

Avice decided to focus on a spot on the wall. "The Queen bears the heir to the throne and demands your service."

"So that's how it's to be? Now? With my hand up this lady's womb?" Plumestra snorted. "Let me guess, I'm to drop everything and rush to her bidding or she'll lop off my head." Her attention shifted to Mira. "Now have a care, we shift gently, you see? But we needs be swift as well, for the fluid's gone and this one needs to be breathing. You push, I'll pull." She lifted her head to the woman on the bed. "Anstra, you just breathe now. Bear down only when I tell ya."

Avice pressed her lips together and waited.

It didn't take long, with Mira and Plumestra working together. There was shouting and pushing and what all, and then the screams of a naked, female infant pulled from the belly.

"Healthy lungs," Plumestra said as Mira beamed. The babe was handed off to one of the waiting women as the other cut the cord, saying the ritual prayers. Plumestra wiped her hands. "Now the work's not done, Anstra. Catch your breath and we'll work on the afterbirth. In the meantime," she turned and glared at Avice.

"That was amazing," Mira bubbled as she watched the babe cleaned and placed on her mother's breast. She wiped her hands and rolled down her sleeves. "A new, precious life."

Plumestra's face softened, but hardened again as she caught a glimpse of the bondmark on Mira's wrist. "And who do I have to thank for bringing me to the attention of the Queen?"

"Guildmaster Forterran," Mira spoke before Avice could stop her.

"Well, I will have to thank the Guildmaster for his thoughtfulness," Plumestra said. "But my answer's still 'no'. Find one of them that serve the nobility and leave me to my own."

Mira went wide-eyed, clearly startled. They were not in a position to accept a "no."

Something the Guildmaster had said clicked in Avice's head. "A charter."

Plumestra turned back, an eyebrow raised.

"A guild charter," Avice repeated, pleased that she'd caught the older woman by surprise.

Plumestra's eyes narrowed. "I suspect Guildmaster Forterran mentioned that as well?"

Avice nodded. "And I'll not pretend I have the authority to offer it. But Queen Satia does."

"And she might," Mira piped.

"I see," Plumestra said slowly.

One of the older females swaddled the babe and took it into the outer room. Cries of joy and delight greeted her.

"I've three women I'm tending the next day or so," Plumestra said. "When I've time and if there are no other calls, I will come to the palace."

"Ask for Mira," Mira offered, but Plumestra had already turned back to the woman on the bed, reaching to pull on the dangling birth cord. "Now push, girl. Let's get this done."

"Oh," Mira was fascinated, but Avice snatched up her cloak and pulled her from the room and out to the street.

"Stand guard," Avice ordered the guards. "Wait for the midwife Plumestra and keep her under guard. See to it that she reports to the palace tomorrow."

"As you say, Lady," the guard acknowledged. "But it's growing late, and this is not the best part of town. Do you want us to escort you back?"

"We can see to ourselves," Avice said. "Come, Mira." She headed down the lane, out of patience with midwives and babies. An altogether messy business.

"I wanted to watch," Mira said. "Did you notice that her belly turned flaccid? After the babe was out?"

"Don't mention that to the Queen," Avice strode on. The shadows were growing longer, and there were no street lamps in this part of town.

People were moving about, closing up shop, heading for their homes. There was enough traffic that they had to press against walls in some places, to avoid the crowd. At one such place, a man stepped out of the shadows in an alley and blocked their path.

"Ladies." He bowed, his smile wide. A gold tooth gleamed in his grin.

"Out of our way," Avice demanded as she moved to walk past.

The man shifted, blocking her once more. "Now, Bondmaiden Avice, don't be like that."

That focused her attention.

"And Bondmaiden Mira." He bowed to both of them.

"What do you want?" Avice demanded, searching the shadows

for others. As far as she could determine, he was alone.

"I'll not waste your time, ladies, but get straight to the point. My master wishes to give your mistress a gift."

"What gift?" Avice took a step into the alley, reaching into her skirt slit for one of her daggers.

"This,"The man kicked a large bundle of rags on the ground. It moaned.

Mira stepped forward and realized a man sprawled there, emaciated and smelling of vomit.

"And what does our mistress need with a wreck of a man?" Avice asked.

The gold-toothed man smirked. "A wreck he surely is and addicted to letheon. Still, blood mages be hard to come by."

Avice went still, but Mira tilted her head with a frown. "Blood mage? This?"

"Aye," Gold tooth flashed his grin again. "A piss poor one, truth be told, but beggars can't be choosers, now can they?"

"The price?" Avice asked.

"Let's say 'good will' and let that rest for another day."The gold disappeared as he grew serious. "We help each other. Queen gets her way and we have disposed of a … problem, shall we say? In the future, perhaps we can deal again."

"And if I refuse this gift?"

There was a shrug as the man faded further back into the shadows. "Leave him to die, it's no matter to me." His chuckle came from even further away, "But then what will your Queen do for a blood mage?"

Rapid steps raced off and they were left with an empty alley and a wretch at their feet.

Mira had him by the wrist. "His heart beats strong," she

said with a wrinkled nose. She reached for an eyelid. "But he's drugged to be sure."

"And no knowing if it's voluntary," Avice scowled. "Or if he truly is a blood mage."

"What's to be done?" Mira asked.

"Not for us to decide," Avice flung her cloak over the mess, hoping it would wash clean. She wrestled the man up and heaved him over her shoulder. "It's for the Queen to say."

## CHAPTER TWENTY-TWO

———◦———

The invitation said nothing of this," Orval stared at the young woman who'd come through the door into the kitchen, catching them all off guard. She'd brought cold evening air—and four warriors—into their warmth. The shiver down his spine had nothing to do with the loss of heat and everything to do with the expression on her face: stern, almost angry.

The invitation had said that a carriage would be sent to bring them to their presentation at the Royal Court and that they were not expected to appear until the babes had been fed and settled for the evening.

The invitation had not mentioned one of the Queen's Bond-maidens being sent to tend the babes.

Orval hadn't caught her name, he was so furious. "We've made arrangements," he said firmly, nodding to Winter, who had retreated to stand behind Amari's chair. The younger woman was nursing Dalan.

"'Tis the Queen's command," the Bondmaiden said, with apology in her tone but none in her eyes. "I am to stay with the twins until you return. To see to their safety."

Orval sputtered at her. "Hardly appropriate, bursting in with no warning."

Winter's face was a blank mask, as if she was trying to warn him to obey.

Amari stood, putting Dalan on her shoulder. "Husband," she said calmly, "the Queen honors us by sending Bondmaiden Nora to care for our twins. I am sure Winter will welcome another pair of hands if both wake at the same time. Lara is already sleeping. Just let me put Dalan down and finish dressing." She moved smoothly to the doorway. "I will need help with my lacings."

"I still don't see … ." Orval let his voice trail off as he followed her down the hall. Once inside their bedroom, with the door closed, Amari's face collapsed.

"Orval, we can't leave them with her," her voice shook as she tightened her hold on her son.

"We can't afford not to," Orval said quietly. "We can't take them with us. Winter will be a witness and will watch over them." He shook his head, resigned, and put his hands on Amari's shoulders, then drew her close, the babe between them. "The best we can do is go quickly and come back as soon as possible. The King and Queen will greet us, then surely he'll quickly dismiss his minor relations, a poor, impoverished scholar and his shamed wife, and we will return to change diapers and feed our babes and try to get everyone back to sleep."

Dalan erupted with a burp twice his size. Amari laughed nervously and lowered him into his basket. Lara was already fast asleep in hers. "You're right. I'm just–" She shrugged and went to the wardrobe for her red dress.

Orval averted his eyes, studying the babes as cloth rustled behind him. "This will be over by the next feeding. We will go and mingle briefly with those powerful, nasty, terrible people, endure their poisonous whispers, bow to the king and queen, and leave. We will come back to our warm kitchen and kavage and our stacks of books."

"And fussy, hungry babes." Amari came into view. "Would you mind?" She turned her back, holding the front of her dress to her breasts.

Orval swallowed hard. The skin of her back was so warm and smooth. It seemed a shame to conceal it under fabric. He focused on his task, taking care to not pull the laces too tight.

Amari took a breath, then turned to him. "Let us be about this."

Orval nodded and shifted to put his lips close to her ear. "You have the token?"

"Here," she whispered, putting her hand to her breast. "Marriage contract?"

"By your kitchen shrine." Orval scowled. "She best not rummage through my books."

That brought out a true smile. "Orval, you are the only one who can find anything in those stacks."

He snorted, then smiled back. "Ready?"

"No." Amari said. "But I am not going to let that stop us."

"Together, then."

"Together."

At least the carriage was well cushioned, though it was easy to see where the airion carvings on the doors had been burned off and painted over. With a warrior escort on horseback, they moved quickly through the town, through the gates of the palace, and up to the doors. Too fast, really.

Orval took a deep breath as the door opened, then climbed out slowly. He could feel the impatience of the guards, but he knew not to rush the leg and fall on his face. Once he was down, he turned and offered his hand to Amari.

She emerged with a grace he'd never had and a beauty all her own. The torchlight danced on her warm brown skin, giving gold tones to the bronze.

She stepped out lightly to the ground and arranged her skirts.

Usually Captain Roth was at the door when carriages arrived. But tonight there were only guards in the Wyvern colors and a courtier to greet them.

"Master Scribe Orval of the House Airion, be welcome." The courtier bowed low. "I am instructed to bring you unto the presence of their majesties for an audience immediately upon your arrival."

"My thanks," Orval said.

"This way, if you will, Master Scribe." The courtier plunged into the crowd of those seeking audience. "Make way," he called out, heading the couple through the doors of the castle. "Make way for Master Scribe Orval and his wife, Amari of Uyole."

Orval huffed. Amari raised a questioning eyebrow as she placed her hand on his.

"Not an honor I am usually afforded," Orval said under his breath as they started to follow. The stiffness in his leg eased a bit as they walked. "Not sure if it's an honor or a way to track the prey."

Amari tilted her head slightly, her face fixed in a warm smile as she looked ahead.

The halls were crowded, filled with the murmur of voices and the sound of music coming from the throne room. The courtier had slowed to allow them to catch up, apparently realizing that Orval wasn't up to trotting along. That was fine, it let Orval look at the changes.

And there were changes.

The blue and white of the Airion Crown were gone, stripped away. The red and gold of Wyvern House had replaced them where possible. The ancient tapestries had all been taken down and the bare stone walls made the palace seem shabby and cold. Hopefully the tapestries had been placed in storage, but Orval wouldn't put it past the Wyverns to have burned them. But there was something else, something–

"So different from when I was here last," Amari whispered. "There is so much tension in the air. So much … fear."

She was right.

Orval had walked these halls, though before the civil conflict had broken into open warfare. He'd greeted friends and avoided the more obnoxious cousins and Aunt Xydell. There had been an ease about the place, then. Now, everyone seemed to be avoiding his gaze, but this wasn't the usual disdain for a poor, crippled man outside the currents of power. Somehow, he and Amari were the center of attention, and not in a good way. Orval hoped that the buzz that arose after they passed was normal, spiteful gossip.

There was a slight wait at the door to the throne room. The courtier tried to attract the attention of the Royal Herald, who controlled access.

Orval caught a movement out of the corner of his eye; it was the Royal Master Librarian.

"Jacoben," Orval called out, pleased to see a welcome face. "Have you fixed your translation of Moravek's *Philosophies* yet? I sent you those corrections months ago."

The man jumped liked a startled deer. He hesitated, then bolted, disappearing into the crowd.

"Odd," Orval muttered. "He hadn't made that many mistakes."

"Did you offend him?" Amari kept her voice low.

"Oh, we always argue," Orval said. "Usually over cataloging or translations. Still, that was odd." Odder still that he hadn't heard Aunt Xydell's shrill tones yet or been greeted by the Royal Housekeeper, Rosalind.

The door opened and the Royal Herald struck his staff on the floor. His deep voice rolled over the room, silencing the music and chatter.

"Your Majesties, may I present Master Scribe Orval and his wife, Amari of Uyole."

Orval and Amari stepped within.

The throne room seemed to stretch for miles, as it always had. Orval was pleased that he did not grimace at the length of red carpet between them and the thrones. Amari's fingers pressed ever so slightly between his as they walked forward together.

It would all be over by the next feeding.

The silence was unsettling as the court watched them draw close to the thrones. When they stopped, Orval managed a steady bow. Amari sank down in a graceful curtsey.

"*Cousin!*" King Xyrath sprang up from his throne and strode forward, his face open and honest in a wide grin. He looked the same as he always had, a picture of energy and vitality. Bold and brash and full of life, his golden hair was more of a crown than the crown itself. Xyrath stood tall and tanned and strong, making Orval feel all his inadequacies. Orval had known Xyrath when they'd fostered together, and while that had been many years earlier, Xyrath would always be Xyrath.

The King wrapped Orval in a huge bear hug, then grabbed him by the shoulders when he staggered a bit. "Orval, it is good to see you. And this must be your charming wife?" Xyrath turned his winsome smile on Amari.

"Your Majesty," Amari said, and curtsied again.

"Charming, charming," Xyrath purred. "Let me make you known to my Queen." Xyrath extended a hand. Amari took it and allowed Xyrath to walk her closer to the throne. Orval followed.

"Satia, beloved, this is Amari, Orval's wife, if you can believe it."

Orval gritted his teeth.

"Welcome, Amari." Queen Satia did not seem pleased. There was something in her eyes that told Orval something was not quite right. Three Bondmaidens stood behind the throne and there was a faint scent of ginger in the air.

"We must congratulate you," the Queen continued, "on the birth of your twins." Satia's gaze dropped to Amari's hand, still in the King's grasp.

The King dropped her hand and sauntered back to sit on his throne. "Twins," he roared. "Didn't know you had it in you, Orval." He started clapping and the entire court joined in.

Orval stepped up to stand next to Amari. "Our thanks, Your Majesties," he said.

"Did you have an easy time of it?" Satia asked, plucking idly at a thread on her skirt.

"I did, Your Majesty," Amari said. "A bit of nausea for the first few weeks, but that faded quickly."

Satia's face didn't change but it was as if the very air had grown colder. The Bondmaidens stirred as if fearing something.

Orval reached for Amari's hand, finding her fingers shaking and cold. But his touch seemed to aid her to gather herself. "We offer our congratulations to you, as well as our blessings and well-wishes," Amari said. "We have heard that you are expecting."

"We are, we are," Xyrath proclaimed. "An heir around the Summer Solstice, to add to the family and strengthen the Blood of Xy." He rose to his feet again and the crowd stomped their feet and gave a hearty cheer.

"Speaking of which," Satia suggested, glancing at Xyrath.

"Yes," Xyrath settled back on his throne. "All of the Blood should be honored. It's not right that one of your learning should be wasted on books, Orval, and not be honored with a title and position."

"Your Majesty, I—" Orval started.

"Save your thanks until you hear our decree," Xyrath grinned. He struck a pose, looking around the room and commanding all attention before he raised his voice with a flourish.

"Orval of Xy, this day do I appoint and declare to you, your Lady, and the heirs of your body, the rights and title of the Lord High Barony of the Black Hills."

# CHAPTER TWENTY-THREE

Orval stiffened, frozen in the middle of a breath.

Xyrath gestured and cymbals crashed; the music started again and the crowd cheered.

Two footmen approached from either side, carrying red velvet robes lined with black fur. Xyrath bounded forward and took the first, draping the heavy garment over Orval's shoulders with a dramatic sweep and fastening the chain at his throat.

The cloak weighed a ton. The chain threatened to choke him.

The footman was cloaking Amari. Xyrath leaped back to stand before his throne. "We will eventually restore all the old Baronies," he announced. "You will act as our vanguard and re-establish our domain over the Black Hills. All hail the new Lord High Baron and Lady High Baroness!"

Cheers rang out, echoing around the room.

"Your Majesty," Orval tried to make himself heard, to protest–

"We are glad to reward thee," Queen Satia interrupted smoothly. Something in her expression silenced Orval's objections. "We will send you and your family to the Black Hills with staff and an escort to ensure your safety." She narrowed her eyes. "You will surely have no trouble putting down those rebels that offer us insult."

Xyrath nodded. "No need for oaths, Orval, not between us. Captain Ussin has all the details. He will escort you to your new lands in the morning."

In the awkward silence that followed, it was Amari's turn to reach for his hand and squeeze; Orval blinked and bowed his head. "As you command, Your Majesty." He stepped back, anxious to leave the royal presence so he could try to make sense of what had just happened.

Hand in hand with Amari, trying not to step on the heavy cloak that dragged on the thick carpet, he almost missed Satia's words.

"One more thing, Lord High Baron."

Orval went still, afraid to look at her.

"You won't have time to pursue your studies as you serve your King." Satia's voice was silk over stone. "It would be devastating if it were to be lost. A lifetime of work."

Amari's gaze met his. Orval wet his lips but found the strength to stay silent.

"For the purpose of preservation, your papers and books will be stored in the Royal Library. Eventually, once the collection is catalogued and copied, we will send the originals to you. In the meanwhile, trust in the knowledge that your work will be waiting for you, safe and secure."

Xyrath laughed again. "You'll have the lands under control in no time, mark my words. You'll have the mines working and stone flowing soon. Send me a hunk of white marble as quick as you can, eh? Enough for a life-sized statue, yes?" Xyrath gave a wave of dismissal. "A safe journey to you, cousin." Xyrath lifted his head, looking over Orval's shoulder. "Ah, Master Sculptor! How good to see you!

Orval couldn't speak, couldn't bring himself to thank the King and Queen. He turned and stumbled, feet tangled in both robe and carpet.

At his side in an instant, Amari somehow managed to subtly take his train in hand, easing the drag as he walked.

"Make way," their escort cried out as they approached the hall. "Make way for the Lord High Baron and Lady High Baroness of the Black Hills."

Their walk through the halls, once again following the courtier, was silent, neither willing to speak where so many might hear. The crowd, however, was filled with whispers and knowing looks.

Captain Ussin was waiting at the carriage. "Get in," he said gruffly. "We'll get you back." He barely waited until they had climbed in before he shoved the trailing end of Orval's cloak in behind him and got in himself, sitting on the opposite bench.

Amari fussed with the cloaks, pulling the heavy velvet over them and getting it up off the floor of the carriage. Underneath the mass of fabric and fur, she reached for Orval's hand and held it tight. Realizing the chain of her cloak was pressing on her throat, Orval reached with his free hand and undid the clasp.

Amari rubbed her throat, then released his own chain before

putting her head on his shoulder with a sigh.

"Rest while ya can," Ussin muttered. "Long journey tomorrow." Never once did he look Orval in the eye.

The carriage rattled up to their home and Orval climbed out first, leaving his cloak behind and offering his hand to Amari. She stepped out, looking so weary it made his heart ache.

"I'll see to the cloaks," Ussin said, grabbing Amari's as it slipped from her shoulders.

They climbed the stairs, Amari taking the lead.

The kitchen was empty. Gone, all gone—tables, chairs, crockery, pots, pans. All gone.

Bondmaiden Nora stood in the center of the room holding a lantern. She curtsied deeply as they stared. "Lord High Baron. Lady High Baroness."

A thin wail came from the bedroom. Amari rushed past Nora; Orval followed as quickly as he could.

Light spilled in from the privy. Winter stood by the bed, the only piece of furniture left in the room. The babes' baskets sat on the bed, a tiny hand waving over the side of one.

"She never touched them," Winter whispered, pale as Orval had ever seen her. "The soldiers swarmed in after you left and swept everything into sacks and crates. She threatened–"

Nora walked into the room.

"Lara just started to fuss," Winter finished.

Amari was busy checking the children, making soothing noises. "Help me, if you would," she said to Winter. "I need to nurse them."

"We need to leave them to get their rest, Madam Winter." Nora made it a command. Winter shot a glance at Orval, then nodded and headed to the doorway.

"We have left what you will need for tonight and tomorrow morning in the privy," Nora said cooly. "You will need to wake early and dress warmly for your journey. Breakfast will be provided and the rest of your things will be packed and loaded in the morning." She held out the lantern to Orval.

He took it quickly, fumbling with the handle.

Nora paused in the doorway. "The Queen wants to make sure that you are not disturbed tonight, so soldiers have been posted within and without for your protection." She curtsied. "Sleep well," she said and swept away, herding Winter before her.

Amari opened her mouth but Orval held up his hand. "Let me help you into a nursing gown," he said.

She closed her mouth and nodded.

He focused on untying the laces so that he didn't have to see her warm skin. While she changed, he averted his eyes, but the only things to look at were the walls of empty shelves.

Gone. Everything was gone.

His home had been stripped of his books, scrolls, and papers. Empty shelf after empty shelf. His desk, gone. His chair, gone.

Amari sat on the edge of the bed and took Lara into her arms. Once the little girl latched on, Amari looked at Orval with wide, frightened eyes.

"I'll see if they forgot anything," Orval said. He stepped into the hall to check the other rooms, his labyrinth of shelves.

———•———

Amari listened as Orval moved off, trying not to crush Lara in fear. The sound of his footsteps echoed eerily against the naked wood.

Everything in this room had been swept up and packed away. Their clothes, baby supplies, the bed and bedding were all that remained. She checked the privy, seeing their things piled there.

She heard Orval speak to someone in the kitchen, then walk back toward the bedroom, his withered leg dragging. Poor man, he had to be exhausted and hurting. When he passed the bedroom door, he shook his head when she made as if to speak. The storage room, he was going to check–

Another male voice spoke: "Keep ya safe this night, milord."

Amari closed her eyes against her panic.

At last Orval returned and sat beside Amari. Dalan was waving tiny arms in his basket and Orval took him up and cradled him. Some of the pain seemed to leave Orval's eyes.

"They left us clothing," Amari offered. "Supplies for the babes."

"They even cleaned out the storage area," Orval said mildly. "There are guards in the kitchen and at the back door. We are safe for the night."

"Don't leave me," Amari whispered.

Orval nodded. "Let's see to the babes."

Silently, they went through the regular routine of feeding, changing, and rocking the infants to sleep.

Amari was settling Lara in her basket when she suddenly stiffened. Concerned, Orval went to her side. "Something wrong?" he whispered.

She shook her head and reached for his hand; her warm fingers pressed his down into Lara's basket. His face changed as the tips of his fingers brushed the familiar leather spine of the *Epic of Xyson.*

His eyes closed and he leaned into Amari and pressed his head to hers. She moved closer, saying nothing as they shared their warmth.

Once they finished caring for the babes, they both went into the garderobe, changing and washing together in that tight space, eyes averted for what little privacy there was.

Amari kept the token clutched tight in her hand as she changed and showed it to Orval.

Orval put his head close to hers. "Use the token and summon the marcusi." His whisper warmed her cold cheek. "They will find a way to spirit you and the babes away."

Her heart clenched at that and tears started. But she nodded and stood in the doorway, clutching the token so hard the edges pressed against her palm. *Help us*, she thought, hoping against hope that "us" meant all of them.

She swayed, weary and frozen. Orval was there, gently steering her to the bed.

Amari shivered, the bedding and blankets feeling cold and clammy against her skin. She tucked the token under her pillow. The bedclothes rustled, and Orval eased in beside her. "Come," he said, holding up the blankets.

She turned to him, feeling his warmth as she tucked herself beside him, putting her hand on his chest.

He covered it with his own. "Sleep," he murmured. "I will keep watch."

She couldn't sleep, she thought, as she closed her eyes and listened to his steady heartbeat under her ear. She laced her fingers with his and sighed. There was no way she could sleep.

Yet she did.

## CHAPTER TWENTY-FOUR

Guyik wormed his way through the gathering crowd, unusual for this time of a morning, when folks were normally starting work. When he got to where he could see, the reason was obvious. Not often you saw a military carriage with a large escort outside a pleasure house.

At least, not in Edenrich.

Keeping a wary eye on the horses, he leaned down to an older woman standing in front of him. "Milady, can I ask the reason for all this?"

She turned but said nothing for a moment, clearly taking in his dark skin and rough leathers, the lute strapped to his pack, the gold hoop in his ear, and the purple and green feathers in his hat. "Songster, aye?"

"Just in from Swift's Port." He gave her a warm smile with the lie. "Always looking for a song or a bit of gossip," he added with a wink.

"With those doe-brown eyes, aye, songster for sure." She pointed with her chin. "Our local scribe's been elevated by the new King. Seems he's been made Lord High Baron and is being sent off to his lands this morning, will he, nill he."

Guyik looked around. "Isn't that a reason to celebrate, auntie? There's no joy here."

"Nay, for the Barony be the Black Hills, filled with more bandits and thieves then ever found in Swift's Port. And all be hating those of Xy." She went up on tip-toe when another would have blocked her view. Guyik pushed the interloper aside so the woman could see, earning a nod of thanks. "And Master Orval just married, with two wee babes, and being sent to his death, or so's the word."

Guyik cast an eye on the number of guards around. "But they go with soldiers?"

Auntie snorted. "Escort, lad. And who hates the Blood of Xy more than the Blood of Xy? Family warring against family can be the worst of the worst, yes?"

"Aye, Auntie," Guyik sighed. "Truth."

A banging at the door at the top of the stairs drew his attention. A man and a woman emerged, bundled in cloaks and scarves and bearing a babe each. They made their way down slowly, the man clearly limping.

The Auntie beside him called out in a voice twice her size. "May the Lord of the Light shine upon you, Master Orval!"

All around, those gathered took up the cry, the noise filling the street. The carriage horses threw their heads and stamped their feet.

The man looked up, startled at the noise, but the soldiers with them didn't let them pause. They were hustled into the carriage and the door securely closed.

Another woman appeared, from the establishment below, wearing silks and not wrapped for the cold. Carrying a large, covered basket, she marched up to the man what looked like the Captain and put her face right into his.

"Oh, Madam Winter, giving Captain Ussin what-all," Auntie was clearly delighted.

"–the least you can do, let me feed them, as you take'em to their deaths–" was all Guyik caught above the crowd's roar.

This Ussin seemed none too pleased, but he took the basket, searched through it with a rough hand, opened the carriage door, and handed it in. Madam Winter turned away, tears streaming down her face.

"Hup, hup," the Captain called, knocking on the side of the carriage to get the driver's attention.

The carriage started off, the escort surrounding it and criers racing to take position at the front. The Captain pulled himself into his saddle and urged his horse to follow, looking grim and ill-tempered. It didn't take long for the party to disappear down the road.

"There they go, then, and us the lesser for it," the Auntie shook her head wearily. "If'n you make a song of that, make it a sad one," she said over her shoulder as she moved off with the dispersing crowd.

"Aye, Auntie," Guyik said, resisting the flow of the crowd. He pressed himself against the building and slid into a quiet alleyway.

There was a chance he could catch them. He pulled off his

pack, took his hat from his head, folded it to protect his feathers, and tucked it away. He checked out the walls above him as he felt for the handle of his climbing stick, pulled it free, and shouldered his pack once again. Old moves, made smooth with time and experience.

With a glance around, he set his hook in the wall and started to climb.

Rooftops were quicker and the buildings in this part of town were so close together it was just a step from roof to roof. With his hood pulled up, and thanks to his dark cloak and leathers, he looked like a shadow in the still-thin morning light. He made good time, running lightly. No tiles to worry about knocking loose and few chimneys to have a care for.

In a matter of moments and he was ahead, trying to figure the carriage's path. They should be heading toward one of the main gates if they were in fact leaving for one of the distant Baronies. Long time to travel, he'd have a chance to learn more and—

Carriage and escort turned toward the palace gates.

Guyik frowned, confused. Why that way? Unless they were getting more men? More supplies? He had to think now, to leap streets, and his travel was a bit trickier as the streets grew wealthier. More slate, true enough, and he had a care, but moved as swift as he could.

He was breathless when he found a place with a good view of the palace courtyard, before the carriage reached the gates. Aye, he could see more men and loaded wagons, and—

Guyik cursed and hid himself low on the roof.

Chained mages, three of them, and one that had to be the Guildmaster himself. What in the name of all the—

For a moment Guyik was distracted by movement above. A

window had opened in one of the towers. A woman stood there, staring down at the courtyard.

The guards were dismounting and blindfolding their horses up as the carriage holding Orval and his wife came into view. The carriage stopped and the horses pulling it were treated the same, for reasons Guyik couldn't figure.

The Guildmaster called something out, the other mages gestured, and a huge white circle appeared, a swirling mass of movement, like curtains moving in a wind that could not be felt.

A portal. He'd never seen one before, but it had to be. His thought was confirmed when the first soldiers led their horses through. followed by the goods wagons, and finally the carriage, with Captain Ussin bringing up the rear.

They were gone in an instant, plunging into the white and vanishing.

The Guildmaster called out again and the swirling circle collapsed in on itself.

And the token at Guyik's breast went silent.

## CHAPTER TWENTY-FIVE

Forever after, all Orval could remember of the start of that day was chaos.

Breakfast was water and bread, shoved into their hands first thing. They'd barely finished eating when they were hustled out of bed and told to dress; they could, the soldiers said to their protests, nurse on the road. Orval was fair certain none of these guards had children. Both Lara and Dalan were crying in their baskets before he and Amari had cleaned the babes and themselves and gotten dressed.

Carrying the babes in their baskets into the cold air, Orval had the impression that a crowd had gathered, but he was focused on getting down the damn steps without dropping Dalan. The cheering was startling but he had no chance to respond, for the guards kept them moving, almost lifting Orval and Dalan into the carriage. Amari and Lara followed and the door was shut firmly.

One bench was free, the other filled with boxes and crates below a mound of bundles and sacks, the whole surmounted by their noble robes piled on top.

Orval and Amari were still arranging themselves on the wooden bench, the babes between them, when he heard Winter arguing with Ussin just outside. The carriage door opened and Orval caught a glimpse of Winter's tear-stained face as Ussin thrust in a basket before practically slamming the door.

With the new basket at his feet, Orval grabbed for Dalan as the carriage lurched forward. Amari had Lara in her arms, trying to comfort her.

"What in the name of the Lord and Lady is the rush?" Amari said as they rattled along.

"More to the point, why are we heading toward the Palace?" Orval tried to soothe Dalan as he looked out the small window in the door. "Another audience, maybe?"

Amari was trying to undo her dress, trying to juggle Lara. "I hope she can latch on," she said.

"The horses can't keep this fast a pace forever," Orval said. "Here, let me take her, until you get settled."

With both babes in his arms, Orval scrunched his nose and pursed his lips, making kissing noises at them. Dalan stopped crying, staring with wide eyes. Lara wasn't fooled, her face scrunched up and fists flailing.

"Come, little one," Amari reached out and took her back. "Let's get some milk in that grumpy belly."

Orval rocked Dalan, peering out the window as streets and

people flashed by, noting the open palace gates as the carriage rumbled through and came to a halt. "Odd, what's the Mage Guildmaster doing here at this hour?"

"There's another carriage," Amari was looking out her side as Lara nursed.

"And another mage," Orval sucked in a breath as he saw the blindfolded horses. "Amari, I think–"

The carriage jerked forward and the world went white.

It lasted for seconds, the glare blazing inside his eyelids. Orval's stomach flipped and his ears popped. The air he managed to take in was cold as ice.

"Orval," Amari sounded shocked. Her eyes were wide, her brown skin ashen. "What was that?"

Both babes started screaming their heads off.

Orval cursed and placed Dalan in his basket. "Just a moment, little one," he said as he got to his feet, careful to keep his balance as he reached up and pulled down the furred cloaks. He glimpsed the outside world as he moved and nearly collapsed at the sight. "Look out the window," he said, almost gasping.

"The city is gone," Amari's voice held a note of sheer terror. "Orval, the city is gone! It's just fields of snow." She whipped her head around to look at him, clutching a crying Lara to her breast. "Cities don't just disappear."

"Amari, we need to think on the babes," Orval said, growing steadier as he focused on the tasks at hand. Your cloak's not enough in this cold, so let's get you wrapped up and Lara seen to."

It took some doing, but at last the furred cloak was wrapped around her from head to toe, even covering her legs and making a warm nest. "Looks like these damn things will be good for something," Orval said as he arranged his own nest and brought

Dalan into its shelter. "Sorry, my little man, but we menfolk have to look after our ladies first, you know." Orval curled his finger and offered the baby his knuckle. Dalan grabbed for it and mouthed the skin, making sucking sounds as he slobbered.

Better than wailing, Orval figured.

"What do you think happened?" Amari had calmed and Lara was sucking strongly.

"A portal," Orval said grimly. "A very expensive way to get somewhere quickly."

"All the faster to see us dead," she said.

"Perhaps," Orval said. "Most like, in fact."

"I'm frightened," Amari whispered, her eyes filling with tears.

"Really?" Orval asked. "Just frightened? Because I am ter-rified."

Her snort was more sob than laugh, but she smiled at him. Orval smiled back. "In truth, lady, I have no idea what to expect from the next hour. But this basket likely has some decent food, maybe a flask of kavage, if I know Winter. We have two babes to care for and ourselves to see to. We will deal with what comes far better if there's food in all our bellies." He reached his hand to her. "We are in this together," he said.

Amari nodded, clasping his hand. Her fingers were cold, but warmed swiftly. "Together," she said before releasing him.

Orval balanced Dalan and started to look through the basket.

"Do you suppose there is pease porridge?" Amari said, a light tease in her voice despite her tears.

"Why ever not?" Orval lifted his chin. "It's warm and filling and cheap, you know."

That time, her laughter wasn't feigned.

A few hours later, Orval had had enough.

The babes were sleeping well enough, but Amari was clearly uncomfortable and well she should be. Orval banged on the side of the carriage and yelled out the window for Ussin.

Ussin rode up, keeping pace with the carriage, with not much more than his eyes showing under his hat and scarves. He nodded when Orval made his request, then urged his horse forward, yelling orders. Wasn't long before the carriage was off the road and stopped.

"Thank the Lord and Lady," Amari said wearily.

Ussin ordered his men to keep their eyes peeled, swords and crossbows at the ready. Some were stomping out a flat area in the snow, for use as a privy. One guard had set up a small metal stove and started a fire in the base.

"You first," Orval said. "I'll stay with the babes." He grabbed her arm. "Don't wander far," he warned her.

Grim-faced, she nodded. When the door opened, she took Ussin's hand to climb down.

"Stay in sight," Ussin said gruffly. "I'll give ya as much privacy as I can, but be quick.

Amari nodded and went off alone in the direction he indicated.

"You want help?" Ussin asked, peering in without meeting Orval's eyes. "We're stopping long enough for a hot drink and to see to the horses. Might want to stretch yer legs while ya can."

Orval hesitated.

"They be well?" Ussin asked, nodding at the baskets with what looked like honest concern.

"They're sleeping," Orval said. "I'll step out, but not far. I want to hear them if they rouse." He winced as he went to stand;

the leg had stiffened up on him. Ussin made no move to aid but made no comment. He closed the door gently once Orval was on the ground. "Keep the heat in," he muttered.

Orval gave him a nod and took a moment to look around. Empty fields as far as he could see, with woods in the distance. The snow was deep and pristine, but the road seemed traveled. Behind him were wagons with what had to be their belongings. Their bed frame was strapped to the top of one, looking forlorn.

The warriors around him all seemed on edge, a wary eye on their surroundings even as they saw to themselves and their horses.

Amari came back, wrapping her cloak close. "All well?" she asked. Her eyes widened as she looked toward the front of the procession.

There was another carriage there, with two people emerging.

Following her gaze, Orval's jaw dropped. "Rosalind? Captain Roth?"

"Privy's there," Ussin pointed. "Stay alert," he roared and moved off, clearly wanting to avoid any talk. Roth helped Rosalind walk toward them.

"Lord High Baron," Rosalind said in greeting. She looked exhausted and cold.

"I rather think that we can skip the formalities," Orval said dryly, "given the circumstances."

"Aye." Roth's eyes flicked to the guards nearby.

"Come," Amari said to Rosalind, gently grasping the older woman's arm. The two of them walked off together.

"There's something you need to see, in our carriage," Roth said.

"Not 'til Amari returns," Orval said. "Our babes sleep within."

"Agreed," Roth pressed his hands into his armpits.

Orval leaned against the carriage, the cold starting to bite through his cloak. He took his turn at the privy once the women were done. When he returned, limping, Rosalind and Roth had retreated to stand by the lead carriage. They were looking at him with grim expressions.

"Lara and Dalan are still sleeping, praise be," Amari said. "But you need to go to Rosalind and Roth."

Orval limped over, careful to watch his footing in the snow. Roth opened the door and Orval looked in.

"Aunt Xydell?" He could hardly have been more surprised.

She was stretched out on a bench and covered by a heavy blanket. Orval struggled into the carriage and put his hand to her cold, pale face. "Is she dead?"

Rosalind had climbed in behind him. "A near thing," she whispered. "She fought them, you see, and they drugged her. Letheon, I suspect. Who knows when she will wake–"

"Or if," Orval growled.

"Hey there, what ya be doing?" came a cry.

Roth turned and Orval lunged for the door, fearing the worst. But Amari was also looking back at the wagons.

Two guards were tussling with a lad, yanking him from between some of the crates. They backed off fast when the boy drew knives and slashed at them.

"Yfin?" Roth roared and charged forward, which was when Orval realized that the man had no sword.

Ussin shouted an order and the guards pulled farther back.

Roth fell to his knees before the boy, who was blue and shaking with the cold. "Lord of the Sun, lad, what are you doing here?" He asked as he took the blades from the child's hands.

"Cap'n, I saw them grab ya and take ya," the boy gestured at Ussin. "An' the old lady bid me follow ya, said there's honor in your sword. So here I be."

Roth shook his head. "Lad, this isn't a good place for you. You—"

"He's here, he stays," Ussin barked, holding his hand out for the knives. "He'd not have a warm welcome if I took him back."

Roth handed the weapons to him and got to his feet, swinging his own cloak over the lad.

Ussin looked at the sky. "We needs get hot kavage in the men and finish up here quick like."

Orval stomped up to him as best he could given the footing, shivering with what he hoped was anger. Ussin stared at him in shock, but could not be half as shocked as Orval himself as he felt himself glaring at the man. "If you're going to kill us, do it now and spare us any more torture in that carriage."

Orval heard the others exclaim with half an ear; he was focused on Ussin, who seemed honestly horrified.

"What?" Ussin gaped as every one of his men watched. "No! Those are not my orders."

"Do I see supplies in those carts? Do I see a contingent of guards under Captain Roth's command?" Orval demanded. "I don't. We are being sent to our deaths."

"There are supplies," Ussin said weakly, spreading his hands wide.

"Doubtful. So if you are going to kill us, do it now." Orval crossed his arms over his chest.

"None of that," Ussin growled, his face reddening. "My orders are to deliver you all to the Keep of the Black Hills and return to Edenrich." But we needs be back to where we arrived, for when the portal opens," Ussin looked about, "to get my men safe home.

"There's no welcome here for us," he said, scanning the horizon. Then he caught himself and gave a big, false grin. "You'll be fine, once we get you to the Keep. So hurry up with that," he yelled at the soldier tending the stove. The water was boiling.

The guards all turned back to their tasks as Ussin stomped off between the carriages.

Orval huffed a breath as Amari came up behind him, pressing her shoulder to his. "Orval," she whispered, and he heard horror and fear in her voice.

"Sorry," he put his head toward hers.

"Kavage," Roth said as he thrust a rough clay mug at Amari.

"Wait," Rosalind reached over and took the mug before Amari could. She smelled the mug, took a sip, then nodded and handed it back to Amari.

"The men are drinking," Orval said. "Ussin wouldn't poison his own men."

"Satia would," Rosalind said quietly as she, Roth, and Yfin drank.

The pit in Orval's stomach grew even as he gulped down his own kavage. His fear rose but he fought it down. "We would be warmer with us all together," he said loudly. "And we could keep an eye on my Aunt."

"Good idea," Roth agreed. "I'll fetch her."

It wasn't that easy, of course, but thankfully Ussin agreed with Orval's decision. The guards help shift the boxes and Roth carried Xydell over, still wrapped in her blankets.

Orval stood and watched, knowing he'd be more hindrance than help. Amari was directing the guards and keeping them away from the babes.

Ussin came up beside Orval and stood beside him in awkward silence, shifting his weight from foot to foot. In the past, Orval might have said something to ease the man, but he remembered the fear in Amari's eyes.

Ussin broke first. "Not that much longer now," he muttered. "A few hours at most."

Orval drew in air and let it out slowly, watching as his breath formed a cloud in the cold.

"You can see it there." Ussin pointed. "Just the towers, on the horizon."

The carriages were ready. Orval left Ussin standing there as he walked to his place.

Just before he climbed in, Orval turned to look where Ussin had pointed. He could just make out the tops of the towers against the glare of the snow.

The Keep of the Black Hills.

## CHAPTER TWENTY-SIX

The carriage started with a lurch, jerking Orval almost from his seat. He and Roth both braced Aunt Xydell, propped between them on the bench. Amari, Rosalind, and the babes had the opposite bench. Yfin was on the floor between all their knees. One fur cape wrapped around them all, the other draped over their laps, almost burying the boy.

"Safe to talk now," Roth said as the carriage rumbled on.

"What did they do to her?" Orval took his Aunt's cold hands in his own and tried to warm them. She wasn't his favorite person, but to see her so frail–

"They came for her last night, before the audience. I was drawn to the ruckus, for she put up quite a fuss. She fought them," Rosalind said, a tinge of admiration in her voice. "Gave them what-for with her cane, hollering at the top of her lungs."

Orval snorted. "Not surprised by that."

"I tried to stop them," Rosalind continued. "But all they said was 'Queen's command'. They got the cane away from her and poured something down her throat. It had to be letheon." Rosalind took a deep breath. "They hauled her off and fool that I am, I followed, protesting, and found myself locked in with her and informed that I now had the 'honor' of being your Steward." Her voice grew bitter. "Queen's command."

"Bastards, to treat you so," Orval shifted so that Aunt Xydell's head sagged on his shoulder. He tucked her cold hands under the fur, seeing bruises on her wrists.

"Much the same for me," Roth said. "Although it was my own men."

"Not all," Yfin piped up, a great grin on his face.

"Not all," Roth agreed and gave Orval a wry look. "My youngest recruit, it appears."

The boy just kept grinning, the edge of the cloak just over his head.

"And what are you grinning for?" Roth asked.

"Warmer now than I was," Yfin said cheerfully. "And with ya."

Roth shook his head. "Not sure that was the smartest choice, lad."

"Old lady said–" Yfin protested but Roth cut him short.

"Queen Mother Tithanna said you should be trained by me, not follow me to some gods-forsaken wilderness." Roth said dryly.

"Tithanna?" Orval asked.

"Aye," Roth looked down at his hands. "We were the last to see her, before–" he stopped and swallowed hard.

"She didn't–" Orval started but Roth was quick.

"She didn't," Roth said. "Don't give it another thought. She was defiant and intended to endure. That she didn't has to be laid to another's hand." Roth rubbed his face. "And to me, for not protecting her."

"She gave you orders," Rosalind pointed out. "And who would have thought … ." her voice trailed off and they all sat in silence for a moment. "They didn't even give her the rites, just said a few prayers as they shoved the coffin into the crypt."

Orval cleared his throat. "Queen Tithanna was a true Daughter of Xy, for all that she was of House Wyvern."

"She told me, she did, to follow him." Yfin said. "His sword has honor, she said." He lifted his chin with youthful defiance. "So I did."

"Such loyalty should be rewarded," Amari said warmly. She reached overhead and produced Winter's basket. "Here."

"Ooh," Yfin said as he dug in, then held up and offered about what was left of their breakfast. Orval was impressed that the lad was willing to share, though he was clearly hungry.

Roth waved the food off and shrugged when Orval caught his eye. "I was informed I was promoted to your Weaponsmaster," Roth said. "Stripped of my own weapons and held secure until I was escorted out to the carriage."

"Better than disappearing." Rosalind said bitterly. They lapsed into silent despair, for what was there to say?

Orval leaned back, shifting so that Aunt Xydell seemed a bit more comfortable. He was just as glad she slept. She'd be sure to have cutting words for all of them, and he didn't want to hear that. But then shame replaced the relief.

He caught a glimpse of Amari, gently smiling at Yfin, watching him eat.

Orval's heart clenched.

He'd failed Amari.

He dropped his gaze down to the stupid cape and plucked at the fur lining. He'd promised her, assured her, and he'd failed to keep her and the babes safe. *Over by the next feeding*, he'd said, so smugly that the memory made him sick.

His eyes fell to the baskets where his babes slept. The weight of his failure settled in his chest. He'd failed them as well, although there was still a chance one of the marcusi would appear. It would just take time. Hopefully not more than they had.

A burbling noise came from Lara's basket. Amari leaned over, cooing at the restless babe.

Orval quirked his mouth, thinking of the *Epic of Xyson* tucked under Lara's little tush. They'd missed that, hadn't they?

What else might they have missed?

Amari nudged his foot with hers and gave him a questioning look. She glanced down at his leg and back up. Orval grimaced and shrugged. It wasn't bad yet, but it would make him pay later.

Her expression shifted to a lovely look of gentle concern. Orval's heart lurched again at the danger he'd placed them in.

He pressed his lips tight as he hardened his resolve. This was Satia's doing, not Xyrath's. He knew Xyrath well enough from their fostering days. He'd always been obnoxious, even as a youth, filled with a sense of his own importance. A rotter, true enough, but a straightforward one. More likely to punch you in the face then stab you in the back.

But Satia was an unknown, something of a mystery. Satia was sly and cunning and about as trustworthy as … a wyvern. Why had she decided Orval was a threat? How in the name of all the elements could a poor scholar be dangerous?

A quote from the *Epic* came to mind. *Beware the learned ones, for not all warriors wield steel.*

Orval spoke before his idea was fully formed. "We need a plan," he said.

"Eh?" Roth looked at him.

"When going into enemy territory, you need knowledge of what lies ahead before you establish camp. Then you see to your warriors needs. 'Shelter, water, fire, food'," Orval recited.

"Where did you learn that? You never had a command, did you?" Roth asked, eyebrows jumping up in surprise.

"The *Epic of Xyson*," Orval said. "There's also a chapter on proper privy placement," he added dryly.

Roth snorted out a chuckle even as Yfin squinched up his nose.

"So, what do we know?" Orval repeated.

"Hmm," Roth mused, rubbing his face with his left hand. "Well, the Barony of the Black Hills rebelled fairly early during Xykahn's reign when the Lord High Baron died suddenly. Around the time that Xywellan was born, if I remember correctly." Roth crossed his arms over his chest. "There were a series of High Lord Barons appointed to bring the region under control with military force. It didn't go well." Roth gave Orval a grim smile. "It was said that any assigned the post of Lord High Baron of the Black Hills was lost before he left the gates of the palace."

Amari sucked in a breath, shaking her head. "All I know is something that Xywellan said once, in the battle camp. He and Kara were talking about the Black Hills." Amari lifted a hand to smooth back her hair. "Xywellan said, 'whatever you do, don't mention it to Dell.'"

"What did Kara say to that?" Orval asked.

"Queen Kara just rolled her eyes and they both chuckled."

"Xydell?" Orval asked.

Amari shrugged apologetically. "I didn't pay too much attention, since I was tending to Dalan."

"The people of the Black Hills have a reputation for being hard and stubborn. They are miners and stone workers, digging for black rock, gems, and marble. They have no love of Xy, Arion or Wyvern. Xywellan and Kara were going to take action to bring the Barony back under the control of the Crown, but the Blood conflict arose, and, well …" Roth shrugged.

"Their forces were stretched thin," Rosalind offered. "They barely held their army together as it was; they couldn't afford to send more warriors to the Black Hills, even if there was a potential for taxes and tithes from the mining charters." She dropped her eyes at their astonished looks. "There is was very little gossip I don't—didn't—hear."

Roth nodded. "There's been no royal presence out here for at least five years. Rebels took the Keep, then the Blood besieged it and reclaimed it. When the Airion forces were pulled back, they left the Keep a ruin. Of no use to the rebels or any others."

"So they may be taking us to a ruined Keep, dumping our 'supplies,' and turning tail to race back to the portal," Orval said. "What can we do to about that?"

Yfin piped up, his mouth full of bread. "I can scout."

"Don't talk with your mouth full," Amari admonished.

That brought chuckles all around, but it also broke the logjam. Ideas spilled out as they talked and discussed and argued.

"Now," Orval said after a time, "let's flip it around. What if there are people in the Keep? What then?"

"Our goals are the same," Roth said. "Shelter, water, fire, food.'" Until we know their intentions towards us."

Orval nodded. "We act as if they are allies until we know different."

They tossed more ideas at one another until Yfin's face cracked open with a huge yawn.

"Boy's got a point," Roth said, moving the cape so he could look out the small window. "Nothing but fields ahead. Might be able to catch a bit of rest before we arrive."

Yfin was already curling up, head down, his hair spilling over his eyes. Amari settled into her corner after checking the babes.

"Here, let me," Roth eased Xydell on to his shoulder. "Take a rest." he said, digging into a pocket and pulling out a loop of string. Orval raised his eyebrows.

Roth huffed. "Old habit. Cat's cradle. Keeps my fingers warm."

Orval nodded, settled back, watching the man's fingers flick through string patterns, trying to think, to plan, to … sleep claimed him quickly.

---•---

Sleep? Rosalind almost shook her head in disbelief; years of training kept her still. How could she sleep? Her heart was racing hard and fast, threatening to leap out of her chest. She'd been torn away from everything she'd known, everything she had worked for. Her keys, the badge of her office, ripped from her belt. She closed her eyes as shame washed over her.

All of her years of royal service, all her work, all her pride of place, gone.

The only thing keeping her from weeping was the quiet strength of the others. They were thinking, planning, not trembling inside.

She flushed, hot and embarrassed. She'd thrown herself at the guards, begged to be reinstated, forgiven. The Bondmaiden had smirked at her tears as she'd taken the keys.

Rosalind felt useless. Nothing in her life had prepared her for this. She'd been raised to serve the royal family; what did she know of war camps? She'd never heard of anything good coming from the Black Hills.

She knew the running of a large household, the standards that things were to be kept to. The history of the palace and its contents. Her passion for the ancient tapestries, their care and preservation: what good was that now?

Orval's leg shifted slightly, and Amari shifted to make room for him, neither opening their eyes. Whatever the circumstances of their marriage—and there had been quite a bit of speculation about that at Court, hadn't there—it was clear they had a bond.

Roth was concentrating on his string patterns, occasionally glancing out the carriage window. Rosalind knew that the patterns had names and stories, but she'd never seen someone so proficient. She'd have to ask him about that later.

Lara fussed in her sleep, yawning and blowing bubbles.

Rosalind gently reached in and stroked the babe's cheek. Such a precious thing, with that shock of black hair that looked like it would be curly.

Lara yawned again and opened her eyes. Fey blue eyes.

Xywellan's eyes.

Rosalind sucked in a breath, frozen in discovery as the pieces of a puzzle clicked together in her mind.

Lara was Xywellan and Kara's daughter.

No, it couldn't be. But her brain was ticking through the gossip, the rumors, as everything fell into place. Amari's shame, Orval's loyalty … .

*"I didn't pay too much attention, since I was tending to Dalan."*

Dalan, fast asleep in his basket, was so much bigger than … .

They weren't twins.

Shocked, Rosalind opened her mouth, the words on the tip of her tongue, then froze. The more people that know a secret means it's no longer a secret.

Lara had fallen back to sleep, her sweet cheek pressed to Rosalind's fingers. Questions raged through her as she watched the precious babe sleep. How had this royal child, heir to the throne, been trusted to a cripple?

Desperation. Queen Kara could only have done this out of desperation and terror.

Which meant it fell to her, Rosalind, to see to the child's welfare.

Awe washed over her. It must be so. She was meant to be *here*, to serve, to protect, to preserve. A new purpose filled her.

"My hand to yours," Rosalind whispered with barest breath. "Bless you, Xylara, Daughter of the House of Xy, Daughter of Xywellan and Kara, Warrior Queen."

Lara blew a bubble of spit.

Rosalind took a calm, steady breath. A new Queen to serve. Her resolve eased her heart. Yes, it would be hard, maybe the hardest thing she'd ever done.

Still and all, she would do it.

Rosalind relaxed into her corner as best she could and closed her eyes, holding fast to her newfound peace.

And courage.

---

Orval startled out of sleep, not sure what had roused him.

Roth was at the small window, pulling back the fabric. "We're slowing," he glanced at Orval.

"The Keep?" Orval rubbed his face as the others roused as well.

"No," Roth said. "A village, maybe? Hard to tell at this angle."

Orval shifted, trying to look out his window, but all he could see were a few outbuildings. The Keep was still in the distance, but much closer now. He leaned forward, straining to see.

The carriage jolted along the road.

"A stop, perhaps?" Amari asked as she covered a yawn.

"Hard to say," Orval frowned. "Do you think they sent word of our arrival?"

"Unlikely," Roth said. "Why give the rebels a chance to gather? I doubt they know who we are."

The carriage rumbled on with their escort moving up to surround it. Orval watched as a wooden palisade appeared. A village then, to have such stout walls. The road appeared to run past, but they pulled to a halt before the main gates.

Ussin's voice rang out, loud enough to be heard by all.

"Hear ye, hear ye, unto the Town of Wareington," the Captain shouted. "By the Royal Decree of King Xyrath and Queen Satia, Lord High Baron Orval of the House of Xy and Lady High Baroness Amari, his lawful wife, have been appointed to the Barony of the Black Hills, to have and hold these lands at their gracious Majesty's pleasure." Ussin's voice seemed to echo through the carriage. Aunt Xydell stirred but didn't wake.

Ussin dismounted and approached the gate with a scroll in his hands.

"The Lord High Baron and Lady High Baroness are here to take residency of the Keep immediately. Prepare to pay thy respects and tithes in the coming days," Ussin boomed out. "So sayeth King Xyrath and Queen Satia, by their order, command, and decree."

With that, he let the scroll open with a flourish, and nailed it to the door with a dagger.

"On," Ussin called as spun on his heel and mounted his horse. "To the Keep of the Black Hills."

The carriage lurched forward.

"Well, if they didn't know before," Orval said, "they know now."

# CHAPTER TWENTY-SEVEN

A mari's stomach had finally adjusted to the rocking of the carriage, though she much preferred to ride a horse on a long journey. But after they left the village, they were in rolling hills, and her queasiness grew again.

"We're getting close," Orval said softly, as he started to pull the velvet capes away from the carriage windows.

Amari sucked in a breath of the cold dry air that spilled inside. It helped somewhat. At least it got her mind off her discomfort. Orval and Roth both peered out, trying to get a glimpse of the Keep ahead. All she could see was the afternoon sun glittering on the snowy hills they passed.

Drawing her attention back inside the carriage, Amari studied

Orval for a long moment. As close confined as they had been these last weeks, there was still much she didn't know about him. Did he prefer a carriage to a horse? Could he ride? She knew that if he didn't take care, his leg would pain him in the night. There hadn't been time to really know him, and yet–

He caught her staring and raised an eyebrow.

"What can you see?" she asked, dropping her gaze to check the babes and hoping the flush on her cheeks didn't show. Dalan and Lara were both still sleeping, thank the Harmony. She covered their baskets so the cold wouldn't reach their faces. They'd need nursing when they woke and she didn't want them to rouse any sooner than they must.

"Not much yet," Orval answered. "Roth?"

Roth had his head at an angle. "No banners or flags, and I don't see anyone on the walls."

Orval stared out his side. "What walls?"

Roth's head jerked, but Xydell was leaning on his shoulder so he couldn't shift to look our the other window. "What do you see?" he demanded.

"There's a huge breach in the wall on this side," Orval said.

Yfin stirred then, shifting the capes around and scrambling to his knees between their feet to share Orval's view. "There's stone everywhere," he marveled.

"Old?" Roth asked.

"Hard to say," Orval replied. "Covered in snow, and quite a jumble."

"I could get over it," Yfin said.

"So, no effort to block or repair the hole," Roth said.

"No smoke, no fires," Orval noted. "It's cold enough that there should be fires burning." He looked at Amari and grimaced.

"If they used catapults to bring down the walls, the gatehouse might still be intact." Roth peered out his side again. "Our best hope, at least."

"Why?" Amari asked.

"Smaller rooms, secured access," Rosalind said. She gave Amari a half-smile as she shrugged at her surprise. "Castles that have been overrun need repairs. Walls are easier than structures."

"Listen," Orval commanded.

Amari held her breath as they all obeyed, listening to the thudding of hooves and the creaking of the carriage.

After a moment, Orval shook his head. "No horns, no hails. It's deserted."

Roth grunted. "Hopefully."

Orval put a hand on Yfin's shoulder. "Yfin, you know the plan?"

Yfin nodded, squatting on his knees. "Run out, quick as I can. Check the main courtyard. Look for wells and buildings, not too far away." He drew a breath and recited. "Don't go in anywhere, just look all around and then report to the Captain."

"Good lad," Orval grinned at him.

"I'll take the gatehouse first," Roth said. "Check it as quick as I can. If it can be secured … ." He looked at Rosalind.

"I'll direct the guards where to put things," the woman said. "There should be enough room on the upper floors. And don't forget, there may be a cellar with a well for water in a siege. Check for that too."

Both Roth and Yfin nodded, but the boy's face was more serious. "I'll check the cover too. Make sure the babes can't crawl in."

Amari's heart lifted and she smiled. "It will be a while before that's a worry," she said.

"Still and all," Yfin looked at the baskets with a frown, avoiding Amari's gaze. Roth caught her eye and shook his head. Amari nodded back and changed the subject.

"I'm to stay with the babes and Xydell," she said, "until you can get us somewhere safe."

"I think we're almost to the gates," Orval announced; he had been keeping watch.

"Help me fold up the robes and get them out of our way," Amari said. The adults all helped shift and roll the velvet and furs into a large bundle while ensuring that Xydell remained wrapped well against the cold.

Amari worried for her. She didn't know much more healing than what one learned caring for children, but it couldn't be good for someone Xydell's age to be unconscious for so long.

The carriage rolled to a stop, followed by the creak of wood and the rattle of chain. "Sally-port, most like," Roth noted.

The carriage rolled through the gate; Ussin's voice echoed around them, as he shouted: "Keep an eye on those ruins. Watch for any movement. You two, keep watch on the road."

The carriage door swung open.

"Lord High Baron," Ussin began, then shouted "hey" as Yfin sprung out the door and pushed past him.

"Boy needed air, being cooped up," Roth said calmly, moving even as Ussin sputtered a protest. "Shall we check the gatehouse?" He stepped down and offered a hand to Rosalind, who managed to look graceful as she scrambled to follow.

Orval grimaced as he struggled to stand. Amari leaned forward, reaching for him, and he took her hand. He glanced out the door as he got his balance, wrapping her hand in his long, warm fingers. "I could see if Ussin would take you and the babes back with him," he offered quietly. " I think it's eating at him.

If I begged–"

"No," Amari held tight to him. "Our place is with you. We are far safer with you than in Satia's hands."

Orval nodded, gripping her just as tightly. "Keep the token close," he whispered before ducking out after Roth. "Don't even think of leaving those crates there," he shouted. "Ussin, what is the meaning of this?"

He closed the door behind him, blocking the chill. Amari pulled her hand under her cloak and pressed her hand to her chest, missing his warmth. She drew a long, steadying breath as she listened to the shouts outside, and the horses stamping, their harnesses ringing as Orval and Ussin argued.

Dalan shifted in his swaddling and started to stir.

"Roth?" Orval demanded.

"Gatehouse can be secured," came a distant shout.

"Very well," Orval snapped. "Get your men to carry these crates and supplies in, quick like. Form a line and *move*."

Amari blinked at his tone, so sure and commanding.

"You heard the Lord High Baron," Ussin bellowed. The pressure in Amari's chest eased slightly. It had worked, Orval had won the day. A tiny triumph, but a triumph just the same.

The carriage door opened and Orval stuck his head in. "Have they roused?"

"Almost," Amari said.

"Let's get you inside, then." Orval grimaced. "Cold and damp, but we can tuck you in a corner so you can nurse." He looked at Xydell, who hadn't once stirred. "Maybe Ussin will forget she's in here?" he gave Amari a sly look. "Take her back with him?"

He was making light of it, but Amari wasn't fooled. That little crease in his forehead told her that. "How bad is it?" she whispered.

"Not so bad. Cold and," Orval looked away and swallowed hard, "empty."

A memory of their old rooms filled her: cluttered shelves, glowing copper lamps, and the warmth of home. "We will fill it," she whispered, and watched as his eyes went damp and his resolve returned.

He reached for Lara's basket. Amari took up Dalan and accepted Orval's help exiting the carriage. She got a brief glimpse of the snowy courtyard before she followed Orval through a heavy wooden door into the gatehouse. The guards stepped back to let her in.

The stone room was very large and very empty and very cold, with a dusty, unused smell. The only light came from the open door. There was a small stool by the cold hearth; Orval moved it to tuck her into a corner, out of the way.

"Best we can do for now," he said, setting Lara's basket on the floor.

"It's fine," she said. The stool rocked on its four legs as she settled in place but seemed sturdy enough.

"All right, then," he said, and turned back to the guards. "Don't just stand there," he snapped. "There's more to unload and we need to get the furniture inside."

Amari set Dalan's basket down and undid her lacings as Orval harangued the guards. Dalan's eyes were wide open and he latched on quickly, sucking greedily. He was warm against her skin and the familiar tug on her nipple was reassuring. No matter what, babies needed to be fed … she wrinkled her nose … and changed.

"Orval, I'll need that sack of nappies," she said.

Orval nodded and squeezed through the door as the guards brought in more sacks and crates. He returned quickly, cheeks red with the cold, followed by men carrying their familiar, old kitchen table and chairs.

"Those can stay here," Orval ordered as he put the bag of nappies next to her. "Put it against the wall with the chairs in front. The rest can go up to the third floor."

Other things were being brought in, things Amari didn't recognize. She looked questioningly at Orval.

"They're from the storage room," he said softly. "My sister's things." There was a flash of pain on his face but he went out the door before she could say anything.

She looked down at Dalan, but his eyes were closed again, his tiny hands curled in pleasure. She rocked a bit on the stool, probably more for her own reassurance than his.

A rattle startled her as pebbles bounced out of the chimney. She stared at the small stones scattered on the kitchen floor.

The pounding of feet on stairs was followed by Yfin bursting into the room, his hair in his eyes, a grin on his face. "They came down?" He crowed when he saw the stones on the floor, then ran over to peer up into the fireplace.

Amari nodded.

"It's clear, then," he reported as he dodged the guards to pick up the stones, his words tumbling out breathlessly. "There's privies on every floor," Yfin blinked at her in wonder. "And outside there's a dovecote, with lots of pigeons. My ma made a real good pigeon pie. And one of the barn cats let me pet its head." He laughed. "It's kinda an ugly cat." He glanced at the hearth. "Cap'n said if the fireplace was clear, we could start a fire."

Amari opened her mouth to protest; there were rituals and prayers for a first fire in a hearth. But Yfin had already darted off again, deeper into the building.

She hugged Dalan and sighed. Not what she had imagined for her first hearth. Sorrow rose in her chest and she fought it down. Given all that had happened, she should thank the Ancestors that she and hers weren't dead in a ditch and beg forgiveness for her ingratitude. Still, the ceremonies were important. She could pray, silently, and sweep the hearth before they laid the fire. As to the water, she could–

"Here," Yfin burst back in the room, all youthful, awkward eagerness. "I brought you this."

There in his hand was a bucket, brimming with water, yet not a drop spilling.

As good an omen for a new hearth as any could ask.

"There's a well below," he grinned as he put the bucket beside her, on the hearthstone. "It's got a good cover too, one with a latch."

Amari smiled up at him as he stood bouncing on his toes. "We'll need firewood," she said. "To start our first fire."

Yfin flew out the door, causing at least one guard to curse him as he plunged through them.

*"A hearth heals in its own way,"* one of her aunties used to say. Amari took a breath and breathed out a small prayer of thanks.

Roth stuck his head in the door. "They're almost done," he said. "Just a few more things. I'll get Xydell."

"Make sure we have those capes," Amari said. "They'll make fine bedding, if nothing else."

Roth gave her a funny look, bowed his head, and disappeared back outside.

"No, take that back downstairs." Rosalind's voice floated down from above. A moment later, she entered the kitchen from the stairs, followed by two guardsman holding a large, wooden box. "It can't be that heavy," she scolded them as they put their burden on the table and fled outside.

"I found some dishware and some foodstuffs they must have grabbed off your shelves," Rosalind continued. Rummaging in the box, she pulled out a crumpled piece of paper with the symbol of the Harmony on it. "I have no idea what this is," she said, studying it.

"I do," Amari said reaching out, her heart lifting.

———•———

Orval watched as the guardsmen struggled to get the last bits out of the wagon, rolls of carpet and a few more sacks of what looked like bedding.

Ussin came to stand next to him. "Got my orders, don't ya know. Need to see to my men. Can't miss that portal."

Orval stayed silent.

More guards came to help with the heavy rugs while others were seeing to their horses and mounting up.

One of the guards heaved up a large sack that clanked. Ussin took a step forward and said, "Here, you, take this'n to Cap'n Roth." The soldier nodded, a quick jerk of his head.

"Roth's weapons," Ussin said gruffly, avoiding Orval's eye. "And the boy's knives."

Orval said nothing. If Ussin was uncomfortable, so be it.

Ussin cleared his throat. "Here's your Letters Patent granting you the Barony of the Black Hills," he said, shoving a heavy scroll at Orval; it dripped with red wax seals and ribbons. "Along with a list of expected tithes," another scroll, "including a piece of pure white marble large enough for a life-sized statue of King Xyrath." Ussin reached into the wagon and produced a cage filled with pigeons. "Send word when the King can expect delivery."

Orval stared at him incredulously. "Xyrath really expects–"

A shriek of horror came from inside the gatehouse. "The tapestries?"

The guards scrambled for their mounts.

"Sun's light be with you," Ussin said over his shoulder as he headed toward his own horse. With sharp commands, the men, carriages, and wagons were gone in a flurry.

Orval just stood there, scrolls in one arm, cage in the other, watching them vanish through the main gates and down the road. The pigeons in the cage fluttered and made grunting sounds at their rough treatment.

So that was that. They were on their own, abandoned and betrayed. Yes, they'd secured themselves as best they could, but it seemed a hollow victory.

He looked up, over the walls of the Keep, to the mountains that loomed over them. The sun etched sharp shadows on their face, making the scene feel ominous and threatening.

The wind picked up and he shivered, feeling the ache in his leg. He'd have pain tonight, sure as anything. He was used to that. But the pit in his chest was new, wide and deep, with no remedy.

An outburst from the open gatehouse door drew his attention. He gathered himself and limped in, dreading the others' anger and despair.

A fire in the hearth made the room glow. Rosalind was sitting on the rolls of fabric that were not carpets, it seemed, but tapestries, her face buried in her hands.

She lifted her face, covered in tears and …laughter. Yfin giggled by the hearth, and Roth was struggling not to laugh out loud as they built the fire up.

"What?" Orval moved further inside, totally confused. Roth shifted to close the door behind him.

Amari was by the table, her face glowing with merriment, tears in the corners of her eyes.

She gestured to the crate on the table.

Orval limped over and peered in, and his own laughter bubbled up in his chest, releasing tension and fears he'd trapped there.

They'd packed the pot of pease porridge.

# CHAPTER TWENTY-EIGHT

—◦—

Caris balanced the breakfast tray and opened the door to the Queen's chambers.

"So, our new Lord and Lady High Barons have left?" Satia asked from her bed, a mound of pristine white pillows at her back, perfect, regal, serene, and clearly gloating.

The morning sun spilled into the room, setting the red and gold carpet alight.

"Yes, Bonded." Caris settled the breakfast tray by the bed, checking to make sure that steam was still rising from the oats. "Early this morning."

Satia smoothed the crisp, white sheets and coverlet over her belly. Her brown skin and black hair glowed against the field of white and she knew it. "And his books?"

"Secured," Avice said. "Every scroll, every piece of paper. I will see to the delivery to the library myself, and watch them boxed and sealed and placed into storage."

Satia tilted her head. "And my little surprise?" she inquired, raising an eyebrow at Avice.

"As you commanded, I had the tapestries loaded into the wagon. The guards have instructions to see that they are the last things dumped on the ground." Avice was heating water by the fire.

Much to Caris's relief, Satia slowly smiled with clear pleasure. Gloating always put the Bonded in a good mood. Caris rattled the tray a bit, drawing her attention, and lifted the honey jar. She let the dipper hover over the top of the jar and raised her own eyebrow.

Satia gave a nod. Caris let the sweet syrup drip down on the oats as she watched. "More," Satia demanded.

Mira opened her mouth as if to protest, but Caris gave her a warning look as she let the sweet honey flow until there was enough covering the oats to make her own teeth ache.

"Just a few nuts," Satia commanded.

Caris put the honey down, and sprinkled nuts from a jar.

"I'll pour the cream," Satia said. Caris bowed her head and put the tray on Satia's bulging stomach, propped with pillows on both sides. She stood close, with clean napkins, just in case.

"Question Captain Ussin when he returns." Satia swirled her spoon in the grains, mixing it with just a dab of cream. "I want to know how she reacted."

"Of course, Bonded," Avice replied.

Satia put the spoon in her mouth and closed her eyes in pleasure. Her contentment radiated down Caris's bond. Perhaps today would be a good day after all.

She glanced around the room, careful not to let Satia see that her focus was elsewhere. The fire was crackling in the hearth with just the right amount of heat. Nora and Mira were putting the Bonded's clean clothes in the wardrobe, folding them precisely as she liked. All was well.

"What of our guest?" Satia asked, swirling in more cream.

"We have him safe. He is not conscious yet," Avice said. She placed the Bonded's slippers and robe by the fire to warm "It might be another day or two."

"Or more," Mira added softly. "If he is in fact addicted to letheon, he may be semi-conscious for weeks."

Satia frowned, staring at her bowl. "I am supposed to enter into subtle negotiations with a powerful blood mage to conduct the ancient family ritual for this babe, and I have to deal with a drug-addled, puking fool?"

The question was rhetorical, they all knew better than to answer.

"Still," she narrowed her eyes. "I have a blood mage. It is a start."

Avice opened her mouth, no doubt to remind the Bonded that they weren't certain that the man was a blood mage. Caris gave her an incredulous look. Avice pressed her lips shut.

Satia slowly swirled the spoon, then scooped up more oats, catching any dribbles on the side of the bowl. She ate a few more bites, her mouth curving upwards in clear enjoyment. "And the midwife you are all forcing on me?" she asked softly.

"She should be attending your majesty later today," Mira said. "One of the women under her care went into the labor early, and that has delayed her."

"Hmph," Satia scraped her spoon on the bowl, sucking up

the last of the sweetness.

Pounding footsteps from the outer chamber. "*Satia! Where is my queen?*" rang out in glorious royal tones.

Caris whipped the tray down and under the bed. The others all donned worried looks as Satia sank down in the bed, looking pale and frail. Avice pulled the curtains closed just as the door burst open and the King strode in with a flair.

"A triumph!" Xyrath paused in the door, clearly coming from the practice ring. His quilted sparring jacket was stained with sweat and dirt, but his tanned face glowed, every golden hair was in place, and his smile rivaled the sun itself. "We should hold a triumph!"

He paused in to doorway, blinking in the dimness. "Oh, beloved, did you not have a good night?" He frowned at the women around Satia as if it was their fault.

"I'm fine," Satia said weakly. "Come, my beloved. Sit here."

Caris bowed herself back and retreated as Xyrath bounded over and seated himself on the edge of the bed, spreading his filth over floor and bedding.

"A triumph," he crowed as he settled down, taking Satia's hand in his. "We will declare a holiday and I will lead my men marching through the streets, crowds cheering, like in ancient times, dragging our prisoners in chains, all through the town."

"You didn't take any prisoners," Satia sighed and smiled wearily. "You released them to their homes." Her eyes narrowed. "With their weapons and armor. Remember?"

"Oh," Xyrath frowned, then smiled wryly. "Ah, well. It wouldn't be nearly as much fun without prisoners." He kissed Satia's hand. "Did you see the portal this morning? We saw it from the practice yard. Awesome, all swirly white. Took four mages to cast. Pretty impressive."

"And cost a pretty penny," Satia grumbled, but that satisfied look was back on her face. "But worth it. Lord High Baron Orval will be all the quicker sending you your marble."

Caris resisted the urge to laugh. The Bonded look so smug.

"When we start our conquest of the outlying baronies, mayhap we could use those portals." Xyrath laughed. "Think of how glorious it would be to emerge from that swirly white circle, me in my gold armor, on a white steed."

"Worthy of you, my King." Satia smiled wanly.

"My precious girl," Xyrath leaned forward to cup Satia's cheek. "Do you think you will be available for audiences this afternoon? Lord Marshal Tarwain is especially insistent on speaking with you. He wants decisions on land grants. I told him that I'd make no final decisions without your advice."

"I will try," Satia sighed. "I just need a bit more rest, my King. I am tired." She cradled her belly, rubbing the mound.

"My poor dearest, bearing the light of the world. I'll leave you to get some rest." Xyrath rose to his feet, heedless of the long smudge of dirt he left on the coverlet. "I'll have a word with Tarwain, remind him that your health is everything."

Satia smiled up at him. "You take such good care of me," she said, holding out her hand.

Xyrath took it gently and kissed it. "Did I tell you that the Master Sculptor Muris has offered to do the initial sketches for my statue?" Xyrath straightened and puffed out his chest. "Nude, of course, with a crown of laurel, to celebrate our ascent to the throne."

"I only hope he can capture your likeness perfectly," Satia dropped her eyes to his groin.

Xyrath let out a hearty laugh.

Satia tilted her head. "Did he happen to mention a cost for his work?"

"Cost?" Xyrath scoffed. "Oh, I am sure he will do it just for the glory of being the Royal Sculptor."

"Of course," Satia said.

Xyrath bowed to her. "Until later, my Queen." He strode out, raking his fingers through his hair. "No triumph, lads," he bellowed to the entourage waiting. "Let's hit the baths."

As soon as the door closed, Caris stepped forward and started to roll back the filthy coverlet. Mira pulled another one out of the cupboard, smelling of sunshine and fresh from the laundry.

Mira reached to plump the pillows up behind Satia as Avice reopened the curtains.

"Everyone has a hand out," Satia murmured as she stared at the door. "All reaching, grasping, clutching, seeking power and riches."

Caris removed the filthy coverlet. "So all do, Bonded," she murmured in response.

"Tarwain is becoming an issue." Satia held out her hands to Avice, who wiped them carefully with a warm, wet cloth. "He whines about that daughter of his and presses for more power and a barony. No patience in that man." Satia nodded to Avice, who started to dry her hands with a warm cloth.

"I told him that he can move on the Black Hills once the Lord High Baron Orval is killed by the rebels, but he wants everything this instant. Men. Don't they realize that planning is all? And success, the reward of carefully thinking things through?"

They all softly indicated their agreement as they finished smoothing the clean coverlet into place.

"Nora, you will tend to our guest." Satia settled back against the pillows.

Nora pulled her hands back abruptly. "Bonded, I am not really the nursing type. Mira deals with that kind of thing far better than I."

Satia raised an eyebrow.

Nora bowed her head. "Yes, Bonded."

"I will release you once he is weaned from the drug and the moon-child arrives to care for him."

Nora kept her head bowed in obedience.

"Now, when can I expect word from the Black Hills?" Satia asked.

"Captain Ussin won't return until midafternoon, Bonded." Caris said. "The mages are to reopen the portal then."

"Fine." Satia stretched, yawned and snuggled back under the blankets. "I need to consider. To think." She took a long slow breath, then curled on her side. "Wake me in two hours," she commanded with a graceful, dismissive wave of her hand.

"Yes, Bonded." Caris reached for the tray as the others returned to their tasks. So she was the one that saw the discontented pout form on Satia's face even as her mouth opened to form a demand.

"Chamber pot."

## CHAPTER TWENTY-NINE

He supposed that if one was going to fail, it was best to do it early.

Guyik moved off over the roofs, not interested in drawing any attention to himself. He started back toward the more common area, away from the palace and the noble houses. Down by the docks would do fine.

He took his time, no need to rush with bad news. At last he settled on a nice roof-top, with three brick chimneys giving off heat and smoke. From the smell, a bakery. He checked the area throughly before taking shelter there. The warmth felt good as he wrapped his cloak around himself and pulled up the hood.

The scent of bread made his stomach growl. Best not to work on an empty stomach; he drew a dried apple and some cheese from the depths of his pack.

The roof offered a view of the ocean, a long, huge swell of water. No matter how many times he gazed on it, it still astonished him. His homeland was vast, true enough, but dry, sand and scrub and little else. The ocean … breathed, in the way Guyik had never seen. He had waded in it, tasted its salt, but hadn't yet dared to venture out on a boat. He'd heard tales of the sickness that could result, and to his way of thinking, boats were best admired from a distance, with their wide sails and webs of rope.

It was fascinating, but Guyik had always had a stronger link to the land, more than any other element.

With the last bite swallowed and a long drink from his flask, he could put off his task no longer. He brought out his wooden scrying bowl and a small pouch of precious earth from the Wastes. He poured just enough to cover the bottom of the bowl.

He placed the bowl in his lap, and the pouch carefully to one side. Cross-legged, he hunched over the bowl, took a pinch of the earth, and rubbed it between his palms. He took a few deep breaths, inhaling the scent of home.

Then he cradled the bowl in both hands and invoked the earth, asking for its aid.

This far from the Wastes, he was never sure of their answer. But the earth sparkled in the depths of the bowl and he fell within, seeking, reaching … .

A breath, then another, and then a voice spoke in his mind. "Guyik," said the Liam.

In Guyik's mind, he could see the Liam seated with others of the Order.

"Report."

Sighing, Guyik bowed his head. "Master, I failed."

"Tell us," the Liam commanded.

He did, going over the details of what he had learned. There were gasps at the use of the portal and the Liam shook his head in despair.

"So they are lost to us," he said, and Guyik shared his grief.

"Not so," another Elder said firmly, calling attention to herself. "Who can say what will happen between the lightning flash and the boom of thunder?"

"There is truth to that, but we have no presence in the Black Hills," the Liam pointed out. "There's been no one of the Blood there in many, many years." He lifted one hand to rub his face.

"Elder, I have failed the Order." Guyik's heart wrenched as he spoke. He'd failed those of the Blood he'd sworn to serve.

"Nay, the failure is mine. I failed to anticipate the Blood's actions. I sent you to Swift's Port because I thought one side or the other would flee there." The Liam's shoulders sagged. "Who could foresee such hate? Or the use of a portal by foul magics?" The Liam shook his head. "Guyik, take no more blame than the rest of us for not being able to peer into the future."

"What would you have me do?" Guyik asked. "Should I travel to the Black Hills? Or return to the Wastes?"

"No. You would be months on the road to no purpose. Xyrath is of the Blood, be it Wyvern. And while that House rejected us long ago, they are still our charge. Stay. Watch and wait. Learn what you can."

Guyik bowed his head in obedience. "Master."

"The skies be with you, Guyik," the Liam said. "Keep yourself safe."

"I will," he whispered, opening his eyes to the bowl of earth in his hands.

He poured the earth back into the pouch with care, saying a ritual prayer before placing them both back in his pack. He sat for a moment, watching the sky.

The sun was rising over the city and a cold wind was rising. The bustle on the streets was starting to get louder. He'd need to make some decisions soon enough.

In truth, he was not disappointed to be required to stay. He loved the Wastes, they were his home. Yet he also loved the city life, if truth be told.

Easy enough for the Liam to give orders, but it was left to Guyik to figure out the details. The Liam was wise, true enough, but he was a dweller of the Wastes. It had been a very long time since he'd been in a city the size of Edenrich—if he ever had. "Watch and wait" was not as easy as the Liam might think.

Guyik carried a few disguises in his pack, and enough coin to get him by for a while. But if he was here for a longer term, he needed a plan.

He might be able to work his way into the palace ... but no. He dismissed the thought almost immediately. Too close to the seats of power and too easy to fall afoul of them. There were taverns that catered to the Palace guard, but he had to believe that there would be suspicion there as well, and men looking over their shoulders. Nay, perhaps in a few months, but not now, when every loyalty was considered and questioned.

He could start at the wellspring, he supposed. Madam Winter's pleasure house. He'd only that brief glimpse, but there'd been some connection between her and all the parties. Perhaps he'd glean a bit more from an evening spent in comfort.

At the very least, he'd obtain a good meal and a warm bed for the night.

Scruffy songster would not do for this, though, although his story of travel from Swift's Port might be enough explanation. Perhaps he had taken shelter in a noble manor during the war and thought to try his hand in Edenrich now that the strife was over. That should work well enough for today, when he'd coin to spend. Tomorrow would care for itself.

Good enough. He lifted his head, pulled back his hood. It looked to be noon, by the sun. Time enough to move far enough away from his goal so as not to arose suspicions when he arrived. He chuckled to himself as he stood. Wouldn't do to drop out of the sky like a thief.

Even if he was one.

# CHAPTER THIRTY

She's plotting something." Lord Marshal Tarwain scowled as he paced before the fireplace in their family chambers. His bootheels rang against the stone floor as he strode back and forth.

Halithe sat on her stool, back straight, hands folded in her lap, eyes down as befit a young lady of quality. She had no doubt as to who her father was referring to. He'd been stewing since the morning meal.

She'd almost rather be sewing.

Almost.

"I was supposed to subdue the Black Hills until she got it into her head to send that scribe there first. I agreed that it was a good way to rid us of a problem, but who knows how long it will take. There are riches to be found there, wealth to be pulled from the very ground."

Halithe made a soft sound of agreement, as she'd been schooled. Long experience had taught her to always be attentive, but never to offer her own thoughts. That didn't stop her thinking, though.

Father was right, something was happening. There had been a flurry of activity in the wee hours of the morning. The Queen had closeted herself with her Bondmaidens, pleading illness, and all the noble ladies had been sent to their own chambers. There was a new tension in the air since the new Lord High Baron had been sent to his barony.

Almost as if others had discovered that they too could be "honored" in such a way.

"I think she's avoiding the council." Father turned on his heel and marched the other way. "She's avoiding all discussion of lands and grants. And the King can't be bothered with details. He spends all his time beating on the pells."

Halithe would have nodded her understanding if her input had been welcome. Instead she kept her thoughts to herself.

"The only way that brainless idiot came to power is through her," Tarwain said, making no effort to lower his voice. Halithe glanced carefully around, seeing no servants. But this was the Royal Court of Wyvern House, where one never knew who watched and listened. Did Father think himself immune?

"She's the power, the brains, the manipulative she-wyvern," Tarwain continued. His voice had changed, ever so slightly, growing deep, sultry—

Halithe closed her eyes, and willed herself not to react. It could not be, her father could not have–

"She is magnificent," he mused.

Halithe must have made a noise, must have unconsciously twitched in a way that drew his attention. He came to stand in front of her, his hands behind his back. "I've strived to bring our family to the forefront," Tarwain groused. "Done everything I could to bring us to a position of power and influence within the Court."

Halithe tried very hard not to imagine exactly what he and the Queen had done.

"And what have you done, chit? These mage lessons are nonsense. The Queen has allowed them for now, for some reason, but you and I both know there's no power for you other than that a woman gains through marriage. A good marriage, one that brings wealth and more influence, should be all that you strive for, all that you want. To build a foundation to pass on to the heirs of your body."

Well, this was familiar ground, and she could ignore the rest, even as he returned to pacing, hurling barbed words at her for her failures. She didn't sigh, didn't shift in her seat, just settled in, knowing he'd have to let her go soon, for the noble ladies were to gather in the chapel in the next hour, to recite prayers for the health of the Queen and her child.

A soft knock at the door interrupted Father's tirade. "Enter," Tarwain barked.

Halithe raised her head as the door opened. Ritathan entered.

How did he do that, she wondered. Glide into a room so quietly, with no announcement, no boots ringing on stone. Just quiet assurance of power, and maybe the smallest clink of his chains. As if to say "I can kill you in an instant."

She loved that.

"Forgive me," Ritathan with a tone that implied anything but a plea. "I need my apprentice for a lesson."

"She's to go to prayers," Tarwain grumped.

Ritathan nodded gravely. "A quick lesson," he assured Tarwain. "There's enough time if we hurry. Come quickly, apprentice."

Halithe rose, curtsied to her father, and went to the door, keeping her eyes down to hide her glee. But once they were in the corridor, the door closed. she looked Ritathan full in the face.

He raised one of those shaggy eyebrows. "Control yourself, apprentice." he said mildly, his eyes twinkling. "Come. We've not much time."

He swiftly led her to a bank of windows that looked out over the Palace courtyard. He carefully cracked open one of the casement windows. "Look," he ordered, tucking his hands into his robes as the cold air flowed in.

She stepped closer to him, close enough to smell the incense that clung to his robes. The cold air snapped at her cheeks. She'd a clear view of all the bustle, normal for the afternoon. Guards, tradesmen, servants going about their chores. All seemed normal, until she spotted four figures coming through the gate.

"Is that the Guildmaster?" she asked, although it clearly was. The portly man was decked out in vibrant blue and green robes; the other three wore black robes, their bond-chains clearly visible.

"Yes," Ritathan said. "The escort sent to the Black Hills is returning. He and the others will open the portal for their return."

Guildmaster Forterran was shouting orders, clearing the area.

"Watch," Ritathan said. "Remember that not everything is as it seems."

"I don't see–" Halithe started, but then snapped her mouth shut when Ritathan's fingers encircled her wrist, cold under the metal of her bracelet.

"*See.*" At that single word, a tingle of power ran through her. The world *shifted.*

Startled, she looked at Ritathan, saw lights swirling around him and glittering among his chains. She felt, saw, sensed his Ramathan's strength, his knowledge, his ... resignation?

"Not me," Ritathan chided and nodded to the window. "Down there."

Halithe's gaze went to the window and beyond, the lovely, wide sky and the world ... she was lost in amazement.

"What do you see?" Ritathan whispered.

She lowered her gaze. "The gates," she breathed.

"Wards," Ritathan explained. "Very old spells, cast deep within the structure. They feed off the energies of those that live within, although they do have to be renewed at intervals."

"The Guildmaster," she frowned as the man started to chant and wave his arms. He glowed then, as did the area before him. "But the others, they aren't really casting, are they?"

"Good," Ritathan said. "Forterran is putting on a bit of a show. He would say he is giving them their money's worth."

Halithe jerked back as a wide, white, swirly circle of energy opened in the center of the courtyard, glowing intensely.

In another breath, blindfolded horses emerged, men at their heads, pulling a carriage. Another carriage followed, with an empty wagon behind, followed by men leading their mounts. The last man through, seemingly in charge, called for a head count. Once he had it, he gave the Guildmaster a nod, and the circle disappeared.

The Guildmaster staggered a bit and his apprentices ran up to offer aid.

"Trust Forterran to add a dramatic touch," Ritathan scoffed.

"You can close the window, now."

Halithe did so with her free hand.

"This," Ritathan squeezed her wrist, "this is what we call mage sense. When you first experience it, it is usually just your sight that seems enhanced. But it can be so much more than that.

"Think of it as more than just an extension of your physical senses, because given time and practice, it may allow you to sense strong emotions."

The wagons and carriages were leaving through the palace gates, as was the Guildmaster. It looked like the man in charge of the expedition was being directed toward the Royal Quarters.

"I have shared my mage sense with you today," Ritathan said, "but you must develop your own. For each of us, mage sense has inner ways, some stronger than others." He released her wrist, and the effect was immediate—the sense dulled, slipping from her grasp to lie just out of reach.

"You must learn to invoke this for yourself," Ritathan murmured. "My spell will linger for an hour, maybe more. You must focus, concentrate on summoning it." His mouth quirked. "Perhaps while you are at your prayers."

The chapel bells started pealing.

"We are done for this day," Ritathan said. "The rest is up to you. Report to me tomorrow and we will continue to work on control."

"Yes, Master," Halithe said as he strode off, his robes flowing around him.

———•———

The chapel was crowded and over warm, since no lady of the nobility wanted to be counted absent. It was said that the Matriarch herself would lead the service, so they stood in silence in the pews, waiting, the only sound the rustle of skirts and the occasional cough.

Halithe felt sweat start to gather on her neck. The sun was beating in the windows and the heat was rising. The chapel wasn't large and none of the colored glass windows opened. She looked around, realizing some recent repairs had been done. Was that to please the Matriarch?

Perhaps politics played a larger role in faith than she had imagined.

A glitter from the altar, drew her attention. The sun disk that hung above the marble glittered again. She focused, trying to invoke mage sense.

The disk flared bright, white and pure and—

A wave of hate hit her, almost like a blow to the chest.

Anger. Rage, deep and furious, but with an odd tang to it. It poured from the gated entrance to the crypts. Halithe focused again, trying to find a source, concentrating as hard as she could–

Then Caris stepped into view and all other thoughts fled.

Caris glowed, as if covered in ground gold and diamond dust. So beautiful that Halithe's breath caught in her throat. Caris was warm amber and Halithe's heart was caught within.

The golden cords of the bond danced with sparks of red and writhed like a silken web that clung to Caris's skin, tight enough to be a trap, a prison, a binding. It moved with her, yet restrained her at the same time.

Caris glanced in her direction and for a long moment their gazes locked. Halithe's mouth went dry as a surge of longing rose up in her soul. A deep, abiding hunger to rip those restrains free.

The hand bells chimed and the call for prayer rang out as the Matriarch led a procession of clerics to the altar. Halithe knelt with all the other women, but her mind was not on prayer.

*I know what I want, Father,* she thought as she bowed her head, *and I will strive for it.*

# CHAPTER THIRTY-ONE

L et me guess. You will strike off my head." Plumestra lifted her chin and sent a pugnacious look directly at Queen Satia.

Mira froze, mouth gaping open, staring at the midwife in disbelief. No one talked to the Bonded that way. Ever.

Satia's eyes narrowed. She was lying on her cushioned couch, propped up on pillows. While the morning had started well, it hadn't been a good afternoon, what with vomiting and avoiding council meetings. Even Captain Ussin's description of events in the Black Hills hadn't lifted the Bonded's mood. The others had been sent off on various tasks, leaving Mira to serve during this interview.

Mira clutched at the knife concealed in her skirts and hoped she wouldn't be commanded to use it.

"You will serve as my midwife exclusively," Satia repeated.

"No." Plumestra folded her arms.

"I will have you executed." The fury in the Bonded's voice made Mira's jaw clench.

Plumestra tilted her head as if in doubt. "That threat loses some of it impact if you repeat it too often."

"I am your queen," Satia hissed.

"Aye," Plumestra agreed. "But your jugs and your womb work the same as all others, noble or common. Waste of my time and skills to be at your beck and call."

Mira grasped her knife's hilt harder.

"I have found that noble-born ignore my advice, act surprised when they run into the slightest discomfort, and don't pay," Plumestra continued. "You have no need to have me dance in attendance, and we would both get on each other's last nerve."

"Your death—"

"You prefer those that serve you to cower, don't you? Dread your displeasure, fear your reprisals," Plumestra observed coolly.

Mira couldn't even breathe.

"I am old enough that I no longer care to play games. Lop of my head if you wish," the midwife said. "A quick death would be fine with me."

"It doesn't have to be quick," Satia snarled. "Or perhaps I will lop off your husband's head. Nightsoil Guildsman, I believe?"

Mira froze.

Plumestra's eyes narrowed. "You go too far, missy." The midwife turned on her heel, her skirts swishing the floor she spun so fast. "Send your executioners. Your guards know the way."

Mira couldn't take it anymore. "What matters most," she blurted out, "is the health and safety of the babe."

The two stubborn women went silent. Mira could not breathe for the weight of that silence.

Satia broke first. "I would ask for your services for the birth of the heir," she said, her tone cool and formal. "I would ask that you take up residence in the Palace perhaps two weeks before the birth."

Plumestra heaved a sigh and turned back to the Queen. "One week," she said, just as cool and formal as the other.

"Very well," Satia agreed.

Mira remembered to breathe.

"I would ask that you take my advice, based on years of experience," Plumestra said, "and forgive my plain speaking."

"Agreed," Satia sagged back on her pillows and grimaced.

"Let see how the babe is doing," Plumestra started to roll up her sleeves.

"Must you?" Satia asked, shifting on the couch. "I–"

Plumestra raised an eyebrow.

Satia sighed. Mira released her grip on the dagger and stepped forward to help pull back the blankets. "You will speak to no one of this," Satia growled.

"Yes, of course," Plumestra said.

Mira watched, fascinated, as Plumestra felt the babe and checked between the Bonded's legs, quickly and surely, all the time asking questions about diet and bowels and activity. 'Twas masterfully done, to be sure. Mira let herself relax now that the weight of the birth was off her shoulders alone. She'd have someone to ask, someone to guide her. The relief was immeasurable.

When she was finished, Plumestra began to pull up the blankets and Mira hastened to aid her. "The babe is well and you don't have much longer to wait." Plumestra started rolling down her sleeves.

"Surely I am in the early months yet," Satia said.

The midwife narrowed her eyes. "If you wish that to be true, so be it. Then I tell you the babe will come earlier than one might expect."

Satia huffed.

"Some women bear easy, some bear hard," Plumestra continued. "From what you have experienced so far, I suspect you will not have an easy time of it. Forget the stories you have been told. Birth is hard on a woman's body."

"I know that." Satia glared at the midwife.

"Knowing and experiencing are two very different things," Plumestra said. "Still, there are things we can do to make you more comfortable. For one thing, laying about like a wounded cow is of no use."

Mira closed her eyes as Satia sputtered in rage.

"Yes, I know, execution," Plumestra said. "Do so after I give the advice that you will certainly ignore. You need to move more. Outside. Long walks. It will aid in the swelling and unblock your bowels. As to your stomach, no more sugar in the tea. Unsweetened weak tea and dry crackers to go with it when the sickness hits. No more sweets of any kind and avoid spices and garlic."

Satia sat, sullen and glaring. Mira hovered close.

"Well?" Plumestra asked. "Up, now, and a walk about the hallways. Or are you like every other—"

Satia grunted, threw back the blankets and struggled to her feet. Mira went to aid her.

"There is another matter," Satia said. "I am appointing you

Royal Nurse. You will oversee my child's household."

"No," Plumestra said firmly. "My skills are not in babe-tending." She hesitated for a moment, then added. "I would, of course, aid you in finding the best nursery maids and wet nurses." Mira noticed Plumestra was watching Satia's face carefully, as if looking for a reaction. "They may be of common stock, but will be loyal and reliable."

"Of course you will do that," Satia gather her robe about her, flinging her hair free of confinement. "Royal Nurse, I command you–"

"There. Well, that lasted longer than I thought you would." Plumestra turned on her heel and headed for the door. "If you don't mind, give me a few days to see to the last of those currently under my care. Then send your guards and–"

Satia drew a breath. Mira started to pull her knife, expecting the command—

"Wait," Satia said.

———•———

Madam Winter herself greeted Guyik as he entered her establishment. The warm air of the sitting room surrounded him with the comfortable scents of supper, with just a touch of spicy perfume. The lady was a pleasant enough looking-woman, but there was a weariness in her eyes.

Guyik bowed low. "Lady, I am Acton, a merchant. I have been long on the road from Swift's Port. Before I begin my business in the city, I would relax, dine, and have my cares seen to. Perhaps one of your ladies would entertain me for a meal and see to my needs?"

"Of course," Winter said. "If you have the means."

He opened his purse and offered her coin. "A meal, some company, and a week's lodging?"

She nodded, took the money, and stepped back. "Come in and be welcome, Merchant Acton. Let us see to your comfort."

In no time at all, he was in a comfortable, padded chair by the fire, with a cold ale beside him. It was early enough that there weren't many other patrons, so quite a few women hovered about, eyeing him with warm smiles.

Guyik stretched his long legs out and relaxed into the warmth, just as any weary traveler might, and smiled back, but gave no signal to any yet. He'd ask one to join him eventually, someone cheerful and plump, who hopefully liked to gossip.

Madam Winter wandered over, gesturing for him to remain seated when he went to rise. "What news of Swift's Port, Master Acton?" At his grimace, she smiled. "Not to your liking?"

"Nay, Madam, salt air did nothing for me, and all the music was sea chanties, and all the food, fish." He screwed his face up in a mocking grimace and drew a laugh from her. "Edenrich is better for a soul now that the war's done," he finished.

Her face went flat. "Not all souls," she said bitterly, and moved off.

Ah. Guyik settled back, satisfied. He knew well enough that it might take some time before he'd learn anything.

A slight ruckus at the door drew everyone's attention. One of the woman was at the door, barring entry, glancing back at Winter.

Madam Winter stood in the center of the room, drawing herself up as if for battle. "Let him in," she commanded. The woman stepped aside and a military man pushed his way in, the one Guyik had seen that morning.

Guyik's interest perked. Perhaps he'd learn more quicker than expected.

"Captain Ussin," Winter's voice rang out as she confronted

the man. "How dare you come here, after what you have done."

"Winter," Ussin's face was red, perhaps from wind and snow-burn. "I had my orders," he said pleadingly. "It's an honor for Orval to be–"

"It's not, and don't claim it is to my face," Winter snapped, her jewelry rustling as her body shook with anger. "The Black Hills are never anything but trouble and death for Xy, and you know it."

"What else could I do?" Ussin asked. "I had my orders. If I refused to carry them out, another would have taken my place."

"Better so," Winter choked out. "If you could have seen Orval's face when he walked in, seen what you'd done–" she stopped herself with a sob. "It will haunt me forever."

"I did what I could," Ussin said. There was more there, Guyik could tell, but the man glanced around and it was clear he wasn't sharing detail. "I had to do it," he continued. "I had to protect my men–"

"And yourself," Winter said.

"Aye, true enough," Ussin said and just stood there, as forlorn a man as Guyik had ever seen.

Winter sagged, old and tired, and stared at the floor. "I don't know who I despise more," her voice the merest whisper but loud in the silent room. "You, for taking them to their deaths, or myself for not doing more to stop it from happening." She closed her eyes.

"Winter," Ussin's whisper was a plea for both their sufferings. Guyik held his breath.

"Come, Captain Ussin," Winter held out her hand. "We will open a bottle and share our grief and try not to hate ourselves quite so much come the morning."

Ussin stepped forward and took her hand and they disappeared together up the stairs.

The room stayed silent. Guyik looked around at stricken faces, filled with fear and indecision. Perhaps a new understanding of life under the House of Wyvern was slowly sinking in.

Guyik took a sip of ale and settled back in his chair to watch.

———•———

Plumestra left the her escort of guards outside and eased the door of her home open. It was a solid, decent home. No velvet, or servants, but them and theirs and a door to close against the world.

The warmth within was not just from the fire. Borre, stood by the table where a meal was laid, a pitcher and mug in his hand. Waiting.

"You heard." She paused in the doorway, seeing the worry in his eyes.

"The gossip beat you home," he rumbled. "My entire guild knew and watched and kept eyes on you as you went about with palace guards, and then to the palace itself. The Queen wants a midwife, I take it."

"Husband, I–" she didn't even know where to start. She closed the door at last.

"You are worn," Borre poured hot kavage. "What food can't cure, kavage can." He held out the steaming mug. "Come tell me of your day, wife."

She started to remove her scarves and cloak, then glanced at the door behind her. Stout and warm the house might be, but hard to know if ears were glued to the door.

Borre nodded his understanding as she took the mug. "I've roasted onions, and here are bread and cheese." He settled his large frame into a wooden chair and she sat opposite him.

They kept the talk light, each telling of their day. Plumestra said that the Queen wished her services and did not to mention the threat of execution.

Borre raised an eyebrow, then nodded. "Of course," he said. "You are the best, and known for it."

Plumestra flushed with pleasure.

Borre finished first and offered more kavage, which she declined. "Have you women in need this night?" he asked as he cleared the plates.

"No, unless I get a summons of distress."

"I too am released from duty tonight. I've a mind to take you to bed, wife."

"And I've a mind to be taken," she said, glowing.

What followed were normal chores, clearing the table and warming water for washing. What made it special was her consciousness of Borre's presence. The warmth as he stood next to her, his soapy hands handing her the dishes to rinse and dry. His scent as he leaned into her space, reaching for a pot as he gave her ear a brush with his lips.

She smiled in anticipation and gave him a nudge with her hip.

He hummed in response though she could see the worry in his eyes.

She went to bank the fire. And her warm, wonderful husband, a caring man, went out and offered kavage and bread and cheese to the guards.

She almost laughed out loud as he walked back in and closed the door firmly behind him.

He shrugged and held out his hand.

She took it and he led her to their sleeping chamber. They made their ablutions quickly, then climbed into the bed to meet in the center where it sagged. The linens warmed as she snuggled up next to him.

"I do not like this," Borre whispered. "I fear for you."

Plumestra raised herself to look in his face. "She offered me a guild charter."

Borre blinked. "Say again?"

"A guild charter," Plumestra repeated. "A full charter, with fees waived, and a royal endorsement."

"I'll be damned," Borre said.

"Imagine it," Plumestra said. "A seat on the guildmaster council. Apprentices, the awarding of a master's badge, a way to teach, to learn through something besides failure? Maybe even a birthing house." She settled back down, putting her head on his shoulder. "Save the lives of countless women and babes."

"I know it's your dream, my plum." His arms tightened around her. "But I do not trust them. There's been body parts found in the waters that flow out from under the Palace, and they did not come from upstream, so far as any knows."

"Borre, it's more than that, don't you see?" Plumestra put her lips to his ear. "They've won and she is in power, whether we like it or not. The Queen is not going to keep the child at the tit for long, if at all. We could influence the next Son or Daughter of Xy through the wet nurses, the nursery maids, the staff. While his mother plots and schemes to gain power and glory, we will take the long view and teach the child a sense of honor and truth."

"In that household?"

Plumestra hummed. "She is not the kind to raise a child, husband, and will pay little attention to the nursery. We will raise the child and instill a strength of character she cannot dislodge."

"It's a risk," Borre murmured.

"It's a risk," Plumestra agreed. "But being within a hundred miles of her is a risk."

"Know this, my wife," Borre shifted on his side to face her. "If aught happens to you, my guild will never clean their cess pits again."

"A terrible thing," Plumestra said with a smile. She pressed her hand to his chest. "Sleep, Borre. All will be well."

Borre scoffed, and shifted, moving to cover her. Plumestra drew in a breath as the heat started to rise in her depths.

"Didn't just take my wife to bed just for gossip," he said as he nuzzled her ear.

"Borre," she sighed with pleasure and rained kisses on his face.

## CHAPTER THIRTY-TWO

Mayor Jerrold stood at the farthest part of the shelter mine and surveyed his people. It seemed nearly all of Wareington had gathered. The glow of dim lanterns was just enough. Not that they were necessary. You live with each other for years with no outsiders, you have no need to see a face.

He decided to wait a bit, seeing that stragglers were still coming in.

This mine hadn't been worked in his lifetime. But it was well-braced and sound. As were Wareington's people.

Jerrold glanced at his mother, sitting on a wooden bench close by, bag of knitting at hand. She watched the crowd as well, gauging their temper, even as her hands reached into the bag. One thing the entire village knew full well, Mother Bercie's hands were never idle. And woe betide ya if she thought yours were.

As he expected. she pulled out a dagger and a whetstone and started to sharpen the weapon. Jerrold felt some of the tension release from his shoulders at the comforting sound of blade on stone. One of his Da's daggers; he recognized the handle. A wave of sadness swept Jerrold, catching him by surprise.

His mother caught his eye, her gaze steady yet full of worry. Those eyes had seen so much death and pain over the years. He glanced at his son, sitting next to her, and felt the same fear. Jerrold drew himself up and looked out over his people and did the only thing he could do with fear.

He faced it.

"Scouts out?" he asked. "Guards in place?"

His captains nodded.

Jerrold nodded. "For years, we've known this day would come," he started, raising his voice. The people grew silent, giving him their attention.

"Those of Xy, Airion and Wyvern, have always tried to take what is ours. Our livelihoods, our resources, our lives, sometimes wiping out entire villages." He paused, swallowing hard. "We will always remember."

"We will always remember," came the response from all.

"After we drove off the last Lord High Baron that dared try to rape us and our land, the Blood entered into its own strifes. While Blood warred with Blood, we of Wareington put the years to good use, preparing as our fathers warned us to.

"It seems that our time of peace is ending.

"It's been days since the royal carriage rumbled past and they pounded their challenge to our gates," he said. "I've sent messages to every village and town in the Hills, spreading the warning. Word has come back from all but the farthest reaches. We're here to share what information we have and decide on a course of action.

"There's no sign of warriors at our borders. All the villages there have promised to restore the signal fires, to warn of movement."

That caused a stir.

"No movement?" Old Lewald asked sharply. "Not the main roads, nor the back trails?"

"Not a sign," Jerrold confirmed.

"So they sent a new Lord High Baron to 'subdue the rebels abhorrent to our realm' without warriors?" Old Lewald snorted. "What happened to those that were with them at the gates?"

"They were seen galloping back down the road, wagons empty." Rasfel spoke up. "Disappeared somewhere between here and the border. No word or sign since."

"Magic," came a dark mutter from the crowd. Unease swept through them all. Talk flared up and Jerrold let that go on for a bit. Best to let them get it out of their systems. The Lord of Light and the Lady of Laughter knew, it still wasn't out of his. The not-knowing ate at his gut.

But his mother was still sharpening her dagger, and he had a job to do.

"Let's focus," he said at last. "I ask the Captains to report on preparations."

One of the portly Vestor twins stood up. "The stores have been checked, plus all the caches in all the shelters. Enough dried food for a year for all. We cleaned out any that went bad. Water barrels are being filled and the wells in the caves are clean and pure."

Another voice. "Haven't moved the livestock yet, but ready

at the first sign. We've sent out more hunters, for fresh meat to add to stores."

"Weapons?" Jerrold asked.

"Every man and woman are equipped. We've fletchers working on more arrows and bolts."

Mother Bercie spoke up. "We've stockpiled healing supplies, salves, medicines, and bandages. We've small kits for any warrior, make sure your people all have one." She looked up and scanned the faces. "All those caring for the little ones know the hiding places."

Jerrold nodded grimly. "No plan survives the enemy's attack. But we are as prepared as we can be, it seems to me." He turned to the leader of the scouts. "Rasfel? You've had eyes on the new Lord High Baron. What have our watchers seen?"

Rasfel had a sheepish look on his face; he ran his hand through his black hair before he spoke. "Well, in truth, our new Lord High Baron seems to be setting up residence in the gatehouse."

Jerrold frowned. "How so?"

"In the time since they've been there," Rasfel said, "we've seen the Lord give his son sword lessons in the courtyard. His wife sits in the sun, sometimes, nursing twins. They've a maidservant and a scribe to aid them."

"Scribe?" Mother Bercie questioned.

"We've taken to calling him that since he carries a small book at times," Rasfel shrugged. "All he can be, really, with that gimp."

"Careful you don't assume too much." Mother Bercie said.

"Seen no others?" Jerrold asked.

"Nay," Rasfel shook his head. "Cirda is one of the watchers," he said, nodding at Jerrold's eldest. "He can confirm."

Jerrold turned to his son.

Cirda stood, tall and grown-up, and to Jerrold's pride, squared his shoulders and spoke clearly. "The son is hunting pigeons. Both women forage in the old kitchen garden for what they can find, digging roots and taking dried leaves."

"That garden always was protected from the deepest snows," Mother Bercie mused. "But it's not been tended in years. Left to run wild years ago. Can't be much there in the dead of winter."

"They all take turns trying to pull stones from the main well."

That caused a grim murmur to run through the crowd. Dropping stones into that well had been a favorite practice of the Wyverns. Crida hesitated but Jerrold gestured for him to continue.

"They are also gathering what wood they can," the young man said. "But I don't think there's enough in the ruins to keep them the rest of the winter."

"Smart lad," Rasfel said. "I think the same thing."

"You have not been seen?" Jerrold asked.

"No, Father," Cirda said, clearly indignant, rolling his eyes at the very idea.

Ah. There was his son. Jerrold suppressed his smile as he spoke. "Of course not."

"Horses may have brought them," Rasfel added, "but there's none to be seen now, nor wagons neither." He gave a sly grin. "The Lord High Baron knows enough sword work to teach the basics. The son needs more practice."

"Should kill them now, before they learn more," an old, querulous voice rose from the back, thumping his cane for emphasis. "Now, if I had my goat cart–"

Old Petro, without a doubt, ready with an opinion or complaint. Jerrold cut him off before the old man could get wound up. "I do not understand this," Jerrold said to the crowd. "To make such an announcement, without force of arms, is either arrogant or stupid."

"The Blood of Xy is not stupid," Mother Bercie reminded him. "Do not let hate blind you. There have been good ones here, before your time, my son. Remember that," she chided him. "Remember who you are named for."

"Aye, Mother," he nodded to her, then turned back to his people. "The Black Hills has suffered and will suffer again unless we make a stand when they come against us. For now, we wait. We watch."

"And maybe prod them a bit?" Rasfel looked eager. "Maybe test them a bit, eh?"

"For now? No," Jerrold shook his head. "We watch."

"And seek answers," Mother Bercie added.

# CHAPTER THIRTY-THREE

The rains turned to snow as Vren and Dust traveled toward Athelbryght.

They avoided the roads, mostly because they both enjoyed solitude. Easier, not to be questioned or observed, and their haste might draw questions. But also because more than once they had spotted groups of warriors returning home from the battlefields, weary, hurt, and angry. No need to give them targets for their wrath.

They took time to hide their trail, but as the days passed, they favored speed over caution.

There was a joy running with Dust, traveling swiftly and with confidence. The marcus and the vore were used to such weather.

They hunted where they could and took shelter when they could find it. Huddling together for warmth, sleeping with Dust's fur in his face, was a delight. Until such time as Dust returned to her human form, it was all he could ask and all that she would ever offer.

Each night he checked the mage key, the ring, and the red blood of the vial he carried. He kept them safe, tucked within his pack, wrapped well in a cloth and then again in oiled leather. Dust watched him every night, and he knew she was amused at his caution. He'd shrug, and she'd shake herself and let her tongue loll.

They found the body on the outskirts of Athelbryght. It was the horse that drew them, tied to a tree and struggling to free itself. A warrior had clearly made a camp, crawled into his bed roll, and died of his wounds.

Dust snuffed at the body, then sat and looked at Vren.

"I'll try." he said with a shrug, and moved toward the horse. "Easy now," he crooned. "Easy."

The horse was having none of it, rearing and snorting and making a fuss. It finally turned at the limit of its tie and kicked out at Vren, who backed off immediately.

Dust huffed. Vren shrugged, got as close to the tree as he could, and cut the reins.

The horse snorted and lunged away, but Dust caught the reins in her mouth and tugged as Vren backed off. The horse quieted, although its eyes rolled toward Vren.

Dust tugged again and led it off, presumably to take it to the near-by stream. The poor thing looked the worse for wear, thin and tired.

Not that Vren knew much of horses.

When she returned, still leading the animal, he raised an eyebrow.

Dust looked at the body and then at the horse.

"You know him?" Vren asked. When Dust nodded, he sighed. "If I remember," Vren coughed, his throat not used to talking after the last few weeks. "There's a village north of here. Think he was headed that way?"

Dust gave a nod.

"They'll know you there?" Vren asked.

Dust nodded again.

"I'll see to him, then, if you think it best." Vren's breath hung in the air. "I'll wrap him up and gather his things and we can take them both to the village. There's enough daylight left that we can risk the road."

Dust held the reins, letting the horse reach fresh browse as Vren wrapped the body and gathered up the gear. It took some doing, with the horse jerking away at every chance, but Vren managed to heave the body over the saddle. He didn't bother with the saddle bags, just threw them over his own shoulder.

The vore wasted no time tugging the horse toward the road. The horse was not thrilled, but it seemed more than willing to go where Dust wished once they took to the road. Vren stayed back, keeping his distance.

The village was fair-sized and seemed to be shutting down for the night.

"Wait, Dust." Vren stood in the shadows and unstrapped the baby sling from his chest. The doll was worse for wear, but still held together. He placed it in his pack. "Ready."

Dust trotted ahead, into the cobbled yard of the inn.

Vren got the attention of the stable-boy, whose eyes went wide at the sight of the body. The boy ran for the Innkeeper as Vren waited in the yard.

"What's this then?" The innkeeper was a tall, skinny fellow; he'd brought two men-servants with him. "Who are you?"

Vren opened his mouth as Dust pushed forward, and gave a bark.

"Dust!" The innkeeper went to one knee. "Well, that's all right then." He scratched Dust's ruff and looked at Vren. "She'd not be with ya if you'd killed him."

Vren nodded. "Found him dead, with his horse fighting his ties. Dust wanted him brought here. You know him?"

"Bring a torch, lads," the innkeeper said, getting to his feet with difficulty. "Damned knees," he muttered as they brought the light and he pulled up the corpse's head. "Aye, that's Widow Harris's oldest. Went off to fight for King Xywellan, Lord of Light and Lady of Laughter hold him close."

"So you've had the news?" Vren asked.

"Aye." The innkeeper shook his head. "Not good news, to my way of thinking." he said glumly.

"War never is," Vren said.

"Aye, well, you and Dust come in to the kitchen and get warm. Give ya a bed and a meal as thanks for bringing him home. There'll be sorrow, but there will be certainty too. We'll take him the rest of the way and break the news." The tall man gestured and the other two took charge of the horse and body. Vren offered them the saddle bags, which they accepted.

"We can pay our way," Vren offered as they watched the sad procession leave.

Dust huffed.

"Reckon I can afford ta feed a skinny one like you on my own coin—and your human," the innkeeper said, laughing at his own joke. He started toward the door, where light and heat spilled out onto the cobblestones. "Dust, I know. What did you say your name was, lad?"

"Dithen," Vren said.

"I'm Ian. Come tell us your news, Dithen, and we'll share what we know. There's been little news of the war so far, and yours will be the first that we trust. Let's keep ya in the kitchen for now. You can eat while I gather a few that need ta listen. Lissa," he bellowed. "Dust is here, with a guest."

————•————

Lissa, who turned out to be Ian's wife, fed them both and kept the curious out of the kitchen until they'd had their fill. Then she ushered them into the main room, where Vren found himself facing the Mayor and what had to be most of the adults in the town. Lissa made Ian move over on his bench and settled herself down beside him.

Dust sat with her back to the fire as the townspeople looked at Vren expectantly.

He spread his hands wide. "I'm afraid I have not much more to tell you. When we left, King Xywellan was dead and Queen Kara had just been defeated in the field before Edenrich. I'm sure that Xyrath and Satia have since taken the throne."

"Well, that's an ill wind," Ian said and heads nodded all around.

"Any word of Queen Mother Tithanna?" asked another. "Now there was a Queen, mind you, took care of all the folk, not just the rich."

"No," Vren answered. "I'd heard no word other than that she was in the castle, awaiting the outcome."

"And our lads?" another asked. "Any word of a pardon for those on the losing side?"

"Dust and I didn't stay to hear," Vren said cautiously, pleased that he received nods of understanding. "We passed a few straggling this way," he offered. "I'm not sure if they're local or not."

"Word is that Satia is not the forgiving kind," came a mutter from the back.

"Athelbryght was neutral to both sides, by the word of the Chosen," the Mayor explained, "but she allowed any that wished to go to make their own decisions."

"Harris's boy had a horse, might explain why he was nearly home," said a man off to Vren's left.

"Now there's a new King and Queen," Ian grumbled, "and sure as I have hairs on my ass, there'll be trouble."

"Ian," Lissa scolded even as chuckles rose all around.

"It's the truth," Ian said glumly. "Aye, our lads returning, but so are those that will turn to thievery. And there's trouble in the Black Hills and–"

"Aye, and it's all gonna end in fire and death," the Mayor said, standing up. "Ian, you fret worse than an old granny. The Chosen and the vore have kept us safe here in Athelbryght for longer that my father's and grandfather's time. So it will continue, yes?"

Worried looks, then nods all around. Vren could hardly blame them. What happened in far off Edenrich touched them rarely— but it might dig sharp claws in now.

The Mayor continued, "Let's be off. Morning comes soon enough and the Widow Harris will be needing our aid." He bowed to Dust. "Our thanks, vore Dust, for this news and your service."

Dust bowed her head in acknowledgment, then rose and headed for the door.

Vren paused. "I would aid in the digging of a grave, if there's a need. Hard work in the winter."

Ian rose and clapped him on his shoulder, pulling the marcus aside. "Ah, no, lad, many thanks. In Athelbryght, we burn our dead. Long tradition. Best you sleep warm tonight and be on your way in the morning." Ian lowered his voice. "With Dust returning, there'll be a Packmoot, most like."

Dust looked over her shoulder and nodded.

"The Chosen lives, Dust, but," Ian hesitated, then almost blurted, "last word is she's slippin'."

Dust huffed.

"Aye, then," Ian walked them to the stairs. "Sleep well. Best you get on first light. You've still a bit to go before you reach the manor give them the news. We'll see ya fed and provisioned in the morning."

Vren hesitated, not wanting to offend, then followed the man, resigning himself to a sleepless night.

The room was small, not much more than a bed, a rug, a nightstand, and a fire in the hearth. The four walls were too close, the ceiling too low.

Dust stretched out on the rug in front of the fireplace.

Vren stripped down, climbed in, and sank into the soft bedding. Even with the warming pan, the bed felt cold and lonely. "You could climb up here," he suggested softly.

Dust didn't even lift her head.

Vren closed his eyes, rolled over, and willed himself to sleep.

———•———

A few days of hard travel found them at the gates of the home of the Chosen.

When they left the village, Dust had led Vren to the road, and Vren had agreed to follow it. There seemed little danger now and speed was necessary. The fact that the roads were lined with fields fully harvested, hay stacks neatly arranged, and livestock behind stout fences gave at least the illusion of peace and security.

Far better than piles of the fallen and weapons littering the ground.

Dust barked sharply as they crested the next rise.

From ahead came an equally sharp bark in response.

"Watcher?" Vren asked.

Dust snorted agreement as she continued, pace increasing to a trot. Vren kept up.

They weren't challenged again until they reached the main gates. The snow-covered lands they were passing through sprawled with wooden trellises supporting mature grapevines, heavy with fruit.

At the gates they were met by two vore and a human, a short man, broad of face and brown of skin. He had dark hair, dark eyes, a goatee and a wide smile.

"Dust!" the man called even as the vore was surrounded by wagging tails and furry bodies.

"We did not think to see you for some time," the human said to Dust. He offered one hand to Vren. "Welcome. I am Aramal of Athelbryght. Be welcome in the Chosen's name."

Aramal was deeply tanned, broad of face, with a wide smile. Vren took his hand. "My thanks. I am known as Dithen, traveling with Dust. We have news for the Chosen."

"Then let's get you both inside, where it can be shared."

Aramal didn't ask any questions as they walked toward the main house. The vore walking with Dust were quiet too, although Vren knew well enough that they had their own way of communicating.

"The Chosen will be in the kitchens, close to the hearth for the warmth. I'll send word to the fields. We are preparing for a harvest, so all hands are in the sheds."

"Harvest?" Vren asked, looking out over frozen fields.

"Icewine," Aramal said. "The very best. But the grapes must be picked at just the right time, and that's now."

"So of course, we arrive," Vren said with a chuckle.

"Such is always the way," Aramal agreed. "But if it weren't difficult, it wouldn't be worth the doing." He pushed open a heavy wooden door. "Latarie, Dust has arrived with news."

"Hush, she's sleeping," came a soft voice. A lovely woman came into view. "Come in, come in, don't let the cold air in."

Dust and Vren stepped into a small stone kitchen where the hearth blazed high, filling the space with heat. In the center of the room was a large, well-worn, wooden table surrounded by benches and chairs; the walls sported shelves full of bright dishes and crockery.

At the far end of the hearth stood a rocking chair, moving back and forth very slowly. In the chair was a figure bundled in colorful shawls and blankets, with thick socks and slippers visible on its feet.

Dust went over, whining softly, and shoved her nose into the midst of the wrappings.

A hand emerged, frail and veined, to rest lightly between Dust's ears. "Dust?" said a quavering voice as one scarf dropped away to reveal an ancient-seeming woman, frail and pale, with hair as white as the snow outside. Long, her hair was braided and wrapped neatly around her head, arranged so that just the points of her ears peeked out.

Vren drew a breath. Elven. She was elven. He'd heard of them but never seen one.

"Dust," the old lady crooned. "How is my Princess Dusty?"

Dust whined and the old lady laughed. "You don't like me telling that tale, do you? Do you remember how little Berla named you all, the first time she laid eyes on you? Red told me the tale, you know." The old woman paused. "But we aren't supposed to call her Red. Not in front of … ." her voice drifted off and her head lifted and turned toward the newcomers, though her gaze seemed to look right past Vren.

"Chosen, Dust and Dithen here bring news," Aramal said.

"Dithen? Do I know you?" The Chosen focused on him, her brown eyes sharp.

"No, milady," Vren bowed his head. "I am newly come with Dust from Edenrich."

"Well, you are welcome," the Chosen said, her voice a bit stronger. "Drop your pack and pull up a chair. Latarie, get this young man some kavage, and make it strong and hot." The Chosen smiled at Vren, her hand still stroking Dust's ears. "If I know my Dust, she kept you moving at a fast pace. Wear a soul out, she will."

"Yes, ma'am," Vren said. He sat and accepted the mug Latarie handed him.

For a time all was quiet. Vren drank his kavage as the Chosen crooned softly to Dust. The door soon opened and others entered, stamping boots and taking kavage of their own.

"Make it quick, Dithen," Aramal said, friendly enough but determined. "We'll talk more after the harvest is done."

Vren spoke then, fast and firm, and gave the basics.

"Well," Aramal said when the marcus finished. "So yet again the Xyians war over land ill used and a city falling apart at the seams. Bad cess to them all, I say."

Mutters of agreement. "Well, enough for now," Aramal said.

"We've a harvest to get in. Dust, I assume you'll tell the others? Lessen you wish to be pickin' grapes?"

Dust's tongue lolled out.

"Thought not," Aramal said. "We'll be all night pickin', Dithen. Rest yourself and we'll have questions later."

The group filed out and Latarie shut the door behind them. "Dust, before you join the others, there's something you need to know." She caught Dithen's eye. "Dithen," she said loudly. "Would you mind fetching wood for the fire?"

There was no need that Vren could see—the wood box was full and the fire burned high. But he nodded anyway and rose from his chair.

"Such a kind young man," the Chosen said.

"The pile's just by the path." Latarie said.

Vren went out into the cold. He could see the lanterns of the pickers in the field, the large, brightly-lit sheds waiting for the grapes. Cold, hard work, he expected, but he'd heard wonderful things about icewine. Indeed, all the wines of Athelbryght had always been praised.

Giving Latarie time to say what she needed, Vren took his ease. After a few minutes he gathered an armful of wood and returned to the kitchen, loudly stomping his feet clear of snow before pushing open the door. The Chosen was still in her rocker, Dust at her side. Latarie was poking the fire.

"And who might you be, young man?" the Chosen asked.

# CHAPTER THIRTY-FOUR

It was with a heavy heart that Dust entered the Packmoot.

The others had already gathered at their traditional meeting spot. The twelve birch trees originally planted in a circle around the small clearing had long since died and fallen to rot on the forest floor. But their seedlings had taken root, and their seedlings had taken root, and the birch grove thrived.

The night was cold and clear, with no wind. The vore could easily hear, in the distance, the vineyards full of ice grapes being harvested.

Fog came up to greet her, and in the way of the vore, spoke. "Dust. You have seen the Chosen?"

"Yes," Dust didn't have to say anything else, her body showed him her sorrow.

Fog nuzzled her muzzle for a moment. "Any sign?" he asked.

Dust shook her head. "No, I found no child born with the dagger-star birthmark."

"Nor did any others," Fog said. "Although those that ventured out to Tassinic and the ancient Elven Kingdom beyond have yet to report." Fog tilted his head. "You returned with a marcus," he observed, his voice neutral.

"Aye," Dust said. "Hard enough to bear news of the human world without a human to speak the words."

"Humans," Fluff snorted, coming up behind her.

"We were once of them," Dust said mildly.

"Once," Fluff growled. "No longer. And I do not think that we should trouble ourselves overmuch with–"

"Let us begin," Whiskers shook herself and took her place in the center of their circle. The others settled around her. "Dust, what tale would you tell?"

Dust told them of the war, of the lack of finding a Chosen. She was honest about Vren and that fact that he was a marcus, but found herself unwilling to share the truth of Xylara's birth. That seemed his story to tell, not hers.

"No one has found a Chosen," Fog summarized. "Although we have not yet heard back from all that we sent seeking."

"We should have sent further, out even into the Plains," Bright Fang growled. "Yes, yes, I know the dangers," he continued when others snapped at him. "But there are humans beyond where we have searched. We could have sent humans to aid the search."

"We have fallen into a trap of hoping," Long Tongue said. "Thinking that a Chosen would be born before our beloved lady passed. Yet a Chosen has not been born and our beloved lady will soon leave this world."

"Piss poor way to determine governance, if you ask me," grumbled Sassy. "A birthmark, of all things."

"We did not ask, nor question, when we gave Red Gloves and Lord High Baron Josiah our pledge," Fog said. "Now that the path grows dark, you would abandon it?"

"I didn't say that," Sassy snapped.

"Then what did you say," Socks said, letting his hackles rise.

"Enough," Fog thundered.

All lowered their eyes, acknowledging his dominance.

"There is still time for a Chosen to appear," Fog resumed. "Our Lady's health is good, even if her memory fades. She is cared for and well-guarded."

"The humans will want to—" Long Tongue started, but Fog cut him off.

"No. There is no mage in Athelbryght and there will be none. We will not allow her to be touched by foul magic."

"And when she dies, for she will die," Whiskers said calmly, "will we leave here? Fade from the lands of man?"

"Leave the people we have aided and lived among for many of their lifetimes?" Fog asked. "Leave them to their fates?"

"I do not know the answer," Whiskers said.

"Nor do I," Fog said. "The time may come when we must find them, but that time is not now. Dust," he said, shifting the Packmoot's attention back to her. "As to your marcus."

"He seeks to return to the Wastes," Dust said. "Through the mountain pass."

"Where we cannot venture," Whiskers said.

"What advantage to us in aiding him?" Fog asked.

"What disadvantage?" Dust asked. "To give him escort and supplies?"

"That trail is narrow and dangerous." Sassy said. "And the dangers of the Wastes are as wide and vast as the grasses it once held."

"Used to be good hunting, though," Long Tongue said wistfully. "I remember—"

"Yes, well, aiding him keeps our options open." Fog said. "Bright Fang, you just talked of spreading our search wider."

"The marcus knows of our need, and would send word if he found such a child," Dust said, then shifted uncomfortably at their glares. "I talked to the Liam," she admitted. "But it was needful."

Fog stared at her and she knew that she'd face more questions about Vren at some point, though for now, Fog just shrugged. "We will aid him then, with supplies and an escort through the pass. Dust, you will take him, but though the marcus is free to venture out there, you are not. You will return and report on the conditions of the trail."

Fog made eye contact with each of the gathered vore. Dust and the others lowered their heads in turn.

"So let it be," Fog said.

———•———

Iris shifted slightly in her tree perch, concealed by wind and rain and dark of night. Sap clung to her cold hands and dripping hair. She'd never be rid of the smell of pine and she was tired almost beyond measure.

But she was downwind of the farmstead. Safe enough from the vore. Safe from *all* the vore.

Who knew there were so many? Who knew that the fields would be filled with farmers harvesting grapes in winter?

Her stomach complained; she ignored it. But she couldn't

ignore the need, the drive, the ache in her bones.

There was no way she could enter the Manor of Athelbryght. Too many guards, too many workers, too many people who knew one another. Too many damnable vore, with keen noses and swift intelligence. A tight community. She'd thought about limping in as a wounded warrior seeking shelter, but there were too many dangers. She wasn't sure she could pass, and if her bondmark was seen … not worth the risk. Iris nibbled at her lip.

There was no way she could do this. Just no way. She'd be found, caught, killed perhaps. The damn vore and their damn senses.

Her heartbeat echoed with her failure. She glanced at the bondmark on her wrist, which quietly thrummed with the demand to hunt. The Bonded seemed content to wait for news.

Iris was not.

She had to admit a grudging respect for the vore and the marcus. She'd lost the track more often than she cared to admit. It had been sheer luck to find a vore print, followed by hoofprint, followed by a booted footprint. From there she had followed them to the village, and staked it out until they left.

It was her first real look at her prey. The vore was bigger than she'd imagined. The human was smaller then she expected, and she couldn't tell its sex. They still had the babe in the sling. She would have attacked on the road, but they moved too quickly for her to catch them alone before they were welcomed to the Manor proper.

How were they feeding the babe? If the marcus was a woman, perhaps she was nursing the babe. Or perhaps the vore?

Or maybe this was one great game of bluff and she was chasing a will-a-wisp.

Iris blew into her cold hands, trying to warm her fingers. It didn't help, so she slipped her right hand under her cloak, below her breast. Through her leathers, she rubbed at her scar.

There had to be a way. The need burned deep within her; she couldn't think of giving up the chase. There had to be a way. It was a litany in her head, a thought she could not free herself from.

The wind died down. She ignored it. There had to be a—

A pig squealed, then another. She turned her head, following the sound.

Pig. That meant a pig sty. That meant pig shit and pig piss and … Iris grimaced. But it might work.

Covered in that muck, she'd be able to move about and maybe learn something. Take no overt action, just scout. Watch. Listen.

She didn't move, not yet. She picked at her plan, thinking it through, looking for flaws.

The harvest wouldn't last forever. She'd strip down, cache her gear. Take a knife, nothing more. Find the sty and soak for a bit in the mess. The pigs wouldn't care, at least she hoped they wouldn't. She could wait there until things quieted, then move about carefully and learn what she could. If her prey left in the meantime, she'd pick up the trail again.

She closed her eyes and tried to picture the maps she'd memorized. There were the main roads, but there was also that mountain pass to the Wastes. It was a fair bet that the marcusi was headed there.

Iris nodded and started to ease down out of the tree. At least the stink of pig muck would be better than the cloying scent of pine.

Well, different, at least.

## CHAPTER THIRTY-FIVE

oyal Master Librarian Jacoben's gut roiled in sick, squirming knots as sweat pooled in the small of his back.

The main doors of the library were open, the chill air sweeping away the warm, sweet scent of paper and ink. He watched as the palace guards with their filthy boots hauled open boxes and barrels of books and scrolls into the Royal Library—*his library*—like so many sides of beef, stacking them willy-nilly on the tables and floors. A chaos of knowledge, treated with utter disdain.

When a page fluttered to the floor, a guard snatched it up and crammed it into his crate.

Jacoben could barely breathe. He opened his mouth to protest, but the sight of the Queen's Bondmaiden, Avice, stilled his words, cleaving his dry tongue to the roof of his mouth. She was a lovely woman, but her was the cold beauty of the blade. Something about the way she moved spoke of a cat, waiting to pounce when the mouse twitched.

He stood stiff and silent at her side, his cold, clammy fingers laced together to keep them from shaking.

There were whispers. Rumors of disappearances.

Of deaths.

"There's more coming," Avice sniffed. "At least another wagon-load."

Another wagon-load? Looking at what had already arrived, Jacoben realized with horror that that would be all of Orval's collection. The Librarian swallowed hard, trying to get moisture in his mouth, trying to protest, to spit on this woman for this atrocity.

Then he recalled his lovely wife, his oldest son—just about to start his apprenticeship, and his youngest daughter, first learning to walk. And the others. Six mouths, altogether, to feed and clothe and nurture and ... bile rose in his throat.

He could not risk it.

He and Orval had their differences, certainly, and the man was definitely wrong in his interpretations of the *Epic of Xyson*. But to strip a man of his books, his life's work.... .

Jacoben looked at the volumes around him, organized systematically, cataloged, the knowledge of the Kingdom.

*His* life's work.

He'd been told—no, warned—that Orval was to be "honored" by the King, told that his staff should be ready to accept the scholar's books as an addition to the Library, but he'd never expected this. A few of the choicest pieces, certainly ... but *everything*?

The worst of it? The thought that burned in the back of his

throat? He'd seen Orval at the Audiences and for one brief instant, he'd dared to think. Dared to warn him, to try to aid him ... .

Instead, he'd fled back to his library. To the shelter of the stacks and shelves. They'd never been friends, though they weren't truly enemies, either. Perhaps adversaries was the better term, but–

Guilt added to the pain in his bowels, which were turning liquid. He clenched his ass tight and tried to breathe.

The Bondmaiden shifted slightly, smelling of ginger and something sour. The silence had gone too long; she was looking at him oddly. He forced words out past the clog in his throat. "We are overwhelmed to be trusted with this amount of material. It will take time to organize and catalog–"

Avice gave him a direct stare from under dark lashes. "No need. The Queen wishes these materials preserved, so we will seal the crates with her personal seal and place them in storage.

Jacoben licked his lips. "We will need to find suitable storage, somewhere dry and free of–"

"Somewhere there is room," Avice said firmly. "Safely under lock and key."

"Of course," Jacoben said faintly. "But we could prepare a list–"

"Of the crates? Certainly." Avice said. "Of the books? Why bother? If anyone asks for access, tell them they will need the Queen's permission. Written permission," she added firmly.

"I see," Jacoben said cautiously.

"Excellent. You should be aware that there are plans to secure additional materials from other libraries in the future."

*Other collections?*

They watched as more boxes were brought in. Then sacks. *Sacks.*

Avice spoke again. "The Queen understands that you receive

requests at times, for research and information."

"Y-y-yes." Jacoben swallowed hard. "The work of this Library and Archive is to provide–"

"No more, Master Librarian. In the future, all requests must be approved by the Queen," Avice said.

"Oh, but," Jacoben glanced at the stacks of pending requests on the shelf designated for them. "But that will–"

"No 'buts,'" Avice said, a threat in her voice.

"No, of course not," Jacoben said faintly. "As the Queen commands, of course." He drew a breath, thinking of his wife, his children, his staff. He knew they were currently pretending to work, bodies hunched over desks but pens barely moving.

"Good. Ah, that's the last of it." Avice nodded as the guards started to bring in lids for the crates. One of them dropped a lid on top of an over-full box and mashed down the contents. Jacoben tried not to wince.

The Librarian never knew where the idea came from; he spoke almost before finishing the thought. "There's one difficulty," he blurted out. "The King has commanded that we search all records for any reference to atira blades."

"Hold," Avice said. The guards obeyed.

Jacoben trembled at his own daring. "Surely he would wish us to search these new collections as well?"

There was a very long pause. Avice didn't even look at him.

"The King is very focused on this goal," Jacoben ventured.

"He is," Avice confirmed. "Is there a chance there is a mention in all this?"

"Yes," Jacoben said firmly. Of course there was a chance. A small chance, perhaps, but a chance nonetheless. Who knew what Orval had locked away? "With the Queen's permission, we could review this collection and seek the information the King has requested."

Avice looked at him coolly and he knew damn well he was not fooling her. But King Xyrath had made it very clear to everyone that he desired an atira blade above all things.

Jacoben smiled weakly, feeling his knees begin to give way. He was useless and spineless, but–

"I will consult with Her Majesty," Avice said. "No one is to touch these crates until I return. You," she pointed at two of the guards, "stand watch while I am gone."

The other guards followed the Bondmaiden out. It felt like the very air grew warmer as she left.

"Master," came a whisper, and Jacoben felt the warmth of other bodies around him.

He came to himself to find he was surrounded by his staff. Copyists, archivists, friends. Worried faces, all looking to him.

"We should return to our duties," he choked out. "These boxes are not to be touched until we receive instructions from the Queen. We will work around the clutter. Move your things and use the desks towards the back."

"Yes, Master." Their voices were quiet as they bowed away, retreating to their usual desks.

Jacoben brushed off the front of his tunic and returned to his desk, glancing at the papers there. "Apprentice Hulbert, did you find that Second Age reference for me?"

"No, Master," came the response from the boy, his pudgy face stark white, his cheeks two spots of red. His dark eyes glanced at the guards, then lowered. "Perhaps it has been mis-shelved. I will look again."

Good lad, Jacoben thought, though he merely nodded. He

returned to work as the others gathered their things and moved away. The pair of guards kept their distance, standing together near the main door, chatting with each other.

After what seemed like forever, Hulbert called from the back. "I have it here, Master. Shall I bring it out?"

"No," Jacoben rose. "I will come."

As he expected, his people were gathered together, huddled among the farthest stacks. They gathered close to him, like stoop-shouldered, ink-stained chicks.

"What shall we do?" one whispered. A few looked over their shoulders toward the main door, their fear plain.

"There are many new faces," another said, wringing ink-stained fingers.

"That new Housekeeper is not to be trusted," a third growled.

Jacoben gathered them even closer, whispering. "We will keep ourselves and the collection safe. We will do as we are commanded."

"But–"

"We will continue the work of this archive. The King has commanded us to search out any reference to atira blades, no matter how vague. The Queen will have little choice but to allow us to go through Orval's collection, or–" he swallowed hard, "any other materials that come into our possession." He took a breath. "And if we organize and preserve as we go, who is to say we err?"

Nods all around.

"We will review all new acquisitions according to our standard procedures," he reminded them. "Through methods that take time and care. In an orderly fashion, so that we do not miss a single reference to atira blades."

They were calming, thinking of the work ahead.

"We will send their Majesties a daily report, to keep their interest and show our co-operation." Jacoben nodded, the idea forming even as he spoke. "We will keep safe and quiet."

"What if we find one?" Ansella, the youngest apprentice, asked, with wide-eyed hope. "Might the King come here? To the Library?"

Hulbert opened his mouth to argue.

"Ansella," Jacoben chided her even as the others chuckled. "It's a myth, from the Golden Age of Xy. Hundreds of years and no one has found an atira blade yet." He straightened, lifting his chin. "Although if one is to be found, I am sure we would be the ones to find the reference."

Soft chuckles all around. They were justifiably proud of their abilities.

"What of those research requests?" Hulbert asked.

"We will send our regrets and explain the new procedures in ways that provide a carefully worded warning. We will note that all requests are reviewed and noted and that there might be … further acquisitions."

Light was dawning in their eyes as they began to understand him.

"But Master," Hulbert reminded him, "The crates will still be sealed, the knowledge contained within still not accessible."

"True," Jacoben smiled grimly, "at least until the page turns. And we all know that there is always another page. And with every turn of the page, new knowledge is revealed, new ideas and thoughts."

He looked them all in the eye in turn, gauging their understanding. He was met with hope and determination.

"So, we will work and strive and keep ourselves and our own safe as best we can." Jacoben gestured them back to their work as the main doors opened. "It's all we can do."

He headed back through the shelves to his desk, changing course when he saw that the Bondmaiden had returned and was awaiting him. Even as she instructed him to catalog Orval's papers, his thoughts kept churning back to the man himself.

Lord High Baron Orval. Married, huh, that had come as a surprise. Still, he wished the new Lord High Baron and his wife well.

They were going to need it.

## CHAPTER THIRTY-SIX

Amari came awake in an instant, staring into the dimness, holding her breath, waiting for the sound that had disturbed her to repeat. When it came, it wasn't one of the babes as she expected.

It was Orval, lying in bed beside her. A swift, pained intake of breath.

"Orval?" she whispered.

"Sorry." His voice was low and strained. "A c-cramp. Trying not to wake the babes."

The small copper lantern they'd left burning still flickered with light. She eased out of the bedding carefully, shivering in the cold air as her toes met the icy floor. She took a moment to check the babes' baskets, finding they still slept, then padded over to Orval's side of the bed as quietly as she could.

Roth and Yfin had chosen to sleep down by the front door, watching over the fire and Xydell. Rosalind had taken the second floor, hiding her pallet amidst the crates and baskets.

She and Orval were on the third floor, in a room with a stout wooden door that bolted on the inside.

'Just in case,' Roth had said grimly.

There were two floors yet above them, but other than checking for occupants, human or otherwise, they'd left them for later.

Orval's face was twisted in a grimace and shiny with sweat. He was holding his breath, as if he didn't dare breathe, the pain would stop; his hands were fisted in the sheets.

"Let me see," she said softly, easing back the blankets and gently pulling up his night clothes, enough to expose his leg but keep his privacy.

The withered leg was thin and wiry compared to the healthy leg. She put her hand just above the knee and felt the muscles, taut and hot beneath her fingers.

"Can't get it to ease up, Orval said through gritted teeth. "It will pass, it usually does."

"You did too much these last few days," she murmured, starting to rub warmth into his skin below the knee.

"Not much choice," he murmured back.

That was when she caught the look of fear in his eyes. He'd been so strong for them all. This wasn't just about the cramps in his legs. She suspected the reality of their situation had hit him; the mental anguish amplifying the physical pain.

"It worked," she said, rubbing down toward his feet. "We have shelter, water, fire, and food. In fact, Ussin left us with more of that than we had in your rooms." She arched an eyebrow. "More than pease porridge."

Orval gave a pained chuckle.

"Roth and Yfin have their weapons and Xydell seems to be coming back to us," she reminded him.

"Do you think she is well enough, sleeping down by the fire?" Orval asked.

"Yes," Amari sighed. "The warmth is the best thing for her now, as well as all the liquids we can get her to drink. The hearth has its own healing." She felt a slight easing of his muscles under her touch.

"Still," he shifted slightly in the bed, "we are still stranded, still alone, with no idea of what lies in wait for us."

"You have met all those first requirements you told us about," she said. "What else does the *Epic of Xyson* say?"

Orval frowned, then his face relaxed as he began to think, to remember. Amari felt more tension leak out under her hands.

"Scouts," he said firmly. "Secure the area around the camp in ever expanding circles."

"So, a plan for tomorrow," she nodded. "You can command Roth and Yfin. Rosalind and I can organize our supplies."

"Command," he snorted, a wry grin on his face, then glanced at the babes in alarm.

"They're fine," she said. "Is it any better?"

He nodded.

"Then let me try something," she said, and without waiting for permission, she dug her thumbs in just under the knee and pressed hard.

"Ah!" Orval jerked in surprise, then relaxed onto the bed, his eyes wide. "Where did you learn to do that?"

"My brothers," she kneaded his muscles, leaning in harder. "Overzealous in their training and of course–" she stopped, avoiding Orval's eyes.

"Eijer?" he asked.

"Eijer," she confirmed, suddenly at a loss for words. How could she explain–?

She met his gaze then and found his eyes warm and kind in the lamplight. She shivered, but not from fear. More from hope. Or maybe … anticipation. She lowered her gaze and started to pull the blankets back over him.

"Did you love Eijer?" Orval asked.

Amari hesitated.

Orval grimaced. "Forgive me," he said. "I have no right to ask that and you're cold." He scooted over to the other side of the bed, holding the blankets open. "Come where it's warm."

Amari hesitated. "The babes," she whispered.

"They're fine," he said after a fresh glance, "for now. Do you think they might sleep through the night eventually?"

"They will," She got into bed, and helped him arrange the blankets over them both. "Eventually."

He chuckled as she settled in, curling on her side to face him. He laid on his back, staring at the dim shadows above them.

"You have every right to know," she said. "The problem is, I do not know how to answer your question anymore."

"Why's that?" he asked the ceiling.

"Eijer was … " she trailed off, not knowing how to proceed.

Orval glanced at her, his blue eyes glittering in the darkness. "Remember, I knew him. We fostered together. Eijer was always Eijer."

"He swept me off my feet," Amari said. "What I thought was

love was more an overwhelming assault on all my senses. I was new to the royal court, and alone, and he swept me off my feet." She hesitated. "At the time, I thought we loved."

"Eijer always had that way about him," Orval said. "He drew you in with his smiles and charm and made you feel like you were important. A friend, a confidant. But Eijer was always looking out for Eijer. He was not one to stand at anyone's side, he always had to be at the forefront."

Amari nodded. "While it's clear to me now that he just wanted a conquest, I would not take back the pain of that betrayal, not one moment of it, for Dalan is a joyful gift in my life." She sighed. "Yet, if Eijer were here before me, I'd curse him and reject him even as he rejected me. So when you speak of love … it's complicated."

Orval nodded.

"There were warning signs, in hindsight." Amari admitted. "I told him my dreams, but looking back, I can see that he didn't listen, didn't build on them with me. What I thought was love was just empty air."

For a time they lay together in the dark stillness, each lost in their own thoughts.

Orval broke the silence first. "What were your dreams?" he asked.

"Hearth mother," Amari said immediately. "With many hearths under the shelter of mine. Ten children, with lands and gardens and livestock and crops as far as the eye could see."

"Ten children?"

Amari laughed at his expression. "Well, Hearths adopt, you know. There are always children in need." She smiled. "And I would preside over all as Hearth Mother."

"A benevolent matriarch, I am sure." Orval said.

"A benevolent matriarch," Amari agreed. She hesitated, then asked. "What of you, Orval? Were there not marriage plans for you?"

"Not for a cripple," Orval's mouth grew tight. "The only ones who wanted to marry me were only interested in the Bloodline. My parents made short work of them. After my parents died, I left the court and I think I faded from memory."

"But you must have had dreams?" she asked. "Surely you had a dream, before all this?"

"A dream?" His voice grew grim. "I did not let myself dream. I intended to live out my life lost in my books. Hadn't thought beyond needing to hole up against the world." He stifled a yawn. "Tell me more of yours.

"Children and grandchildren and great grandchildren running about my feet," Amari said. "Gardens and herds of fat cattle. Dogs and cats, horses and pigs. All sprawling around a huge manor house."

"All those children," Orval yawned, blinked at her sleepily. "You will need a school and teachers. And maybe a library."

Amari smiled, watching his eyes slowly drift closed. So different from Eijer, in every way. So smart and kind. His strength was different, too. He'd offered her a contract without a hesitation, to protect her and the babes.

She relaxed into the warmth of the bed, reaching out to touch him lightly on the shoulder with her fingertips. Maybe her dream could include—

Orval's eyes fluttered open. "Sorry. You were saying?"

"Sleep," she said.

"But your dreams," he protested.

"We should sleep while we can," she said. "Shared dreams

are lovely, but dawn comes with something I'd let myself forget. All the work that dreams require."

Orval gave a slight snort as his eyes closed again. "You are not alone in that. No one ever wants to think of the work."

Amari watched as he slipped into sleep. Such a lovely man. He was everything that Eijer wasn't, and so much more.

She yawned, relaxed into the bed and closed her own eyes. Perhaps a bit more sleep–

Dalan's hungry cry cracked the air.

## CHAPTER THIRTY-SEVEN

—•—

Heard you're leaving us tomorrow," Aramal said.

Vren looked up from his seat on an overturned bucket. Aramal was standing in the stall door, looking relaxed, a harness in his hands.

Vren smiled at the man and gestured him in. "Harvest done?" he asked.

Aramal had understood that Vren couldn't sleep within four walls. He'd offered an empty stall in the barn, used to store feed. Warm, what with all the animals. Vren had spread his bedroll on a pile of hay and slept like a rock.

There was only one horse in the barn, thankfully, an old plow mare in a box stall. Vren made sure to keep his distance from her as he came and went.

"Aye, and it looks to be a good one." Aramal seated himself on a barrel across from Vren and began to check the leather straps for wear. There were no idle hands in Athelbryght. "You sure it's a good idea, heading up into the mountains now? What of the weather?"

Vren shrugged. "I've a need to get home."

"First I ever heard anyone call the Wastes 'home,'" Aramal said. He pulled some tools from his pockets and began to work, then paused to gesture at the blanket where Vren had emptied his pack. "So what's this about, then?"

Vren had tossed most of the contents of his pack into the center of the blanket and now was sorting everything, spreading the items out. "Been traveling for a bit, and one acquires things, more than ya know. Just checking to see what needs repair."

"Like your boots?" Aramal jerked his chin towards Vren's foot.

"Aye," Vren wiggled his toes in the hole. "And to see what I need to leave behind."

"So? Worried about weight?"

"No," Vren smiled. "The Wastes tolerate nothing forced by the hand of man."

"So the stories are true?" Aramal's curiosity was clear.

"Truth," Vren said. "Step into the Waste with this," he held up his steel dagger, "and it will return to the elements. I need to rid myself of that as well as things like this." He held up a small tin box holding flint and steel.

"And I have to sharpen these," he added, digging out his set of bone knives.

"Ho, now, those are lovely," Aramal set harness and tools down and reached for the blades. Vren gave them up willingly.

"The handle's horn, isn't it?"

"Aye," Vren said. "But they don't hold an edge like steel does, so I have to keep sharpening them."

"You don't use stone?"

"Never," Vren said as a shiver ran down his spine.

Aramal didn't seem to notice. He ran his fingers over the yellowed blades. "An odd sort of life, seems to me," he said slowly.

"The one I know best," Vren said.

"What are the Wastes like?" Aramal asked.

Vren took a moment to think.

"I'd not offend," Aramal said quickly, into the silence. "I've never been out of Athelbryght and only travel to trade at our borders. I had a chance to leave once but … I didn't take it. Not that I have a reason to leave, mind, but sometimes I get an itch to know."

"No offense taken," Vren said. "Just not sure I know the words. To your eye, the Wastes would seem desolate. Plant growth is sparse and scrubby. Trees don't get much taller than me and the ground is stony, full of grit and sand. Water's scarce." He shook his head. "Shades of brown, yellow, tan.

"And the heat?" Vren rolled his shoulders at the memory. "At the height, sun burns like the hottest fire. I come to the border of the Wastes, I won't be wearing leathers." He reached into the depths of his pack and pulled out a cloth tunic and trous, and a rather battered straw hat.

"I'll not tread in the full sun, either." Vren smiled. "Walk early in the mornings, or after the sun peaks."

"What about snakes?" Aramal asked. "And I heard tell of creatures called gurtles that hunt in packs."

"Well, you always walk with both eyes open," Vren said.

"'Cause everything in the Wastes is trying to kill ya."

"Why live there, then?" Aramal asked, eyes alight with curiosity.

Vren hesitated. How to explain ancient oaths that bound them? "There's a beauty to it," he said, settling on something Aramal could accept. "In the Spring, after the rains, the Wastes become alive with color and the scent of growing things." Vren lifted his head and flashed Aramal a grin. "And ya might be cold, but ya never find yourself balls deep in snow."

Aramal laughed and returned Vren's knives. "True enough, friend."

"It is home," Vren said; the longing in his voice caught him by surprise. "I am called to return."

Aramal nodded. "As I would miss the scent of the harvest, and maybe, just maybe, the snow as deep as my balls."

They shared a grin.

"What about that doll, then?" Aramal asked.

Vren turned to look. He'd forgotten he'd propped it against the wall, wrapped in its sling. "A distraction," he grinned. "For any who might pursue me."

Aramal shook his head. "Well, I'll not pretend to understand, or ask for explanations. Just know you'd be welcome to stay, if you wished it."

Vren shook his head and Aramal nodded, accepting.

"Still, it must be a hard life." Aramal returned to his leather stitching. "No metal for tools, pots, or pans."

"We've bone and stone," Vren shrugged. "Glass too, and pottery."

"But isn't glass forced?"

Vren shrugged again. "The Elders think it's because glass is formed of sand and heat and then shaped. 'When the Blood turned on the Blood and the wrath of the elements fell upon us, there was no reasoning with the forces of wind and fire. We adapted to their ways, at their command.'" He dug into his pile of possessions and held up a glass disc. "So we make fire with this."

"I can see good parts and bad parts to that," Aramal mused. "Mostly having to do with cloudy, dark days.

"Again, we adapt," Vren said. "I welcome my return to the Wastes tomorrow."

"It will take more than a few days to trod that path. I've a good piece of cow hide that might work to fix those boots." Aramal set his work aside. "Let me fetch it."

"My thanks," Vren called after him, then waited until his footsteps had faded before digging out the most precious of his burdens.

The glass vial was still well stoppered with cork and sealed with the wax that Queen Kara had dripped on it. The blood within gleamed bright red.

The small key that he'd wrapped with it was also still safe. He didn't know what it was made of, but it was worked metal and probably magic at that. "You'll not survive the Wastes," Vren told it. "I'll cache you with my sword and daggers until the Liam figures out what to do with you."

He wrapped the items up again and placed them back in his pack, along with his cloth garments, then continued to sort through his belongings. Funny, how so much metal wormed its way into his pack on his travels. Buckles, pins, spoons. Yet they were easy to shed, once his focus returned to the Wastes.

As his fingers worked, he considered his options.

There had been no sign of pursuit for some time. He'd thought of back-tracking and killing her. The vore might aid him in that, even if Athelbryght was neutral.

But that wasn't his goal. He wanted the pursuer to fail, to report back that he'd escaped with the babe into the Wastes. Anything to pull their attention away from Orval and Amari.

So he'd play the prey a bit longer and wear the sling.

Just in case.

———•———

Iris knelt by the rough wood of the barn wall and pressed her ear close. She was numb and shivering, naked, every inch of her dark skin covered with a thick layer of muck from the pig sty. She stifled her curses at the wind, and the cold, and the muck, and idiots who slept in a barn instead of a warm bed. It had taken many a miserable night to learn that much.

But he was in there. She could hear the men talking, but their words were muffled. She leaned in, seeking a crack, holding her breath, hoping to hear something. Anything.

The wind died.

The local spoke, his voice deeper, louder, asking about the wastes. Then the breeze picked up and she heard little of the marcus's reply.

At least now she knew her target was male. Which just made her more determined to cut off his private parts.

Iris found another crack, a bit wider, with more light. She checked her surroundings, then pressed in close. The words became clearer.

*"What about that doll, then?"*

Iris caught her breath.

*"A distraction for any who might pursue me."*

Rage shook her so hard that she lost the rest of the conversation. Her vision darkened and it took everything she had not to rise up and kill them both. Muck-covered, naked avenger with naught but her gleaming knife in her hand, teeth bared, as she slit their throats.

He had no babe. *He. Had. No. Babe.*

Her whole body shook at the fury of being fooled. Fierce hate filled her.

Death was too good for him; she'd inflict such pain as she was able.

Reason asserted itself. No, she couldn't do that, not yet. There had been a babe born; she'd seen the evidence of that herself in the Airion command tent. The Bonded had commanded and she would obey.

A wisp of words reached her ears.

*"I welcome my return to the Wastes tomorrow."*

Iris allowed herself a moment of triumph. That mountain path. The smug fool would sleep warm this night and head out in the morning. But she'd start now, this moment, circle back to her cache, skirt the manor house and its fields, steal a bit of food, maybe more blankets.

Iris eased away from the wall and crawled to where the shadows were deepest. Suddenly the cold, the wind, and the dung mattered not a wit.

The Bonded needed to know where that babe was. It had to be somewhere back in Edenrich. The marcus would tell her as she carved him into pieces.

He might have the vore with him, and that made her think. She'd have to find a place to attack well before the trail headed down to the Wastes. A good ambush site, then a crossbow bolt for the vore and her knives for the man.

She wouldn't bathe. The stink would last.

She grinned mirthlessly. For all their reputed abilities, marcusi were still human. They suffered pain, as any did.

Iris was good at pain. He would tell her what she needed to know. And after, well, she might get a bit of revenge for all the trouble he'd put her through.

Then she could bathe and sleep and take the vore's fur back to the Bonded.

It was as good a plan as any.

—◆—

Vren lay in his bed of straw and blankets, eyes wide open. The barn was quiet and dark, with nothing stirring but a few mice, being hunted by barn cats. Moonlight filtered through the old boards, giving everything an odd glow.

Vren was free to wrestle with his conflicts.

He should not do this, he had no right and no desire to offend, but when would he have such a chance again? He was leaving at dawn, and who knew if he would survive the journey. And if he did, when would he leave the Wastes again?

Before he could talk himself out of it, he flung back the blanket, rose to his feet, and donned his patched boots. He straightened his clothes as best he could, brushed himself off, and ran his fingers through his hair. His care might not make a difference, but then again, it might.

Vren took a deep breath, stepped into the main corridor, walked a few steps it took, and faced the open stall.

The old plow horse stood there, her shaggy winter coat more grey than brown. The moonlight seemed to make it glow.

Her large head turned, eyes dark. It stamped one forehoof, hard. "No farther," it seemed to say. Old it might be, but a horse that size could do harm.

Vren swallowed hard, moved one step closer, then sank to his knees. He bowed his head. Carefully, slowly, he raised his hands, palms open. "Spirt of the Horse, hear my plea, and in my voice, hear the plea of all those of the Wastes."

The only sound was the rasp of his breath and the beating of his heart in his ears. "Forgive us," he whispered. "Forgive us for what was done by our ancestors." Vren crossed his hands over his chest, resting his fingers on his shoulders. He expected nothing, for the prayers and petitions of his ancestors had always gone unheard. Guilt and shame flooded through him, at the past, at daring to plead. He'd rise to his feet, back away, and return to bed.

He lifted his head and lost all ability to breathe.

The mare was now a gleaming warhorse, eyes bright, tail swishing in anger, saddled and bridled, armored in gleaming metal that reflected the moonlight. Its gaze was not friendly.

The woman standing beside it was also clad in armor, top to toe, her eyes bright under her helm, a huge, two-handed sword on her back. In the shadows behind her, Vren caught a glimpse of a man in leathers, little more than an impression of bright hair and kinder eyes.

Vren went still, for there was power here, and fear that that power might strike him for his nerve. He sank lower, bowed his head almost to the floor.

"Far from home, wanderer," came a voice that climbed up the hairs on the back of his neck. It was a woman's voice, yet not, echoing yet clear. "Long time since we have heard this plea."

Vren swallowed hard. He didn't dare speak.

"You are of the Tribe of the Horse. Faint, but traces remain of the old blood within you."

Vren licked his lips. "Yes," he breathed a whisper.

"Change will come. You will not see it, Vren of the Horse." her voice held a hollowness of truth and dread.

Sorrow gripped him.

"But you might be the spark that ignites the wild grass fire," she continued.

Hope forced him up, made him stare right into the glitter that surrounded her.

"You plead to have the Wastes restored to what was, wanderer. To have the horses return, to flourish and grow. For forgiveness of the betrayal so long ago.."

"Yes, on behalf of all my people," he said breathlessly, tears in his eyes. "Yes."

"It requires much," she said. "The price is high."

"Yes," Vren said again.

"Even if you do not see it in your lifetime?" she pressed.

"Yes," he said for the third time. "Even so."

The Spirit turned her head ever so slightly. The male figure behind her nodded, giving assent.

"Let it be so," she said, and now there was warmth in the hollowness. "Willing sacrifice, willingly made. Not an easy thing, but you will have a choice to make, wanderer. You will know when the moment comes. Remember us." She put her hand on the horse's shoulder. The warhorse shook its head, rattling its barding, and stamped its hoof.

Brightness flared all around them. When his sight returned, they were gone. All that was left was an old plow horse, who snorted and turned its head away.

Vren, mouth dry, backed away, shaken, his heart racing. He returned to his pallet, buried himself in the blankets, and tried to convince himself that what had happened had not truly happened. He stared at the beams above him, his heart pounding, his breathing coming faster and faster as a panic he'd never felt before overcame him.

The plow horse snorted again and stamped her hoof.

Peace washed over him, and with it, sleep.

# CHAPTER THIRTY-EIGHT

That's enough for today, Yfin. Fetch us some water."

Orval looked up from his book as Roth and Yfin ended their sparring session. They'd begun by clearing a large space in front of the guardhouse, sweeping the thin snow from the cobblestones. This was followed by work on developing Yfin's fighting skills. The sounds of their practice had been an oddly peaceful backdrop to Orval's study of a section of the *Epic of Xyson*.

Now he checked the baskets at his feet, where the babes slept in the sun, bundled against the chill. Here in the courtyard, out of the wind, it was warm enough to give them a bit of sun and air.

It also gave Amari and Rosalind a bit of privacy as they saw to Aunt Xydell's needs.

Yfin ran off to the well inside, bucket in hand.

Roth settled on the bench next to Orval, removing his helmet and pushing his sweaty hair back. He lowered his head, hiding his face and making a fuss over checking the helmet's lining. "They're watching us," he murmured.

"Oh? Where?" Orval looked around.

"Don't do that," Roth growled.

Orval flinched. "Oh, yes, of course." He pretended to focus on his book.

"You are the oddest combination of book smart and street stupid," Roth said.

"Sorry," Orval said.

"You don't look for watchers. We don't want them to know that we know," Roth said. "As far as I can tell, they aren't there now. Probably getting their nooning and giving a report. They've been watching for days."

"I guess I shouldn't be surprised." Orval bit his lip. "Are we at risk?"

Roth snorted. "We've been at risk from the moment we were abandoned here," he reminded Orval grimly. "So far, they are just watching from a distance. A few high in the Keep windows, some from the far walls. No threat. Yet." Roth set his helmet down. "We are going to have to confront them at some point."

"No," Orval said firmly.

"No?" Roth asked, shocked.

"I want them to see us," Orval glanced at Roth. "I want to look … harmless. Not vulnerable, mind." He pointed with his chin at the swords beside Roth. "But not a threat."

"Confusion to our enemies?" Roth asked.

"More like curiosity," Orval said. "They know even less about us than what we know about them. We have limited ability to seek them out, so I need them to come to us."

"You hope not in the night, with daggers out."

"I hope that instead of attacking us outright, they will want answers." Orval said. "So it's a good sign that they are watching."

Roth gave him a long, steady look, then nodded. "You've brought us this far," he said grudgingly. "But time is against us," he added, brushing his hair back off his forehead. "We've food for another, what, five days?"

"I know," Orval said.

Yfin emerged from the gatehouse and headed toward them, full bucket in one hand, dipper in the other.

"The lad seems good with a sword." Orval said.

Roth nodded. "He comes to it late, but he's learning. He's better with his knives. Learned that when he was on the streets."

Orval raised an eyebrow and Roth lowered his voice and answered the unspoken question. "He was running with other children, all orphaned by the Sweat, for a long time, Finally King Xywellan had the guards round them up and put them to work."

Yfin set the bucket at their feet and offered Roth the dipper. "Did ya see?" he asked Orval, wiping his forehead with his hand. "I almost scored on him."

"Almost," Roth snorted, but Yfin's grin was infectious. Orval grinned back at him, sharing his delight.

"Good for you," he said as Roth offered him the dipper. Orval set his book aside and drank deep of the cold, sweet water.

"What ya reading?" Yfin asked.

"The *Epic of Xyson*," Orval said, and waited for the usual eye-roll and exclamation of disdain. Yfin just cocked his head.

"What's it about?" he asked.

"Didn't you read it in–" Orval started but stopped when Roth nudged his knee. But Yfin wasn't embarrassed at all; he just looked curious.

"It's a very old, epic saga from a very long time ago, of a King that went to face his enemies." Orval glanced at Roth. "You can read it, if you wish."

"Can't read," Yfin shrugged. "Never learned."

"Well," Orval said. "We will have to see to that."

Yfin gave him a skeptical look. "Reading is for smart folk."

"Reading is for all folk," Orval said. "It just takes practice."

Yfin wrinkled his nose.

Roth spoke up. "If you're going to insist he learns to read, then he should teach you some knife moves. Only fair."

Yfin perked up.

Orval gave Roth an uneasy glance. Weaponsmasters in the past had tried to "teach the cripple to fight." He wasn't eager to deal with that again.

Roth shook his head, as if reading his mind. "Knives, not swords," he said, and there was understanding in his eyes.

Orval still frowned. "The boy needs to know how to read."

"You need to know how to defend yourself," Roth added. "All it takes is practice." He repeated Orval's words with a grin. "You can learn from each other."

Yfin's frown probably matched his, but Orval couldn't help himself.

Roth laughed, his voice echoing on the cobblestones. The door to the gatehouse opened and Amari and Rosalind emerged. Rosalind carried a tray of food, Amari a basket of wet clothes.

"What is so funny?" Amari asked. She'd stripped down to her bodice and skirt, leaving her arms bare. She put down her basket and started to spread the freshly-laundered clothing out on the cleared cobblestones so it could dry in the sun.

"The goose and the gander both cook in the same grease," Roth said, then explained.

Rosalind was setting out their meal, with Yfin's eager help. But Orval only had eyes for Amari.

She was brilliant, there in the sun, dark skin glowing against the snow and stones. She moved with unconscious grace, absorbed in her task.

Catching him staring, Amari smiled widely. Orval flushed and looked away. "How is Aunt Xydell?" he asked to cover his confusion.

"She's clean and warm, sleeping by the hearth." Amari's smile vanished. She spread out the last few tunics and continued, "We got her to take some porridge and water. She even managed a few steps to the privy."

"She barely stirred when we bathed her," Rosalind sighed. She folded up to sit on the ground by Yfin. "And she's not talking to us at all. Not sure she knows us. That letheon is dreadful stuff."

"It's not good at her age to lay about like this," Amari came to sit on the bench beside Orval, who shifted to make room. "She just doesn't seem to be all there."

Orval tucked his book safely between them, feeling the warmth of her body. "As nasty as Aunt Xydell is, she didn't deserve this."

"There is still hope," Amari reassured him. "The hearth heals in its own way."

"The warmth?"

"And the life around the hearth."

"Where there is life, there is hope." He frowned at Amari.

"Umm - are you - umm - warm enough, like that?"

"Hard work," Amari said. "I'm fine for the moment." She checked the babes in their baskets, still sweetly sleeping. "It's warm enough here in the sun, for now." Her gaze drifted to the well in the center of the courtyard.

"That still bothering you?" Roth asked gently as Rosalind handed out bowls from the tray, filled with hard crackers, sausage and cheese.

"What kind of people fill a perfectly good well with stones?" Amari's eyes were shadowed. "What kind of hate sparks that kind of cruelty?"

"It was done to prevent anyone from sheltering here," Roth said. "A common enough tactic, I'm afraid."

Orval nudged Amari to take her bowl from Rosalind.

"This is the last of the spicy sausage," Rosalind told Yfin.

Yfin bit into a link. "Is good," he mumbled, then cast a look at Amari and straightened, chewing with his mouth closed.

"You can have mine." Amari laughed, adding one of her links to Yfin's bowl. "I've enough flour to make pigeon and dumplings."

Yfin nodded, then swallowed before he spoke. "I love pigeon n' dumplings. My ma made the best, but," he hurried to assure her, "yours is good too."

"There's only so much pigeon a man can eat," Roth said. "Maybe we could try to snare some rabbits."

"Rats are good," Yfin piped up. "There's quite a few rats."

Orval wasn't the only one to look at him with horror.

"No really," Yfin said. "You gut them and then roast 'em whole. Stinks something terrible as the hair burns off, but they taste really good."

Orval started choking at Amari's expression.

"No rats," she said firmly.

"But–"

"No," Amari said.

Roth was looking off into the distance, clearly trying not to laugh out loud.

Yfin looked so disappointed.

"It's a good thought, Yfin." Orval said. "Shows you are considering all the possibilities."

Amari and Rosalind gave him horrified looks.

Orval bit his lip, trying not to laugh, but the truth was, if they had to, they would. Best to change the subject. "You haven't killed the royal pigeons, have you?" he asked.

"Nay," Yfin said. "Been feeding them and watering them, like you said."

"Good," Orval said. "I am tempted to send a message to Edenrich. 'All's well. No marble to be found. Yours, sincerely, Orval'."

Rosalind snorted out a laugh, spewing crumbs, then covered her mouth, her eyes dancing. They all joined in, merriment with just a touch of hysteria.

Lara stirred in her basket.

Amari brushed the crumbs off her lap and reached for her. "Time to go back inside. We'll need to build up the fire." She arched an eyebrow. "And you gentlemen are overdue for a bath yourselves."

"Really?" Yfin said with dismay.

"Yes, really." Rosalind confirmed. "But before you do, help me hang the last of the tapestries. They do warm a room, and it's better for them than lying heaped on the floor."

"Will you tell me more of the stories?" Yfin asked. "The one about Uppor stealing the stars?"

"Of course,"

As they gathered the tray and the babes, Roth lowered his head again. "Our watchers are back, no, don't look," he said to Rosalind with a long-suffering sigh.

Orval hated the way that the light drained from Amari's eyes as her sense of safety—false though it might be—disappeared.

"Higher in the Keep," Yfin twisted to pull the bucket of water closer and offered the dipper around. "Not sure how they get up there."

Orval looked at the Keep towering over them. "How much of it is sound, do you think?"

"Not sure," Yfin said. "Some walls tumbled," he explained. "I couldn't get much higher than the second floor. Lots of moldy cloth and broken furniture and bats and pigeons. There's a weird room with a lot of pillars. There are stars painted on the ceiling."

"An old shrine to the Lady of Laughter," Orval said. "I'd like to see that."

"There's stairs," Yfin warned him, then added, "They're fairly clear. I can take ya."

"No," Orval shook his head and brushed crumbs from his own lap. His stomach was in knots but he could see no other path forward. Needs must when the snows come. "Let's get you all inside. I was just telling Roth I hoped they'd come to us, but I don't want to wait any longer. If they won't come to us, the Lord High Baron must go to them. Alone."

Roth glared at him and stood, looking around. "We need to move inside for this argument. Now."

## CHAPTER THIRTY-NINE

Orval found himself hustled inside. The others followed, and the door had barely closed behind them before Roth started yelling.

"Are you out of your gods-damned mind?" the Weaponsmaster asked, his face turning red. "Have you listened to anything I have been saying?"

Orval stood quietly as a storm of protest erupted from everyone, including the babes. Between crying infants and upset people, it was loud. He hoped no one outside could hear; the stone walls of the gatehouse should have muffled the sound.

"No," Amari said, glaring at Orval. She settled on a stool and put Lara to her breast.

"Not just no," Roth growled, arms crossed over his chest. "Hells, no. You are not going out there, and especially not alone. Are you mad? You just cautioned patience."

Rosalind was trying to comfort Dalan, who was shrieking furiously.

"I swear this boy's voice can pierce castle walls," Orval shook his head as he limped over and took the babe from Rosalind. "Hush, my boy," he crooned, offering his own glare at the others.

Amari shut her mouth into a thin, angry line.

Roth at least lowered his voice. "Your wits are gone with the winds."

Rosalind went to check Xydell, sleeping on a pallet near the hearth and showing no signs of rousing at the noise.

Yfin stared, wide-eyed, at all of them.

"I have perfectly sound reasons for doing this," Orval said, prepared to review all of his logic.

"All of them stupid," Roth responded.

"They might yet come to us," Amari insisted, desperation in her voice, but it was the fear in her eyes that hit him hard. "They might knock on the door tomorrow morning. There is no need to risk yourself."

"Amari," Orval rocked Dalan, stroking his cheek to get him to quiet, "remember our contract. Above all else is the safety of our children. Roth and Yfin can protect you, and I won't risk you or Rosalind."

Dalan grew quiet but alert, eyes shining as if he was listening. "If things were different, I might set Xydell on them, like a mastiff after a bone." Orval gave Amari a smile.

It was not returned. She was fierce and angry, but he could see resignation creeping into her eyes. "I –" she started, then stopped.

"I am the Lord High Baron. I am the best choice. The only choice," Orval said.

"And I am your protector." Roth said flatly as he moved to block the door, his arms crossed. "I can't allow you to do this. Unless you let me go with you, I will keep you in here until you regain your wits."

"Roth," Orval said, "I have to do this. Our position is not defensible, we are running out of food and firewood, and—"

"You are the last of the Blood, Orval of Xy," Roth's voice cracked. "You and Xydell, The last of the House of Airion."

"Roth," Orval said, exasperated, "you give me no choice. I command—"

"No," Rosalind said, startling all of them. "Tell him the truth, Lord High Baron."

Orval froze, jerking his head around to stare at her.

"Tell us all the truth of who we are protecting." Rosalind stood tall and straight, one of the tapestries spilling from her hands to lay on the floor.

Orval glanced at Amari, lifting his eyebrow. *Did you tell her?*

Amari gave a slight shake of her head. *No.*

Roth caught the exchange. "Tell us what?"

Orval turned to Rosalind. "What do you think you know?"

"Gossip," Rosalind said, "from the Court. Dates. The babes themselves." She gestured at Dalan. "Tell him."

Orval drew in a slow breath and looked again to Amari, who nodded.

Roth waited, watching them both.

"Lara and Dalan are not my blood-children," Orval started.

Roth's eyes narrowed.

"Dalan is Amari's true son." Orval glanced at Amari, who gave a quick shake of her head. "His father is of no import." Orval took a breath and said, quickly and clearly, "Lara is Xylara, Daughter of Xywellan and Queen Kara, of the House of Airion. True heir to the Throne of Xy."

Roth sucked in a breath. "How is that possible?" he breathed out. "They are twins, you said–"

Amari rose, supporting Lara who was still suckling. She put her hand on the stone hearth, right below her small shrine. "I swear it by the hearth of my home and the harmony within. Lara is not the child of my body. Queen Kara retained me to act as wet nurse. With the aid of the marcusi I smuggled Lara out of the Airion camp when Queen Kara went to her death."

"What's a marcusi?" Yfin asked, darting wide-eyed looks at all the adults.

"Kara trusted Amari and I trust no one more," Orval said. "She is a woman of honor and my Hearth Mother."

"This is Tithanna's granddaughter?" Roth asked, stepping closer to stare at the child in Amari's arms. His voice was choked, tears in his eyes. "Truly?"

"Yes," Orval said. "My daughter in name, my third cousin, once removed, in truth." He drew himself up, trying to look as stern as he could with Dalan waving his tiny hands about. "You must swear yourself to her, and to her cause, Roth, you and Rosalind both. If you can't swear to that, then I demand your silence, all of your silences, for if any others learn of her heritage, Xyrath and Satia will have her killed."

Roth reached out a rough and callused hand to the babe, gently touching her shock of black hair. "How do I know this to be true?"

"Why would I lie?" Orval tried not to let his impatience show.

"So I can go out and face my death? I swear it by the skies, and if you wish I will swear it under the open sky, with fire in one hand, water in the other, and my bare feet on the earth."

Roth stared at him. Orval met his look steadily.

It seemed many heartbeats before Roth bowed his head and dropped to one knee before Amari and Lara. Surprisingly, Yfin moved as well, taking the same position beside him.

"Yfin, you don't—"

"Swore to the old lady." Yfin's mouth was set, his gaze firm. "Where my cap'n swears, I swear."

Rosalind flicked her wrists and the last of the tapestries spread out before her, showing an airion in a battle with a wyvern, its beak cutting into the wyvern's bloody neck. The colors were vivid, the red of the blood bright where it welled on the wyvern's neck. "Seems appropriate," she said as she also knelt.

Roth cleared his throat.

"Please, take a seat, Amari," Orval said softly, stepping to her side.

When Amari did, Roth reached out his hands, palms up. Yfin and Rosalind copied his gesture.

"My hand to yours," Roth and Rosalind chanted together, with Yfin stumbling a beat behind, copying them. "Bless you, Xylara, Daughter of Xy, Daughter of Xywellan and Queen Kara, Warrior Queen."

A thrill passed through Orval as he responded to the ancient words. "On behalf of Xylara, Daughter of Xy, my hand to yours. Blessings upon you, Warriors of the House of Xy."

A soft murmur from Xydell drew their attention, but her eyes did not open. Rosalind rose and went to her.

Yfin bounded up. Roth climbed to his feet and wiped his face with his hands. "Command me, Lord High Baron."

"I am going out there," Orval said. "I will try to come to terms with them, but if I have to–" he swallowed. "If I offer myself as sacrifice for the lives of my wife and children, you will take them, leave the Black Hills, and head to Athelbryght. It's strong and remained neutral in the struggles."

"Whatever you do, Lord High Baron, don't stop reading *Xyson*. It shall be as you command," Roth said. "You should at least take a knife or–"

Orval shook his head. "Harmless is the best look for me."

"We need a code and a counter-sign," Roth said. "So we know it's safe to open the door

 when you return." He offered suggestions and Orval listened absently and nodded, but really only paid attention to Amari. She had collapsed back on to her bench, tears in her eyes.

Orval passed Dalan to Rosalind and limped over to sit beside Amari.

"Orval, no, I can't let you do this," she whispered even as he opened his mouth to speak.

"You can, Hearth Mother." Orval put his arm around her shoulders, felt her trembling against him. Lara's tiny face was pressed into Amari's soft breast as she suckled fiercely. He drew in the scent of Amari's hair, of her skin, of baby and milk, and his heart cracked wide open.

Warmth flooded into his chest, so lovely it hurt. His old, book-lined life had been swept away and he had no regrets. If he needed to offer his life for hers and the children, he would do it without hesitation and not regret the going.

Orval's heart twisted then, as he realized the truth. He would indeed regret the going, for he wanted more; he was greedy for more of life with this wonderful woman at his side.

"You can't go," Amari looked ill; her eyes were wet with tears. "You can't do this."

"Our duties," Orval whispered. "As Hearth Mother, your duty is protecting the hearth. Our babes must have their mother."

Amari nodded then, and he shifted to risk pressing a kiss to her temple. But she turned her head and met his lips with her own warm ones. "Please come back to us," she begged against his mouth.

Her lips were sweet and salty on his. Orval did the hardest thing he'd ever done; he pulled away from her. "I will use every weapon I have, to return." Orval forced himself to release her and rose to his feet. "Besides, it might take a few trips before they approach me."

They were all staring at him and he found his courage in their steady gazes.

Straightening his tunic to cover his own concerns, Orval asked, "Where, exactly, is this shrine to the Lady of Laughter?"

———— ◆ ————

The sun hadn't yet set but the walls and the Keep created patterns of deep shadow and light. Orval slipped out the door and walked toward the main doors to the keep.

With a clunk, Roth and Yfin bolted the door behind him. It sounded so … foreboding. Still, Orval walked on through the courtyard.

This seemed so much easier in the books he'd read. Famous warriors never spoke of knots in their guts or of fear. When stories were told, no one mentioned a desire to puke. Orval paused, swallowed hard, and resolved to think of something else.

Pigeons fluttered in the rafters. Something scurried in the

dead leaves that lay swirled in the corners by the wind. Scurrying rats, most like. He caught a brief glance of red fur and the bright eyes of a startled fox running off. Seemed Yfin had competition.

Orval stopped to admire the main doors, sagging from rusting hinges. Old wooden doors, warped by water and time. Despite being richly engraved and carved, they somehow looked lost.

He stepped into the main hall. Dead leaves rustled though no breeze stirred the air.

Rats, Orval assured himself. Just rats.

The stairs were off to the left, as Yfin had said, a circular stair with arrow slits that let in enough light to see. Cobwebs clung to the rough stone.

A Lady of Laughter shrine would be something to see. Few enough remained after the purge by the clerics of the Lord of the Sun. He'd read about the shrines, of course. Even seen a rare sketch. Orval frowned, trying to remember which book he'd seen that in, as he started up the steps.

Nowadays, the Lady of Laughter was rarely worshiped or invoked. The Church of the Lord of the Sky referred to her as the Lady of Darkness. A source of evil and chaos. But it hadn't been that way in the old days.

Orval paused to catch his breath. The stairs weren't that steep, and there was a clear enough path through the rubble and accumulated rubbish. Still, Orval took his time, resting one hand on the rough stone to make sure of his balance.

The first entrance he came to was dark, but he could see a bit of light ahead. Why hadn't he thought to bring a lantern? He couldn't linger long, since he didn't want to lose the light. Besides, there didn't seem to be anyone here but him.

He stepped in, looked up, and gaped in admiration.

Stars. The ceiling was covered in stars that glittered in the fading light.

He wandered forward without really looking where he was going and stumbled over the raised lip of a reflecting pool that had white marble pillars at each corner. No water now, of course, but in its day it would have been full, its waters and dark tiling designed to reflect the stars above. All white marble, now dirty and stained with time.

Orval stood in the center and stared up, turning in a circle. The stars seemed to wheel above him, still bright, although it looked like someone had scraped at a few to see if they were actually silver. Silver paint, perhaps. Did they reflect actual star patterns? Orval wasn't sure but–

A rush of steps behind him was his only warning. They were on him fast, grabbing his arms and forcing him back violently against one of the pillars. Orval lost his breath at the impact, seeing nothing as a sack went over his head.

The sack smelled of tubers and dirt and was tight on his face.

Orval jerked back instinctively, banging his head on the pillar. When he tried to relax, he felt something sharp prick at his throat. He froze. In the stillness he only heard his ragged breaths and those of his captors.

An older female voice grated in his ear, grating and vicious. "Talk, scribe. Tell us of your master."

"Uh," was really the only thing Orval could think to say, trying to slow his heart and his breath. He wet his lips, feeling the rough cloth against his face. "Hard to talk with a blade to my throat," he rasped.

"Harder to talk without a throat," one of his captors snarled.

"There seems to be a misunderstanding–" Orval started.

"No misunderstanding what we have seen with our own eyes." A woman's voice rang out, sharp and hard. "We seek answers, scribe, not your blood. Answer our questions and you may return to your master."

"I'm not a scribe, well, I am but—" Orval started to explain but they tightened their hands on him and forced his arms farther back. Anger shook him, then. Bullies, all of them.

Their sweaty hands grasped his wrists, their breathing was just as ragged as his. Fear was everywhere, and that which is feared is to be harmed.

"Answer her questions," came a hiss.

"She hasn't asked any," Orval snapped, letting his temper get away from him.

His arms were jerked back yet again, painfully pressing him to the pillar behind him.

"Tell us of the Lord High Baron," came the demand. The same female voice—and there was no fear in it. "He is clearly a warrior. How many are his forces and from which direction will they come?"

"None," Orval said. "He – I – have no forces."

"What sort of fool comes here to claim a barony without support? Brings only his wife, his son, his babes, one handmaiden, and a scribe?" Her disdain was clear, and Orval stiffened.

"The sort of fool who comes out to talk instead of flourishing a sword." Orval's anger grew. People always did this, assumed that he was a nothing due to his lack of weapons.

The woman scoffed. "What kind of Lord High Baron sends a scribe to his death?"

"The kind of Lord High Baron that risks himself to seek out his watchers to ask questions."

"What?" From the confusion in her voice, it seemed that maybe she was finally listening.

"I am the Lord High Baron of the Black Hills," Orval sucked in sour-tasting air through the sack. "Orval of the Airion House of Xy."

There was silence then; he could almost hear them thinking it through.

"Any movement from the gatehouse?" she asked.

"No," a different man's voice, from farther off.

"There won't be," Orval said. "They're bolted in, safe, waiting for my return."

Breathing. Boots on the floor.

The sack was pulled off swiftly and Orval found himself blinking into the light of a lantern. He could see nothing else but the bright glare. Then the sack was back over his head, stifling him again.

The knife edge returned to his throat, cold against his skin, the point sticking into the bottom of his jaw. Orval felt a slow trickle of something wet and warm start down his neck.

"You have the look," the woman said slowly. "The eyes, for certain."

"And the hair," Orval said ruefully. "Do we still need the sack?"

The blade pressed deeper. He sucked in a breath.

"We could kill you now," she said, "and be rid of–"

"I came out to talk, didn't I?" Orval interrupted quickly. "So I will talk. Xyrath and Satia want you to rid them of the Airion bloodline." He sucked in another stale breath. "They hope you kill me, my wife and children, and my aunt. End the Airion bloodline and give the Wyverns an excuse to send an army to subdue you and claim this Barony."

"You lie," another voice, male this time.

"No," Orval said. "The one thing I can promise is that I will not lie to you."

The only sound was his own breathing. He was sweating profusely and his stomach was tight with a need to hurl. All he had were words, so he used them. "If you kill me, kill the newly appointed Lord High Baron, conveniently ridding them of the last of the Airion bloodline, Xyrath and Satia will use the excuse of avenging my death to lay waste to this Barony."

"We are ready," a younger male voice this time, passionate and eager. "We will fight them off as we have in the past, as did my father, and his father, and—"

"At what cost?" Orval asked. He shifted, trying to ease his weight off his leg. "There might be a way we can help one another. If I am not dead, Satia and Xyrath have no reason to attack, to send another as Lord High Baron."

"They will find a reason," the woman said.

"They might," Orval admitted. He thought of the list of tithes back in the gatehouse and decided now was not the time to mention them. "They might not."

"Trust a Xyian?" the oldest male asked, a bitter undertone in his voice. "Either Airion or Wyvern?"

Orval drew another breath of close, stilted air. "Then, if you must kill me, spare my wife and babes. Amari is from Uyole and does not deserve your hate. She is a woman of honor, and the children," his throat closed. He forced the words out. "The children are innocent. Make out that you have slain us all, but let them go."

"You offer us your life for theirs?"

"If you won't consider other options, such as an alliance or truce, then yes," Orval closed his eyes, feeling the sweat dripping down his face, the blood running down his neck.

His breath was deafening in confines of the sack. He heard nothing else for a long moment.

"There was one we trusted, long ago, she and her Lord High Baron," the woman paused. "They were good people. But they died and left us in the hands of another Lord High Baron, known best for his cruelty and greed."

Orval frowned, trying to remember his baronial history. "Which Lord High Baron could you trust?"

The woman sighed and Orval swore he heard a shrug. "Lord High Baron Jerrold and Lady High Baroness Xydell. I remember them well."

The cold shiver of shock and disbelief hit Orval hard, and a laugh escaped him. Xydell?

"What's so funny?" came this hiss.

"Aunt Xydell?" Orval asked.

"Aunt?"

Orval cleared his throat. "There is someone you should meet."

## CHAPTER FORTY

Amari watched, shivering, as Orval left her, slipping out through the wooden door on his mission. Roth closed it behind him and threw the bolts with a resounding clunk. She was terribly afraid for him.

Lara yawned and released her nipple, blinking with sleep.

"I'll see to her," Rosalind said, offering Dalan in exchange. "I'll get her cleaned and lay her down upstairs."

Amari nodded, heart too full to speak. Dalan stared whining and she took him to her breast. The little boy latched on quickly and she settled down to nurse him, her thoughts in turmoil.

Rosalind headed to the stairs. "Come, Yfin, you can hang that tapestry while I see to Lara."

"Don't linger," Roth said. "In case–" he nodded toward the door.

Yfin nodded and dashed after Rosalind.

"You need to go up too," Roth said, and Amari looked up, startled. "You need to be bolted in upstairs," he continued. "In case they try the doors."

"I just–" she caught herself. "When Dalan's done," she agreed, and then cast a glance at Xydell, still and quiet on her pallet. "Should we move her?"

Roth hesitated. "Better for her to be warm and covered," he said, "but yes. I will carry her up." He settled on one of the rickety chairs. "Let's wait and see how this goes. Nothing might happen."

Amari nodded and tried to focus on the babe in her arms. Dalan sucked loudly, clearly determined to feed well. She rocked him, feeling the stool move with her, rocking faintly on the stone floor.

She could faintly hear Rosalind and Yfin, above, as they talked. Amari rolled her shoulders slightly. All would be well: Orval would return and she would be able to breathe again.

Maybe she could bake a risen loaf over the fire. She'd need a starter, and it would take time for the yeast to grow, but it would be a nice change from the flat breads. Besides, she felt a desire to knead, and the thought of dough calmed her.

The hearth required other chores, of course, and they would need to– Amari started, remembering. Dalan lost the nipple and whined.

Roth looked at her, raising an eyebrow.

"We left the laundry out," Amari said as she got Dalan resettled..

Roth chuckled. "Well, nothing says 'harmless' like drying

laundry. I will get it when Orval returns." He knelt by the fireplace. "Need more wood," he said. "He'll be chilled when he comes back."

Amari nodded. Maybe she should use the last of the kavage tonight, to warm them all.

Roth didn't go back to his seat, instead beginning to pace. "He won't be gone long. He said he'd wander around a bit and then return."

Dalan released the nipple with a whine, so Amari shifted him to her other breast. Her hands were trembling, and she held him tight as he latched on. No matter what, babes needed feeding and changing and—

*"As Hearth Mother, your duty is protecting the hearth. Our babes must have their mother."*

*Hearth Mother.* Amari's heart skipped a beat.

She'd never once called him Hearth Father - never …. she hadn't thought he wanted that commitment, hadn't dared think that—

And now he was out there, wandering around, making himself a target for whoever might come across him, be they friend or foe—

Her heart was in her throat, her fear tearing at her, her regret a rock in her stomach.

He'd gone out there alone. She'd never said anything, never told him– Her breath caught and tears welled. She was an idiot and he'd gone out, maybe to his death, and she'd never said, never told him–

Dalan lost the nipple and complained and she focused back on the babe in her arms. Dalan's tiny hands grasped at her breast, as if sensing her distress, her need to get up and bring her man back safe.

Amari knew what she wanted now, knew with all her heart what she burned to have. His heart, his smile, his joy in his stupid, odd obsession with ancient texts. Harmony above, below and within, she loved that stupid, stubborn, pig-headed scholar.

She looked at her shrine, her bit of parchment bearing the symbol of the Harmony. She closed her eyes in prayer. *Lord and Lady, let him return to me safe and sound and I will build such a Hearth with him at my side and offer you such honor... .*

Dalan released her nipple and gave a tremendous burp. She smiled down at him and he sleepily echoed her, his tiny lips curving.

Rosalind came down the stairs, Yfin close behind. "Lara's asleep. If he's done, I'll take him." She reached out for Dalan.

"I want to put water on for kavage later," Amari said, handing over the babe.

"We need to shift Xydell," Roth said to Yfin. "Upstairs would be safer."

A knock at the door froze them all.

"Roth? It's me," came Orval's voice through the door.

Yfin and Roth moved to flank the door. Rosalind took Dalan and ran up the steps. Amari began to follow, then paused in the doorway and held her breath.

"Orval?" Roth asked. "Are you alone?"

"No," Orval sounded slightly flustered. Amari took a few steps forward so she could hear him better.

"Give me the sign," Roth demanded, drawing his sword.

"Ahhh," Orval stalled. "I forgot about that. Wait, just give me a minute."

Amari choked on a laugh as Roth rolled his eyes. Yfin's face was screwed up, as if he was trying not to giggle. It wasn't funny, it really wasn't, but—

"Damn it, Orval," Roth said. "Who is with you?"

"I'm with … er, well, friends isn't the term I'd use. Or they'd use." Orval said. "But they haven't killed me yet and they did take the sack off my head."

Amari covered her trembling mouth with her fingers. What had they done to him?

"That's not reassuring." Roth responded.

"It had something to do with pigeons, didn't it?" Orval asked.

Amari stepped quickly to the main door. "Orval, if it's safe, tell me a lie. What did you give me at the well?"

"Oh, well, a kiss, sort of," there was such joy in his voice. "And a bracelet, leather braided with red jasper."

Amari's eye welled with joy. He was alive and talking and—

Roth was shaking his head in disbelief, eyes closed as if in pain.

"A walk to the well is tradition in Uyole, for babes three months old," Orval said, clearly explaining things to his kidnappers. His voice trailed off; Amari could just imagine their faces. "Oh, I was supposed to lie, wasn't I?" Orval said. "Well, I'm not very good at this. Let's try again."

"Enough," a woman's voice came through the door, loud enough that Amari took a step back and Roth raised his sword. "I am Bercie of Wareington of the Black Hills. I come in peace, offering no injury or insult to the house."

"Bercie?" came the softest whisper. Amari turned to see Xydell's face turned toward the door. "Bercie?"

Amari and Roth stared at one another, then turned again to see Xydell's pale hands pulling at her bedding. "Bercie?" It was a soft, fragile whisper.

"I will come in alone," the woman's voice continued. Other voices, all male, were raised then, clearly in protest.

Roth looked at Amari, who nodded, and retreated to the inner doorway. Yfin, knives in his hands, he pressed himself to the wall, out of sight of the main door.

"I will open the door," Roth called out, readying his sword. "But none but the Lord High Baron and the woman enter."

"Leave the door open," a male voice responded. "So that we can see within. Any treachery will be met with the same."

Amari held her breath as Roth opened the door.

Cold air spilled in as Orval came inside, followed by a woman in leather armor. She was older, gray, wrinkled, with a no-nonsense, commanding look.

No matter, Amari forgot the woman as she took in the sight of Orval. Disheveled, sweaty, oh dearest Harmony, there was blood trickling down his neck. She must have made a sound, for he looked at her, and with a few brisk steps was at her side, taking her hand. His fingers were cold and clammy and she gripped them hard. He shook his head at her worry. "I'm fine." he whispered.

He was, he was, he was standing beside her, safe. She put her head on his shoulder and felt the weight of fear come off her chest.

"My Lady?" The older woman, Bercie, stood in the middle of the room, staring at Xydell. Amari knew it must be an odd sight, a woman cushioned and wrapped in ceremonial robes, all crimson velvet and black fur. The wrong colors for an Airion as proud as Xydell, but all they had.

A rustle of cloth and Xydell roused, smiling, her eyes half-open and misty. "Bercie, is that you?" One frail hand reached out, shaking.

"Lady High Baroness." Bercie took a step forward, staring as if she had seen a ghost. "They told us you were dead."

"Am I home?" Xydell's smile was wistful. "Did you have your baby, Bercie?"

Bercie hurried over to her. Both Roth and Yfin reacted, but Orval held them back with a raised hand.

Bercie took Xydell's hand and slowly knelt at her side. "Oh, my Lady High Baroness, I did, I did, I had a son. We named him Jerrold after—" her voice choked off with tears.

"Oh, lovely," Xydell's face lit up. "Jerrold will be so pleased … ." She blinked in confusion and her face crumpled. "But Jerrold's dead, oh Bercie, he's dead and I lost my babe the same day he died, and they wouldn't let me return, they wouldn't let me come home."

"We sent letters, pleading to know what had happened," Bercie wept. "But they would only say you both had died, and the Barony went to a Wyvern who—"

"I could do nothing," Xydell wailed weakly. "I was ill for so long and they told me not to worry my head about such things." Her voice was brittle, bitter, and angry. "Tithanna tried to help, but no."

Bercie took Xydell in her arms, and Xydell went willingly, both women hugging and rocking each other in grief as everyone stood in stunned disbelief.

Amari looked at Orval. *Did you know?*

Orval shook his head slightly.

Their tears trailing off, Bercie helped Xydell settle back in her bedding. "A fine thing, to find you on the floor in a bed of velvet and fur," she said. She looked over her shoulder at Orval. "Your ceremonial robes."

Orval shrugged. "Thought it was more important to keep her warm than worry about my so-called dignity."

Xydell snorted, tugged at Bercie's hand. "My nephew," she explained. "He's a good lad, but no sense of the proper order of things."

Orval glanced at Amari, his lips in a wry smile.

Xydell yawned, her eyes closing. Bercie went to rise but Xydell tugged at her hand. "Don't leave me," she whispered as she faded to sleep.

Bercie eased back down. "I will watch over you," she said gently. Then she gave all of them a glare and her voice hardened. "There is much I want to know."

Orval nodded and gestured to the men outside the door. "Come in, come in, let's all get warm and talk this out."

Roth stiffened, but to Amari's surprise, the men, both young and old, sheathed their swords and started to obey.

"Cirda," Bercie called. "Take word to your father. He's waiting nearby." The youngest nodded and headed off.

Amari heard a shuffling behind her as Yfin casually emerged from hiding, his knives sheathed. Orval caught his eye and jerked his chin up. Yfin nodded and headed up the stairs.

Amari gathered her wits. "I'll brew kavage to warm us." She released Orval's hand after one last, heart-felt squeeze, and headed to the hearth.

Bercie's men settled around on the floor. Roth closed the door and took a chair. Amari noticed he kept his sheathed sword at hand.

"What was done to her?" Bercie demanded softly.

"As to the past, I cannot speak to that." Orval settled on a bench close by and stretched out his leg. "As to the present," he drew a breath and began, telling almost all. It took time, and all their kavage, but Amari thought it was well worth it.

When Orval reached the part about the letheon, Bercie growled low. "Oarno," she snapped. "Go fetch Wethe and tell her what you have heard." One of the men rose and went out without a word.

Orval continued, explaining what had happened. The kavage was gone by the time he finished.

Bercie tucked Xydell's hand under the crimson robes. "Help me up," she commanded, and rose stiffly with aid from one of her men. Once up, she faced Orval. "The Black Hills hates Xy and all it stands for, Airion, Wyvern, makes no difference to us."

Orval got to his feet and Amari moved to stand beside him. He would have spoken then, but Bercie raised her hand to forestall him.

"For the love of my Lady," Bercie looked at Xydell and her expression softened, "Orval of Xy, we offer you respite. Shelter, food, and aid, such as we have." Her grey eyes bored into both of them. "We do not acknowledge you as Lord High Baron." she said curtly. "And I make no promises for the future."

"Let it be so," Orval said, nodding. "There is still much we need to know about one another before we can come to an agreement."

"Hmm," Bercie looked at Orval. Amari could see her puzzlement.

They waited in silence then, until there was a knock at the door. "Mother Bercie? It's Wethe."

Roth didn't look happy, but at Orval's nod, he opened the door. A stout woman walked in, with a younger girl behind her. "Who has a need?"

"Here." Bercie stepped back, giving her access.

"What am I dealing with?" Wethe asked, frowning down at Xydell. "And why is she on the floor?"

As Bercie started to explain, Rosalind appeared on the stairs and looked at Amari, who leaned closer to Orval. "I am going to go to the babes."

Orval nodded. "I'll come up when they're gone," he whispered, squeezing her hand.

"Good," she smiled, pulling her fingers slowly from his. "Don't be long." She turned and went up the stairs, eager to get the babes settled. And make her own preparations.

It wasn't over an hour before Orval knocked, slid inside their room, and closed and bolted the door behind him.

He looked exhausted, sagging back against the wooden door. "They're gone," he said. "They should return in the morning with food and things to make Aunt Xydell more comfortable."

"I am fairly sure Mother Bercie thinks a knife in my ribs would be a comfort to her." Orval shuddered. "Her hate is almost palpable."

Amari stood from where she sat on the end of the bed and started toward him. He was disheveled, his curls all this way and that, and the blood had dried on his neck.

He looked wonderful.

"Turns out the mayor is Bercie's son. Should have seen his face. It went from hate at the door to confused by the bedside. Orval wiped his brow. "Mind, the hate is not for us personally," he gave her a weak smile. "But for Xy, for any authority, actually. All I can offer them is the truth of how bad things are," He chuckled. "They keep looking at Roth for directions; I think I confuse them."

He stood straighter, looking at the baskets. "Babes fed? Are you hungry? Rosalind managed to make some—" he blinked as she stepped closer. "Amari?"

Amari touched his neck. "Does it hurt?" she asked, seeing the bruising, the split flesh. "Did one of the healers check it?"

"No, no, just a small nick, really." Orval stood still, as if wary. "The healers were busy with Xydell, said they would be back in the morning as well." He paused. "Are you angry with me?"

"For risking your life for us?" Amari asked.

"For forgetting the password." Orval sagged. "Roth had a few things to say, after everyone left."

"You were so strong," Amari whispered.

"Never so frightened in all my life," Orval whispered back.

Amari pushed him back against the door and kissed him.

## CHAPTER FORTY-ONE

Orval's heart filled with joy even as his arms filled with Amari, warm, wonderful woman that she was. Orval returned her kiss with all the passion in his heart. He wrapped his arms around her, felt her breasts press to his chest, and fully engaged in a moment more precious than all the others in his life.

Until she murmured "Hearth Father" in his ear, and dashed cold, icy reality on his dream.

"Amari, no, no." He broke off the kisses, and eased her away from him. The warmth of her body was replaced with the chill of the truth.

"What?" Amari's eyes were wide with confusion, her breathing ragged. She reached for him but he caught her hands.

"Amari, this is just the heat of the moment, the elation that we succeeded." Orval tried to control his own reaction. "This is not what you want." He had to make her understand. He wanted this, oh, how he wanted this - but it was not right to take advantage. He wanted what was best for her, and he was not—

"It is," she insisted.

"It's not," he answered, smiling sadly, reaching up to cup her cheek. "You are making a mistake you will come to regret."

"Orval, I—"

"I understand, I do," he said earnestly. "But I won't take advantage of you this way, not in the flush of success, of our survival through this whole thing. The last few months have been the best of my life, even with the threat of death," he looked over at the babes. "They are okay, yes?"

"Yes, of course," she started. "But—"

"No 'buts,'" Orval drew a deep breath. "I'm not going to let you make this mistake. I am not right to be one of your Hearth Fathers, and after a few days you will know that and regret this." He managed to step away from her. "Now, go get under the blankets, or you will catch a chill. I'll just be a moment."

He didn't flee to the privy, exactly, but he didn't linger. The distance seemed to take forever, but that was only because his leg was tired. Exhaustion was washing over him. Or was it grief?

He didn't look back at Amari.

With the privy door closed behind him, he went to the shelf where a pitcher of water and a basin waited. He splashed water on his face, trying to get himself under control.

He'd convinced her heart, he was certain.

Now he just had to convince his own.

Amari plopped down on the end of the bed, and stared at the privy door.

Had she misread Orval's interest?

She flushed. Maybe. She wasn't untouched, after all. She'd had a baby and she wasn't a virgin any longer. Her body wasn't perfect by any stretch of the imagination; it had changed, from pregnancy and birth. She pulled her robe closer around her.

On the other hand... . for one brief, glorious moment, he'd returned her kisses. And she'd felt him responding to her.

Amari bit her lip as confusion overwhelmed her. Maybe he was right, maybe it was just the stress of the moment, the tensions of the last few months. Maybe she–

The door opened and he stepped out, looking somehow both sheepish and determined.

Warmth flooded through her, settled in her chest, and bloomed. This wasn't a spur of the moment thought, it wasn't an impulse.

Her hearth stood before her.

"We should get some sleep." Orval didn't look at her as he limped to his side of the bed. "We need to talk to the elders tomorrow and hopefully Xydell will finally wake up. It would be good if she could tell us more about these people."

He was babbling nervously as he pulled back the bedding and climbed in. He stretched out on his back, staring at the ceiling. "Did the babes feed well?"

"Yes," Amari stood and pulled back the bedding on her side. "How is your leg?"

"Not too bad tonight," he said quietly as she lay down and covered herself.

Amari curled on her side to face him, staring at his profile. She took a breath, determined to speak.

"No," Orval forestalled her. "We are not going to discuss this. The marcusi may appear tomorrow to get you and the babes to safety. I am not going to let you make a mistake out of gratitude. I know that you should choose your Hearth Fathers for their ability to defend the Hearth and–"

He blithered on, but Amari had stopped listening. "Hearth *Fathers?*" she said with a frown, interrupting his declarations. "You mean, more than one Hearth Father?" Had he said that before?

"Yes, of course," Orval said. "I know your people take multiple fathers into the Hearth, and I read the standards that you should follow. We would be fooling ourselves if we … ."

He kept talking, but the joy in her breast drowned out his words. She propped her head up with her hand, and looked at him, staring at the ceiling, rattling on.

She moved her foot, tucking her toes under his calf. Orval gave her a startled look.

"My toes are cold," she said, keeping her face straight. "Do you mind?"

"Er, no, it's fine." Orval said and continued on with a list of why he wasn't suitable as a Hearth Father.

She rubbed her foot up and down his leg, and tucked her other foot under as well.

Orval darted a glance at her, but kept on until he finally wound down.

"What book did you read?" she asked. "About Hearth Fathers?"

"Oh, well," Orval relaxed, as he always did when discussing books. "It was *Uyole: A Fine and Noble Land* by Verismet. I also had a copy of *Birth Rituals of Foreign Lands* and *Rare Matriarchal*

*Cultures*, which went into detail about the bracelets and their significance." He sucked in a breath as she rubbed his skin with her toes. "Are your feet warm yet?"

"No," she said, and kept rubbing. "All this time," she mused aloud, "all this time, you thought this? You cared for us, and preserved us, and all this time you thought this about yourself? That you are not worthy?"

Orval blinked at her, then returned his gaze to the ceiling. "Of course," he said. "It has always been so, you know."

That calm acceptance of what was, with no trace of blame or self-pity, cracked her heart.

"Orval," she whispered. "How old were these books of yours?"

"Oh, well … ." Orval's brow furrowed in thought. "Well, *A Fine and Noble Land* is fairly recent, within the last twenty years or so. I don't recall the date of *Rare Matriarchal Cultures* but it has a reputation as a fine translation." He finally turned his head and looked at her. "Why? Is there a problem? My sources are primary and–"

Amari moved then, sliding to lie on top of him, pinning him to the bed. "It's my turn to school you in history."

"Amari," Orval put his hands on her shoulders, as if to move her off.

She resisted, placing a finger over his lips. "In the time of what you call the Mage Wars, yes, it's true that a woman would have multiple hearth fathers. At one point, my forefathers feared that our people would die out, or inbreed past saving, so great was the destruction."

Orval stared at her.

"Now, how long ago was that?" Amari asked.

"Hundreds of years," Orval whispered, and she could see

understanding dawning in his eyes. "Customs change?" he asked hopefully.

"Customs change," she said, cupping his cheek with one hand.

"I got the part about the bracelets right, though."

"Yes, you did."

"But no multiples?" She ached at the hope in his voice.

"I won't say that it doesn't happen," Amari said. "There are multiples, but that is the exception, not the rule. People contract for marriage as they please."

"Oh," Orval said and swallowed hard.

"And I please," Amari kissed his jaw. "To have one Hearth Father. My hearth is here," she put her hand on his chest, felt his heart beating wildly under her palm.

"Oh." Orval was wide-eyed, staring at her.

"So, my chosen Hearth Father." Amari brushed her lips against his. "You of the tremendous heart and mind and whose body I desire, may I kiss you?"

The tears in his eyes caught her by surprise. "Are you sure, Amari? Please be sure. Because the last few months, with all the chaos it has brought, have been the best months of my life." His breath was ragged. "I can't imagine not having you at my side."

"I am sure, so sure, beloved." Amari teared up as well. "Unless you do not desire me, my body is not perfect and—"

"You are wonderful," Orval scolded her. "And perfect and beautiful. But we could be killed tomorrow, the marcusi may come, the people of the Black Hills may kill us. Life is so uncertain, with no promises, no assurance beyond our next breath."

"Yes," Amari smiled through her tears. "And the babes might awaken at any moment. Our lives are fraught and fragile. But our hearts are strong and steadfast."

Orval nodded, reaching up to wipe the tears from her cheek. "The only certainty is how we feel for each other. We will build on that."

"Our hearts are one. My hearth is here, in the beating of your heart." Amari said. "So, are we done now? Have I convinced you?"

"Yes," Orval said. "Yes, a thousand times yes."

"Good," she said. "Because we have wasted enough time." She shifted then, pressing her hips down on his hips, feeling his body respond as his eyes went even wider.

"Amari," Orval gasped as she sat up, tossing back the bedding and pulling her night shift up and off. "Oh, skies above," he gasped, looking at her with every bit of desire that she could ask for. "Amari, yes, please, but I don't - I've read but I haven't–"

She leaned in. "I know," she whispered back. "And I claim the privilege. I want to ravish you." She brought his hand to her breast. "But maybe we should go slow, for your first–"

Orval shifted his hips under her. "No, no, please feel free to–"

She leaned down and kissed him hard, pressing her lips to his and sliding her tongue into his mouth. Hot, warm, and so sweet.

All the sweeter for the need for haste, but she wouldn't really ravish him. That word was too harsh for what she intended.

Because she intended kisses, long and slow, all over his body as she eased his night robe off. Orval's initial shyness faded as she caressed him, admiring his pale white skin that seemed so frail in comparison to her strong brown, but was not.

She intended touches and strokes, letting him explore her body, showing him what pleased her, when to be gentle, and when to be firm. She arched up, urging him on as he explored her depths with his hands. Hesitant at first, Orval grew confident as she guided his fingers; her release caught her by surprise as she clung to him and moaned.

"I did that!" Orval's pride was clear and she laughed softly and nodded, and kissed him, easing him back so that she could sit astride him once again. She wanted him hard, and wanting, before she–

"Precautions?" he whispered. "Do we need to worry about–"

"It's fine," she whispered, loving him even more for the thought. "I'm nursing," she explained.

"Oh, okay–" then reason fled his eyes as she moved.

And because she intended joy, she took him inside herself, his flesh firm against her, and moved, listening to the smart, rational man beneath her babble endearments as his eyes reflected the wonder of it all. When Orval clamped both hands on her hips and arched his hips up, gaining his release deep within her, she rode the waves of her own pleasure before collapsing at his side.

He pulled her close, their breathing slowing together as the sweat dried on their bodies.

Orval covered her face with kisses. "Amari, that was ... I have no words."

She chuckled, putting her head on his shoulder, infinitely pleased. "You? Wordless?" she kissed just below his ear, taking in the heady scent of their bodies.

"I think I might need to create a few," he whispered and they both laughed. Orval moved his arm to pull the blankets over them. "Perhaps in the morning–"

Dalan shrieked.

They both jerked in surprise, then Orval laughed again. "I'll get him," he said and climbed out of bed, presenting Amari with a lovely view of his backside. She admired him as she pulled herself up and propped pillows behind her.

Orval clucked at Dalan as he carried him back. "Are you hungry, little one?" He handed him to Amari, then turned back to get Lara.

Dalan sucked fiercely; a pleasant pain. Amari cradled him close.

Orval returned with Lara, just starting to wake. He placed her on the bed beside Amari. "I'll just see to a few things."

He lit more candles, brought cold water for them both to drink, then retrieved his night robe from the floor and placed it at the foot of the bed. Finally he crawled back into bed with her and made sure to cover them all in a warm nest. Orval rested on one elbow as he looked at them all with the oddest look on his face.

"What is it, love?" she asked.

"Oh, it just occurs to me," Orval said, as Lara reached to grasp his finger. He looked at Amari, his eyes shining. "There are some things not to be learned from books."

## CHAPTER FORTY-TWO

Orval felt the warmth of Amari at his back as they stood in the common room together and watched Wethe tend Xydell.

Bercie had made good on her promise. Xydell was on a bed now, still by the hearth in the main room, but with proper blankets and bedding. Rosalind had stored the ceremonial robes after folding them carefully. Bercie's people had brought food and firewood and the gatehouse was warmer and brighter as a result. Xydell was more responsive, more aware of where she was and who was with her.

But Wethe's face as she turned toward them let Orval know that the news wasn't all good.

"I'm sorry," Wethe said. "It's her heart, you see. I have a few draughts that will make her comfortable, but she's not going to get better."

"You could talk to me, you know," Xydell's thin, wavering voice rose from the bed. "I'm right here. Not dead yet."

"I already talked to you," Wethe said patiently. "Now I am telling them."

Orval grimaced, but he had to ask. "How long?"

Xydell snorted. "Not long enough to be a bother," she said.

Wethe gave her patient an exasperated look and shrugged. "It's hard to say," she hedged. "Tonight? Next week? A few months? That is in the hands of those that watch over us."

"Enough. I really don't have time for this." Xydell coughed, then waved her hand to regally dismiss the healer. "Ask Bercie to come to me."

"Of course," Wethe bowed to Xydell. "I will return later to check on you."

"If I'm still here," Xydell muttered.

Roth ushered her out, took a long look around the courtyard, and then closed the door.

"Our guards still out there?" Orval asked.

"Aye," Roth threw the bolt. "Still not sure if they are here to protect us or kill us."

"So much anger," Xydell whispered. "So much hate." She sighed, plucking at the blankets. "We're finally alone?"

"Just us," Orval pulled up a stool.

"Bercie was my dear lady's maid," Xydell smiled briefly. "But she has grown as bitter as I have. I fear for you all, after I am gone." There was no joy on her face now.

"No, I am sure–" Orval started.

"Don't pretend otherwise, you're not stupid," Xydell snapped, a little of her old fire burning in her eyes. "Listen to me. My Jerrold cached things around the Keep and its surrounding. A pouch of coin, a dagger, or a sword. A few trail rations." She drew a slow, harsh breath. "He always said that you never know when you might need one or the other at hand."

"You should rest," Orval said. Her paleness worried him.

"Fool," she rolled her eyes, "I've more than enough rest coming. Bercie knew of some hiding places but not all. My Jerrold was canny. He marked these caches." She paused. "I wish I could remember, but–" she shook her head. "Tell that boy to go exploring. You might need whatever he finds."

"I will, I promise," Orval said.

"If he forgets, I will remember," Roth added.

"Good, good," Xydell sighed. "At least you have a few smart people around you, Orval." She took another breath. "Amari–"

Orval stiffened. "Aunt Xydell, I won't let you–"

"Hush," Xydell frowned. "Amari," she held out a hand toward his wife.

Amari moved forward and gently grasped the old woman's hand. "Xydell."

"I heard," the former Lady Baroness said, then took a few quick breaths. "I think I heard … is it true? What you did for Kara?"

Orval exchanged a glance with Roth in consternation.

But Amari plunged ahead. "Yes. But it's also true that I had a child with Eijer."

"Dalan is Eijer's boy?"

"Yes," Amari confirmed.

"Ah," Xydell said. "A good bloodline, but watch out for his mother."

Orval raised his eyebrows. Was she wandering in her wits?

"I am sorry, lass." Xydell's fingers grasped Amari's so hard they turned white. "I said awful things to you, and I regret them. Forgive me, child." She gasped a bit, trying to catch her breath.

"All is forgiven," Amari knelt down and wiped the tears from Xydell's face. "Do not fret."

"I regret so much," Xydell whispered, still weeping.

"Auntie, it's fine, we will be fine," Orval said.

Xydell pressed her lips together. "No surety of that, young man."

"But surety of love," Amari said. "Between us, and around us, and through us, and abiding at all times within this hearth."

Xydell gave a nod, her gaze set on something distant. "My blessing to you both," she said. "After I am gone, I want you to give me to the mountain, Orval. Here in the Black Hills."

"We could send you to Edenrich," Orval whispered. "To be interred with Uncle Jerrold in the Palace chapel. I am sure Satia and Xyrath would allow it."

"Pfft, more like they would feed my corpse to the pigs. No, nephew, no need to go to that effort." Xydell closed her eyes, and her smile was soft and peaceful. "My Jerrold will find me in the snows."

There was a knock at the door. Orval helped Amari to her feet as Bercie came in, with her son, Jerrold. Bercie only had eyes for Xydell, but Jerrold glared at everyone.

He especially frowned at Roth. "You ever war here?" he asked gruffly.

"No," Roth answered, looking him straight in the eye. "Never set foot on this land or shed blood in this place."

"Peace, son," Bercie chided.

"For now," Jerrold grumbled.

"Wethe has told you?" Orval asked Bercie.

"Bercie, don't waste time with him," Xydell rasped. "Come talk to me."

Bercie nodded and walked over, taking the stool Wethe had recently abandoned. Xydell smiled, reaching for her hand. "Oh, Bercie, let us tell each other tales of old times."

"There were good ones," Bercie said, taking the offered hand. "I'd hoped for more time with you," she continued, her words sounding thick. "I despise what the Blood has done to you."

"My heart was broken long before this," Xydell whispered. "When Jerrold died and I lost the babe, I also lost my mind. I failed the Black Hills, should have fought harder to return, to champion the cause–"

"Hush," Bercie said. "None of that."

"I will not fail you now," Xydell said. "I leave you Orval and his family. If you still think of me as your Lady High Baroness, then I name him my heir."

For a moment, the only sound was the crackle of the fire. Then Jerrold said, sharply. "Here, now–"

Bercie held up her hand to silence him. "Lady High Baroness, I–"

Xydell nodded. "I know, Bercie, I know. So much pain and death and hate won't make it easy for you or the Black Hills." She closed her eyes and gave a weak chuckle. "The Wyverns thought they were sending us to our deaths." Xydell opened her eyes with an air of determination. "It may be so for me. But let it not be so for them.

"He is a good man, even if he gets lost in his books now and then."

Orval exchanged an eye roll with Amari, who added a hint of a smile, as if to say, *She knows you well.*

"I want to be interred in the mountain, Bercie. With the hidden ones." Xydell looked at her. "It's still there, yes?"

"Yes," Bercie kissed Xydell's hand as her eyes welled with tears. She glanced at Orval and looked as if she would have spoken, but Xydell kept talking.

"I am sorry to bring up old sorrows. Just wanted you to know my wishes. Now tell me of your family. Your son I know," she nodded at Jerrold. "But daughters? Grandchildren? Share the joy of your life with me, Bercie."

Bercie leaned in on the bed, and started to talk, her voice soft and quiet.

Amari excused herself, probably to check on the babes with Rosalind. Roth had settled into his guard position by the door. Jerrold leaned against the wall, his arms crossed, as if determined not to be budged. Orval drifted over.

"I was wondering," Orval said quietly, not wanting to interrupt the two women. "Does anyone in town have the supplies for sending a message with a pigeon?"

"Maybe." Jerrold looked at him with dark eyes. "Why?"

"At some point, after we come to an agreement–"

"If."

Orval ignored the implication. "I want to send a message back to Edenrich," He said. "Don't worry, you can read it before I send it. I'll need your help because I've never tied a message to a pigeon's leg before."

Jerrold snorted. "Clearly." He glanced at the bed and the two old friends.

"Mother will have to approve."

"Oh," Orval smiled, "I don't think that will be a problem."

## CHAPTER FORTY-THREE

If Queen Satia had to walk, everyone walked.

Caris suppressed a smile, following the Queen as the Guildmasters puffed alongside Satia, trying to make their arguments heard.

"A Guild charter, Your majesty?" huffed Merchant Guildmaster Evens. "Is this really necessary? Childbirth is only a woman's matter, and usually handled by the women of the family. Surely there is no need for–"

Ah. Word had gotten out. It had taken time to draft the charter, but Plumestra had started at once to advise the Queen. Twice daily walks through the Palace. At least a quarter of an hour in the gardens in the sun. Plain tea and dry toast. Satia had not taken it well, but she had done as she was told. Not that she would admit it was working.

But it was.

"Are you saying that a woman's health and care in childbirth are not important?" The Queen asked in a mild, dangerous tone. Caris noted that she picked up her pace a bit.

"No, of course not, your majesty," Weaver Guildmaster Mator chimed in. Thin as a rail, he was having an easier time keeping up. "But these are matters of the body, usually addressed by the physicians and apothecaries."

Evens was breathing hard. "Guilds govern matters of craft or trade and–"

"The safety of the Queen and her child are paramount," Caris interrupted before they could keep digging the hole they were in. She kept her face demure, her eyes down, but put a threat in her tone. "Above all other concerns."

"But Plumestra will sit on our Council," Evens blurted out in a plaintive tone.

Ah. Caris had suspected that was the crux of the matter.

Queen Satia stopped suddenly and gave Evens a long look, with an arched eyebrow. "Guildmaster Plumestra."

"Oh, yes, of course, your majesty," Evens stammered. Both men bobbed their heads nervously.

"I fail to see how this threatens your Guilds or your livelihoods." The Queen lifted her head imperiously. "I would hope that you are not placing your discomfort over my health."

"No, of course not, your majesty," Evens stammered again and started wringing his hands.

"The matter is settled. Good day, Guildmasters." Queen Satia started off down the hall, leaving the Guildmasters open-mouthed in her wake.

Caris bobbed a curtsey to the men and followed.

This hall was lined with courtiers and nobles, some with actual business, some there just to be seen. Everyone cleared a path for the Queen, bowing and greeting her with her titles, wishing her well.

Few things pleased the Queen more than adoration; Caris could feel her contentment through the Bond. Satia strode the length of the hall, even stroking her belly to accent its roundness.

Nora appeared from the crowd and joined Caris.

"How does our guest?" Caris asked softly.

Nora rolled her eyes. "Men," she scoffed. "He's incoherent, claims he is dying, moans in his suffering. We just got through the latest round of puking. He's asleep."

"And if he wakes while you are gone?"

"He can lie in it until I return." Nora said.

"What does Mira say?" Caris asked as the Queen resumed walking.

"That while she has no experience with this kind of thing, she doesn't think he is dying."

They walked side by side behind the Queen, careful to keep in step.

"You need to have a care," Caris cautioned her. "The Bonded needs him."

Nora sniffed.

Mira came up from behind, holding an armful of velvety white fur. "The Queen's new cloak," she whispered. "Isn't it lovely?"

They parted to let her pass and present it to the Queen.

Satia made a show of stroking the white fur of the collar. The crowd of courtiers around them murmured their admiration.

"What of your other tasks?" Satia asked her Bondmaidens under her breath.

"I met with the midwife, and she gave me lists of potential nursemaids and wet nurses." Mira assured her. "She also recommended an expert seamstress to make a new blessing gown, since we haven't been able to find the ancient one."

Satia's smiled never wavered but they felt her displeasure.

Mira looked miserable. "The craftspeople did press as to the cost of the materials for this," she lifted her arms to indicate the cloak. "And for the gown, especially if you want the silks–"

"Of course I want silks," Satia snapped.

Mira dropped her gaze.

Satia huffed, turned on her heel, and headed toward the gardens.

This hall was not quite so crowded, undoubtedly due to the draftiness of the windows. Caris shivered a little as they walked.

"My Queen!" came a call from behind.

King Xyrath came striding up, clearly fresh from the baths. His entourage followed close behind, all smelling of soap and sandalwood. Caris demurely lowered her eyes as they drew close, avoiding their gazes. Lord Marshal Tarwain was toward the back of the group, looking only at the Queen.

Xyrath held out his hands to Satia. "Beloved," he kissed her cheek. "How do you this fine morn? Out for your morning stroll?"

"Yes, my love." Satia gave him an admiring glance. "How did the sparring go?"

"Great fun, great fun. Ran them all around the practice grounds." Xyrath dropped his hands to her belly. "And how does our heir apparent?"

Satia's smile was more genuine this time, as she covered his hands with hers. Caris felt her glow of pleasure. "Very well, beloved."

"Good, good, then you can join us in council this afternoon," Xyrath smiled.

Satia blinked. "I thought we had said that–"

Xyrath nodded. "Yes, yes, I know, but that was a while ago," he reminded her. "We need to talk things over, to make plans – there are so many questions." He lifted her hands and kissed both of them. "I need you at my side."

"Of course," Satia said faintly.

"Besides," Xyrath lit up, "there is news. Look," he snapped his fingers and a thin, old man stepped forward, looking nervous. Caris caught a whiff of something … odd. The man held a small strip of curled paper out toward the Queen.

"Look at this," Xyrath snatched up the paper and unrolled it. "Came in this morning from the Black Hills."

Satia perked up.

"Turns out we have a pigeon house," Xyrath held the paper so she could read it.

"Coop, your majesty," the thin man corrected.

"Whatever," Xyrath said. "Hundreds of pigeons, and this man cares for them."

Caris tried to hold her breath against the foul smell.

"The teeny-tiny handwriting," Xyrath marveled. "Orval certainly knows how to say quite a bit in a few words."

"Orval?"

Caris didn't need to hear the distaste in Satia's voice. The cold ice of the Bond was more than enough.

"Oh yes, all good," Xyrath said. "He's established himself and his family in the Keep, if you can believe it, with the help of the locals."

"Did he," Satia said flatly.

Caris glanced at Tarwain. His face was bland, but his eyes were dark.

Xyrath continued, oblivious. "Also says they are searching for the best, pure white marble for our project, still needs to be quarried, mind you. Asks for credit against taxes and tithes." Xyrath let the paper roll back up. "Smart man, my cousin."

"Yes," Satia said darkly.

"I asked the pigeon keeper here if we could send the pigeon back, with a note, but apparently it doesn't work like that."

"It doesn't work like that," the man squeaked. "The birds need to be trained, and then–"

"Yes, yes," Xyrath grimaced. "Best we can do is get a messenger off, or even better, send Master Sculptor whats-his-name with our message, so he can supervise." Xyrath puffed up a bit. "He's already made fine sketches. He's including a sword, a shield, and a few skulls of my enemies at my feet."

Satia took a very long breath.

Xyrath frowned at the slip of paper. "Takes forever for messages to travel. Maybe we should have the Mage Guildmaster do another portal or two, it would save months of travel time."

"The cost," Satia said through a clenched smile.

Xyrath nodded. "You are right, dearest." He raised her hand for another kiss. ""Another thing to discuss at council, I will see you there." He bowed and headed off.

"Come, lads," he called. "Let's go see the Master Sculptor. He will be thrilled. And you, pigeon keeper. Walk with me and explain how we can whip these birds into shape."

There was an odd silence as the King departed. Satia watched him go with narrowed eyes.

Lord Marshal Tarwain lingered behind and broke the silence with a bow. "Could I escort you to the gardens, Your Majesty?"

"My thanks," Satia extended her hand. "Perhaps you could stay and talk for a while?"

"Alas, I cannot," Lord Tarwain said as they began to walk. "The council meets before the formal session to discuss how to approach your majesties concerning the issue of taxes. I thought I might sound out some of the councilmembers, see how they feel about the cost of the army, the fact that the treasury must be maintained."

Caris and the others followed silently.

"You will support us?" Satia asked.

Lord Tarwain made a noncommittal humming sound that grated on Caris's nerves. "It now appears that I will not be the Lord High Baron of the Black Hills," Tarwain said.

"I am sure it's a temporary—"

He interrupted the Queen. "My daughter is still taking the lessons with that mage."

"Who I am still paying for," Satia responded, nettled. "With no luck searching for the key."

"How does he get away with defying you?" Tarwain asked mildly.

Caris shivered at his tone.

"My daughter's marriage would solidify my wealth," Tarwain continued. "And yours, Your Majesty. A reward for my efforts on your behalf."

Though Caris kept her eyes down, she managed to exchange a glance with Avice. Had there been a threat in those words?

"Both the King and I believe in rewards, Lord Marshal," Satia said as they approached the doors to the garden.

"I am grateful to hear it." Tarwain bowed over Satia's hand as they paused before the doors. "I fear that I must leave you here, your majesty," he said. "Until the council meeting?"

Satia graciously nodded and he walked off, boots ringing on the stone floor.

Avice and Nora opened the double doors to the garden. Cold air flowed in as Mira placed the fur cloak around Satia.

"It snowed," Mira chirped. "But the gardeners stamped out a path. There's a brazier for warmth, and hot bricks in your footstool, so you don't take a chill."

Satia made no comment, seemingly lost in her thoughts as she shrugged the cloak into place. Her head turned as she surveyed the garden. The noble ladies of the court were stationed about, looking fairly miserable. Caris wondered how long they had been waiting in the cold.

She caught a glimpse of Halithe on the far edge, with just a hint of a scowl on her face. Something tingled inside her and Caris looked away quickly before she was caught. Halithe would have something pithy to say about this later, she was sure.

They hadn't had a moment together since their encounter in the chapel. Caris's tingle grew stronger at the recollection of the intensity of the look they had shared.

A focused needle of anger and cold rage echoed in the Bond. Caris's attention was brought back to the Bonded in an instant.

"Tea, of course, and crackers," Mira continued, then hesitated, no doubt feeling the same prick of the needle. She glanced at the others as she tried to keep talking. "As the midwife directed … ." her voice trailed off as the bond darkened.

The four women froze in place as Satia paused in the doorway.

Satia framed herself in the doorway as she surveyed the snowy garden.

The noble ladies stirred. Heads turned in her direction and they all started to rise, faces white, cheek and noses red from the cold.

Satia didn't bother to acknowledge their courtesies. She swept forward, striding to her cushioned chair, settling in with her furs, placing her feet on the warmed footstool.

The ladies fluttered about, offering praise for the furs and compliments on how she glowed. Her Bondmaidens finally settled the woman back to their sewing and Mira started to make tea.

Satia pondered.

They were going to have to start settling lands, titles, and rewards in order to keep their followers loyal. There were marriages to arrange, and also wardships, for the newly orphaned, wealthy children. And there was the not-so-small matter of Swift's Port.

Satia sighed, trying not to feel put-upon. High Barons, minor lords, warriors: their impatience was almost as strong as their greed. Many hands grasping for what they deemed as their due.

The problem was that she wasn't sure of anyone's loyalty.

Xyrath's approach of reward-them-and-then-kill-them-if-they betray-us wasn't ideal.

Satia caught sight of Tarwain's girl, wrestling with a simple hem. It made her grind her teeth, reminding her that Ritathan refused her commands, yet instructed that chit. She seethed with frustration and resentment, and there was little she could do—

Or was there?

Satia accepted a cup of tea from Mira and breathed in the scented steam. She closed her eyes and thought of possibilities.

Her Bondswomen went still around her, turning their heads

to her like flowers to the sun, feeling the anticipation as they waited for instructions.

"It's a risk," Satia murmured to herself. "But there would also be advantages. There might be a cost …"

Oh, but it would make her feel so much better.

"Worth the risk." Saitia murmured. "Worth the cost." She allowed a lovely, dark smile to float over her lips. She could find a way to use it, to create more delay in intricate mourning rituals.

She gestured to her women to draw near.

They leaned in, heads close to hers.

"Ritathan," Satia said under her breath, as she nodded and smiled to the ladies about her. "Kill him."

## CHAPTER FORTY-FOUR

aris and the others bobbed swift curtseys before leaving the Queen.

They had their orders and their target. Calm settled over Caris; it was good to have a clear and concise goal. It brought a strange clarity to her world.

In perfect unity, they turned to one another, clustering as handmaidens do on being released from duties, as if giggling over a lover, or a hairstyle–

–Or planning a death.

"Most like in his tower, at this hour," Nora murmured.

"Alone, most like," Caris added, and nodded to the garden. "His student is without." She felt a flicker of relief at that, for there could be no witnesses.

The Bonded never wanted witnesses.

"I've master keys," Avice said.

They drifted down the hall as if returning to the Queen's chambers, aware of the eyes on them.

"Never killed a mage before," Nora said, her eyes getting that special wild look.

"We must be fast," Avice said firmly. "Do not give him a chance to speak or cast his sorcery."

"He is chained," Mira said.

"He is permitted to defend himself," Avice reminded them.

"These skirts," Nora muttered, and they all nodded. Not easy to be a swift killer in their cumbersome dresses. They had slits for their daggers, but still it was an issue.

As was the blood.

Memory flared for Caris, of a sweet, hidden kiss in curtained shadows. Her heart hurt with the barest flicker of regret. Halithe, her hopes, her desires—

The need of the Bond asserted itself. "There's a concealed alcove," she offered, focused now on the target. "Close to his office."

"That could work." Avice nodded as she took the lead.

"We could poison him," Mira said, then shook her head. "Never mind." No doubt she too felt the urgency of the Bond. "If it's to be done, we'd best be quick. Every blow must be a fatal one." Mira looked at Nora. "Take no risks."

"I don't," Nora insisted.

Caris gave her a sidelong look which Nora pointedly ignored. Her dark eyes glittered. "Iris will be sorry to miss this," Nora said.

Avice kept them moving along. "Do we know the room?"

"Door at one end, windows at the other," Nora answered

quickly. "Chairs in front of a desk, then his desk chair. Room is lined with shelves that stick out, making good hiding places. Books everywhere and a cage of songbirds on the corner of the desk." Nora smiled. "He's old and slow and–"

"Make no assumptions," Mira scolded as they moved into a new corridor, away from the halls of power.

"We will try the 'message from the Queen' routine first." Avice led the way briskly, now that they were out of sight of the courtiers. "I'll go in first, Caris distracts, and you two come in fast and low."

She paused on the stairs. "You might be able to use those chains against him," she suggested. "That would please the Bonded."

They all nodded and started up the stairs.

There were no guards posted in this hall, which was mostly lined with small residence chambers. The courtiers who occupied them were nowhere near, undoubtedly busy about their duties. Caris pulled aside the curtain over the alcove.

Nora and Mira slipped in, whispering to each other as they stripped down to their underthings.

Caris stood near Avice, keeping watch on her end of the hall. Her hand slipped into the slit in her skirts, checking her knives.

Avice watched the other way and kept a wary eye on Ritathan's door. Ever the cool one, was Avice. No sign that her blood was up or that a kill was pending.

Caris bounced on her toes ever so slightly, trying to settle her racing heart. Excitement hummed through her, making the world bright and sweet.

Avice gave her a quelling glance, but her eyes were just as bright.

The curtain behind them shifted. "Ready," Nora whispered.

"Clear," Avice set her shoulders back and stepped to the door of Ritathan's chambers. She rapped sharply with her knuckles. "Mage Ritathan, a message from the Queen."

"Come."

Avice opened the door, swinging it wide. She took a few steps in and curtseyed.

Caris followed, stepping to the right.

The room was as Nora had described. The chairs, the desk, the shelves. Sunlight streaming in the windows. Songbirds chirping in the cage on the corner of the desk.

Ritathan stood in front of the windows, dressed in his dark robes, his chains running from neck to wrists to waist to ankles. He was reaching to open one window, a dark outline against the light. "Yes?" he asked over his shoulder, pushing the window wide.

Avice stepped forward, extending a hand, her smile bright. "M'lord, the Queen sends a message–"

Nora and Mira came in, crouched low, moving swiftly, their feet silent on the stone floor.

"What?" Ritathan turned. Caris couldn't see his face, but she saw the glitter of his eyes. "What is–"

Caris hurled her dagger at his face, aiming for that glitter.

The knife bounced off something unseen, a shield of some kind. That was fine. Her goal was not to strike but to distract.

Ritathan flinched back, raising one hand in front of his face instinctively, his chains rattling. But that glitter grew hard. His other hand lifted, a dark, pulsing glow seeming to come from his palm. "The contract is broken," he spat.

Nora vaulted the desk, legs straight, toes pointed. She kicked the bird cage as she passed, without breaking momentum. Her feet hit Ritathan squarely, just below the ribs, throwing him back against the glass of the window. The man lost whatever breath he had in an explosive "oof."

The cage toppled, fell, and burst open. The songbirds screeched and fluttered about, colored feathers floating in the air.

Nora twisted to land on her feet.

Ritathan staggered but didn't fall. The pulsing glow dimmed for a moment, then flared bright.

Caris froze, eyes drawn to the threat as he reached for Nora.

Mira came in from the side, grabbed the mage's chains, and yanked them toward her.

Ritathan stumbled, then braced, then surged toward Mira, hands outstretched, fingers spread.

Mira scrambled back, releasing the chains.

Nora leapt, sinking her hands into his robes and using his own momentum to bear him to the floor. She and the mage disappeared from sight, falling behind the desk.

The birds were calling frantically, circling, some already escaping out the open window.

Caris saw Nora's hand raise, her fist and knife dark against the light for an instant, until it plunged down.

There was a grunt, male, low and pained.

Mira's blade was out as well. She dropped to her knees near Nora. Blocked by the desk, all Caris could see was the rise and fall of their daggers. All that could be heard were the wet sounds of knife thrusts.

Avice had closed the door and thrown the lock. She stood calmly, watching. "Enough," she finally said. "Dead?"

"Dead," Mira said.

Nora stood, breathing hard, a sheen of sweat on her skin, satisfaction written all over her face.

Avice stepped forward then and Caris followed. The last of the songbirds were gone, flown away, and cold air spilled into the room from the open window.

"You might have avoided the face," Avice observed. "Hard to display the body and claim a heart attack now."

"Well, his heart did fail," Mira chirped, and they all chuckled.

Caris felt herself relax at the old joke. "His robes seem to have soaked up all the blood," she said. "No splatters on you. Even the floor seems clean."

Nora and Mira checked themselves over then knelt to wipe their blades on the thick cloth.

"Best we take care of the body ourselves–" Avice said but an unfamiliar noise caused them all to stiffen. "What was that?"

The body shifted slightly. Something hissed from its mouth.

"What?" Nora pulled Mira away.

"Back," Avice barked.

Something dark oozed out, covering the mutilated face. There was a hissing sound as the body twisted. An evil black cloud rose, carrying a foul stench, driving them all back.

Avice ran to the door, throwing the bolt and opening it wide. The warm air of the hall flowed in, creating a draft.

The smoke dissipated, although the putrid smell hung in the air. Mira was retreating, coughing, but Nora was focused on the body. "It's ... melting," she said in fascinated horror.

Caris covered her nose and mouth and risked stepping closer.

The body was collapsing in on itself, the robes glistening with the wetness of blood and something far more slimy. The entire mass seemed to writhe, forming an oozing, festering pile. The silver chains lay glinting in the mess, which dissolved into a disgusting puddle, bubbling on the stone floor. As the Bondmaidens watched, it dried and dissipated and faded away.

Leaving nothing but the glistening chains.

They stood there, speechless, looking at one another and the floor.

"That was—" Mira grimaced.

"Fascinating," Nora chimed in. "Even his robes are gone. Do you suppose that happens every time you kill a mage?"

Caris frowned at her, knowing full well her thought. "Don't you dare kill that blood mage just to find out."

Nora shrugged.

"Well," Avice said, looking out into the hall before closing the door. "Apparently we don't have to dispose of the body."

Other than the broken birdcage and some shifted furniture, there were no signs there had been a struggle. She nudged the chains with her toe.

"All right, then," Avice said, sounding more confident, "we need to report. We should take the chains."

"I'm not touching those things," Nora said, taking a step back. Mira did the same, shaking her head.

"Fine." Caris scooped them up. The silvery metal was cool and dry against her hands, the chains thinner and lighter than she'd imagined. She could easily hold them in one hand and hide them in the folds of her skirt.

"We came to deliver a message and found him ill and dying." Avice said. "Mira tried to aid him, but alas... ."

"His heart failed," Mira said, but the joke didn't seem quite so funny the second time.

"We offer no specifics," Avice said. "He gasped, died—"

"And dissolved into goo," Nora finished.

Avice nodded. "Get your dresses on, then put the room to

rights." She looked at the shelves. "I suppose the King will want all this taken to the library as well," she muttered. "Come, Caris. Try to keep those out of sight until we reach the garden."

Caris followed.

———•———

The Queen and her noble ladies were all still clustered in the garden, as if no time had passed.

Queen Satia was sitting, a cup of tea in both hands, breathing in the steam. She turned her head slightly as they entered the garden, raising an eyebrow.

Avice and Caris both curtsied. As Caris rose, she shifted her hand to let the chains be briefly visible.

Satia's lip curled and her pleasure swelled the Bond.

"Avice?" she called, putting her cup down. "You look as if you have news."

Avice moved forward and Caris followed, basking in the warmth of the Bond, enjoying the glow of satisfaction for a job well done.

Something shifted. Out of the corner of her eye she saw Halithe start, her eyes wide.

For the swiftest of moments, like the trill of a tiny songbird on the wing, Caris felt regret.

Until she saw Satia's face.

"My Queen, I regret to inform you," Avice said, the lie flowing from her as smooth as silk. Caris watched in admiration as the Queen's face artfully reflected her shock and horror at the news as Caris displayed the chains for all to see.

The ladies cried out in dismay, their voices rising. Above the other rose one sincere, anguished cry. Caris was careful not to look around.

Not to see Halithe's grief.

"What a tragedy!" Satia started to struggle out of her chair. Avice rushed to assist her. "We must plunge the Court into mourning for such a wise and good man, so loyal in his service to the Crown." On her feet, she started toward the doors, summoning all four Bondmaidens with a gesture.

"Ladies, I must leave you, but let us do him every honor."

Avice rushed forward to open the doors for her.

"Let every member of my court don black and let any festivities be cancelled. Send word to the King, for we must cancel the council meeting for this afternoon."

Satia paused in the doorway. "We must also send word to Guildmaster Forterran of this terrible tragedy," she added. Then, with a twirl of her fur cape, she was gone.

Caris followed, eyes down, silver chains in her hands.

## CHAPTER FORTY-FIVE

Vren walked up to the very edge of the precipice and looked at home.

The Wastes stretched out before him, dry desert and scrub in all the shades of brown and gray known. He took a deep breath of the hot air rising in his face, smelling sand and stone and acrid, bitter air.

His heart swelled with the quiet joy of home.

To his left lay the start of the switchback trail that led down to the lands below. Rough going, true enough, but far better than the sheer drop before him.

Dust whined behind him, sitting back aways, guarding his pack at the edge of the cleared area that marked the trailhead.

Vren walked back and knelt at her side, pulling his pack close over the loose gravel. "We made decent time," he said softly. "Fairly sure we've lost our pursuer. You'll need to be careful on the way back."

Dust huffed.

The baby bundle was still strapped to his chest, a bit worse for wear. He removed the sling and set it aside carefully, still in the habit of treating it like an actual child. Amused at himself, he opened his pack and started to pull out the items he would cache here, among the rocks and scrub. Knives, buckles, the ring, and most important, the mage key.

Dust backtracked a bit and started digging at an old animal hole between some rocks, making it wider. Vren wrapped the items in leather and tied the bundle tightly shut. Dust moved aside as Vren knelt, crammed the package into the hole the vore had created, then filled it with dirt, gravel, and small stones. Good enough for a casual eye, especially up here, where few ventured. He brushed off his hands and stood. Mingled with his joy at homecoming was pain.

Time to say good-bye.

He knelt again beside his pack. Dust came to lean slightly against him.

"I wish you could go with me," he said, closing and tying the pack. "I wish I could show you the beauties that are to be found in the Wastes."

Dust nudged him with her nose.

"I know," he said. "Too dangerous." He stood, looking any-where but at her. His sadness was an ache in his heart. "I don't know when I will see you again, Dust. I have enjoyed our travels, and I don't want to leave you, but–"

There was a wet thud, followed nearly instantly by a horrible, hurt whine.

Dust collapsed on her side, a crossbow bolt in her chest.

Vren spun.

There, on a rock above them, a woman was raising another crossbow.

*She'd gotten ahead of them.* Vren dodged, rolling, tumbling away, the grit of gravel under his shoulder. The next bolt hit the ground where he'd been standing.

Vren regained his feet and threw his pack at the woman, drawing his bone knives while the pack was still in the air.

She dodged, dropping the crossbow as she dropped to the ground. She'd a knife in each hand, same as him, and a look of hate in her eyes.

Same as him.

Vren snarled, she echoed him, and they began the dance. Moving this way and that, feinting with blades high and low. Watching for the first mistake, the first chance–

Her eyes drifted to the baby bundle on the ground.

Vren lunged, slicing at her eyes while trying to catch her wrist. He nicked her forehead, slicing deep. Blood flowed, but she was fast, very fast. She twisted in his grip and would have hit his heart if he hadn't retreated.

She followed, teeth bared, and slashed, cutting deeply into his wrist. Vren ducked and got inside her reach. He butted her hard with his shoulder, knocking her to the ground.

The woman sprawled near Dust's body and the bundle. She was braced for his attack, but he backed off to catch a breath.

Blood dripped from her forehead and down the side of her nose. Her face was contorted with rage.

With a roar, she grasped the doll, tearing into it with her knife. Vren laughed at her expression as dried pease flew everywhere.

"Where is it?" she demanded as she rose to her feet. "Where is the babe?"

He shrugged and grinned. The bitch could just wonder. He planted his feet, aware that the footing had changed.

She glared. There was something in her eyes, an anger that told him this one didn't deal well with failure.

"Not here," he taunted.

"Where is the babe?" she roared as she lunged, clearly not really interested in an answer, wanting only his blood.

She slipped on the pease.

Vren sliced up as she slid, cutting through her leathers. He managed to slash deep, scoring a thin line of blood under her breast, cutting through what looked like an old scar.

With a hiss, she grabbed at him and pulled herself up by bracing herself on his body. She clamped down on his wounded wrist, twisting his arm back, getting the knife away from her.

For long moments, they struggled, hot breath in each other's faces, then Vren moved, trying—

It didn't matter. This time he was the one betrayed by the dry pease. He went down on his knees hard.

She was behind him in a moment, locking one of his arms in the air, her blade to his throat. They both went still, breathing hard. Vren jerked but could not break her hold.

She leaned down to whisper in his ear. "I can make it swift or slow," she rasped. "Where is the babe?"

The blade was cold on his neck, the edge sharp. He felt the warm blood start to flow as she dug in harder. They were close to the edge, very close. If he could force her back, the wastes might destroy the blade and he could maybe get free. A desperate chance, but the only one.

"Where is the babe?" she demanded again, her head lowered, so close her hair framed his face.

She didn't see what Vren saw: Dust staggering to her feet and running toward them, the bolt still in her chest.

Brave friend, unfailing warrior.

Vren braced, about to sink down, to give Dust a clear shot at her throat when her head came up, when–

The Wastes sang.

It was the only way Vren could describe it. An elemental pulse, a long note of longing, of waiting, of wanting … her. The woman.

*'Willing sacrifice, willingly made.'*

Vren forced himself up, rose to his full height, dropped his knives and opened his arms wide to catch Dust, hugging her close, taking the force of her forward movement.

As the woman's blade sliced into his throat, he bent his knees and thrust back with all his might, combining his momentum with Dust's to plunge them all off the cliff's edge.

For a moment, all he knew was the feeling of flying, the rush of warm air like a lover's embrace, the sun blazing bright, brighter, brightest. He felt the woman pressed to his back, the vore's fur tickling his nose.

Then there was falling, and twisting, and … nothing.

## CHAPTER FORTY-SIX

They made sure Xydell was never alone.

During the day, someone was always in the kitchen; cooking or puttering. At times Xydell was talkative, especially during Yfin's reading and writing lessons. She seemed to like the boy, perking up whenever he laughed.

There was a small stream of visitors as Mother Bercie would bring one or two people who remembered the Lady High Baroness and were known to her. Xydell's face would light up, she'd extend a frail hand, and they would all sit in the warmth of the kitchen and talk in hushed voices. Orval noted as the days passed that some of the looks he got were kinder, or at the least he detected less malice.

But as the days went on, Xydell drowsed more, rousing only long enough for a bite to eat or a sip of kav. She always made an effort when Mother Bercie arrived, but afterwards Xydell always slept deeply. So deeply, in fact, that once or twice Orval checked to make sure she was still with them.

Wethe was true to her word, bringing possets and mixtures that helped ease Xydell. Once, outside, she looked Orval in the eye. "Have you seen death?" she asked softly.

"Yes," Orval said. "My sister, of the Sweat." He looked away. "I sat with her."

"Ah," Wethe said. "This won't quite be the same. Your Aunt won't be feverish or fretful. I suspect she will slip from us quietly, so long as she is comfortable. Perhaps best then that you take the night shifts, yes?"

He'd nodded. It was no real burden for him. Every night, he'd see Amari and the babes to sleep then relieve Rosalind and sit by the fire with the *Epic of Xyson*. For the last few weeks, he'd enjoyed the quiet, so rare these days.

Not tonight.

Tonight, he opened the book, stared past the words, and looked his troubles in the eye.

Mother Bercie, her son, and the entire town—none of them trusted him. Bercie was paranoid and suspicious, and from what Orval had learned of the history, she had every right to be. They all did. The Black Hills had been fought over like a carcass being fought over by wolves fighting a mountain lion. The land and its people were the worse for it.

Jerrold was grim and hard. Orval was fair certain that without Amari and the babes, he'd be dead.

A log in the hearth collapsed. Orval rose, sucked in a breath waiting for his leg to support him, then added wood to the fire.

True enough, the people were seeing to the newcomers' basic needs. But for how long would that continue?

He had promised Bercie and her people that he wouldn't lie, but he hadn't shared the truth of Lara's parentage and wasn't sure he ever would. Safer that way, although to be honest, he had the unsettling thought that too many people already knew the truth.

He sat back down by the bed, stretching his bad leg toward the warmth. It hurt, to be hated for what he could not change. He couldn't change his blood, his leg, or the past.

He trusted Roth and Rosalind. They would both die before betraying the secret and Yfin would follow Roth in that regard. But Rosalind made Orval uneasy for reasons he couldn't quite put his finger on. He thought she favored Lara over Dalan, but he wasn't sure. He hadn't mentioned it to Amari yet because … .

He drew in a breath, not wanting to face it, but Amari was his other worry. No, more of a fear. The last week or so, she'd been acting different. Pulling back from him, not meeting his eyes. A few times, he caught her staring at him, her mouth open as if to say something, but then she'd turn away.

Orval frowned, staring into the fire. It was hard, to be husband and wife. He'd thought it would be easier somehow, that having a relationship meant that you knew the other's thoughts and feelings. It wasn't like that at all.

Vren had said that a marcus would come. So it was still a possibility that she would leave and take the children with her. Orval knew they'd be safer away from this place, this strife, but he couldn't bear the thought of losing her.

It wasn't just the nights, oh, the nights when they took pleasure with one another. But the days, with her sharp wit and her laugh and her tenderness to the babes. And the babies themselves, Dalan and Lara were such joys. He smiled wryly to himself; how had he ever lived without them?

Well, he hadn't, had he?

He grimaced then. He didn't have the courage to just come out and ask her what was wrong, to press her to tell him what was troubling her. Fool that he was, coward that he was, all he could do was wait and see.

Xydell stirred and opened her eyes.

"Aunt Xydell." Orval closed his book and leaned over. "Can I get you anything?"

She turned toward him and smiled. She looked relaxed and so much younger. "Orval," she said, reaching out a trembling hand. "You love Amari."

"I do," He took her hand in his. It felt so cold and frail. "And even better, she seems to care for me." He smiled, still trying to understand the wonder of it, and hoping it was still true. But his doubts were not something he was going to discuss with his Aunt.

"Good," she whispered. "That's good." She yawned and sighed. "Sometimes it seems this has all been a bad dream. All the pain, all the grief, since my Jerrold died."

"Perhaps, if I hadn't buried myself in ancient history, I wouldn't have ignored the living history before me," he said, voicing his own quiet regret.

Xydell sighed. "Perhaps, if I had let my bitterness go, I might have been willing to talk of the past." She plucked at the blankets with her free hand, "Old people can be so stubborn."

"Life is wasted on the young," he said. They shared a smile.

"Go back to sleep," Orval said softly. "And dream a better dream."

"It's good to be back home." She closed her eyes and murmured something faintly.

Orval leaned in to hear.

"The fire has warmed me." Her words were nearly breathless, a final struggle.

He'd never been sure of his Aunt's beliefs. It wasn't much talked of in the family. But Orval knew the ancient words; he'd learned them at his mother's knee.

"We thank the elements," he recited.

"The earth has supported—" Aunt Xydell drew a ragged breath.

"The earth has supported you," Orval finished for her. "We thank the elements."

Her lips moved, following his words.

He drew a breath as she slipped into sleep, her breathing growing shallow. "The waters have sustained you. We thank the elements." He kept his voice soft, not wanting to disturb her. "The air has filled you. We thank the elements." He paused, then gave the traditional ending.

"Go now, warrior. Beyond the snows and to the stars."

It was only when he stopped talking that he realized she had stopped breathing.

The silence seemed endless; the only sound the crackle of the fire. There should have been an outcry, the peal of a horn or the crack of a glass shattering. But there was nothing like that, just something precious and quiet gone from the room.

There was a ritual, actions to take, words to speak, but his throat closed and the tears came. He allowed himself a breath, and then another, then wrapped his fingers around Xydell's thin right wrist.

"Xydell," he called softly, his voice cracking. "Xydell of the Blood of Xy, answer me."

There was no response.

Orval shifted, reaching for her left hand. Those pale, frail fingers. "Xydell, Daughter of the Blood, answer me."

Left, foot, right foot, each time calling her name. He knew she was gone far beyond his voice, but as with all who suffer this loss, he hoped for her to wake, to open her eyes and scold him for being a dolt, for probably getting the ritual wrong.

Finished, he put his hands in his lap, acknowledging his pain and grief, and, to be honest, keeping her to himself for just a moment longer.

Then he rose and went to the door, opening it wide to let in the cool night air, and offered his tears to the wind and the glittering stars.

Finally, he drew a deep breath. He'd need to wake the others, and send word to Mother Bercie. He went to close the door when the thought occurred.

*The Black Hills have no reason to keep us alive.*

———•———

Orval hadn't mentioned his fear to the others, but the tension was there as they watched Mayor Jerrold bring a wagon filled with women at dawn. "We've come to see to her, for the washing and the laying out." Mother Bercie said as the others climbed down from the wagon.

"She is of the Blood," Rosalind's voice was strident and fierce. "She must be honored properly."

"We do not honor her for her Blood," Bercie snapped. "We honor her as Our Lord High Baroness, who cared for her people and suffered for them."

There was a pause, then Amari placed her hand on Rosalind's arm. "We thank you for your aid." Amari said gently. "She is within, and we have water warming by the fire."

"The men can wait outside." Bercie announced, and started toward the gatehouse.

Orval walked over to the bench and sat, Roth followed but remained standing. Yfin wandered, shoulders hunched, kicking at stones.

"See to Yfin," Orval said.

Roth glanced toward Jerrold, who was seeing to the horse.

Orval just shook his head, and nodded to Yfin.

Roth heaved a sigh. "I'll see to him," Roth said softly. "Hey, Yfin," he called. "Let's go hunt a few pigeons, shall we?"

At the lad's nod, Roth patted Orval's shoulder and headed off toward the old stables, Yfin in tow.

Jerrold had finished his work, and had walked to the well.

"It's still filled with rocks," Orval called, wrapping himself tighter in his cloak. "The only water is the well in the cellar," he pointed at the gatehouse with his chin.

Jerrold gave an abrupt nod, then looked at loose ends.

"I have a question," Orval ventured. "What did Aunt Xydell mean by 'with the hidden ones'?"

Jerrold glanced at the door, and for a moment Orval was certain that the man was going to refuse to talk to him. But with a shrug, Jerrold drew closer, taking a defiant stand in front of him.

"Years of war have taught us well." His deep voice made it a pronouncement. "Seeing our wells filled with stones, our fields burned, our dead desecrated, we learned to hide our dead, among other things. Where is none of your concern."

"Ah," Orval shifted on the bench, glancing at the well. "We

tried to shift the rocks out you know, but they are too deep and heavy for us."

"I know," Jerrold said. "We watched."

"Yes, of course," Orval glanced at the gatehouse.

"We will treat her with respect," Jerrold said. "More respect than the Blood of Xy has ever shown us."

Orval craned his neck to look up at the man, genuinely surprised. "I never doubted that. I am truly grateful."

From behind them, in the depths of the Keep, came a triumphant shout from Yfin and the fluttering of wings.

Jerrold relaxed slightly. When Orval gave him a questioning look, he shrugged. "He sounds like my son," Jerrold said gruffly.

Orval nodded his understanding, then nodded toward the gatehouse. "How long will that take, do you think?"

Jerrold shrugged, and sat on the other end of the bench, adjusting his scabbard. "About an hour, maybe a bit longer."

Orval nodded.

After another moment, Jerrold spoke. "I have a question."

Orval met his gaze with a raised eyebrow.

"What is it you really want, Lord High Baron?" The disdain in his voice was clear.

In his mind's eye, Orval was back in their apartments, an ache of homesickness for crowded shelves, copper lanterns, the smell of pease cooking. Amari's delightful laugh and the gurgle of babes in arms. Those precious days before all of this had crashed down on him. On them.

Orval drew a breath. "I want a place," he said slowly. "Where I can build a life with my wife and children where we need not fear the knock at the door or want for our basic needs."

"Not power?" Jerrold asked. "Not wealth, dominion, or glory?"

"No." Orval said, dying to launch into all the historical, philosophical, and practical reasons behind his answer, but shut his mouth firmly.

Jerrold grunted, then went silent. Orval was more than willing to do the same, for fear of offending the man. They sat in the sun, listening to the occasional shouts from Yfin, of both success and failure. At one particularly loud string of curses, Orval couldn't help but chuckle. He glanced over to see a half-smile on Jerrold's face.

It was a start, maybe.

When the door finally opened, Mother Bercie emerged with Amari. Orval could hear, in the gatehouse, women's voices raised in a chant.

Jerrold rose to greet the women. Stiff from sitting, Orval struggled to get up. Jerrold extended a hand to aid him and Orval took it with thanks.

"It's done," Mother Bercie said, coming to stand in front of them. Amari nodded to Orval to confirm.

"Thank you," Orval said.

"Others who wish to honor her will be here shortly," Bercie continued. "We will escort her and see her entombed." She looked at Orval. "You cannot come."

"I know," Orval said. "The Blood of Xy—"

"No," Mother Bercie stopped him with a raised hand. "The path up into the mountain is narrow and torturous. With your leg … ."

"Oh," Orval said.

"And Amari should not risk it." Mother Bercie decreed.

Orval expected a protest, but Amari's head was down, her gaze firmly on her shoes.

"The others would be welcome, to witness the honor we give

her." Mother Bercie finished.

"Mother–" Jerrold started.

"No, my son," she said firmly. "These two need to know from those they trust that we did her right and proper." Bercie sighed, her eyes going to the Keep behind them. "As she deserves." She huffed out a breath and focused on Orval. "I tell people that hatred blinds, but I seethe at what was done to her. Past and present, like she was nothing but a tool."

Orval nodded. "I would hope that the enemy of my enemy is my friend," he said cautiously.

"Not yet, Orval of Xy," Berice said, "not yet. But we can agree to be uneasy allies."

Amari spoke. "With an uneasy truce?"

Bercie snorted. "Truce?" But then she shrugged. "You may both, in fact, be worth more to us alive as the token Lord and Lady High Baron. Time will tell."

"I do have some coin," Orval said. "We could pay for food and services."

"We will see," Bercie said. She looked back at the gatehouse. "You should make your farewells."

Orval nodded and started toward the door. Rosalind was waiting, tears in her eyes. "Come see," she said, opening the door wide.

The fire in the hearth was a strong, steady glow. Orval stepped within to a room ringed with women of all ages, chanting softly.

Xydell lay on the table, her face at peace, her white hair braided around her head like a crown.

Orval caught his breath.

Xydell was covered in a traditional airion blanket, of blue and white wool, with embroidered airions dancing in a smattering of clouds. It glowed in the firelight, and he could swear that the creatures' eyes glittered as if alive.

"Where—?" He barely dared breathe.

One of the women spoke up. "My Gran smuggled it out of the Keep when the Wyverns came. Said it was woven by her hand, and damned if any would ruin her good work." She reached out and touched the cloth. "I remembered it when we heard the Lady Baroness had passed. I think Gran would have wanted it used this way. Seems fitting, don't you think?"

"Yes," Orval wiped at his eyes, suddenly feeling the loss. "You honor her and us with this."

The woman nodded and resumed chanting. Orval went closer and pressed a kiss to Xydell's forehead before he pulled the blanket over her head as the music flowed.

From the look on her face, he was sure she had already found her Jerrold.

## CHAPTER FORTY-SEVEN

—◦—

The men of the village lifted Xydell's bier onto the back of the wagon. To Orval's eyes, the blanket seemed to glow an even brighter blue in the sunlight.

A fairly large crowd had gathered at the gates. As the wagon passed, they fell in behind, walking in silence. Roth, Rosalind, and Yfin fell in as well, welcomed by the other mourners.

Orval stood at the gate, shoulder to shoulder with Amari, glad of her support. He noted that other people, mostly older, were also watching, unable to accompany the wagon, which was an odd comfort. He wasn't the only one who couldn't make the journey.

They all watched as the procession disappeared over a hill.

Then the crowd started to dissipate, heading to the village. Some glanced over their shoulders at himself and Amari.

Not all the looks were kind.

"Will they be safe?" Amari asked.

Orval put his arm around her shoulder. "Roth slipped Rosalind a dagger, and Yfin has his knives." Amari jerked, but Orval continued. "But I doubt that they would dishonor Xydell with a slaughter at this time."

Amari shivered next to him.

"You're cold," Orval said. "Let's get inside."

The room seemed empty without Xydell. The fire had died down and the faintest odor of the herbs that they had used hung in the air.

"Let's leave the door open for a bit," Orval suggested. "Air the place out."

"Please," Amari said. She propped the door open, then removed her cloak and placed it on the bench by the fire.

"There is something else, she said hesitantly. "A simple cleansing ritual. It won't take long."

Orval nodded, starting to add wood to the fire.

Amari smoothed her hair and faced the hearth. She bowed her head for a moment, then took the salt cellar from the mantle. With graceful movements, she circled the table where Xydell had been laid out, scattering salt on its surface.

Orval watched, lost in her grace.

The salt cellar returned to the mantel, Amari took a dipper of water from the bucket and poured it into a small wooden bowl. Again, she circled the table, flicking water droplets onto its surface with her lovely hands. She took a drink from the bowl, then offered it to Orval.

He drank, finding the water clean and cool.

Amari placed the bowl on the mantel.

The room was colder now, with the door open, despite the blaze in the hearth. Amari took a piece of kindling from the wood box and set the tip to the flame. Once again, she circled the table, waving the smoldering stick over the table.

With her round completed, the stick went into the fire.

"What are you doing?" Orval asked quietly.

She shook her head at him, signaling for silence. Taking a clean cloth from the nappy basket she kept by the fire, she started to rub the wet salt into the rough wood of the table. There was nothing gentle about this, the table rocked with the strength of her arms. Again, she circled the table, scrubbing every inch of its surface.

She went 'round again with the water, until the wood was cleaned of the salt.

Once she was done, she turned back to the hearth and bowed her head. The cloth was hung from one of the pot hooks to dry.

Then she sat, wearily, on the bench opposite Orval. "An old custom," she said. "From Uyole. The salting of the table after a death in the house." She glanced at the cloth. "I will burn that after it dries."

"Can I close the door?" Orval asked.

"I will," she said and rose to do just that, throwing the bolts. "I need to check the babes."

Orval nodded, adding another piece of wood to the fire. The room warmed quickly with the door closed. He could hear Amari moving about, but other than that, the gatehouse was filled with a rare silence. He poked at the fire, thinking. Couldn't help that persistent little doubt that he wasn't enough for her.

"Still sleeping," Amari said softly as she returned. She looked so tired and worn that Orval's heart hurt for her. For all his fear of asking the question, fear of hearing her answer, what mattered was her, wasn't it? Even if it was a truth he didn't want to know. He couldn't go on, not knowing.

She sat on the bench, checking to see if the cloth had dried.

Before he could lose his resolve, Orval said, "Amari, won't you tell me what is troubling you?"

She jerked, her eyes wide, and stared at him for a moment before bursting into tears with a wail. She covered her face with her hands, sobbing.

"Amari—" Orval was shaken by her response. Amari, who was so strong, so resilient, who had fled a battlefield with two babes, and dealt with every blow she'd been given. "Amari, please tell me what–"

"I'm pregnant," she gasped.

His shock was followed by a joy that bubbled up in Orval's heart and spilled into a huge grin and a laugh that he could barely restrain. But he held it in as she wept, huge, gulping sobs that shook her body.

He wanted to comfort her but he wasn't sure how. He felt at a total loss, not knowing what to say. But he had to try. "Amari, are you not pleased?"

She nodded. "I am, I am," she said, then burst into fresh tears, trembling like a leaf.

Orval waited, hesitant. "Help me understand."

She drew in a deep breath and when she spoke, her words tumbled over one another. "I told you I was nursing, that I couldn't quicken, but Wethe scolded me for an idiot for believing that old wives tale, but I did believe it and I didn't mean to add to our troubles, with another baby and this—" she waved her hands around, indicating the room, the gatehouse, the whole situation for all Orval knew.

"This is no place for babes and we've no stocks of food and we are barely scraping by and–" She sucked in a breath. "And, and the last time—" she couldn't finish the sentence and put her face back in her hands, refusing to look at him.

It took Orval a moment. "And the last time you told a man you were expecting his baby, he rejected you in the cruelest way possible."

She didn't look up, just kept crying, wiping her face with her hands.

For a long moment, Orval didn't move, afraid to say anything that might hurt her, unsure that he could even find the right words.

At last he struggled to his feet, limped over, and took a nappy from the basket by the hearth. He sat next to Amari and offered her the cloth. She took it, staring at him, all bleary-eyed and teary.

"You can dry your face with that, if you like," he said. "Or I can dry your face with kisses."

She snort-laughed, choking, stared at him for an endless moment, then threw herself into his arms.

Orval managed to brace himself with his good leg as he took her weight, then held this warm, wonderful woman tight. He didn't try to shush her, just let her cry. Once her sobs eased, she tried to pull back, but he held her tight for a few seconds longer before releasing her—just enough to rain kisses over her face.

Which made her smile and push him away enough that she could mop her face with the cloth. He kept his arm around her shoulders.

"I was so afraid," she whispered.

"How long have you carried this fear alone?" Orval asked.

"Since Wethe confirmed my suspicions." Amari drew a breath. "Orval, it's early yet. We could–" Another breath. "It might be smarter to take the medicines and … ." her voice trailed off. Her next words were a whisper. "With all the dangers we face."

"True, it's dangerous to bring another child into the world," Orval reached for her hand. "But–" he started, then stopped. "It is your decision, Amari. I support any choice you make. But oh," his voice broke, "I so want another child with you. This child."

"So do I," Amari confessed. "With your eyes," she whispered.

"No, with yours. Dark and sweet." Orval choked back a sob. "The best reflection of both of us."

She brought his hand up and kissed it.

"You are right," he said, weak with relief. "We face challenges. But you are strong."

"We both are," she chided him. "In our own ways."

"Yes," Orval said. "The future holds no promises for us, be-loved, owes us no obligations, that's true. But we have our promise to each other, and if we hold true to that, we will find a way to build a Hearth." He cleared his throat. "To that end, Hearth Mother, it would appear that we have met the requirements of entering into a formal marriage contract."

She sat back, her eyes still wide, but shining now with hope. He brushed her cheeks with his lips.

"We will get paper and ink and draft it together, you and I." He pressed his forehead to hers. "We will craft wonderful words, whole paragraphs and clauses, together, you and I, that will honor your traditions and mine."

"That would be wonderful," she breathed.

"This time, you will have to tell me what kind of bracelet," he said dryly.

That brought a wet chuckle.

"There's something else," Orval said. "Something my Aunt reminded me of, before she passed. There are old words," he took a breath. "Not used much these days, but a tradition in my family."

You have honored my ways," Amari said. "I will honor yours, if I can. Tell me these words."

Orval hesitated. He'd never thought to say these words, never thought to find a companion, one who was willing to share his life, one who he could trust with his heart. But he wanted this, more than anything, and he tried to put his feelings into the ancient words.

"Amari Misalyn Anouk, flame of my heart, I would bond with you." Orval said. "Be my star, my flame, my night wind and my morning sun, to the snows and beyond."

Amari caught her breath, looking at him with eyes that shined with love.

"Orval of the Airion House of Xy, flame of my heart, I would bond with you." She pressed her forehead to his. "Be my star, my flame, my night wind and my morning sun, to the snows and beyond."

They kissed, and kissed again, each flowing into the other with quiet joy. The fire popped and crackled as if it approved.

"The babes will wake soon," Amari whispered.

Orval nodded, drawing her head to his shoulder. "But not just yet. For now, for this moment, just let me hold you here in the warmth of our Hearth.

Amari nodded, pressing close.

"When the babes wake, when the others return, we will face

our challenges." Orval said.

Amari reached for his hand. She wove her fingers into his. "Together."

"Together."

## AFTERMATH

———◉———

The Liam knelt in the sandy soil of the Wastes, feeling dirt and sand shift under his knee. The peoples with him fanned out, searching. Two stood with him, bearing witness.

Vren's crumpled and broken body lay sprawled on the ground before him.

The weight of failure settled on the Liam's shoulders, pressing him down as he sighed. He was the leader, the teacher, the wise one. He was supposed to instill hope and courage, to lead his people with confidence into the future.

All he had within him was empty, hollow despair.

"I will see to him," he forced himself to say. "Aid the others in their search."

Instead, they moved closer, offering silent support. Which crushed him even more. Even in defeat, they stood by him.

He was not worthy, did not deserve … the sun's heat burned his shoulders, even through his clothes and straw hat.

What had happened, that it had come to this? He tried to reconcile it, even as he reached for Vren's right hand, taking it in his own. "Vren of the Horse," the Liam spoke, clearly, loudly, trying to speak with hope, knowing it was hopeless. "Vren, sworn of the marcusi, answer me."

Those cold, parted lips did not move. There was no heartbeat in the wrist.

"Vren," he demanded. "Vren, the Liam calls. Answer."

There was no response.

Hands reached out to aid him in shifting the body so that he could pull the left arm from underneath. The Liam grasped Vren's left hand. "Vren of the Horse, defender of the Blood of Xy, answer my summons."

Only the wind, and the soft movements of small creatures in the brush around them.

As they straightened the legs; the Liam could hear the grind of broken bone. Left foot, right foot, he repeated the ritual, each time calling Vren's name.

But the silence was absolute and final.

The rite complete, the Liam sat back on his heels. "His pack?"

He knew, the moment he put his hand on the wrappings, that the vial was intact. The Liam breathed a sigh of relief as he stood.

"The others?" he asked as he started to carefully pull the wrappings off the precious package.

"Dead," came the response. The Liam nodded as he peeled

back the last bit of cloth and revealed the vial, intact, the blood bright red in the sun.

His first impulse was relief; the vial was intact. His next thought vanished, driven out of his mind by the vivid color of the fluid.

It took a breath for the implication to sink again, and he looked down at the corpse, almost expecting to see signs of life. But no–

"Check them again," he commanded, sure he would be obeyed, as he hastily re-wrapped the vial.

"Master," came a loud shout, both hopeful and horrified. "Master, they live, but barely. Their injuries–" the sounds of urgent efforts cut off the rest.

The Liam looked up quickly, scanning the skies. It would not do to attract a swarm of wyverns now. His gaze was drawn up, up to the top of the escarpment far above them. It was not possible, and yet—

Had the Wastes, the elements, taken a hand in this?

He took a breath, felt grit in his eyes as the wind took his tears. Just for a moment, he let his grief fill his breath. Then hope rose, a wild, uncertain possibility. *For every ending, there is a beginning,* he could hear the ancient wisdom in the wind.

"Forgive my doubts," he whispered to the wind, but as always, there was no answer and he did not wait for one. "Gather them up," he commanded. "We will render aid."

He saw the glances exchanged among them, saw their doubts. But confidence returned to his voice. "Quickly," he urged.

Others moved, but one gave voice. "Will they survive, Master?"

The Liam placed the wrapped vial in his own pack. "Well, we will see, won't we?

## THE END
*but really*
*just the beginning …*

## ABOUT THE AUTHOR

Elizabeth Vaughan is the *USA Today* Bestselling author of *Warprize*, the first volume of The Chronicles of the Warlands. She's always loved fantasy and science fiction, and has been a fantasy role-player since 1981. By day, Beth's secret identity is that of a lawyer, practicing in the area of bankruptcy, a role she has maintained since 1985. More information can be found at her website, WriteandRepeat.com.

Beth is owned by incredibly spoiled cats, and lives in the Northwest Territory, on the outskirts of the Black Swamp, along Mad Anthony's Trail on the banks of the Maumee River.

www.ingramcontent.com/pod-product-compliance
Lightning Source LLC
Chambersburg PA
CBHW030919120726
47906CB00002B/393